TAKEN
BY
SURPRISE

BOOK REVIEW
HILLCREST SHOPPING CENTER
1618 HWY 52N
ROCHESTER MN 55901
(507) 285-1600

TAKEN BY SURPRISE

SUSAN JOHNSON
THEA DEVINE
KATHERINE O'NEAL

KENSINGTON PUBLISHING CORP.
http://www.kensingtonbooks.com

Contents

From Russia with Love

Susan Johnson

Chapter One

Russia, 1570

Ivan the Terrible had begun very early to show the streak of sadism that marked his life. As a child, he'd throw small animals from the Kremlin towers for amusement. When he was old enough to ride, he would travel the streets of Moscow slashing people with a whip and if anyone offended his sight, he had their head struck off. In the course of his reign, so many subjects were tortured and killed on his orders, it was said only God knew their names.

Perhaps Ivan's paranoia was understandable. Only three when his father died, his mother had ruled in his name until she'd been poisoned by men who wanted the throne for themselves. In fear for his life, humiliated by the nobles at court, powerless and defenseless against the magnates who ruled the land, Ivan managed to survive. At seventeen, he seized power, executed or exiled his enemies and placed the crown on his head.

But conspirators were everywhere, plots to usurp his sovereignty constant.

The great boyar families all had some claim to the throne and everyone knew that power could change hands as swiftly as sinister alliances could be formed, poison could do its work, or the thrust of a sword could end a man's life.

It was a violent time.

An uncertain time.

No one was safe.

In the midst of this chaos and savagery, a beautiful, young noblewoman was wed to one of the most ruthless men of that age, the marriage arranged as was customary for the time— and sanctioned by the tsar. Ivan IV had offered the orphaned heiress as a reward to his henchman, Prince Igor Shuisky for his fealty to the crown.

While the prince had no need of a wife, the vast estates the woman brought as dowry were reason enough to please the tsar. The bride and groom met for the first time at the altar where Igor took one look at Tatiana, and churlishly noted that she looked too frail for breeding. Buxom women were more to his taste.

But regardless of his crude observations, the groom asserted his conjugal rights with a casual brutality on their wedding night and with cruel diligence afterward, intent on impregnating his wife as soon as possible. Scarcely a month after their marriage, he was given the news he was waiting for. His wife was with child.

He immediately sent her back from whence she came, to her country estate that was now his. She could await the birth of the child far from Moscow and whether she survived the event was of no consequence. He had her wealth.

In due time, a daughter was born with the raven black hair and brilliant blue eyes of her father. The news was not pleasing to Prince Shuisky, who had expected a son, and as a sign of his displeasure he didn't respond for some months. When he finally did reply, he specified that his wife was to continue her exile until such time as he deigned to re-admit her into his good graces.

When young Tatiana received the message, she was relieved, although she took care not to expose her feelings to the man her husband had sent from Moscow.

But the moment the young lieutenant was led away by her steward, she returned to her rooms and standing before the precious icon of Saint Gabriel she had carried with her to her wedding, she offered up a prayer of thanksgiving. Then, because pagan beliefs were still strong, she knelt before the small shrine dedicated to the earth spirits, touched each stone and bit of grass, dipped her finger in the crystal container of water, inhaled the delicate scent from the small cedar bough framing the talismans, and thanked the spirits of nature as well.

Only then did she truly smile.

She kept to her rooms for the remainder of the messenger's short sojourn. As a woman, she wasn't expected to personally offer him hospitality, although conventions varied on that issue. But, as a woman who had recently given birth, she had every right to remain aloof if she chose.

And she did.

She had no wish to become better acquainted with anyone from her husband's household.

Chapter Two

Two days later, on a bright spring forenoon, the messenger took his leave, bowing to the princess as she stood on the porch with her infant daughter in her arms. His troop was waiting in the courtyard, already mounted, and Prince Shuisky's lieutenant swung up onto his fine Kurland charger in a flash of light mail and glittering weaponry. In the country near Pskov, the tsar's friends had their detractors and any man who served Ivan best travel with a strong escort.

Tatiana watched the forty men until they disappeared into the birch groves at the end of her drive. And then she muttered, "Good riddance," and smiled down at her daughter, Zoe.

"I'll have the house and outbuildings washed of their stench," her steward, Timor, noted, his lips curled in disdain.

Glancing up at the old man who had served her family for as long as she could remember, Princess Tatiana nodded. "And put guards on the road to the village so we have warning the next time the prince interferes in my life."

Orphaned two years ago when her parents died at the hands of brigands, who may or may not have been in the pay of the court, her staff was her family. Timor smiled at the princess who had grown to womanhood under his watchful eye. "With luck, we may not soon see them again."

"With luck, perhaps never. I'm told my husband has a son now, born to one of his buxom mistresses."

Timor made the warding-off sign for the devil. "I'll pray for your deliverance, your highness." Timor had traveled to Moscow with Tatiana and had seen the evil prince firsthand.

"At the moment, I *am* delivered—it's a gorgeous spring day, and once Zoe is ready for her afternoon nap, I'm going out for a ride."

The buoyant note in Tatiana's voice reminded the old retainer of better days and happier times before Prince Shuisky had entered their lives, when Tatiana had spent every spare moment on horseback. "I'll have Volia saddled and the grooms readied to escort you."

"I want to ride alone." She lightly touched the dark silky hair on her daughter's head and was rewarded with a gurgling smile. At four months, Zoe's smiles were instant and generous. "They're all gone, Timor. I'm safe."

Even if he wished to offer demur, in good conscience he couldn't. Tatiana was adored in her corner of the world. A princess in her own right, an heiress to a boyar family that had lived near Pskov since time immemorial, she was as much a part of the land as the green grass and white birches. And as revered.

In fact, the Bishop of Pskov had tried to intercede in Ivan's marriage plans for Tatiana, knowing full well the vile reputation of her husband-to-be. But even the servant of God hadn't had the power to withstand the will of the tsar. But he had personally made the long journey from Pskov to baptize Zoe when she was born and he continued to be Tatiana's advocate in all matters that pertained to her welfare.

"Tell me how far we are from Moscow, Timor," the princess said, lighthearted and gay, gently swinging her daughter in the cradle of her arms.

"Six hundred versts, my lady."

"Tell me again," she insisted, grinning.

"A world away, my lady. An entire world away," he replied, smiling himself at the joy in her eyes.

"Yes, yes, yes, *yes!*"

Zoe giggled and gurgled and drooled in response to her

mother's jubilation, her bright blue eyes focused on Tatiana's face.

"Isn't this a beautiful, happy day!" Bending low, the princess kissed her daughter's dainty nose.

And cooing spit bubbles trailed down Zoe's chin in blissful agreement.

Chapter Three

An hour later, Tatiana was riding along the southern shore of the great Lake Peipus that ran along her land for miles. Her Friesian mare was galloping in a loose-reined loping stride, enjoying the fine breeze and sunshine as much as her mistress. The winter had been long, and the sun seemed to be waking the earth from its slumber. Great flocks of birds were flying across the skies, traveling north in their spring migrations, the sound of their wings a distant roar. Colorful wildflowers raised their dainty heads through the new green grass. The lake sparkled like blue diamonds in the sunshine.

She was truly home, Tatiana thought, inhaling deeply of the pure, fresh air. She had a beautiful daughter she adored. Her staff was loved and loved her in turn. Best of all, she was far, far from the misery of Moscow.

She laughed out loud from sheer joy, the light trilling sound soaring upward in the wind, sailing over the gently rolling grassland.

Catching the ear of a troop of horsemen in the distance who touched their sword hilts in an automatic gesture of defense.

A woman would have an escort.

And these were troubled times.

* * *

They waited just inside the protective shelter of a birch grove, each man's gaze trained in the direction from which the woman's laughter had come. Their well-trained mounts remained utterly still under their rider's knees; no man spoke, their hands on their sword hilts.

The small troop wasn't equipped for battle. Lightly armored in padded leather, they wore no helmets and only carried small arms. But even without insignia, it was obvious who their leader was. He sat his sleek bay stallion with ease, his right hand raised slightly in signal to his men. He was fair, his muscled shoulders wide beneath his red leather jack, his powerful arms tanned where the soft white linen of his shirtsleeves were rolled back against the warmth of the day. His raised hand was gloved in embroidered violet leather fit for a king. And he was half smiling as though looking forward to the coming encounter.

When Tatiana rode over the crest of a rise a half-verst distant, his green eyes narrowed faintly. As she drew closer, her tawny hair became more visible, her skirts hitched up over her knees revealed shapely legs and green leather boots, her breasts beneath an embroidered jacket swayed gently as she rode. And her black Friesian mare was almost as beautiful as she.

But he waited, watching to see if she was reckless enough to be out riding alone. Moments later, when no escort appeared, his smile broadened and he dropped his hand. Half-turning in the saddle, he spoke softly to his men. Then nudging his horse with his heel, he rode out from the shelter of the birch grove to meet the rash and glorious young woman trespassing on his land.

The horseman seemed to emerge from the dappled grove before her like an apparition, but strangely the princess felt no fear. The man was fair of face and hair, his sleek, golden locks brushing his red-leather-clad shoulders. He was tanned and strong as an oak—the phrase from childhood stories coming to mind. She found herself comparing him to the pantheon of legendary heroes that had peopled her nurse's bedtime tales.

And now here he was.

One of them.

Smiling with perfect white teeth that gave further cause to think him unearthly.

But when he reined in before her, and spoke, his voice was deep and clear and real. "Good afternoon, my lady. Have you lost your way?"

Volia came to a halt of her own accord, as though she recognized authority in the tenor of the man's greeting. Tatiana shook her head. "I've ridden this land all my life."

"I own it now." But he spoke with kindness, not malice. "You're in Livonia."

"The borders keep changing," she said, as though she spoke to someone she'd always known; his Russian was without accent. "The Glinsky lands are mine."

"Ah."

He said it as though he knew everything. But how could he when she'd never seen him before? "You're new here, aren't you?" she asked.

"In a manner of speaking."

"How new?"

He smiled again so beautifully she was reminded of angels, an altogether incongruous thought with a man of such formidable strength.

"The lands came to me at Christmas."

"A splendid present."

"Hard earned though," he said, softly, the wind ruffling his hair as though in emphasis.

She knew what he meant. All lands were awarded for valor in battle or favors at court and he didn't have the sly look of a courtier. "Congratulations."

The woman was unutterably natural and open, showing neither an iota of fear nor apprehension. "Do you ride alone often?"

"You say that like I shouldn't."

He sighed in the faintest of breaths. "A woman alone can be open to misfortune."

"But I know everyone, present company excepted, of course. I'm quite safe."

"Really," he said, his gaze clearly taking issue with her statement.

"I'm Princess Glinsky."

"Princess Shuisky, you mean."

He watched her gaze turn afflicted.

"Court gossip reaches Livonia as well?" Russian suzerainty was fitful in Livonia.

He smiled. "Everyone has their sources. It's a matter of survival, is it not?"

Ivan had his spies everywhere; every powerful family did. Was he someone of Igor's cadre? Should she not be speaking to him? "Tell me your name."

"Stavr Biron."

Her brows rose. Her surprise registered, but not her relief. The Birons were archenemies of her husband.

"One of the lesser branches of the family, my lady," he noted with a quirked grin.

"I didn't know *lesser* pertained to the Birons." The Birons had ruled vast areas of Livonia and Kurland for centuries.

"As you see," he murmured, opening his arms in a lazy gesture that brought his prominent muscles into play and strongly belied his words.

She felt a curious ripple of warmth streak through her senses and had she not been less naive about the congress between the sexes she would have recognized its cause. She didn't of course. "We're neighbors then," she simply said with a smile.

By dint of his physical graces, Stavr had considerable experience with women and he recognized the faint flush on her cheeks. But he wasn't a predator by nature—and she seemed unaware. Young women of good families were often kept convent-pure until they wed. He'd met Shuisky; the prince was hardly the style of man to awaken a virginal wife. "Would you like to see my modest farmstead?" he asked, even while he knew he shouldn't be contemplating anything even remotely sexual in terms of this virtuous young woman.

FROM RUSSIA WITH LOVE / 13

"Is it far? I have to return soon." She blushed more deeply.
"My daughter is napping, but she'll soon wake . . . and—that
is—er—"

"She'll want to nurse. You don't believe in a wet-nurse?"

"No." Her mouth set in a firm line.

"Do I detect some controversy over wet-nurses?"

She suddenly smiled. "I'm sure you're not interested."

"My farm is just past the stream ford. Why not tell me
about it on the way? I'll have you back home in an hour."

She looked at him with an open gaze. "An hour, now
you're sure?"

"Less if you like."

"Very well," she said, smiling.

He felt the full force of her smile in the pit of his stomach—
or perhaps slightly lower. But he'd spent enough time at the
courts in Warsaw and Vienna; he knew the necessary graces.
"I'm honored," he murmured, tipping his head in a faint bow.
"Allow me to introduce you to my men." And so saying, he
whistled a soft bird sound and a dozen men rode from the
birches into the meadow.

Tatiana's eyes flared wide, her mouth formed into an astonished O.

"They could have been brigands, my lady. I'll see that you
have an escort home."

"Thank you," she breathed, still half-startled and then she
turned to the men who had ridden up. They were young men
like her neighbor, but seasoned veterans of battle from the
look of their weapons and armor, from the vigilance in their
eyes.

"The princess is coming to visit," Stavr explained, beginning the introductions. And his voice was such that his men
took care to be on their best behavior.

Not a single smirk gave evidence of their thoughts.

Chapter Four

What Stavr had referred to as a farm turned out to be much grander. The main house was a large three-story manor in the Italian style, its stucco walls painted a pale yellow, the broad, large windows more suited to southern climes, the entrance distinguished by twelve-foot-high carved double doors. The gardens that bordered the drive gave evidence of a woman's touch and for an odd second, Tatiana experienced a disappointment.

"My mother has promised to help me with the gardens," her host noted, as he rode beside her. "I'm told the roses in summer scent the land for miles."

"Your mother," the princess murmured, her mood curiously lightening.

"She lives in Riga," Stavr replied, charmed by her artlessness. She was really quite transparent; it almost made one reconsider the merits in virgins. "You'll have to meet her sometime."

"I'd like that." How long had it been since she'd enjoyed the company of someone other than her staff?

"She's promised to visit when the roses are in bloom."

"You must both come and dine, then."

"Thank you, we will." He made a mental note to send a message to his mother reminding her of her promise. And while his designs on the princess were inchoate, or marginally so, perhaps even nonexistent, he was already looking forward to the roses blooming.

He wasn't in the habit of serving tea; his was a bachelor establishment. In fact, he and his men had only recently returned from a campaign fighting the Turks. He planned to stay on his estate for the summer, seeing to his crops, letting his men and mounts recuperate in body and spirit before returning to the hostilities in the south.

Summoning his cook when they entered the house, he gave her orders for tea. The plump peasant woman gazed at him, then at Tatiana with a knowing smile as he issued directives, then nodded her head and bowed. "Humpf, tea, indeed, my lord," she was heard to say under her breath as she walked away.

As her rotund form disappeared down the hall, Stavr turned to Tatiana, his smile rueful. "My apologies. The servants came with the house."

"My servants are as unceremonious. One becomes immune."

Was her comment ingenuous or insinuating? "So you pay no heed."

"It depends, I suppose, whether I want my dinner on time," she replied with a grin. "Although, I much prefer their informality to the cunning address at court."

There was his answer. She was a guileless young girl, quite unaware of the significance of his cook's comment. And he would do well to remember that. "How true. I would rather face a regiment of Turks, than one scheming minister at court. Come, we'll wait for our tea." Gesturing toward a small parlor, he began unbuckling his jack.

Moments later, they were seated across from each other on a pair of settees upholstered in crimson silk. "I feel out of place in a room like this." He indicated the muraled walls and chandeliers. "I'm much more comfortable in a tent in the wild."

"That sounds very appealing at the moment." Well out of reach of her husband, she thought.

She shouldn't have spoken in such a breathy tone. While he doubted it was intentional, his reaction was intense—thoughts of the innocent Tatiana in his tent in the wilds entirely lewd. "It's not the life for a woman," he murmured, abruptly coming to his feet and moving to a nearby table. "Would you like some wine?" Without waiting for an answer, he lifted a decanter from a silver tray, poured some wine into a glass and quickly tossed it down.

Heavy drinking was a way of life at court and outside, so Tatiana wasn't surprised. But she'd not been raised in such a household. "No thank you. I'll wait for tea."

She was virtuous, indeed. Ordinarily, he was uninterested in virtue, but he found himself curiously intrigued. Perhaps her splendid beauty overruled his normal inclinations, or her sweet candor. Maybe the fact that she clearly disliked her husband made her a fascinating pawn in the animosities that had long existed between the Shuiskys and Birons. Then again, perhaps he was as perverse as her depraved husband and simply wished to blemish such unsullied innocence for no other reason than he could.

But a second later, he dismissed such uncharacteristic thoughts, vowed to have tea and then quickly send her home.

No doubt, he'd been on campaign too long.

And she wasn't like the women one met while campaigning or at court for that matter. She was naive as a nun.

Pouring himself another glass of wine, he returned to his chair, his desires sensibly in check. "Have you met the tsar?" he asked, considering conversation about the demented ruler sufficient to distract his mind from other more illicit thoughts.

"Once, briefly. At my wedding."

"And?"

"I wouldn't wish to comment."

He smiled. "Are you always so prudent?"

"About some things," she said, her gaze suddenly drawn to his, as though they both suddenly found the word, prudent, equivocal. Or maybe she'd never seen such a wondrous, warm smile. Or a man lounging like that in casual invitation, golden-haired and full of grace, exquisitely virile, alluring—unlike her husband who was rough and crude and black as sin through and through.

He dropped his gaze before the longing in her eyes because he knew better than to take advantage of such innocence. And his voice when he spoke was neutral. "In terms of the tsar, prudence is always sensible. I have the advantage of being nominally beyond his reach in Livonia."

"How fortunate for you." She'd had time to compose her sensibilities. If what she was feeling was some attraction to her splendid host, surely she must resist it.

He took note of a servant entering the room with a sense of relief. He couldn't remember when he'd last had to restrain his sexual impulses. "Ah, here we have it," he said, exhaling softly.

Muttered comments aside, his cook had outdone herself. Numerous servants arrived with numerous trays of sweets and confections, an enormous silver samovar and several choices of tea, compliments of the active trade with China that had long existed. The princess selected a favorite tea, a servant readied it for them and served the steaming liquid in porcelain cups so fragile they were almost transparent.

"Your hands are very large," Tatiana noted, smiling at the cup dwarfed in his hand.

And yours are very small, he wished to say if he could allow himself a personal remark. "An advantage when hoisting a sword," he said instead.

"Do you fight for Russia?"

"Sometimes. More often for Lithuania or Poland." The boyar clans had a tradition of seeking service where they chose, offering their sword arms and cavalry units wherever they could best secure their privileged rights or strengthen their family position. In order for cadet branches and individual hetmen such as Stavr to prosper, they occasionally had to range farther afield. "I'm recently back from the Ukraine where Sigismund the Second is seeking to enlarge his domains. I return in the fall."

"Oh," she said, the small sound shimmering in the air for what seemed an endless moment.

"Will you be staying?" He shouldn't ask, but without reason, he wanted to know.

"I'm not sure." She grimaced faintly and plucked at the azure linen of her skirt. "I serve my husband's whims."

While he didn't personally have spies in Moscow, his uncle kept ears at court. Prince Shuisky figured prominently in all the tsar's debauches. "Court life is busy, I suspect."

"One can but hope." She lifted her cup to her mouth and drained the remaining tea.

"I see."

"You needn't look at me with pity. I'm no different than other wives."

"Of course not." But it was a shame to waste such beauty on a brute like Shuisky.

She suddenly flushed, then gasped and for a second he wondered if he'd spoken his thoughts aloud.

"I really must go," she said, nervously.

Following her glance, he took note of two dark stains beginning to form on the natural linen of her jacket directly over her nipples. "Would you like one of my shirts or jackets?" he quickly offered.

The color on her cheeks deepened. "I'm so embarrassed."

"Please, don't be. My sister has five children. I've seen infants nursed countless times. Allow me to lend you—what?— a shirt or jacket?"

Her gaze met his fleetingly, then veered aside, her lashes shuttering her eyes. "A shirt if you don't mind. I seem to have more milk than my daughter needs," she added, turning bright red as the stains widened.

From anyone else but the chaste young woman before him, his answer would have been obvious. In fact, his body was overlooking her chastity with a vengeance and he was debating how best to call for a servant without having to rise. "That's good, is it not?" he said, a new tautness in his voice. "Some women are not so fortunate."

"And some women at court apparently prefer wet-nurses," the princess said, pettishly.

"Your husband sent one from Moscow?" Shouting for a servant might call more rather than less attention to his condition, he decided, opting for a brief respite before summoning a servant.

"She was so filthy, I wouldn't let her touch Zoe. I sent her back."

The princess had autocratic tendencies, it seemed. Perhaps her modesty was confined to sexual matters. "How old is your daughter?" he asked, needing a moment more to compose himself before coming to his feet.

"Four months. She's an absolute angel."

"Why wouldn't she be with you for a mother." It was a spontaneous remark, one he would have made to any charming woman, but her gaze dropped and she looked so agitated, he quickly added, "My sister might come to visit with my mother. She's sure to want to see your daughter."

"That would be lovely, but I *really* must go."

"I'll call some men to see you home."

"I-if—you don't mind—er—the shirt . . ."

"Of course." Rising, he quickly turned from her and walked to the door.

She watched him as he moved away, taking in the splendor of his tall form, wondering what it would be like to live with a man like Stavr Biron who was actually capable of having a conversation with a woman. He even spoke to his servants kindly, while her husband treated everyone with cruelty and scorn. Not that she should even consider making comparisons.

"They'll bring you a shirt in a moment," Stavr said, returning.

"Thank you." Nimbus-like in the sunlight, his golden hair framed his face, his benevolent gaze and warm smile evocative as well of saintly grace, while his powerful body reminded her starkly of the militant saints on precious icons. All reasons perhaps why she was so profoundly moved, why his presence alone intoxicated.

She couldn't have known all women were sensitive to Stavr's charm, although rarely impelled by saintly motive.

She couldn't have known he was the darling of every hot-blooded woman who crossed his path.

Tatiana only knew what she was feeling was temptation. And she must resist.

Chapter Five

Once the shirt arrived, Stavr helped Tatiana don it, holding it out as she slipped her arms into the sleeves. Her scent was sweet in his nostrils, her small form inches away, only sheer will keeping him from drawing her back into his body and testing her modesty. Would she bolt if he were to run his fingers through her tousled hair? What would she do if he were to kiss her rosy cheek half-turned to him? Would she sigh in surrender or cry out?

He knew the answer. His seductive skills were well-honed.

So the question was rather Would he dishonor her?

For a hovering moment he held the shirt between his fingertips . . . then he let it drop on her shoulders.

There were women aplenty in the neighborhood who would tax only his stamina not his honor. He drew back, not one step, but two because the demure Princess Tatiana was the veriest of temptations and he was keenly tempted.

"My men are waiting outside, my lady."

The minute edge in his voice brought her head around and she glanced at him over his shoulder with the faintest of drawn brows. "I appreciate your kindness," she said softly.

"My pleasure."

His bow was unconscious, a small, refined motion and she wondered where he'd learned such civility. The Russian court from her brief observation was not so discriminating in its conduct.

Uncomfortable under her scrutiny, struggling to keep his desires in check, he said, gruffly, "This way, my lady," and waved her to the door.

Was he suddenly angry with her? Had she done something of which he disapproved? She had no experience to draw from, no easy conversation to smooth over the moment. So she preceded him out of the parlor, past the servants in the entry hall, through the grand outer doors held open for them.

Their mounts had been left waiting on the drive.

Another awkward moment ensued as Stavr debated lifting her onto her saddle. He wasn't sure he could deal with even so simple a gesture.

She stood by her mount, uncertain, hesitant.

Drawing in a breath of constraint, he grasped her around her slender waist, tried to ignore her large, full breasts almost brushing his chest, and tossed her up onto her saddle without making eye contact. Then he signaled his waiting men forward.

"My troopers will see you home." There were eight of them, fully armed this time. "Thank you for a pleasant visit." He wasn't capable of nonchalance in the presence of his men who knew him too well and he wasn't about to physically embarrass himself by prolonging the conversation. "I'll send you a message when my mother arrives."

"I'd like that." Even if she wished to say more, it was impossible. They were virtual strangers.

He could have said more. Unlike the princess, he had experience with dalliance. But that was precisely what he was trying to avoid. "Until the roses bloom, then," he said with a nod.

Taking her cue, Tatiana nudged her horse forward and Stavr's men fell in behind her.

He stood on the gravel drive, watching her ride away until

she was a tiny speck on the horizon. Restless, consumed with longing, he wasn't entirely sure why he was attracted to such innocence. Certainly, she would be gauche and awkward to bed, perhaps even frightened. He had no illusions about Shuisky's tutorial skills; the man was a pig. Running his fingers through his hair, he exhaled in frustration and reminded himself there were any number of ladies nearby who were more than willing to entertain him.

So forget about the sweet princess with milk-heavy breasts.

He swore under his breath, the erotic image that sprang to mind not likely to inhibit his whimsical predilection for the luscious Tatiana.

He needed a drink or ten or twenty and then perhaps he could blunt his iniquitous cravings. Walking back into the house, he called for more wine. "Bring the bottles into the armory," he ordered, moving down the hall to the room where he and his men were most comfortable. There were always troopers present in the armory—gambling or readying their weapons, passing the time of day in idleness. Numerous whistles and ribald remarks greeted his entrance.

It was a man's world not only in the armory, but everywhere.

Although male amusements were the current focus of attention here with his men on leave. "We didn't think we'd be seeing you anytime soon, Stavr. Didn't she like you?"

The young hetman surveyed the various droll looks and roguish grins, his brows drawn into a faint frown because the worst of it was she did like him—even if she didn't realize it. "She's married," he grunted.

"The best kind," someone replied. "You don't have to marry them."

"She's Shuisky's wife."

"So? He's eighty hours of hard riding away."

Stavr slumped into a chair, lifted a wine bottle to his mouth, muttered, "Unfortunately, she's virtuous," and poured a long draft down his throat.

"Don't say you're losing your touch," another man noted, grinning.

He lifted his bottle toward his men."Gallantry forbids me."

"Since when?"

"Since she looked at me with such innocence I was reminded of a wide-eyed child."

The room went still; regardless of their intemperance, they adhered to a code of honor.

"Let's ride to the crossroads tavern tonight," a trooper interjected into the silence. "The women there are all old enough to know what they want."

"Hear, hear!" A dozen voices took up the chant.

"Go without me," Stavr murmured, waving them off. "I'll drink myself into an oblivion here."

Another moment of silence ensued. Their leader never drank alone.

Stavr looked up at the sudden hush. "I'll join you next time."

"You're not sick, now?" There was genuine concern in the trooper's voice.

He shook his head. "I'm just not in the mood for tavern company."

The men looked at each other with shock. Tavern life was usual, customary and habitual to their existence.

"Don't look at me like that. I'm fine." Pulling a purse from his pocket, he tossed it on the table. "Drink with my compliments tonight."

A brief interval later, alone in the silence of the armory, Stavr slid lower in his chair and with a disgruntled sigh contemplated his moral dilemma. Clearly, the lady could be seduced. Such innocence would submit to smooth blandishments with ease. And being married to Shuisky only made her more susceptible to kindness from a man. So the question wasn't whether she could be persuaded to join him in bed, but rather whether he could in good conscience ruin her.

He exhaled in frustration, unfamiliar with curbing his lust. If he was sensible, he'd put her out of his mind and content himself with experienced bed partners who understood the game. Reaching out, he lined up the wine bottles on the table, setting them close at hand. And then he proceeded to drink himself into a stupor in some misguided attempt to forget the Princess Tatiana who was clearly and emphatically outside the pale.

Chapter Six

While Stavr forwent sleep for drink, Tatiana's night was sleepless for reasons of her own. Her thoughts were consumed with tantalizing images of a tall, fair-haired man with an angel's smile and no matter how she tossed or turned, she couldn't displace the tempting visions. Recalling each word he'd spoken, every movement he'd made, she dwelt on their time together from every possible perspective—the imagery all consuming, bewitching, potent lure to a chaste young lady starved for affection.

But beneath the pleasing fantasy, she understood how compromising her musings were, how scandalous, and she greeted the sunrise with relief. Daylight would expose the practical, mundane aspects of her world, and she would be reminded of the true nature of reality.

But even as she rose at first light, conscious as she was of the mortal sin of desire, she was nevertheless filled with an irrepressible sense of expectation.

Stavr saw the sun rise as well, although his view was marginally muted by bleary eyes and a befuddled brain. Perhaps more strangely to a man who viewed himself as an archpragmatist, he felt a piquant, skittish anticipation without cause.

Or more to the point, without useful cause.

He should have gone to the tavern last night and assuaged his lust.

Maybe he should see who was available, here, now. Surely between the household staff and the several hundred peasant families on his estate, there might be a woman or two who was interested in sleeping with the master.

Although, strangely, where such a casual liaison would have been employed without thought in the past, he found himself curiously selective. Violet eyes and tawny hair, an artless smile and the sweet, alluring uncertainty of virtue were what he craved.

Which made him a damnable fool.

And perhaps no less depraved than her husband if he took advantage of such innocence.

"You finally emptied the bottles, I see. Would you like breakfast now?"

He turned to the sound of the grating voice a trifle too fast and winced.

His cook, who apparently had some seniority in the household from her tone of voice, stood in the doorway of the armory, looking cross. Either she disapproved of drink or of sleepless nights.

"Do you want breakfast here or in the breakfast room?" she inquired, sniffing the cloying wine fumes with disdain.

Immune to disdain, particularly immune to a servant's censure, the count slowly surveyed the disorderly array of empty bottles before him because any sudden movement of his eyes was painful. "The breakfast room," he muttered and heaved himself out of his chair. Groaning softly at the jolt to his brain, he slowly began to move toward the door.

He wasn't in the habit of overimbibing; the princess was to blame, he resentfully concluded, each step jarring his senses.

As she was to blame for his mental distress and unsated lust.

Not that blame was likely to mitigate his dour mood *or* his lust.

He wasn't sure even a practiced courtesan would suffice, which meant something was terribly wrong, he decided, sourly.

Not presently capable of debating the merits of experienced versus inexperienced females, he concentrated on walking with as little movement as possible in an effort to mitigate the hammering in his brain. And when he finally reached the breakfast room, he carefully eased himself into his chair. Blinking against the glare from the windows, he half-raised his hand. "Shut the drapes," he directed. Then, turning aside to avoid the blinding sunlight, he noticed an object laying beside his plate.

A silver baby rattle.

Glancing at his cook who was standing at his side, looking coy, he flicked a finger toward the article. "This has some meaning, I presume."

"You haven't seen the nursery yet, my lord. You might find some items there that would be of interest to you"—her smirk was blatant—"or to the princess."

"I hardly think so." His voice was curt. "I prefer ham to sausage—take the sausage away. And no kvass this morning, just tea."

"Yes, my lord. But look at the painted cradle. It's very fine."

His scowl sent her scurrying from the room to do his bidding. But she was smiling because the servants had observed their master with his visitor yesterday—spying on one's betters was not only sensible but rewarding—and bets were being taken by the staff on when the princess would return.

Damned interfering servants, Stavr grumbled silently. Why the hell would he want to look at a cradle? Shoving the offending rattle out of his line of vision, he reached for his tea.

Several versts away, Tatiana's maid was hovering over her as she ate her breakfast. Since the maid slept in an adjacent room, she was aware of the princess's restless night. Also, the maid wasn't an innocent like her mistress, and Tatiana's return in the company of the Biron troopers hadn't gone unnoticed. She had her own notions apropos of Tatiana's sleeplessness. Hadn't Timor said she'd met the hetman? Wasn't he the object of fantasy for every female within twenty versts?

"What do you think of the new owner of the Kettler estate, my lady?" Olga watched her mistress's face closely as she offered her a plate of sugared apricots.

"He's very pleasant." Tatiana picked up a glazed fruit, trying not to blush.

The maid took note of the color rising on her mistress's cheeks. "He's just arrived, I hear."

"So he said. Apparently, he's back from campaigning in the Ukraine. A soldier for hire, I believe." She tried to speak in a bland tone.

"He's at the service of the Polish king, they say. But then noble families always take care of their own."

Tatiana looked up, a hint of surprise in her gaze. "He made no mention of a title." Hetmen were more likely soldiers of fortune than aristocrats.

"His father, the late count, served the Lithuanian royal family. His sister married into rich merchant dynasty in Riga. His mother lives on his family estate."

Tatiana put her spoon down and pushed away her plate. "How do you know all this?"

"My cousin has a friend who works at the merchant's house. It is very grand. With glass windows from floor to ceiling and soft carpets from the east on every floor. She says they're rich like mongol khans."

Why hadn't Stavr mentioned his title? Or more to the point, why couldn't she get him out of her mind? It was imperative that she do just that. She was a married woman and married women did not cherish memories of handsome young men outside the bonds of matrimony. Not only was it dishonorable, it was criminal.

And with a husband like hers, such an indiscretion could be

deadly. "Olga, would you see if Zoe is up yet?" She required an abrupt diversion from her thoughts; she needed to be reminded of all she could lose. "If she's awake, bring her down."

"Yes, ma'am. Will you go riding again today?"

Tatiana shook her head. "I'll take Zoe to see the orphaned wolf cubs the huntsman is raising. She adores them."

Once Zoe was fed and bathed, Tatiana concentrated on entertaining her daughter, putting aside dangerous longings. She and Zoe went to see the wolf cubs, paddled their feet in the stream running through the orchard, swung on the swing hanging from the huge pine tree near the small lake fronting her house; they even spent some time in the kitchen arranging the menus for the coming week.

By deliberately focusing on the ordinary activities of her day, she was able to forget for a time the memory of a handsome golden-haired man who was much too tempting for her peace of mind. Not to mention her mortality.

And perhaps she would have successfully withstood temptation had not a servant come to her asking whether she wished the count's freshly laundered shirt returned to him by messenger?

The obvious answer was yes. A woman of conscience would have said exactly that. A woman sensible of the dangers inherent in pursuing any future friendship would have. Instead, Tatiana found herself saying, "Zoe and I will return the shirt. Have my horse saddled and two grooms readied to accompany us."

Chapter Seven

After eating a substantial breakfast, Stavr felt as though the pounding in his head had diminished enough for him to comfortably rise. Although he carefully tested his hypothesis, coming to his feet slowly. After taking a few preliminary steps, he came to the conclusion he was sufficiently recuperated to deal with the duties of his day.

Standing motionless in the shadowed breakfast room, he debated what was first apt to require his attention. Several possibilities came to mind; his was a working farm, after all, and the spring planting was in full operation. He bit his lower lip in contemplation or perhaps consternation. Deciding discretion had never been his strong suit, and the spring planting would go on without his immediate supervision, he walked from the room.

As the cook and those servants conscious of the latest gossip suspected, the count took the stairs to the second floor. After opening various doors fronting the main corridor, he eventually found the nursery. Standing in the doorway, tight-lipped, he surveyed the sunny room. The cradle was indeed beautiful, carved and painted, embellished with gilt, the smiling sun and moon at its head and foot forcing a grudging smile from him.

Tatiana might like the whimsical object, although, she no doubt had a cradle if her daughter was four months old.

Furthermore, if he had half a brain, whether she did or not, would be irrelevant. He should shut the door and get on with his life.

But he didn't. He moved into the room and walked about, examining the various articles and furniture common to a nursery: a painted rocker, a small table and chairs, shelves of toys in wood, silver, gold and colorful enamels. A bed, built low to the ground for a child old enough to sleep alone, rested in one corner. A very small wooden rocking horse, with a real horsehair mane and tail held a place of honor in a window alcove. And dolls of every type were ensconced on the pillows of a canopied swan-shaped crib.

The last owners of the manor had died without heirs, their children having succumbed to childhood diseases or the ravages of war in adulthood he'd been told. They'd left behind a collection of beautiful possessions that had come to him because he'd led a cavalry charge that had been decisive in gaining victory for Sigismund II, perhaps even saving his throne. "Blood spilled" in the military service of a king or prince as they said.

And this was his reward.

It was a much larger estate than the modest one he'd inherited, a prosperous estate with three hundred peasants to work the land, in addition to a village that was the center of commerce in the area. The lake was near with its thriving fishing industry. And from each undertaking, he collected his share of taxes. Such flourishing holdings almost made one consider settling down.

If he wasn't twenty-six.

If he still didn't have battles to fight and booty to gain.

He smiled. Mostly, if he wasn't twenty-six.

Picking up a delicate painted doll, he surveyed its brightly painted wooden face, tested its moveable arms and legs, smoothed his finger over it's little embroidered dress brilliant with colorful silk threads. His smile broadened. Tatiana's baby was four months old; she might like a little doll. Tucking the toy into his jacket pocket, he bent to pick up the cradle. Maybe the princess could use two cradles.

Chapter Eight

After bathing in the bathhouse, the count quickly dressed and a short time later, he and his small escort of troopers cantered down the drive.

At the same time, Tatiana and Zoe, along with her grooms were midway in their journey. Zoe lay asleep in a sling suspended from Tatiana's shoulders, the gentle rhythm of the horse, and the sound of her mother's heart under her ear conducive to sleep. Stavr's freshly ironed shirt was folded in Tatiana's saddle bag and she was rehearsing her initial words of greeting.

Something casual would best serve, she thought: We were out for a ride and thought you might like your shirt back; Zoe loves to ride so I thought we'd ride your way and return your shirt; It was such a beautiful day—I hope you don't mind we rode over.

Oh, Lord, what if he looked right through her or worse was offended? What if he wasn't home? Or perhaps he might be entertaining, or terrible thought, he might have a woman keeping him company? She'd heard bits of gossip in the kitchen about his seductive appeal. Not that she hadn't found a modicum of reassurance in those rumors. It helped to know she wasn't the only woman susceptible to his good looks and charm.

Or was it reassuring when she shouldn't be susceptible at all?

She flushed at the impropriety of what she was about to do and for a moment she debated turning her horse and returning home. But something indeterminate stopped her—a feeling, a need, a compulsion so powerful it wouldn't be contravened.

Then Zoe suddenly woke and smiled and gurgled at her mother as though telling her all's right with the world.

It was a sign.

Stavr rode ahead, preferring not to converse with his men when his reasons for traveling into Russia were beyond explanation. They seemed to understand and withheld their usual teasing. They knew something had changed.

They could understand courting a woman with gifts.

But not cradles and baby toys.

The cradle was strapped on a packhorse tied to Stavr's saddle, the wooden doll suspended from his saddle pommel and while he'd been silent about all but their destination, he was bathed and perfumed and wearing his finest linen shirt for this visit.

His troopers had armed themselves well; they knew Shuisky took pleasure in killing. He was the tsar's comrade in arms on his nocturnal excursions to the torture chambers beneath the Kremlin, and even in a brutal culture, the number of men who found amusement in torture were few.

It would have been more sensible had Stavr chosen someone else to court. But then none of them were sensible. If they were, they would have been farmers.

Stavr saw the princess first, his keen eyesight often lifesaving to a man of his calling. He recognized her horse from its color and gait, took note of the sun gleaming off her pale hair. Was she coming to see him? Or was this just a lucky coincidence? Perhaps the lady was less virtuous than he thought. The latter possibility intrigued him most, he decided, smiling faintly. Spurring his mount, he set off to greet the woman who had become a fever in his blood.

* • •

Moments later, when Tatiana's grooms called her attention to the troopers approaching and she caught sight of Stavr's powerful form in the lead, all her apprehensions melted away. Perhaps she wasn't alone in her feelings of bewitchment. Perhaps, she thought with a shiver of delight, he felt the same. But even as a thrill of excitement raced through her senses, a niggling voice reminded her of the possible dire consequences to such a friendship.

He raised his hand in greeting just then and even from afar, she could see the flash of his smile. An inexplicable jubilance warmed her soul and jettisoning her misgivings, she waved back.

How could it matter if she simply talked to him?

She had Zoe and her grooms with her.

She was safe.

Stavr slowed his mount as she approached and they met on a windswept meadow, under a blue, blue sky so pure and bright it could only be a reflection of their cloudless joy. Their escorts, less imprudent than their masters, took the measure of each other while those they were there to protect remained a blissful island unto themselves.

The breeze off the lake swirled about the two young nobles in eddying currents, ruffling their hair, the fine linen of their garments, the horsetail whips hanging from their saddles. "Did I say what a pleasure it is to see you again?" Stavr said, reaching out to brush away a ringlet from Tatiana's cheek.

She shook her head and smiled. "But I could tell."

For a moment he thought she meant something lascivious until she added softly, "You have the nicest smile."

He hadn't heard a woman say anything so sweetly naive in a decade. "Thank you. I had reason to smile when I caught sight of you. And you brought Zoe," he murmured, his attention drawn to the infant who was observing him with the mindful look babies reserved for strangers.

Tatiana stroked her daughter's little hand clutching the fabric of the sling. "She likes to go riding."

A shadow suddenly swept over them and glancing up they saw an eagle soaring overhead, its broad wingspan silhouetted against the sun.

"It must be a sign," Stavr murmured, with a smile. "Not that I needed one."

"It's my name day, too," Tatiana said, shyly.

"Perfect."

For a magnetic moment their pagan sensibilities met, and the quixotic reasons that had brought them here were suddenly resolved.

"I would have come earlier, but I restrained myself," the count said without artifice.

"I as well," Tatiana replied. "I told myself it was a sin."

"No, never."

She sighed softly. "Even if it is, I don't care."

"It isn't, believe me." Long a participant in the world of opportunistic savagery, he better than most understood the definition of sin.

Their escorts had dropped back as though they knew they were de trop and Stavr and the princess sat their horses knee to knee, the warmth of her leg pressed against his.

"Send your grooms away," he said. "I'll dispatch my men as well and we can be alone."

She glanced at her daughter, then at him. "I shouldn't." Her words were barely audible.

"I've thought of you every minute, every second."

Her gaze dropped against the heat in his eyes and her heart suddenly began beating like a drum.

Arching her little back, Zoe languorously stretched, pushing her pudgy fists skyward with a babbling exhalation of sound.

Shifting the attention to her, effectively diffusing the taut moment.

"Forgive me," Stavr said with a rueful smile. "I'm too rash."

"You aren't alone, my lord. I rode over today on the pretext of returning your shirt."

He smiled. "We're both impetuous, then."

"I'm not as a rule. Actually, I'm not at all," she added in further disclaimer.

Her frankness was unutterably charming. He could have said, he didn't as a rule court virginal women, but such bluntness might alarm her and she was indecisive enough. "Since, unfortunately, I'm much too presumptuous, I shall endeavor to restrain my urges," he said, bowing faintly, "and speak of more agreeable things." He brushed his gloved finger over Zoe's cheek. "She looks like you."

"Thank you." No one had ever said that, their coloring so different, her husband's mark strong on his daughter. "I think so too."

"I brought her some toys." Lifting the doll from his saddle pommel, he gently swung it before Zoe's wide-eyed gaze, chuckling as she grabbed it. "I brought a cradle too, although you must have one already." He indicated the packhorse behind him. "If you like we can put Zoe in the cradle under those trees over there and I'll tell you"—he smiled—"in the most respectable way, how you ruined my night."

She smiled back; it was impossible to resist his charm or his gallantry in trying to put her at ease. "We could compare notes on ruined nights."

His eyes sparkled and he tipped his head in the direction of her escort. "Tell them to go."

"Not too far," she returned, caution in her voice.

"Far enough so they can't see us."

Her eyes flared wide for a moment. "I can't."

"Far enough so they can't hear us, then."

She drew in a deep breath, glanced at her daughter who was giggling as she played a gentle tug of war with Stavr over the wooden doll. "You know of my husband."

"Your servants are loyal to you are they not?"

"Of course, but—"

"We'll just talk. Nothing more."

"There can be nothing more."

When in the past, he would have said something teasingly seductive, he said, instead in the gentlest of tones, "I would never cause you harm."

She hesitated a moment more and then turned to her grooms and raised her voice enough to be heard. "Wait for me near the lake."

Stavr simply nodded at his men; their understanding was superb.

And the Biron and Glinsky men rode toward the lakeshore together.

Stavr released his grip on the doll and Zoe promptly brought it to her mouth to taste. Waving toward the tree line bordering the meadow, he said, "After you, my lady. My cook packed some food you might like."

"What if I hadn't come to see you?" Tatiana nudged Volia with her heels and turned her toward the trees.

"We could have eaten under the shade of *your* trees," he murmured, keeping pace beside her mount.

"I might have had company. What then?"

"Can't a neighbor visit?" he returned, smoothly.

She glanced at him, her small nose wrinkling in consternation. "You may know what you're doing, but I don't in the least."

"You mistake me, princess. I'm completely out of my depth."

Her smile was instant and glorious; he almost leaned over and kissed her from sheer delight.

"I'm so very glad," she said in a small breathless voice. "I shouldn't be, but I am. And I have no reasonable explanation for my joy."

"As I have no explanation"—his brows rose—"for neglecting my duties at home. The planting season is critical."

"But I'm more critical."

Her voice was playful and for a moment he wondered whether she was that outrageously naive or simply a cunning little seductress.

"I'm sorry," she said, taking note of his examining look. "I only meant it in jest and now, I've offended you. My mother always said I was too outspoken for a woman." It was a time when many well-born women in Russia lived their lives in the enclosed and protected part of the house known as the terem.

"Not in the least," he replied, thinking he'd find out soon enough whether she was sly or artless.

"Oh, good, because another reason I didn't know if I should come to see you was that gossip has it you're much in demand with the ladies. And I know nothing of such things."

Untouchable madonna or seductress, she spoke with shocking directness. "Gossip is much overrated, my lady, I assure you."

"I can see why the ladies would like you, though. Surely you're aware of your good looks."

He was currently putting his money on her ingenue status, because none of the seductresses he knew would have been so pointed in their flattery. "Good looks don't help you much in battle," he replied deprecatingly.

"Well, I find them very appealing. You're absolutely glorious, you know, like the golden heroes of my childhood tales."

"Hardly, my lady—although, in terms of glory, I doubt you have equal. You must have dazzled Ivan's court." Her expression instantly turned grave and he quickly added, "Forgive me. I spoke out of turn again."

"Please don't speak of . . . *him.*"

"Never again. Tell me, does Zoe roll over yet?"

She softly laughed. "You're so very adept, aren't you?"

"Does she?" he countered, not wishing to discuss his adeptness.

"Yes . . . in the most lurching, tottering way. And it's always a surprise for her when she accomplishes the feat."

"I remember seeing my sister's babies struggling to master the process."

"Do you see your sister often?"

"When I'm home, I do."

This home or the home near Riga, she wondered, her

maid's narrative coming to mind. "Why didn't you tell me you were a count?"

"Does it matter?"

"Not in the least."

She *was* naive. It mattered considerably in the world at large.

"Zoe and I don't care about titles, do we, darling?" she murmured, turning away from his scrutiny.

"Very sensible," he tactfully replied. "Ah . . . here, we have some shade." Drawing his horse to a stop, he gestured toward a stand of birch, not in the mood to discuss the inequalities of society—he more interested, when the time was right, in reducing the inequalities between himself and a virtuous woman. Quickly dismounting, he moved to her side and raised his arms to lift her from the saddle, cautioning himself to behave. But as she threw her leg over the saddle pommel, the glimpse of her pink thigh not only brought a sheen to his brow, but severely tested his chivalry. She seemed unaware though, so he forced himself to keep her at arm's length as she slid into his waiting arms.

Zoe's presence was further curb to his intemperance. He was, in fact, grateful for the baby's company. Without her, it would have been difficult restraining himself.

"Your servants are all Glinsky staff?" he questioned, as he led her to a quiet spot under the sheltering trees, his query partly urbane and partly defensive.

"They're like members of the family. I trust them implicitly."

He nodded.

"But I'm not—I mean . . . I wouldn't want you to think that—"

"Of course not."

While she should have been content with his response, she found herself minutely chagrined at his dismissive tone. Was she not as pretty or charming as his numerous lady friends? Was she not as alluring? But as quickly as she took issue with his response, she reminded herself that such thoughts were entirely inappropriate, not to mention improper. "I appreciate your understanding," she said in what she hoped was a casual, unconcerned tone.

Not sure her understanding and his were even remotely aligned, Stavr chose to evade further discussion of the subject. "This spot should do," he murmured. "Let me get a blanket to sit on." As he moved away, he refused to contemplate what else might be done on a blanket; the lady was too uncertain.

Returning with the cradle, he set it down and lifting out a blanket, spread the brightly striped fabric on the ground. "Let me take Zoe from you," he remarked, turning back to Tatiana.

"I don't think she'll let you touch her."

"I have a trick that never fails," he said with a smile and proceeded to whistle a lively little tune filled with warbling runs that mesmerized Zoe. He was able to lift her from the sling without her noticing, so intent was she on the sounds issuing from his mouth.

Tatiana's brows rose in admiration. "You certainly know what you're doing."

Turning Zoe so she could see her mother, he grinned. "Babies like me."

It was tempting—a line like that, but even a tyro like Tatiana knew better than to tell him she liked him too—when she shouldn't.

A small silence fell.

"Why don't you look in that basket and see if you find anything that appeals to you," Stavr remarked, keeping his voice neutral. "There's some foods for Zoe too."

"How did you know I would bring Zoe?"

"I was planning on seeing you at your home."

She blushed.

"But I'm pleased you rode over instead. Very pleased," he added, as Zoe grabbed a handful of his hair and stuffed it in her mouth. "We have more privacy here."

"Don't say that."

"Well, my men will enjoy their luncheon out of doors, then.

Is that better?" He lifted his arm and turned his shirt cuff toward Zoe to distract her. She immediately released his hair and reached for the shiny gold button.

"Let me take her. She's going to ruin your shirt."

"Why don't you find her another toy? And relax. You're making me nervous."

She laughed. "Am I really? I wouldn't have thought you the type."

"Sit down," he said with a half-smile, "stop looking over your shoulder and once Zoe has some toys to amuse her, I'll tell you what type I am."

And over the course of the next hour, they talked of any number of things while Zoe played on the blanket with her new toys. They ate the cook's array of cold foods, drank wine, and talked with ease—as though they'd known each other forever. Perhaps the Birons and Glinskys had been in residence in the area so long their frames of reference were the same. Perhaps they were simply kindred spirits. They found they both preferred the country to the city. Neither missed the machinations of the court; they both adored horse racing; and when it came to children, they agreed they were infinitely charming.

"And yet you have none, when you're so very good with them," Tatiana noted, smiling at him as he lay on his back holding Zoe on his chest, his large hands remarkably gentle with the baby. Zoe was intrigued with the red embroidery on the collar of Stavr's shirt. She'd tasted each cross-stitched star until the fabric was soaked with her drool.

"Some day," he murmured. "When I'm done with campaigning."

"Some men never are."

He gazed at her from under his lashes. "If all goes well, I might be finished with war after this next campaign. Provided, no one invades my estates."

"Will the rewards be sufficient to retire?"

"We ride into the Crimea."

"To bring home Ottoman wealth."

"God willing and give Sigismund a larger domain in the bargain."

Zoe began whimpering, no longer satisfied with embroidery.

He glanced down at Zoe's fretful expression. "That sounds like a hungry cry to me."

"You're very perceptive for a soldier."

Rising to a sitting position with an effortless grace, he handed Zoe to her mother. "Remember, I lived with my sister for a year." He hadn't mentioned that he'd been recuperating from serious wounds. "One learns any number of cries."

"You can't look," she directed, lifting Zoe from his hands.

He was smiling. "Yes, ma'am."

"I'm serious."

Rolling over on his stomach, he faced the lake, his back to her. "I'm not looking, now. You're quite safe."

For a flashing moment, she wished she didn't have to worry about being safe. She wished she could say, "I don't want to be safe. I want to hold you and touch you and kiss you," although she wasn't entirely sure how to do any of those things. Her sheltered upbringing hadn't prepared her for intimacy with a man, while her husband had terrorized her completely. But Stavr was different; he made her happy in a strange and delightful way.

"Tell me about your sister," Tatiana said, loosening the ties on her blouse. "You never told me what she looks like. Is she fair like you?"

During the next half hour while Zoe nursed, Stavr conversed with Tatiana as casually as possible considering his willpower was taxed to the utmost. The baby's soft sucking sounds strummed through the young hetman's brain, the image they evoked so arousing, he found it difficult to keep his mind on their conversation. His erection was pressed hard against the ground, aching, his desires unsated and he found himself questioning his sanity. He was too old to be captivated by innocence.

But captivated he was—for inexplicable reasons. Maybe it was a phase of the moon or spring madness or something in the air, but she tantalized him to the point of obsession. And not so inexplicably, he wanted what he wanted.

So they talked of his sister's family, of the trading guilds of Riga that were controlled by nobles like his brother-in-law; they spoke of trade on the Baltic and on the Black Sea; they even discussed the practicalities of farming with the short summers in their region. But beneath his politesse and tactful rapport ran an undercurrent of speculation. What would happen if he rolled over—if she saw the extent of his desire? Would she be frightened? Horror-stricken? Offended? No doubt, all three. Although, after having shared Shuisky's bed, it was also possible *nothing* could offend her.

But the hetman wasn't adored by women far and wide because he was a brute. He was also pragmatic to the core—an important asset in a commander. So he reminded himself that he had the entire summer before him. The seduction of the princess needn't be accomplished in haste. The lady was intrigued—that he knew.

He could wait . . . or at least he could *try*.

By the time they had discussed Stavr's sister and Riga's trading establishment at length, Zoe had nursed her fill and was dozing in her mother's arms. And while Stavr hadn't been able to focus fully on their conversation, Tatiana's thoughts had been wandering on occasion as well. Particularly since she'd been at liberty to contemplate Stavr's lean, athletic body with complete freedom. He was remarkably fit, the raw power of his muscled shoulders conspicuous as he rested on his elbows, the fluid beauty of his back the epitome of graceful virility, the strength of his thighs stark reminder of his cavalry career. And when he shifted in his pose from time to time, the play of muscle rippling down his back and buttocks and thighs inspired a striking shiver of response.

But it was a fervent, warm shiver that had nothing to do with fear.

It had to do instead with an impetuous expectation. She was feverishly tempted to touch him.

What would he do if she gave in to impulse and touched him, say, on the light sprinkling of golden hair on his forearms?

Would he take offense?

He'd not turned around once.

And she couldn't decide if she was pleased or displeased by his obvious gallantry.

Even though she'd requested he look away, he could have offered demur, she irrationally reflected. It wasn't as though nursing a child in public was completely improper. Peasant women nursed their children without concern for appearances. And while the upper classes aspired to finer sensibilities—although her visit to court hardly confirmed such niceties—her body seemed to be responding today in a completely immodest way. She was feeling a particularly bewitching warmth . . . a molten heat flowing downward between her legs leaving her strangely restless.

Capricious in mood when she never was, she decided she really should return home. She'd stayed longer than she intended. But a second later, she fitfully decided that the beautiful young count was such glorious company, and Zoe *was* sleeping, it made more sense to wait until her daughter woke again before riding home. Furthermore, she'd not used the beautiful cradle Stavr had brought her. He might think her ungrateful. All sensible reasons for staying, she rationalized.

Alert to every nuance of Tatiana's movements, Stavr had heard the baby's breathing turn into the soft respiration of sleep. He'd heard the princess rise to her knees in a rustle of crisp linen and his pulse had begun racing as she moved to the cradle and placed Zoe inside.

When she returned, his senses were so acutely attuned to her presence, he felt the air stir as she settled back down on the blanket. A moment later, he was aware she'd lifted her arm because the cloisonné bracelets on her wrist jingled faintly. And a second after that as the light pressure of her hand rested on his shoulder, he went utterly still.

She ran her hand down his back in a gesture so tentative, the pressure barely registered on his brain receptors. His sensual receptors, on the other hand, were instantly aroused.

Then she traced a return path upward, with more sureness now, and he began to relax. It appeared the lady was beginning to enjoy herself.

But he didn't move, conscious of her inaptitude for amorous adventure. Remaining motionless, he listened to her draw in her breath, hesitate, and then her hand came to rest on the crest of his shoulder. The sound of birdsong, crickets, the wind in the trees seemed deafening in the sudden hush. Expectation and temptation hovered in the air. Then she exhaled, her hand lifted from his shoulder and a moment later, he felt her fingers slide down his hair.

He half-turned, twisting at the waist and covering her hand with his, drew it across his cheek, slowly—so she had an opportunity to resist if she chose.

"You're scratchy," she whispered, half-smiling.

That was license, whether intentional or not, and he smiled back. "And you're soft as silk," he murmured, bringing her hand to rest against his mouth, gently kissing her palm.

She shivered faintly.

"Are you cold?" His voice vibrated against her skin.

She shook her head.

"Warm?"

She nodded when she shouldn't, when she should rise from this blanket in this shaded glen and take her daughter home. But the hetman's large hand was engulfing hers, holding her captive and the warmth flooding her body was heavenly.

"That's good," he murmured and she felt his words strum against the overwrought nerves in her palm. Then he traced a wet path upward with his tongue to the soft pad at the base of her thumb and lightly bit the tender flesh.

Her gasp was the smallest of stifled sounds, shock and pleasure in equal measure, her utterance sliding away into a wistful sigh at the last.

He knew what ladies wanted when they made that sound. He'd heard it countless times in countless countries; he knew how to satisfy that breathless longing. Quickly rolling up to a sitting position, he placed himself between Tatiana and the shore, shielding her from view.

She took no notice of his gallantry; her eyes were half-closed, her breath coming in little pants, her large breasts straining at the fine fabric of her blouse on each rapturous inhalation.

It took every shred of willpower he possessed to keep from tumbling her down and plunging into her without preliminaries. A lady who was panting like that, chaste or not, was ready.

But he wanted more than a quick tumble.

So he kissed her instead. Prelude, as it were, to what exactly he didn't know. He'd never craved a virtuous woman before. But as his kiss deepened, she responded with increasing passion, moaning softly against his mouth and he decided to see where fate took them. He drew her closer and she squirmed, her hips moving in a small rotating undulation that encouraged him in his fateful journey. Increasing the pressure of his lips, he slid his tongue into her mouth, gently explored its sweetness, plunging deeper as though testing her readiness. She whimpered, the distinctive needy sound affecting his erection in a highly predictable way. As his penis surged upward, swelling larger, he glanced at the baby out of the corner of his eye.

Sleeping. He delivered a silent prayer of thanksgiving.

"Do that again," Tatiana breathed, her eyes tightly shut, her breasts rising and falling in agitation.

He was thinking about doing a whole lot more.

"Kiss me, please . . ."

He swore under his breath, not sure he had the strength, or was so saintly to confine himself to kisses.

"I'm sorry," she whispered, misinterpreting his lack of response. Her eyes opened. "I should go home . . ."

"No." A low growl, an order perhaps, at the very least a polite refusal. He traced the curve of her bottom lip with his finger and smiled at her. "Don't go just yet," he said, softly.

"Are you sure?" Her smile was tentative, uncertain.

"Oh, yes ... very sure." He bent his head, their lips touched and he felt her shuddering reaction with profound pleasure. "Hold me," he murmured, taking her hands and placing them on his shoulders, wanting more like she. "Kiss me back."

"I shouldn't," she breathed, but she leaned forward, hungry, yearning, and her mouth brushed against his in a butterfly kiss. "Did I do that right?" she inquired, her lips wet and pink, her expression artlessly hopeful.

"Absolutely perfect," he murmured, taking her face in his hands, drawing her back, kissing her this time with a fierce, wildness that ate at her mouth, showed her what flame hot feeling did to one's senses, brought her to a panting frenzy in a few brief moments.

He was wondering how far he could take this passionate encounter within sight of his men—not to mention her sleeping child. It was mildly off-putting even for a man of his considerable experience; he raised his head to reconnoiter.

"More, more, more," she panted, pulling on his shoulders.

"More what?" He was perfectly willing, but he needed her sanction in the event she was as chaste as she'd given him reason to believe.

"I don't know—I don't know," she sobbed, quivering, her eyes shut tightly, her hands on his shoulders clutching him in a viselike grip.

Christ, if she was that virginal, he wasn't about to mount her in these equivocal circumstances. Too many things could go wrong. Cupping her chin in his palm, he whispered, "Look at me."

She did, although her lashes were only marginally raised and her gaze focused somewhere beyond his shoulder.

"I'm going to touch you intimately," he said, very deliberately so there would be no mistake. "Do you understand?"

She nodded, her gaze still not meeting his.

"Tell me you understand." Was she aware of what he was saying?

"Touch me . . . please, yes, I understand."

"Remember, we have company. You have to be quiet."

She nodded again.

He felt oddly uncertain himself, the woman before him so intensely aroused and so unaware of the ramifications of her desires. It was curiously alarming; he had no idea how she'd react. And for a second, he debated stopping.

But she suddenly cupped his face in her hands and kissed him in an openmouthed frenzy that was both unnervingly gauche and highly arousing. Virginal frenzy was definitely a first for him. He felt the jolt of desire from his head to his toes and everywhere in between—his rock-hard penis particularly affected.

If he hadn't suddenly heard the whinny of a horse in the distance, he may have jettisoned caution in favor of flagrant exhibitionism. He still might have if not for the presence of Tatiana's grooms—an unknown to him.

But they were within sight, certainly within hearing and there was no guarantee the lady would be quiet. Which left him resentfully aware that he would have to be self-sacrificing today. The lady's ardor, however, could be assuaged in other ways.

Moving her hands from his face, he placed them on the blanket and whispered against her mouth, "No matter what you do, don't scream."

"Yes, yes, yes . . . whatever you say."

It was not what he cared to hear at the moment, and it took enormous self-control to bring his inflamed urges to heel. Soon, he told himself, promising himself a rendezvous with the delicious Princess Shuisky when time wasn't an issue, nor excessive company.

But for now . . . he'd offer her at least a minimum taste of pleasure.

Lifting her skirt the merest distance, he slipped his hands under the fabric and let his palms rest on her knees. "Don't move," he said, his voice like velvet.

She shivered faintly, but obeyed.

She was sitting cross-legged before him, her thighs open and he slid his hands slowly upward, taking his time, watching the flush of passion rise on her face. Her nipples were visible through the white linen of her blouse, the swell of her full breasts pulling the fabric taut and if he'd had more time and less possible interruptions, he would have stripped her blouse away and kissed each ripe, hard nipple.

Soon, he promised himself.

Forcing his thoughts back to more immediate matters, he slid his hands higher in a deliberately languorous motion, forcing her thighs wider as he moved upward. She was wet. He could see the drops of pearly fluid on the golden hair of her cleft, the tracery of her slit glistening in welcome, the resplendent curve of her swollen labia waiting for surcease. For him. Or in this case, a lesser part of him, he reflected, easing his thumbs into her sleek tissue.

But the instant his thumbs were buried in her succulent flesh, she went rigid and he paused to see if she would balk. One second, two, passed, breath-held, and then she squirmed against his thumbs in a silken undulation of liquid flesh and unchaste friction, forcing the nub of her clitoris against his fingers. She cried out in the softest of sounds, muzzled and low, and moved against him again—wanting more. He knew exactly what she was searching for and shifting one hand, he slid two fingers in to replace one thumb and forced his hand upward until his palm came to rest against her pelvic bone. She moaned deep in her throat in a breathy exhalation of need and capitulation, and leaned back on her hands, offering herself openly.

"More," she pleaded in a frantic, unknowing way. "More, more, more . . ."

A man could only take so much. It was a physical fact of

life, particularly for young hetmen who lived by a warrior code that presumed women were made for a man's comfort. Freeing one hand, Stavr reached for his trouser buttons and just as he was about to slip the first button free, he heard the unmistakable sound of a wolf call. A familiar, too familiar sound.

He swore. His men were getting restless or the princess's grooms were, he suspected, and his men were warning him. But he hesitated still, debating the equation of time against consummation against discovery.

A sensible man already knew the answer—the question was rather: How sensible did he feel?

Perhaps the glimpse of the cradle appearing in his line of vision more than anything forestalled his wilder impulses.

He let his hand drop from his trousers.

Slipping his fingers back inside her honeyed wetness, he took solace in her blissful sigh and his ardent vow to have her all to himself very soon. Kissing her flushed cheek, he forced his fingers deeper and whispered, "Is that what you want?"

"Oh, yes." She was finding it difficult to talk with the wild, thrilling rapture gripping her senses.

"So you want more?" he asked, sliding in another finger.

"Oh, oh, oh . . . yes," she gasped.

She seemed not to hear him after that and he brought her to climax with masterful finesse, intent on his mission, aware their time was limited, her small sighs rapidly turning into frantic whimpers until she came in a shuddering orgasm that drenched his fingers.

He glanced around as he slid his fingers free, taking in the position of their guards.

Fortunately, they were still in place on the shore.

He briefly shut his eyes against the intensity of his own desires. Desires that would have to wait for a more opportune time.

A time free from children and watchdogs.

He'd always avoided women with encumbrances in the

past; perhaps he should reconsider the princess's temptations when there were women aplenty he could have for the asking.

But she leaned forward just then and slid her arms around his waist and murmured, "Thank you, thank you, thank you," against his chest and her hair was scented with lily. His favorite flower.

Not reason enough perhaps for stupidity.

"I've never felt so wonderful," she said with a blissful sigh, holding him tighter.

Altruistic impulses were commendable were they not?

"Could you do that again some time?" she murmured, gazing up at him with the plaintive look of a wistful child. Or perhaps, not precisely childlike, he decided, the weight of her breasts pressing into his chest. "Is that possible?" she added.

Not only possible, but highly likely, he decided in a flash, any element of scruple abruptly dismissed. "Whenever you like," he said.

"Truly?"

Her soulful gaze nearly undid him. Now, he almost said, right this minute and for as long as you like or until I die of excess—whichever comes first. But he hadn't survived as long as he had in an uncertain world by being foolhardy. The summer stretched before him—a paradise with his own virginal Eve in residence and he could wait. "Truly," he said. "I promise you."

"I'm going to hold you to that."

And I'm going to hold you down and fuck you until neither one of us can move, he thought. "At your service, my lady," he said instead.

"That was astonishing. Really," she added, wide-eyed. "*You're* astonishing."

He laughed. "It gets better, darling."

She went still.

"It's not a sin," he noted, gently, "if I call you darling, or sweetheart, or the princess of my heart. It's allowed."

"I'm not sure it is."

"I'll be sure for both of us," he murmured, kissing her in a lingering, sweet, infinitely tender kiss.

Sighing against his mouth a moment later, she twined her arms around his neck. "I'm so happy . . . so very happy." She arched back so she could see his face and smiled, "I'm glad it's allowed."

Chapter Nine

Tatiana rode home in what could only be described as a blissful haze. She acknowledged her daughter's babble with an automatic affection, but seemed unaware of her escort—a fact the grooms remarked on when they returned home. A fact that became an absorbing topic of discussion at the servants's supper that evening.

Stavr's introspection on his ride home was only to be expected his men noted, considering the extraordinary impact the princess had had on their commander. And if he chose to keep his thoughts to himself, that was his prerogative. But as they approached the stables and Stavr said, "I'm riding out tonight. You men are excused to pursue your own pleasures," they took issue. They weren't about to let him disregard his safety for some bit of fluff, no matter his fascination.

"If you're going to Shuisky's, you'll need an escort," his lieutenant, Dimitry, disputed.

"A large one," another man added, gruffly. "Her grooms are already spreading the tale of your afternoon tryst."

"Sorry. I go alone." Stavr's voice was firm.

"If she didn't have a small army of retainers and Shuisky wasn't the devil's spawn, going alone might be safe enough. However—"

"Her staff is loyal," Stavr interrupted, his brows drawn together in a scowl, "Shuisky's in Moscow and I have no intention of arguing about this."

"Moscow or not, there are spies everywhere," another man warned, ignoring Stavr's brusqueness.

"I don't care."

Their hetman's tone of voice curtailed any further argument. While the crack cavalry units functioned informally as a band of brothers, at the end a leader always had the last word. So they nodded and said good luck and offered other more ribald comments as well.

Stavr's blush was evident even beneath his tan.

The men were shocked. Their commander was in love.

And while all the lusty young men who rode at his side wished him good luck with the woman, they weren't crazy enough to surrender his life to Dame Fortune when a Shuisky was involved. So when Stavr rode out that evening, a small party of his troopers trailed him—at a circumspect distance.

Not sufficiently circumspect, however, for Stavr rode out from the shadows as they rounded the first curve in the trail and brought them to a halt. "I should have you whipped," he murmured, his half smile visible in the moonlight. "You disobeyed orders."

"We need you for the Crimean campaign," Dimitry replied. "Who else knows the routes through the Dnieper marshes?"

Stavr didn't reply for a moment, weighing practicality against his own selfish motives. "Very well, come if you must," he finally said. "But you have to wait at the northern border of her land. If I'm not back by cockcrow, you may come and get me. Not before."

"If her husband's there, you could be dead by cockcrow."

"He's not. Nor will he be; the marriage suits neither of them."

Stavr's reply was met with a low grumble of discontent, but in the end he had his way and at the north fence line, he took leave of his men.

* * *

When the count neared the main house, he left his mount at the kitchen garden gate and carefully moved through the well-tended grounds to the front of the house. While he doubted the princess had need for defense, she may have a night patrol on the premises and the moon was full. But he reached a good observation point without incident and standing at the base of a slight rise, surveyed the sprawling log structure. A porch stretched across the first floor facade, two decorative balconies embellished the second floor exterior and the windows facing one balcony were dimly lit.

Might she still be awake?

Sprinting up the rise, he came to a halt in the shadows of the porch and debated how best to reach the lighted window. The porch pillars were heavily carved, offering excellent footholds and moments later, he pulled himself over the balcony railing, landing lightly on the plank floor, moved to one side of the arched window and glanced in.

A flickering oil lamp on a wall bracket faintly illuminated the nursery. Zoe slept in the cradle he'd given Tatiana that afternoon. She must have liked his present, he reflected with a smile, and with luck, him as well. The baby's nursemaids were deep in sleep as well, each in their own corner cupboard bed.

A nursery meant the lovely Tatiana must be near, he pleasantly reflected.

A moment later, he leaped to the opposite balcony, teetered on the railing briefly before regaining his balance and dropped to the floor. Moving silently to the darkened window, he peered through the glass. Silvery moonlight streaked the floor, altered the shadows to a wanly hue, shimmered across the white coverlet on the bed.

Where the princess lay asleep.

Alone.

No maidservant or babushka, no lapdog or husband.

He smiled.

Turning to glance at the moon, he gauged his time and easing the window open, stepped into the room. Lifting his holstered musket from his back, he leaned it against the wall, pulled off his gloves, dropped them on a painted chest and moved toward the bed.

She'd been dreaming glorious dreams peopled with a handsome young hetman so when she opened her eyes and saw Stavr, she wasn't surprised.

His pale hair glistened in the silvery light of the moon, his smile flashed white. "You changed," she murmured. "Your shirt . . ." He'd been wearing a red shirt in her dream.

His smile creased his face. "You look the same—beautiful as an angel."

She squealed, not expecting her fantasy to give voice, her high-pitched cry cut short as Stavr clamped his hand over her mouth.

Putting a finger to his lips, he slowly drew his hand away.

Her eyes wide with alarm, she scrambled into a seated position and eased backward as though putting mere inches more between them would save her. "You can't be here," she hissed.

"No one saw me. No one knows."

"They might, they could!" she whispered, glancing at the door, the window, suddenly realizing she was in her night robe, hurriedly pulling the sheet up to her chin.

Her modesty was charming, considering their intimacy that afternoon. Was it possible she'd forgotten? "I missed you," he murmured. "I wanted to see you again."

"I was dreaming of you; I didn't think you were real." Her shock unabated, she was only half-listening. "But you shouldn't be here. Truly you shouldn't."

"I won't stay long." He sat down on the edge of the bed; he had no intention of leaving.

She inched back until the headboard stopped her. "No . . . no . . . it's impossible! The servants could hear!"

"They're sleeping. The baby's sleeping. You're safe." He spoke in a low soothing tone, careful not to make any sudden moves. "I won't stay long," he repeated, his senses in a ramming speed mentality that overlooked everything but the covetous desire that had brought him here tonight. That kept him here when she didn't wish it. "I brought you something," he added, as though remembering that gallantry was required for seduction, when in the past such niceties were normal courtesies. But then, nothing about his feelings for this sweet young woman were even remotely normal.

He pulled a gold chain from a small purse at his belt and held it out to her.

A blood-red ruby set in gold hung from the filigreed chain.

"It's from the lands beyond the mountain passes, from the Indus valley."

"Were you there?"

She was a strange little bird, he thought. Usually, women took his gifts with smiles and fulsome thanks. "Not quite. I was almost there once. But the mountain passes were still deep in snow and we were turned back."

"You shouldn't give me gifts."

"A friend is allowed."

"Are you a friend?"

"Yes, of course. You have rubies, I suppose."

"No."

"Then allow me, your excellency," he murmured, leaning forward to slip the chain over her head. "For friendship," he whispered, bending low, kissing her gently. "For the sweet pleasure you bring me," he added, his words warm on her mouth.

She tried to push him away, her hands a small heat on his chest.

He wouldn't have had to move; she wasn't a match for him. And for an equivocal second he debated pressing his suit—before easing back.

"Please, Stavr." Her eyes were huge in the moonlight. "You must go!"

"What if I were to say no?"

"This isn't my house anymore. It's his and I'm terrified. You shouldn't be here. You shouldn't."

There was an undercurrent of wistfulness in her voice and a

longing he recognized even if she didn't. "If I leave, you must promise to come and see me tomorrow."

"I can't. Don't you see, it's impossible—even if we were to overlook the scandal. What if word got back to Moscow?"

With relief he took note that her arguments had nothing to do with her feelings, but rather with impropriety and fear of her husband. Both reasonable apprehensions. "If I were to make certain no one knew we were . . . friends," he said, his soft emphasis on the word friends bringing a flush to her cheeks, "and if I could guarantee your husband would never know, would you agree to meet me again?"

She looked down, her gaze shielded from his and her voice when she spoke was barely audible. "You can't guarantee that."

Sliding his forefinger under her chin, he lifted her face. "I have a small dacha deep in the woods, not far from here. You and Zoe could come and we could be alone. My men will guard us; I'll see that scouts are in place on your estate and on the road to Moscow. At the first sign a messenger from Moscow is within twenty versts, I'll have you home. Your servants are faithful." He smiled. "What do you think, your excellency? Have I forgotten anything?"

She bit her lip and sighed. "It sounds like the veriest paradise. But—"

"I'll have the entire nursery transported there for Zoe," he said, interrupting her remonstrance. "Every toy and bed and pillow. I'll have nursemaids in place as well if you wish."

"Someone you can trust?"

How could so mundane a question have the unmistakable ring of triumph? "They will be completely trustworthy. How many do you want? Two, three, more?"

"I don't know." She was clearly equivocal, vacillating on more than the number of nursemaids.

"I'll take care of everything," he quickly declared. For a man who had lived off the land during years of campaigning, nursemaids were not a serious issue. "I'll come for you in the morning. I'll be at the orchard gate at ten." He would have preferred saying sunrise, but restrained himself. She had agreed. All else paled to insignificance beside that glorious affirmation.

"What do I tell my staff?"

I'll talk to them he wished to say; I'll tell them I can make you smile and laugh and forget about your husband in Moscow. "You can tell them anything," he said, simply. "They love you."

"I can't stay long."

"Whatever you want."

"If only you could give me what I want."

"Let me try," he said very, very softly.

Her sudden smile lit up her eyes. "Beginning tomorrow at ten?"

He grinned. "Beginning then." He rose from the bed because if he stayed another second with temptation smiling at him like that, he might jeopardize their dacha holiday.

His bow was graceful, the small movement setting his niello dagger scabbards hanging from his belt swinging, the cabochon emerald dangling from his left ear visible as he stood upright once again and his hair swung back. "Your servant, ma'am."

"Do you believe in God?" she asked.

An unexpected question, but he answered honestly. "Sometimes." He smiled. "Particularly now."

"Then go with God," she said in the gentle manner of the time.

He dipped his head. "May his blessings fall on you as well, my lady."

She sat in her bed after he'd gone and asked herself whether the brief, fleeting happiness he could give her was worth her life?

She was surprised how easily the answer came.

Chapter Ten

In the morning when Tatiana woke, she called for Olga and Timor and explained to them that she and Zoe were going on holiday alone. The horse tracks at the kitchen garden gate had already been reported to Timor—a cavalry mount, he'd been told. But he kept his counsel.

"I should be gone a day or so."

"But you can't possibly go alone!" Olga wailed. "Who will arrange your hair and dress you? Who will help care for the baby?"

"My friends have servants available."

"But they may not know what you like for breakfast or what Zoe—"

"Olga, that will do," Timor ordered, cutting short the maid's protest. "When will you be leaving, my lady?" he inquired, understanding Tatiana's need for privacy. And while it wasn't his place to question his mistress's plans, he was already making contingency arrangements for the armed men under his jurisdiction. The princess's safety had always been his responsibility.

"At ten."

He didn't have to ask with whom or where she was going. He already knew the man's identity after the grooms's stories of yesterday. "I'll have Volia saddled," he said, bowing faintly.

"Thank you, Timor."

"We'll watch the road to Moscow," he added, his words without inflection.

Tatiana took a small breath but her voice was as mild as his when she spoke. "Thank you, Timor. What a good idea."

She dressed that morning with more care than she had for her wedding. It mattered more. She wanted to look her best for this man who could make the sun shine brighter, who could make her heart sing, whose mere presence could bring her joy.

She wore a linen gown of pale yellow, her chemise of the finest batiste, embroidered at the neckline with butterflies and banded at the hem by yards of handmade lace. Her low boots were soft crimson leather, buckled in gold. And she wore Stavr's blood-red ruby around her neck.

Stavr hadn't slept. He'd directed an army of retainers who worked through the night readying the dacha. Food and supplies had been brought in, six nursemaids had been driven to the site, his serfs had set up tents for his men, all discreetly out of sight, but close enough for safety. He'd also had a gaily striped silk tent erected on the lakeshore, the interior lavishly furnished and outfitted should they choose to sleep out-of-doors.

When everything was in place, he'd quickly bathed in the lake, dressed and set out for Tatiana's. He was running on adrenaline, wide-awake, in extreme good humor, consumed with images of the bewitching princess. As a sop to his men's concerns for his safety, he had two of his men accompany him. But in his heart of hearts, he felt invincible today. Nothing could touch him.

He arrived early at the orchard gate and found there a household servant of obvious status. The man was well dressed, tall, lean, aged but not infirm. He was Timor, the princess's steward, he said, introducing himself and while his voice was courteous, he had none of the humility of a subordinate. "We are concerned with our lady's welfare," Timor declared once the perfunctory courtesies had been exchanged, his gaze direct and unyielding.

Stavr sat his horse, looking every inch a powerful hetman in his prime. "I'm equally concerned with the princess's welfare."

"*How* concerned is the question?"

Stavr surveyed the elderly man for a moment, not in the habit of being interrogated by a servant.

"The princess has been in my charge since her birth. I would die for her," Timor said in the softest of voices.

"Ah."

"I thought you should know."

"I will keep her safe." Leaning down, Stavr offered his hand to Timor. And when after a second's hesitation the steward took his hand, the young count smiled. "I would die for her too, old man. We're on the same side."

Timor stepped back again and gave warning. "Her husband will kill you both without a qualm, should he find out."

"I know. I have a troop of cavalry at my back."

"If he comes, he'll come without warning."

"I have scouts posted on the road to Moscow. Are the princess's staff loyal?"

Timor looked affronted.

"Good. Since I'm new in the area, I can't speak for mine with such certainty. I've taken precautions to see that no one leaves my estate until I return. Should you need to reach the princess, send a man to the Suni rapids. One of my patrols will be stationed there." Stavr's gaze flicked up. "We'll talk again. She's here."

When Tatiana rode up a moment later, she glanced at Timor with a small frown. "Are you spying on me?"

"No, my lady. I was out for a walk and happened on the count."

"I introduced myself," Stavr said with a small smile. "I hope you don't mind."

"Speak to no one of this," Tatiana ordered, a flush of color on her cheeks.

"Of course not, my lady."

Baby Zoe caught sight of Stavr from within her sling and lifting her arms to him, smiled and babbled in greeting.

For a child who was cautious of everyone other than her mother and nursemaids, her unusual familiarity caught Timor's attention. He watched in wonder as Stavr leaned over, lifted Zoe from her sling and settled her into the crook of his arm.

It was a profound shock Timor reported on his return to the house.

"Might the hetman be bewitching the mistress and babe?" Olga whispered.

"By his grace and charm at least," Timor said, drily.

"Is he as handsome as they say?" one of the scullery maids breathed.

"As if Timor is concerned with his looks," the cook snorted, "when our princess might be in danger."

"She's in no danger from him—except for possible gossip." The steward surveyed the servants clustered round him. "And there will be no gossip from this quarter. I promised him that."

"As if we'd put our darling princess at risk," the cook sniffed. "When her husband is one of Satan's own. They can pull out my tongue before I'd say a word to hurt her or her new friend."

"He be more than a friend, I'd say," one of the maids murmured with a titter.

"There will be no more such talk," Timor snapped, his voice sharp as a whip. "And I want everyone to be vigilant while the princess is away. We must have warning if any stranger comes near."

But regardless of Timor's stern warning, the princess's new liaison was the foremost topic of conversation that night—in the maid's quarters, in the male servant's quarters, in the small apartments where the cook and Timor lived. In fact, late that night when the cook and Timor sat at the kitchen table sharing a small jug of wine, they spoke of nothing else. Everyone wanted the best for their beloved mistress who had suffered so by the hand of her husband. "Tell me again about our precious Zoe," the cook said with a doting smile. "Did she really jump into the hetman's arms?"

"Like a fish going up a rapids. And he didn't mind one bit."

"It's a good man who's kind to children."

"Perhaps fate has taken a hand in our lady's happiness."

"She deserves it, poor little bird."

"Aye. And it's up to us to keep her safe."

Chapter Eleven

That same evening, Stavr and Tatiana were on the small porch of the dacha, seated side by side on a swing made of birch that was sanded so smooth it was like velvet to the touch. White mist rose from the surface of the lake in wispy trails, sparkling fireflies darted in and out of the tall grass bordering the lawn, crickets and frogs serenaded each other in chirruping chorus, and the air was sweet with the scent of wild cherry blossoms.

"Everything's perfect," Tatiana murmured, her head resting on Stavr's shoulder as he held her close. "Thank you for all you've done to make this earthly paradise a reality."

"My pleasure," he whispered, bending to kiss her cheek. "Thank you for coming."

"How could I not," she simply said.

He knew what she meant because he would have moved heaven and earth to have her here like this; in a small way he had. And he'd indulged and coddled his guests that day because he wished to please Tatiana, to see that she and her daughter were both delighted with his playhouse in the forest. They'd rowed a little skiff on the still, small lake; they'd fished under the weeping willows, bright chartreuse in their new spring leaves. They'd dozed in the shade of an alder bush lean-to after a choice, tempting luncheon served on Anatolian carpets laid on the grass. They'd explored the stables and barn, the curious grotto built of shimmering clam shells, the exquisite silk tent filled with luxuries from the east; they'd laughed and talked and played with Zoe and had come to know each other better.

Because, above all, he wished to put her at ease.

And when night came and Zoe was well asleep, he would take her to bed and make love to her tenderly because she was still afraid. It showed in small ways—her startled glance at the sound of a horse whinnying, her quick hushing of Zoe's cries as though the utterance might give them away, the relentless tension in her spine.

"Do you think the servants are sleeping?"

It didn't matter whether they were or not, he wished to say. "I'm sure they are," he said, instead. "It's late."

"I'm not tired."

"We had a nap this afternoon."

"Umm . . . that was nice."

"Would you like to go for a walk? The stars are bright enough to light our way."

"I don't think so."

"Do you want to stay here?"

She shook her head.

"What do you want to do?"

She didn't answer.

"Would you like to go somewhere else?" She nodded and his pulse began racing. Easing his arm from around her shoulders, he came to his feet and held out his hand. "You haven't seen the chandelier at night. I had it lit for you."

He didn't have to explain which chandelier; the sultan's tent held the most exquisite Venetian chandelier. But as he drew her to her feet, she nervously asked, "Will the nursemaids—"

"I gave them orders to fetch you should Zoe wake."

"You didn't say . . . I mean—"

"Dimitry is my liaison, darling. They know only to speak to him should they need you." He drew her close and kissed her gently. "No one will gossip. My word on it. We're alone;

you're completely safe." He could feel her relax, the tension in her shoulders lessening under his hands and her sudden smile was captivating.

"What if I hadn't wanted to see your chandelier?" she asked, a playful note in her voice.

"Then I would have offered you some other adventure." Her eyes twinkled in the moonlight. "Do you have many?" He grinned. "Enough to keep you interested."

"I'm interested in anything as long as you're with me."

His head dipped and the look he gave her from beneath his lashes was warm enough to cause a distinct craving in a woman who hadn't previously known such feelings existed. "May I say, my lady—the feeling is deeply mutual."

"You're much too charming."

Her words were half-breathless, the blush on her cheeks tantalizing.

"And you're much too alluring; I'm bewitched, besotted, and"—he grinned—"out of my mind for wanting you."

"Then you must have me," she said, intoxicated with pleasure, drawing him toward the porch stairs.

He laughed out loud. "How easy you make it sound."

She looked up at him as they descended the stairs, stark adoration in her eyes. "I've wanted to be with you from the first moment I saw you, before I even knew what my feelings meant."

"I know. Like a gypsy charm."

"A very, very good one," she happily declared.

"As good as they get," he muttered and suddenly impatient to reach the tent on the lakeshore, he swung her up into his arms. "If I begin to frighten you in any way," he said, his voice taut with restraint, "just tell me."

"You don't frighten me."

"Good," he replied, exhaling softly. "Good," he repeated, half under his breath and then without breaking stride, he kissed her with the wild, ravenous urgency of a man too long denied.

But she didn't take offense; she twined her arms around his neck, held him in a fierce, strong grip and gave herself up to him.

A dilemma of sorts, in his current rapacious mood—that unconstrained willingness. How long could he act the gentleman when she was offering herself to him with such provocation—without the timidity and diffidence he'd been expecting? How long could he last?

But when he set her on her feet before the tent, perhaps the breeze off the lake cooled his lust, or perhaps her large winsome eyes curtailed his most reckless carnal impulses.

"I like when you kiss me," she said.

Good God, he thought, undone by her sweet naivete. What had he gotten himself into?

"But I like even more what you did, you know, yesterday afternoon."

An enormous weight suddenly lifted from his chest and he could breathe again. "Would you like me to do that again?"

"Would you please?"

He nodded, not able to speak properly while beating down a brutish urge to pick her up, carry her inside, toss her onto the bed and plunge inside her.

"Oh, good," she said, beaming.

And not for the first time since he'd met her—he was struck by the wildly provocative, the utterly tantalizing nature of innocence. Lifting the tent flap, he gestured her in, not sure he could speak in a normal tone of voice considering the combustible nature of his emotions.

This was definitely a new experience—this wooing of untainted virtue.

Standing under the blaze of the Venetian chandelier, he debated how best to accede to the lady's wishes when he felt as though he'd explode if he didn't climax soon.

"This must be hard for you," she murmured, touching his arm with a brush of her fingers. "Being so polite to me."

The word, *hard,* wasn't helpful in his current frame of

mind, the faint contact of her fingers triggering wholly outrageous impulses. Exhaling softly, he lifted her hand away. "It's certainly different."

His rebuff, however gentle, made her even more conscious of his constraint. "Maybe," she said, softly, not quite meeting his gaze, "you should—er—satisfy yourself first and then, well, I could wait."

"Satisfy?" He didn't know he could talk so softly.

"I would be more than willing to"—blushing, she looked away—"accommodate you."

A faint scowl marred his countenance, the image she evoked off-putting. "What if I don't want to be . . . accommodated?" Like your husband, he refrained from adding.

Her blush heightened. "I thought that was what men wanted."

"That?"

"You know," she said, turning cherry red.

"Sex, you mean."

She wouldn't look at him. "Please, must we talk about this?"

His lust momentarily checked by her well-meaning but odious offer of *accommodation* à la Shuisky, he said, gently, "Sex isn't a sin, darling. It's a pleasure—as you discovered yesterday."

"But that wasn't . . . I mean—"

"Yes, it was. Come." He took her hand. "Sit with me."

"But I don't want to sit. I want—"

"And you'll have what you want, darling." As soon as he could dislodge the image of Shuisky from his mind. "We'll just talk a little." Leading her to two low cushioned chairs upholstered in magenta silk shot with gold thread, he handed her into a chair, dropped into the other in a sprawl and surveyed her for a restless, perturbed moment. Was he truly ready for such artless naivete? Did he seriously want to deal with Shuisky's emotional damage? The answers were not only expeditious but unequivocal. Which meant it was only a question of how not if—or perhaps more to the point—a question of how much the lady wished to offer. "Tell me what gives you pleasure."

"My daughter, Zoe; marzipan; a cup of tea in the morning; and you, not talking," she replied, managing to sound both impudent and imperious like a spoiled young princess might.

"You're angry." He smiled faintly as he lounged opposite her, his booted feet crossed at the ankle, his powerful body in repose.

"Why shouldn't I be? You're too far away and I want kisses."

His brows arched in sardonic assessment. "And what would you do with just kisses?"

"I want more, too."

"Then, tell me what you want and I'll see if I can accommodate you," he said, unaccountably goading her.

Her lush bottom lip protruded in a pout. "I won't. And you're being . . ." she paused, searching for an appropriate word, "unkind," she settled on, her scowl pronounced.

He understood the comparison she was making, what her hesitation implied, that *unkind* was a polite choice of words for what she was really thinking. "I'm not like him," he declared, bluntly. "And if you think I am, feel free to leave." He could be imperious too.

A small silence descended, repressed passion and aristocratic umbrage strumming in the candlelit brilliance.

"What if I don't want to leave?" she challenged, patrician hauteur in her violet gaze.

"Would you be staying for sex?" Each syllable was infused with cheekiness.

She lifted her chin a fraction. "I suppose I would."

"How nice. What kind of sex did you have in mind?"

"Stavr! Stop it, this instant!"

"Yes, ma'am, of course, ma'am, your servant, ma'am."

There was something in his tone. "You aren't going to, are you?"

"A person can climax even without anyone touching them," he offered, silky and low. "Did you know that?"

Her lashes snapped up in astonishment, but when she spoke her voice was tart with censure. "Why are you telling me this?"

"So you won't think everyone's like your fucking, brutish husband," he said, gruffly. "There are infinite kinds of sex. Even words alone."

"I don't believe you."

About sex or your husband, he wanted to say. "Suit yourself," he said, instead. "But I can make you come without touching you."

She didn't reply for a lengthy moment, the tumult of her emotions evident—temptation plain in the tiny nibbling of her bottom lip. "Like yesterday?" she finally queried, her gaze examining. "I'd feel like that?"

"Better," he said with brazen assurance.

Wonder displaced temptation in her eyes. "Very well," she said, clasping her hands in her lap, taking a deep breath, nodding her approval in tight-lipped affirmation.

He laughed out loud. "It's not Chinese torture, darling. If you'd rather not," he added, but he was already sliding up in his chair, beginning to pull off his boots.

"Apparently this is all very diverting for you." Unclasping her hands, she scowled at him. "I'm gratified you find me amusing."

He looked up. "On the contrary, I find you the greatest temptation I've ever encountered." Tossing his boots aside, he pulled his chair closer and leaning over took her hands in his. "I want you and I don't want you and I want you even more a second later. And you're here"—he grimaced—"because I couldn't resist temptation . . . nor live another day without having you with me."

"Really?" she said, whisper soft.

"Really," he replied, knowing he was the worst kind of fool to become involved with a woman such as she—chaste and pure, completely beyond the pale. And this time, he was the one who took the deep breath, because he knew if he were sensible, he would send her home. He knew as well, he wouldn't be sending her home any time soon. Releasing her hands, he leaned back and smiled his practiced, charming smile. There were times when it was better not to think too much. "Sit back and relax, darling. Let me make you feel good."

The simplicity of his words was infinitely enchanting to a woman who had known only cruelty from her husband.

"Then I'll make you feel good." Her smile was sunshine bright.

Inexperience aside, it was a pledge from her heart and he accepted it as such. "You already have." He grinned. "Your work is done."

"Just so long as yours isn't," she replied, with an answering grin, resting against the cushioned chair back, spreading her arms wide on the soft upholstered arms, looking at him from under her long lashes like the most seductive of courtesans.

Some women had a natural talent, he thought pleasantly. "I'm here for the duration, sweetheart. You tell me when you've had enough."

"How tempting you make it sound," she purred, shifting faintly on the down cushions. "You mean I can have you entertain me for as long as I want?"

How often had he responded to that husky note in a woman's voice. "Absolutely." This wasn't the time to mention Zoe, or morning, or even think about the practicalities. "But before the entertainment begins," he said, his voice soft as butter, "you must tell me—are you feeling wet?" He glanced at the juncture of her thighs and nodded, as though they were discussing the weather. "I mean there . . . where I touched you yesterday? Would my fingers slide over your silky flesh with ease?"

She made the smallest sound deep in her throat, shifted faintly so the folds of her skirt shimmered in the candlelight.

He watched the pink creep up her throat, saw her lashes drift downward, took note of the raised imprint of her nipples through the pale linen of her bodice. "Are you beginning to feel warm? Just a little?" he whispered, surveying the rising flush on her cheeks. "I could untie the lacings on your gown and lift it over your head if you like. The night air would cool you. And if you were still too warm, I could slide your chemise off to make you more comfortable. If you were completely nude, that would help, wouldn't it?" Her eyes had opened on the word nude and he held her gaze for a heated moment. "If you were naked," he went on in a raspy murmur, "the silk fabric of the chair would slide easily against your hot slit. You could rub against the cushion—ah, that's the way. Is your sweet little cunt beginning to throb?" He wasn't expecting an answer because her eyes were almost closed once again, although her gentle rocking motion perhaps was answer enough. "I can see your nipples through your gown. Your breasts are straining at the fabric. Can you see that? Look. You have to look, darling," he ordered softly and she reluctantly opened her eyes. "Do you think the material might tear with the pressure of your swollen breasts? I'm getting hard just looking at them."

She quickly glanced at his crotch from under the screen of her lashes.

"See how stiff and long you've made my cock? Look at it swell." His gaze came up and met her furtive glance. "It's all right to look, darling. We're alone; we're both in a rut—I can smell you from here . . . like the mares in the fall. I'm feeling hard-pressed not to mount you. What would you do if I slid into you—all the way inside and drenched my cock in that luscious scent?" At her stifled groan, he smiled. "Does that excite you? Answer me, darling, or I won't let you come."

She opened her mouth, then shut it again.

"You want to come don't you? Just say yes, that's all you have to say."

She nodded.

"Say it." A teasing whisper.

"Yes." It was the merest of sounds.

"Good. That's a good girl. I'm thinking I might suck on

your nipples first. If I were to suck on them, I know you'd climax. Would you like that?" he murmured, watching a small secretion darken the fabric over her nipples. "You're leaking just like you did that first afternoon when we were having tea. You made me hard just looking at you. All I could think about was sucking on your large, taut nipples. Like now. Should I unlace your gown? Should I relieve you of some of that excess milk so it won't drip like that? Zoe won't mind. It looks like you have enough milk in those huge breasts for ten babies."

She was leaning forward slightly, her gaze focused on the obvious bulge in his trousers, her breathing labored. He wasn't sure she'd heard him.

Touching himself, he ran his fingers up the enormous length, her fascination with his prick gratifying. "All you have to do is ask and you can have it," he murmured.

She nervously shook her head, a quick, tense movement.

So she was aware of what he was saying.

"I could use my fingers instead," he suggested, softly, "like I did yesterday." One step at a time, he warned himself. However heated her desires, she still had qualms. "You liked what you felt then, didn't you? You liked when I slid my fingers way up your pulsing little cleft; you squirmed and panted for more. You really liked when I gently stroked your tender little nub. You whimpered and turned liquid around my hand. Do you remember the aching pleasure—how it felt when you climaxed—how the fierce spiking rapture pulsed upward in waves, how the orgasmic ripples flowed up through your cunt and belly, spread like molten heat through every nerve and tissue? You wanted the orgasm to last and last, didn't you? Would you like that again? Are you wet enough? You're trembling. Does that mean you want to come?"

She whimpered, her half-shuttered gaze hot with longing.

"I know, I know," he gently soothed. "I'm here . . . I'll take care of you; I'll let you come. Don't cry, darling. Look, my fingers are sliding in past your pouty lips, into your slippery little cleft; I'm forcing them upward—relax, darling, I don't want to hurt you. There . . . there—see, I'm in all the way now, I'm in as far as I can go. Can you feel my fingers filling you, stretching you? Close your legs tightly around my hand so you can feel the imprint of my fingers in your tight little cunt, and I'll suck on your nipples while you come. I'll suck on them so hard the spasms will jolt your senses, the pressure of my lips will reverberate down to your quivering hot core and you won't be able to tell if you're coming because I'm sucking on you or because my fingers are crammed inside you." He half-lifted his hand. "Show me your nipples."

In thrall to unsated desire, she quickly obeyed, grasping her nipples, lifting them to him.

"Ah, perfect." His voice was whisper soft. "So beautiful and hard. Are you holding your legs together? If you don't, you won't be able to climax."

She immediately complied, tensing her thighs, lifting her hips slightly to heighten the bewitching sensations coursing through her heated flesh.

"My fingers are sliding back in again," he whispered, "way, way in and I'm taking one of your nipples into my mouth. That's not too hard is it? Hold your nipple up just a little higher so I can reach it better. Am I biting too hard?"

She was moving against his imaginary hand, her hips, her bottom, grinding, rocking, reaching, reaching . . .

"Can you feel the slick friction—are my fingers completely submerged? Can you feel me sucking all the milk from this ripe, heavy breast? My fingers are all the way in now, my palm is jammed against your pulsing slit. Lift up to meet me—that's right, now, perfect . . . now lift up your breast too . . . umm, you like that don't you? Now, I'm going to withdraw my fingers slightly . . . don't cry, darling—here, you can have them back again. Hush, darling. There. Is that better . . . am I pressing hard enough? Am I deep enough. No? Is that better? Ah, you like that when I have four fingers rammed all the way in. Wait, wait, I'm not finished yet. Wait."

But she didn't wait. She couldn't.

And it took every ounce of willpower he possessed to remain seated when every lustful impulse urged him to tumble her down, mount her, and drive his cock hilt deep into her climaxing cunt.

In due time . . . while he watched her, white-knuckled and resentful, her panting cries slowly subsided and her breathing stilled.

Her lashes eventually lifted, too, and she said, breathy and low, "That's not fair."

"I agree." Narrow-eyed and sullen, he surveyed her pink-cheeked dishevelment.

"It wasn't enough."

"We agree once again," he growled.

"You're angry."

"I'm trying not to be. I'm trying to be understanding."

She couldn't help but smile. "And apparently not succeeding."

He grunted, slid lower in his chair and silently cursed virtue in general and virtuous women in particular.

He didn't look up as he heard her rise from her chair; he was feeling put-upon and surly.

"I think it's my turn to make you feel good."

His gaze came up and he took in her graceful kneeling pose only inches away, her sweet smiling face, the perfect arch of her brows raised impishly. "I'm not in the mood to be toyed with," he grumbled, unimpressed with sweet smiles at the moment.

"I still have this insatiable hunger. Do you think you could help me?"

He glanced at his erection and then at her again. "No problem there."

"Should I undress?"

"I'm not sure it's entirely necessary."

"Will I like it even clothed?"

"I've never had any complaints."

"Don't say that."

His brows flickered briefly, but he still hadn't smiled. "You'll like it with or without clothes."

"Will I like it better if you smile?"

He shrugged, but the smallest of smiles tugged at his mouth. "Honestly, I'd say no, but for you"—he shrugged again—"I'm sure you'd prefer a smiling fuck."

"Now you're being rude."

"You don't know what pressure I'm under."

She glanced at his erection and couldn't repress a gasp. "Are you going to explode?"

"Damn right."

"But the question is where."

"Actually, no that's not the question. I know where."

"On the bed?"

"Very funny."

"Well, I'd like it on the bed." And so saying, she rose to her feet and moved toward the cushions piled on the carpeted floor, pulling the laces open on the sides of her gown as she walked.

She'd not taken more than a few steps when she was lifted off her feet and swung up into Stavr's arms. "This is going to be way too fast the first time, but I'm damned near crazy. Do you understand?"

"You're not alone in your insanity. I'm completely frantic."

He came to a sudden stop. "You are?"

"If I'm not feeling your beautiful enormous—er—"

"Penis."

"Thank you. Inside me within the next few seconds, I'm going to die of longing."

"You're sure, now? Once I start, I'm not going to be able to stop."

"Please don't."

Setting her on her feet, he said, "Don't move," and stripped off her gown and chemise in a flashing moment.

As ravenous as he, she didn't need further invitation. Dropping down on the silk cushions, she gazed up at him. "If I didn't think you were faster, I'd take off your clothes myself."

He visibly wrenched his gaze from her lush beauty, muttered, "Right," and proceeded to rip off his clothes in record time. "My apologies in advance," he murmured, lowering himself between her legs, forcing her thighs wider with a brush of his palm. "I'll make it up to you next time."

But he didn't have to.

"I just love feeling like this," she'd purred the instant he'd entered her. "Tell me what to do."

He didn't have to tell her much as it turned out; she had a natural bent for rhythm. Nor did he have to play the gentleman for long. Fortunately, she was as easily aroused as he and as orgasmic as he.

Or perhaps they had both waited too long.

A number of multiple orgasms were mutually enjoyed.

Although, he'd never felt as though he were dying when he'd come.

She, on the other hand, had always felt as though she were dying when she came. But how would she know any better?

And he did suck on her luscious breasts and partake of some of Zoe's sustenance before the night was over. And he was right. He could make her climax by sucking on her nipples. Twice, then three times, and it wouldn't have been fair to shortchange one breast—so, four times. Four unbelievable, incredible, screaming orgasms.

Her screams brought Stavr's men to attention, but when no ensuing wolf-call echoed in the night, they smiled at each other, sheathed their swords, and wished their commander good fucking.

That first night at the dacha in the forest, set the pattern for a summer of bliss. Entertaining Zoe filled their days, her growth that summer astonishing, her bubbling laughter a constant, the two adults in her life devoted to her.

But when she fell asleep, the nights were theirs.

The young hetman and the beautiful princess were deep in love; sleep wasn't a necessity.

Timor sent messages from time to time; Stavr ran his estate through his steward. He even cancelled his mother's visit with a polite excuse. Nothing mattered but the precious time they had together. Nothing mattered but their love.

Stavr wanted them to marry, but Tatiana was always evasive when he talked of marriage and not wishing to mar the perfection of their small paradise, he refrained from pressing the issue. Her husband figured in an occasional conversation as well in the course of those summer months, but any mention of him made Stavr want to kill him, so that topic, too, was avoided.

The future was too pitiless; their moments together too fleeting. They preferred dwelling in the enchanting present.

And there was no more beautiful place on earth than their secluded acres of green forest and glen.

Chapter Twelve

But as September neared, Stavr could no longer delay his departure. His men had been in readiness for some time, their impatience increasing with each passing day. Sigismund's army was marching south in less than a fortnight and they would have to use whip and spur to reach the rendezvous in time. A point Dimitry had made, tight-lipped, but well-behaved enough not to mention they were all cooling their heels for the sake of a woman.

"I know, I know," Stavr had muttered. He didn't mention Tatiana either or the fact that he was in love for the first time in his life. His men wouldn't understand. "I'll be ready tomorrow."

The next morning, he ordered the tents taken down and the dacha closed. Although his staff and men were capable of handling the details of their departure, he still had a number of personal affairs to deal with. Tatiana and Zoe came with him to his estate. The lovers couldn't bear to be apart with so little time left to them, but conversation was fitful with the specter of separation a brooding presence between them.

On reaching Stavr's house, though, the sheer press of activities tempered the gloomy focus of their thoughts. Stavr immediately called in his senior servants and discussed their duties in his absence. Then he gathered his campaign maps and letters of credit and had them packed. He wrote to his family and business agents giving them a general indication of his itinerary. The village elders were brought to the house so everyone was clear on their responsibilities. During most of the day, Tatiana remained with him, helping where she could, trying desperately not to cry and embarrass him. Stavr would look her way from time to time and smile or make some innocuous remark as though he wished to deny this might be their last day together.

And when she remarked, once, after he'd ushered another of his numerous visitors from the study, "If I'm in the way, I'll leave," he'd swung around from the door, scowling. "Absolutely not!" He'd quickly apologized for his brusqueness. "Don't even think of going," he said, moving to where she sat. "And if I could carry you away with me, I would."

She bit her bottom lip to stem her tears. "The world seems very unfair at times."

"We'll make it right, my word on it." Bending low, he took her face between his hands and gently kissed her. "No zealot or fanatic could feel more strongly than I do," he assured her. "We're going to be together, you and I."

"And Zoe."

Standing upright, he smiled. "And darling Zoe."

It was very late before the last detail had been finalized, the last message delivered. The remains of their dinner was still on Stavr's desk, the candles were burning low. Rubbing his hand over his eyes, he leaned back in his chair. "Done, I think." Glancing at Tatiana who was curled up on a chair, he smiled. "I couldn't have finished without you. Have you ever considered the life of a clerk?"

"For you, perhaps. Otherwise"—she smiled—"my days are rather busy running my estate."

"And I've kept you from it this summer."

She shook her head. "I chose to do what I did this summer."

"Yes," he murmured, his gaze warm, "as did I."

"We chose well, I'd say," she purred.

"The night's almost gone," he said, husky and low as though recognizing a cue.

"Not quite."

He grinned. "So then . . ."

She stood up and dipped her head faintly in his direction and he came to his feet and took her hand and led her upstairs.

They made love almost tearfully, the thought that this might be their last time together impossible to overlook. He was infinitely tender and she tried desperately not to cry. And they both stored the poignant memory, the feel and touch and scent of each other against the troubled future.

He held her close afterward as the final hours ticked away, reluctant to go and leave her. "Come with me," he whispered, as he had so many times that summer. "I'll find you apartments in Cracow. You'll be safe. I promise."

"I can't. You know that." How many times had she wished she could say yes. "When you come back in the spring, I'll go with you."

"The bishop won't be able to help," he muttered. "Not against the tsar."

"We disagree." She was more hopeful than he. Or perhaps she wasn't as capable of disregarding the world. The Orthodox church recognized divorce in rare circumstances; why not for her?

"It makes no difference to me if you're divorced or not."

"I know." But it mattered to her because she wished to rid herself of her vicious husband, and marry the man she loved. A romantic vision, perhaps, but then she was young and naive.

"We could marry in Cracow before I leave for the Crimea. Who would be the wiser?" The Orthodox church had no means of imposing its authority in Catholic Poland.

She softly sighed. "I would be the wiser, darling. Please, let me at least try to arrange a divorce. The bishop in Pskov has far-reaching influence."

"Not enough, apparently, to keep you from that fucking, depraved Shuisky."

"I don't want to fight." Her husband's treatment of her was always a sore point with Stavr. "If the bishop can't help, I'll go with you in the spring—gladly . . . with an open heart." She touched his grim mouth. "Please, darling, indulge me."

And like all the other times they'd argued about her marriage, Stavr gave in—because he loved her, because he knew how much it mattered to her that she strike a balance between principle and love. She knew so little of the unscrupulous world, he reflected with a mute sigh. She still believed in justice.

Although with no guarantees he could return to Cracow during the campaign or perhaps at all—realistically—she'd be more comfortable in her own home than in Poland. So he set aside his selfish wishes. "Forgive me. You're right, of course. I wish you good fortune with the bishop." And then he kissed her gently, his heart full of love. "I'll be back when the cherry blossoms bloom," he whispered, storing away the scent and feel and taste of her against the uncertain future.

"I wish you didn't have to go." Her tears spilled over; she knew the awful dangers he faced.

"It's just a few months. I'll be home before you know it," he soothed, wiping away her tears. "Don't cry."

"I won't." But fresh tears welled in her eyes.

"I'm glad to hear it," he teased and her small smile gave him heart. "Tell me what you want from the Ottoman bazaars: silks, jewels, a slave to comb your hair and bathe you?"

"Why do I need a slave when I have you?" She tried to match his teasing tone.

His smile was sweet, close, and so beautiful she'd remember it always. "That's what I was thinking. So, it's silks and jewels then?"

She suddenly lost her battle to be strong; tears poured down her cheeks. "I don't . . . want presents," she sobbed. "I just want you," she whimpered, choking on her tears. "Promise me—you'll be . . . careful."

"I promise," he lied, this man who always led his men into battle. "Don't worry."

Rising before dawn, he took care not to wake her as he dressed. Kissing her lightly as she slept, he stood beside the bed for a moment, wanting to remember every nuance and detail of her fair, sweet beauty, because fate was capricious and the Turks would be waiting for them.

He finally turned away and moved to the door. With his hand on the latch, he looked back one last time. If he were a more brutal man he would have abducted her and brought her with him. Many commanders had women in their trains; the pashas brought their harems on campaign. It was an age where power and force of arms prevailed and he'd been sorely tempted. But she was staying here because she wished it, and he wished to please her.

Holy Father, keep her safe, he silently prayed.

Make my sword arm strong and sure.

Be merciful to our love and all we hold dear.

Swiftly crossing himself, he opened the door and a moment later gently closed it behind him.

As he strode away, an ominous sense of doom enveloped him. He shouldn't have prayed, he reflected, shaking away his disquietude. He never did. And God had nothing to do with survival, anyway. Taking the stairs in long, leaping strides, he dismissed his brief lapse into sentimentality.

All a good hetman needed was a fleet mount, a keen-edged sword, and his troopers at his back and he could take on the Devil himself.

In the entrance hall, he buckled on his jack, slid his belt with his daggers around his waist, slipped his sword baldric over his head, picked up his musket and slung it on his back. His armor and helmet were on a packhorse, readied earlier by the grooms. He glanced up the stairway, debating one last kiss, then blew out a breath and quickly turned to the door. A moment later he stepped outside into the cool dawn light.

His men were waiting in the drive, armed and mounted. "I hope you haven't been waiting long," he said, striding to his waiting charger.

"Just all summer," Dimitry muttered.

Stavr grinned. "Besides that, I mean."

The communal guffaw rippled through the still morning air.

"Sigismund promises us much booty this time."

"God willing," his men replied in ritual response.

"Or perhaps the lax Turkish defenders will more likely come to our aid. In any event, I'm thinking this could be my last campaign. Booty or not." Stavr leaped onto his waiting horse, nudged his bay with his heel and turned his mount down the drive. His troopers fell in behind him, each man furtively making the sign of the cross. It was bad luck to talk about retiring. Retiring could mean dying as easily as not. Stavr knew the superstition as well as anyone; he was recklessly tempting fate. Just as he'd tempted more than fate with his summer-long liaison. The princess was married to one of the most unspeakable monsters in all of Russia; he could have been more discreet.

Women were the most perilous distraction to a soldier.

Hadn't Stavr always warned them of the danger?

To a man, they were relieved to be leaving Livonia.

Chapter Thirteen

As soon as Tatiana returned home, she began making plans for her journey to Pskov. She wrote to the bishop, asking for an audience. While she didn't overtly mention the word divorce, she did indicate she wished to discuss the burden of her marriage. While the Orthodox church disapproved of divorce, it did not expressly forbid it. Furthermore, Russian canon expanded the grounds for divorce when a woman's physical or economic well-being was at stake.

The bishop knew what her husband was like; he would help if he could.

Timor and Olga would accompany her, along with nursemaids and grooms and a troop of armed men. Timor was currently busy seeing to the conveyences and supplies. The roads were poor, but they could travel by carriage at least part of the way. And the slowness of the journey would allow her adequate time to prepare her arguments.

But on the day they were to leave for Pskov she woke up feeling nauseous. She told herself it was simply nerves as she lay in bed trying to keep from vomiting. She tried not to dwell on the fact that she'd felt exactly like this in the early months of Zoe's pregnancy. Women didn't get pregnant when they were nursing. It was practically a hard and fast rule. Or was it? Letting out a stifled little yell, she suddenly leaped out of bed, raced for the chamber pot and reached it just in time. A few moments later, white-faced and shaking, she sat on the floor and knew it was too late to see the bishop.

She couldn't approach him now—like this . . . an adulteress.

She couldn't pretend her summer friendship with Stavr had been platonic.

The bishop couldn't pretend either, even if he wished to. Church courts were slow and circumspect. A divorce required hearings and complaints, testimony from both parties, witnesses and examination before a panel of clerics who would then deliberate on the most prudent resolution to the marriage.

And she could no longer afford to wait.

Almost immediately, a more fearsome thought came to mind. If her husband were to discover her pregnancy . . . she shuddered in dread. Taking a deep, calming breath, she reminded herself that Igor had never visited her estate, Moscow was far away, his mistresses were close at hand and the probability he would wish to see her was less than remote.

Having momentarily assuaged her apprehensions, she allowed herself to consider the sheer wonder and joy she might be having Stavr's baby. Could it be true? Was it possible? Shutting her eyes, she imagined him smiling as she told him, imagined the excitement in his eyes, knew he would welcome the news with delight. And if it was truly uncommon to conceive while nursing, was this indeed in the nature of a small miracle? Were the spirits bestowing their blessing on their love? Would those same benevolent spirits keep Stavr safe and bring him home?

She started counting on her fingers.

He might be back in time.

He might be home for the birth of their child.

She felt like laughing and crying and shouting with joy.

She'd send him a message. He would want to know.

Oh, God, how could she find him?

Timor would know.

She screamed for her steward.

Chapter Fourteen

Prince Shuisky woke at the soft footfall and reached for the dagger under his pillow. As his body servant materialized in the dim light, he released his grip on the handle. "What's the meaning of this?" he growled. No one intruded into his personal quarters unless called for.

The young man's bow was so low as to be almost prostrate and his voice trembled slightly as he spoke. "I have important news, Your Excellency." No one had wanted to deliver the message, not even the spy who had come with it.

Igor shoved away the nude woman beside him in bed and snapped his fingers, dismissing her. As she fled the room, he sat up and reached for the wine bottle on the bedside table. "This better be important," he muttered, bringing the bottle to his mouth. "Or you'll have thirty lashes for waking me."

"Victor said you would want to know."

Igor set the bottle back down untasted. His factotum, Victor, ran his spy system. He was a coward at heart, but cunning as cowards often were—and very good at his job.

"It concerns your wife."

Prince Shuisky relaxed against the headboard and half-smiled. "He bothered me for that innocuous bitch? Perhaps *Victor* should have the thirty lashes."

"She's with child."

The prince's smile disappeared. "It's not possible," he muttered, tossing the covers aside. "Am I surrounded by incompetents?" Coming to his feet, he towered over the servant, nude, covered with hair like a huge black bear. "Well?" he snapped.

The prince was always dangerous, quick-tempered, and volatile and it took all the young man's courage not to turn and run. "It's—true—Your Excellency," he stammered. "Vasily—rode—here himself. He saw—her."

The prince spun around and strode to the door. Wrenching it open, he bellowed for Victor and Vasily in a voice that shook the walls. He didn't choose to dress, but paced the outside corridor until the two men appeared and then he closeted himself with them in his apartments. Even through closed doors, the thunder of his voice could be heard.

Within the hour, he burst from his rooms, dressed, armed, booted and spurred. And ten minutes later, he and a menacing troop of cavalry were galloping through the St. Nicholas Gate on their passage north.

Chapter Fifteen

Prince Shuisky set a new record on his journey of reprisal, running scores of mounts into the ground in his headlong pace. But horseflesh was incidental to a man who viewed human life as expendable. And fury drove him.

Tatiana had only brief warning of his arrival, her guards having galloped cross-country to reach her with the news that her husband, together with a formidable troop, was riding fast in her direction.

Strangely, Tatiana felt no fear, only a galvanized sense of urgency. Since the detachment was too large to defend against, she immediately gave orders for her staff to flee to the Biron estate. Kissing Zoe goodbye, she handed her over to her nursemaids. "I'll come for you as soon as I may," she explained to the terrified women. "Under no circumstances return until then. A note from me isn't sufficient. I will come myself or not at all," she said with soft finality. She and Stavr had been realistic about the dangers they faced and had made what plans they could for those eventualities—one of which she currently confronted.

"We must also leave, my lady." Timor stood in the doorway, holding her fur-lined cape. "Volia is saddled and waiting."

The princess and Timor had made plans to serve as decoys,

luring their enemies away from the fleeing servants. Two riders could more easily disappear in the pine forests where Timor knew every deer path and hidden glen. They would be risking little. And despite the November cold, it hadn't yet snowed; tracking would be difficult.

So as her staff took Zoe to safety, Tatiana and her trusted steward waited at the entrance to the estate, watching for Prince Shuisky's troop. As the first riders came into view, the princess and Timor wheeled their mounts and galloped toward the sheltering tree line.

A moment later, a volley of gunshots rang out—a useless gesture at that distance. But seconds later, the hum of arrows filled the air. The longbow was imminently more effective at long range and Tatiana and Timor bent low over their horse's necks in order to make as small a target as possible.

Tatiana was plainly recognizable with her sun-streaked, flowing hair and her vengeful husband had no intention of letting his erring wife escape. "The horses!" he shouted. "Shoot them!"

The animals fell under the heavy flight of arrows, tumbling their riders to the ground.

A faint smile twitched the prince's lips.

Quickly coming to her feet, Tatiana ran to Timor. He lay in a gruesome sprawl, his legs pinned beneath his mount, one arm twisted at an unnatural angle. "Run, my lady," he gasped, spittles of blood exploding from his mouth.

There was no point in running. She'd be overtaken long before she reached the forest. "Soon—there's time." She knelt beside Timor, wiping the blood from his mouth with her sleeve. "Everyone from the house escaped. We accomplished that, you and I," she murmured, watching a pool of blood spread beneath his head. She gently stroked his cheek. How often had he comforted her in her youth? How many times had he listened to her childish troubles? And now his eyes were clouding over, his life draining away because of a ruthless tsar and a brutal husband who wanted her fortune. She bris-

tled at such wanton waste, at the injustice of her plight and resolved in the disintegrating moments of her existence to take
matters into her own hands.

An icy calm pervaded her soul as she knelt beside the man
who had served her so well. She tenderly closed his lifeless eyes
and came to her feet. Curiously untouched by fear, she
brushed the grass from her skirt and cape, shook out her rumpled garments as though she were greeting guests instead of an
armed host of horsemen.

The casualness of her gesture startled Shuisky as he reined
his mount to a stop and he scrutinized the woman who had yet
to acknowledge his presence. She was straightening the embroidered cuffs of her riding gloves, her nerveless indifference
striking fear into his soul. It was an age of superstition and fa-
natical piety, fear of God and the most brutal of acts coexist-
ing in the heathen spirit of men. Was it possible God's grace
shielded his wife? Neither shot nor arrows had touched her.

She finally looked up and he flinched before the implacable
rancor in her eyes. "My friend Timor is dead," she said, her
gaze turning his marrow cold. "For this good man's needless
loss," she said, raising her hand and pointing at him with
avenging zeal, "God will smite you dead."

She had the look of Hel, the goddess of death, swathed as
she was in her dark cloak, her gaze piercing, the chill of the
grave in her voice.

The prince paled beneath his dark beard and swarthy skin.
But one of his men snickered, and he stiffened his resolve. "Or
perhaps he might smite you, madame." His gaze drifted over
her rounded belly. "For *your* sins." The evidence of his wife's
iniquities goaded his vengefulness, mitigated his fear; his expression turned grim. "When I return with your lover's head,
you may kiss him one last time before you die."

Tatiana shook her head. "I can see Stavr now. He's smiling
at your puny efforts." Sweeping her arm in an encompassing
arc that took in all the assembled horsemen, she added, softly,
as though she need not raise her voice to be heard, "He curses
you all for your feeble impotence."

A murmur of dismay issued from the prince's men. With her black cloak whipping about her ankles, her tawny hair swirling in the wind, her pitiless eyes that seemed to enter a man's soul, she appeared a black sorceress putting a curse on their manhood.

Even the prince's mount shifted restlessly as though touched by her witchery. Tightening his grip on the reins, Igor cursed the tsar for wedding him to this fiendish harpy. Uncertain, inchoately fearful before such fanaticism, the prince resorted to bluster. "I guarantee your hetman won't be smiling once we find him."

Tatiana lifted her chin and pinned her husband with an uncompromising gaze. "You can't touch him."

Abruptly jerking on his reins, he wrenched his mount around and kicked his horse into a canter, unwilling to continue a discussion that could humiliate him before his men—or worse, put him victim to his wife's diabolical malevolence. He could feel his wife's gaze burning a hole through his back and if she were indeed touched by God's hand, she could be dangerous. Something Ivan apparently overlooked with the lure of her fortune blinding his judgment. Perhaps it might be wise to consider a more circuitous manner of dealing with the Princess Tatiana. He could lock her away in a nunnery, keep her prisoner on a remote estate, quietly divorce her. All options that wouldn't put him at risk from any of her possibly vengeful gods.

Although, the hetman would die. He need not equivocate there. For having lain with his wife even the judgment of Heaven absolved a husband from murder.

Spurring his horse, the prince and his retinue pounded south.

According to reports, Count Biron was participating in Sigismund's campaign in the south. The fluid borders between Russia and Poland allowed easy access to Sigismund's field army. It should prove simple enough to pass as one of the Slav factions cooperating with the Polish king.

Within the week, Prince Shuisky's band found Sigismund's cavalry units encamped north of the Dnieper. They were waiting for additional regiments to be brought up before advancing on the Crimean Khan's upgraded defenses. An opportune postponement for Shuisky; he preferred not riding into the Crimea.

Since Count Biron was one of the celebrated young lions under Sigismund's command, finding the hetman would be only a matter of following his illustrious fame.

Which famed young lion had been visibly chaffing at the unexpected and extended delay. Stavr wanted nothing more than a swift campaign and swifter victory so he could return to Tatiana with all speed. His priorities had changed; his life had new meaning, new direction, and he wanted above all for this campaign to be concluded. Restless and impatient, a tactician of note, he cursed Sigismund's caution.

Stavr's men, however, were more than content to drink away their idleness, their days of leisure running together in a pleasant, inebriated blur. Philosophically accepting their fate, they knew that the Khan would be in his sumptuous city enjoying the delights of his harem whenever Sigismund deigned to attack. His taste for vice was well known. In the meantime they were enjoying the local, albeit less splendid female attractions to the full.

On the day after Shuisky arrived in the area, word finally came down from the overly prudent generals that the advance on the Khan was set for the coming dawn. Stavr was profoundly relieved. Mentally tracing their march, he constructed a reasonable timetable of operations that would bring him home in three months—four at the most. And then he began resisting his men's invitations for a last night of carousing.

Pitted against his men's relentless wheedling and cajoling, however, he eventually succumbed. But he drank little that night, not in the mood for debauch. He particularly excused himself from his mens' sexual revels . . . not an easy task when he was the object of intense interest to all the convivial females in the tavern. But politely insistent, he informed the women that he was in love, which only served to make him more attractive. Handsome officers who actually acknowledged they had a heart were infinitely appealing.

It was after midnight when Stavr finally persuaded his men to relinquish their pleasures. Although additional prodding and occasional manhandling was still required before every man was outside and mounted. They would be marching five days into the Crimea; his men knew they had plenty of time to recover from their drunkenness. To a colorful rendition of a drinking song, they fell into line behind their leader in a meandering, haphazard formation that strung them out in rambling array on the narrow country road. The new moon cast a weak, wane light, its rays barely breaching the enveloping shadows. But the route was familiar and for those half-dozing in the saddle, their horses knew the way back to camp.

Completely sober despite the late hour, Stavr was the only one vigilant enough to catch the glint of armor in the darkness of the forest bordering the road. He dismissed the transient flicker at first. There were soldiers enough in the vicinity. It could be a picket. But a moment later, at the sound of birdsong, he slowly drew his sword from his scabbard. Birds didn't sing at night. Holding his sword high as a signal to his men, he felt the hair on the back of his neck rising. "Prepare to engage," he murmured, the quiet command resonating down the line from man to man.

Movement was clearly visible now behind every tree and shrub.

"To arms!" Stavr shouted, his mount beginning to prance in anticipation, sensing the ambush.

And suddenly waves of mounted troops poured out of the darkness, galloping at them with swords drawn, bellowing the Shuisky battle cry.

"Hold! Hold!" Stavr cried, relegating his shock at Shuisky's presence so far from Moscow for future contemplation, needing his men to hold fast against the unending swarm of riders. And despite their befuddled senses, his troopers rose to the occasion, instinctively responding, defending themselves with extraordinary valor against overwhelming odds. They met the onslaught with clashing steel, savagely carving their way through their attackers with a cut-and-thrust rhythm they'd honed to a fine art, offering a fierce, murderous resistance. But regardless their courage and bravery, the prince's superior numbers eventually took their toll. Stavr's men began to fall one by one until his troop was reduced to a handful of men.

And after another bloody interval, to only one.

Prince Shuisky's contingent was badly mauled. Many of his men were dead and those who remained had been disappearing into the darkness, taking advantage of the concealing shadows to save themselves. Most had no wish to give up their lives for a man they served only through fear. Whether Shuisky didn't notice or whether he could have curtailed their flight if he had, as the battle stilled, he found himself standing alone.

At last, Stavr thought, trying to catch his breath, the man he'd been wanting to kill for a very long time was only a few feet away.

How young he was at close range, Shuisky noted in surprise, taking the measure of his wife's lover. And favoring his wounded left arm.

Both men were ravaged, bloody from wounds, on foot now and breathing hard. But murderously intent.

"We finally—meet . . . Cossack dog." Shuisky's voice was a breathless rasp. "You took—something—of mine."

"I *have* something—of yours."

"Not . . . for . . . long." Shuisky brought his sword and dagger up, gauging the distance to the hetman's wounded arm.

"After—tonight. Forever," Stavr panted, tightening his grip on his sword and dagger, ignoring the pain in his left arm, wanting the man who had brutalized Tatiana dead by his hand. He launched himself at the prince, his blades flashing.

The clang of steel rang in the moonlight, Shuisky desperately parrying the hetman's blows, both men understanding they were fighting for their lives. There would be no compromise, no quarter asked or given, no one to call halt to this death match.

As different as night and day, the two men contested the other's right to live, their struggle ferocious, pitiless, their strength so evenly matched the outcome was moot. They lunged and parried, cut and thrust, driven by rage and vengeance, first one on the attack and then the other, both inflicting damage, but neither able to strike the fatal coup de grace. Their strength waning, only sheer will kept them upright. Even reduced to the use of his right arm, the hetman's youth and litheness was proving too much for Shuisky. He knew his life was in peril. Resorting to cunning and treachery, he gasped, "You'll—never—live . . . to see your bastard born."

A child! Tatiana was going to have his child! In that moment of joy, Stavr's guard lapsed infinitesimally.

And the prince ran him through.

As the hetman fell mortally wounded, Shuisky swayed on his feet, trembling, near collapse. Too weak and debilitated to even experience triumph at his victory, the fact that he'd survived the emotion filling his brain, the prince barely had strength to haul himself up on his horse. Once in the saddle, he slumped over his horse's neck and fainted.

When he revived sometime later, he knew there was no possibility of fulfilling his vow to bring back the hetman's head. But he'd take pleasure in telling his wife that her lover was dead.

And after that, she and her bastard were next.

He turned his mount for home.

Chapter Sixteen

God, however, took pity on Tatiana who had never sinned against His laws unless loving too much was a sin. By His merciful grace, or perhaps as vengeance for the prince's black deeds, Our Heavenly Father saw to it that Prince Shuisky succumbed to his wounds on his journey home.

But the princess received word of her husband's death with mute indifference.

It was too late.

Everything was too late now.

Her life was over.

In the days following Sigismund's report of the massacre, Tatiana's staff had feared for her sanity. She didn't sleep, barely ate, gave no notice of day or night. She hardly seemed aware of her daughter. Her lover was dead and she was mad with grief. As days turned into weeks, Tatiana's voiceless anguish gave way to tears and she would cry for hours at a time, until she became drawn and pale as a ghost. When the tears finally came to a stop, she took to staring out the window as though waiting for someone they all knew would never come.

On Zoe's birthday, the young child uttered the word, "Mama," for the first time. Tugging on her mother's hand, the toddler smiled up at Tatiana and repeated the newly formed word over and over again in childish delight.

The princess turned from the window and spoke in a normal tone of voice for the first time since Sigismund's messenger had ridden away. "How clever you are, darling," she said, lifting her daughter onto her lap, smiling at her rosy-cheeked child. "How sweet and clever and wonderful you are."

It was like a glorious resurrection and the servants all crossed themselves and gave up thanks to the Lord. Then they breathed a collective sigh of relief at their mistress's reawakening and began talking above a whisper for the first time in months.

"What day is it?" Tatiana asked, and when she was told, she inquired next, "What month?" Her eyes had flared wide when she'd been told.

It was a turning point, as though a door had suddenly opened, allowing light and warmth into the darkness of her mind. She even brought herself to visit Timor's grave that day, kneeling before the gravestone for a lengthy time, talking to him as though he were alive.

In the servants's pagan world, speaking to the spirits was commonplace and they only nodded their heads, pleased their mistress had recovered. Life returned to a semblance of normal after that, although the princess's smiles were still rare. But in the days that followed, she once again became engaged in the business of the estate and before long, she was driving everyone at a frantic pace. But no one complained. They understood her need for constant activity. It was a means of keeping her demons at bay.

Then, on a mild, warm day in April, the princess gave birth to a son—a beautiful, blond, green-eyed boy who by the ancient laws of Russia became heir to Tatiana's dead husband, Prince Shuisky. Who, in fact, became the *new* Prince Shuisky.

She named him after his father, not caring what the world might think.

And she built a new life around her two children, devoting herself to them, finding solace in motherhood.

But she never stopped grieving for the great love of her life. Although she took care to do her mourning in private, understanding how difficult it had been for her staff to see her so distraught. She wished as well, to spare her children. But at night, in the quiet of her room, she cried for all that she'd lost—her greatest love, her happiness, her future.

At summer's end, when the birds were flocking up for their return south, one evening, just as the sun was setting, a lone rider appeared at the end of the drive.

Tatiana and her children were on the porch, enjoying the lingering warmth of the day. At the nursemaid's exclamation, Tatiana looked up and her breath caught in her throat. The rider's pale hair shimmered in the sunset, the set of his shoulders struck a chord of memory and for a wild moment, Tatiana thought she was losing her mind once again. But the nursemaid pointed; clearly, she saw the rider, too, and Tatiana knew the man was real. With her heart beating at a furious pace, she handed the baby to its nurse, bent low to speak to her daughter, then turned and took the steps in a flying leap.

She shouted his name as she ran down the drive, tears streaming down her face, her high-pitched cry scattering the sparrows in the trees.

He answered, but faintly, and bringing his horse to a halt, slowly dismounted. She could almost feel his pain as he eased himself from the saddle to the ground.

Racing toward him, she didn't care that he was limping noticeably, she didn't care if he could walk at all—he was alive!

Stavr stopped before she reached him, opened his arms and moments later, she flung herself at him. He sucked in his breath at the impact, his face went ashen, but his arms closed around her and they stood in the golden sunset, laughing and crying, kissing, murmuring love words, feeling giddy and transported, feeling whole again.

"I'm home," he said at last, his breath warm against her mouth, his words balmy with joy.

She didn't ask where he'd been or how he'd gotten here even though his struggle with death was deeply etched on his features. She only said, fierce and low, "Promise me you're home . . . forever. Say it, Stavr! Say it this instant!"

His smile was radiant. "Forever and always."

She laughed, a jubilant, triumphant sound, reminding him of the first time he'd heard her laugh two springtimes ago. Then she took his hand and said with pride, "Come. Meet your son."

When father and son met, green eyes met green, smiles large and small formed on faces that bore the same distinct features and when Stavr bent to kiss his namesake, he met a sweet gooey gurgle in welcome. A moment later as he lifted his son into his arms, even Zoe who rarely took note of anything not specifically related to her said with two-year-old insight, "Baby weally wikes you."

"How can you tell?" Stavr asked, squatting down, drawing Zoe closer. "Do you know what his gurgle means?"

Zoe beamed. "He saying he wikes you. I do too. Wook at me; you wike my pink swippers?"

With such a cue even the most obtuse would take notice. Stavr immediately handed the baby back to Tatiana. "I'm looking, sweet pea," he said, smiling at her. "You have the most beautiful pink slippers. I'll bet you can run really fast in them."

"Faster than you." She pointed at his legs. "You tan't walk good."

He laughed. "I'll be able to soon. Tell me, has your mother been keeping you busy while I was gone?"

Zoe immediately proceeded to describe all her daily activities in great detail, keeping up a running commentary even as they moved into the house at Tatiana's urging. Stavr's gauntness was horrifying. She'd ordered supper for him.

Delighted with her captive audience, Zoe sat beside their guest as he ate, and entertained him with nonstop conversation. When Stavr couldn't eat another bite despite Tatiana's coaxing, Zoe insisted he come see her toys. Leading the way to the nursery, she sat Stavr down on the floor and began showing him all her favorite playthings, explaining how each worked, what its name was, why she particularly liked it with the egocentric assurance of childhood that assumes everyone is interested in one's activities. When her collection of toys was finally exhausted, she ran to where her brother lay in Tatiana's lap, patted his head and said with a smile, "Mine baby," adding him to her possessions. Turning her cheerful smile on Stavr, she wiggled a finger in his direction. "You . . . daddy—mine too?"

"Yes," Stavr said, without hesitation. "I'm your daddy."

"I know dat," Zoe said, her childish certainty putting the stamp of approval on any reservations Tatiana might have had about being truthful. "Ollie tell me."

Tatiana's brows rose infinitesimally. Her maid, Olga, apparently had no such scruples about honesty.

Stavr winked at Zoe. "Ollie is very smart."

Zoe vigorously nodded her head, her dark curls bobbing in assent. "She know—oops"—she put her hand over her mouth and whispered between her fingers—"secret."

Stavr laughed and even Tatiana couldn't help but smile when she remembered how the servants had been her closest friends in childhood.

"Sometimes it's hard to keep secrets, isn't it?" Stavr murmured, smiling at Zoe.

With lips tightly compressed, she only nodded.

"I know something that isn't a secret. I know that we're going to ride to my house tomorrow and you can see my ponies. Would you like to ride one?"

Zoe was immediately full of questions about this new house and ponies. What color were his ponies? Hers was little because she was little; were his? Did he have another family at his house? Did he have pets and toys?

Stavr answered all of Zoe's queries with good humor and great kindness, explaining to her as well all they would do and see the next day. And then he lay on the floor beside her and partnered her in her childish play, making her laugh and giggle, astonishing Tatiana with his capacity for make-believe. She was touched by the attention Stavr gave to her daughter. How considerate he was to a little girl who had never really had a father. How thoughtful and indulgent. How incredibly blessed *she* was to have him home once again.

As though aware of her regard, Stavr's gaze suddenly came up. Winking at her over Zoe's head, he mouthed the words I love you.

She smiled and silently formed the words in return, a palpable happiness shimmering between them.

Zoe's high-pitched voice resonated in the candlelit room, the baby's soft cooing counterpoint to his sister's childish discourse. With a flash of a smile, Stavr bent low once again to listen to Zoe explain to her doll that the red dress was for parties.

Tatiana's heart was filled to overflowing.

She had a family again—entire and whole, the love of her life was returned from the dead; she understood the meaning of bliss.

Much later, when the house had quieted and both children were sleeping, Tatiana and Stavr walked hand in hand down the corridor to her bedroom. His pace was slow, his limp more pronounced with the lateness of the hour, but his smile was as bewitching as ever.

"Have I mentioned how grateful I am for my son?" he said, squeezing her hand.

"Not more than a thousand times."

He grinned. "I see I've been derelict."

She laughed and touched his cheek as she paused at her bedroom door. "You may tell me a thousand times more tomorrow. *Now*, I'm going to put you to bed. You look exhausted."

He glanced up and down the hall, as though taking stock of his surroundings and then slowly exhaled. "Just think, we're going to bed like normal people."

"Miracles do happen," she whispered.

He nodded, drew her into his arms and held her close. And two souls so recently without hope savored the sweetness of the most commonplace of events.

"Speaking of miracles," he murmured, taking a step back, his expression changing before her eyes, becoming constrained. "I'll have a priest marry us first thing in the morning."

Her brows rose; his voice was unnecessarily brusque.

"If you agree, of course," he added, quickly, taking note of the sudden wariness in her eyes.

"Why did you say it like that?" His harsh tone reminded her of Igor; she was instantly on guard.

His lashes fell and when he looked up again, he didn't quite meet her gaze. "I'm sorry. I don't know why." Impelled by a tumult of emotions, none of them benign, he struggled to understand his motives. Terror perhaps. Or possessiveness. Maybe he'd been a hetman too long.

"You're supposed to ask, not tell." With her disastrous first marriage not yet a distant memory, she was apprehensive of dictatorial males. "As a widow, I have a degree of independence. I don't want orders. I definitely don't."

"I understand. Forgive me. I must be tired." He offered her a polite smile.

She stared at him for a moment, and then said, "Very well."

In a grating sort of way he found himself stupidly thinking. A small silence fell.

While he had every intention of making her his wife, struck by some irrational agitation, he found himself momentarily disinclined to propose. Marriage had always seemed like a remote, perhaps even dubious eventuality and after that condescending, *Very well,* suddenly all his former convictions were clamoring for more time.

Don't be absurd, his voice of reason challenged. If you recall, it was your love for Tatiana that gave you the will to survive, that brought you from the brink of death.

And convictions of a lifetime aside, he loved her with all his heart—that he knew.

Taking a small breath, he exhaled, grimaced, ran his fingers through his hair and finally said in a rush of words, "Willyou-marryme?"

Her gaze narrowed. It was impossible not to have seen his doubt. "You're uncertain?"

"No—no, God, no. It's just that, I mean"—he shrugged—"I never—"

"Planned to marry this young?" she inquired, mildly.

"No—yes, yes, but this is different," he said, flushing like an awkward adolescent. "Jesus, I'm sorry. Really. I'm absolutely sure."

She scrutinized him for a lengthy moment. She'd never seen him other than self-possessed and so deep in love herself, she wanted no less from him. But he'd spoken in the early days last summer of all he planned to do, of the campaigns and distant lands, of the joy of riding with his men, of the exhilaration in victory. Did it matter that he was unsure now? Did she doubt his love for her? Could she consider life without him? Did she even want to contemplate such an existence?

Her answers were swift and sure. "Your priest or mine?"

His brows rose. "Does it matter?"

"My priest is closer."

"Yours then. Good. It's settled." His relief was apparent.

"No lengthy marriage settlements or engagement or lawyers arguing about dowries?" Her gaze was amused as she moved past him into her bedroom.

"Our son perhaps precludes the necessity of a lengthy engagement," he replied, drolly, following her in, all the ambiguities vanquished. Shutting the door, he leaned back against it. "As for a marriage settlement, have everything—I don't care so long as I have you."

"How sweet." Her lashes half-lowered. "And imprudent your business agent might say."

"My business agent has no voice in the affairs of my heart."

"Affair of the heart—singular—if you don't mind. Is that clear?"

"Very. I might ask the same of you, as well." His smile flashed white in the candlelight. "Don't look affronted. Think how we met."

She had the grace to blush. "You're right. Singular. I agree."

"'Til morning then," he said, a roguish light in his eyes. "Which gives us plenty of time . . ."

"Absolutely not!" She put up her hand in a warding-off gesture. "You're barely walking. You need your rest."

"I don't think so." After narrowly escaping the grave, sleep wasn't high on his list of priorities.

"You should recuperate for a few more days, darling," she said, gently, as one would to a recalcitrant child. "Lie down while I unpin my hair and then we'll discuss it."

His shadowed eyes glowed with amusement, this man who had ridden a fortnight from the Dnieper on sheer will alone. "We could do that, I suppose," he murmured, dropping onto the bed. "I haven't had the opportunity to actually discuss having sex with you before. You've always been in too much of a hurry."

"Very amusing, I'm sure," she retorted, sitting down at her dressing table, trying very hard not to be selfish. "I'm not currently in a rush, however, and you're really much too unwell to even consider such activities. One of us has to be practical."

"Practical . . ." His voice was a lazy drawl. "Interesting choice of words." Not precisely his choice on his first night home, but he was willing to wait until she had her hairpins out. And while the candlelight flickered and the night winds echoed through the trees, feeling himself the luckiest of men, he lounged on the bed and watched her pull the amber pins from her hair and take off her jewelry piece by piece—her pearl earrings and Scythian rings, the ornate gold chatelaine at her waist, the ruby-encrusted Greek cross at her neck. She smiled at him in her mirror as she combed out her hair and blew him a kiss.

Deftly catching it, he pantomimed tucking it away in his pocket. "Life doesn't get any better than this," he murmured.

Swiveling around on her chair, she gazed at him, a rush of

tears welling into her eyes. "I didn't know I could be this happy. I never *knew.*"

His golden hair, half-grown back after the fever he'd survived, was rough-cut and spiky in the lamplight, his raw-boned strength softened by shadow. "Wherever you are is paradise, sweet Tatia." He'd come back from the very edge of the abyss; he knew.

Her tears spilled over. "I prayed every day for this."

Instantly coming to his feet, he closed the distance between them in two strides, took the comb from her hand, set it down and pulled her into his arms. "I must have heard you," he whispered, gently kissing away her tears.

"You can't ever, *ever* leave me again."

Her sniffling command brought a smile to his face. "Don't worry, darling. I literally rose from the grave to come back to you. I have no intention of pressing my luck." The memory of that frightening moment still brought him awake in the night drenched in sweat.

"The grave?" A look of horror crossed her face.

"The dirt hitting my face brought me back to consciousness." The unforgettable stench of death was suddenly pungent in his nostrils. Forcing down the terror that always assailed him at the memory, he tried to speak in a normal tone of voice. "When I realized I was being buried alive, I screamed your name over and over again." A tick appeared high on his cheekbone, recall of his inability to gain the attention of the men burying him still capable of causing an inexpressible panic. "My cry was so weak," he went on a moment later, having regained his composure, "the men burying me said they wouldn't have heard it if they hadn't stopped to look up at an eagle circling overhead."

"Your eagle," she whispered.

"*Our* eagle."

"Our good luck charm; I remember every second of that day." Every smile, every touch and word, every heated desire. "He found you for me and sent you home." Her face was wet with tears. "I wish I would have known. Someone should have sent word." She would have packed up the entire household if need be and set out to fetch him no matter if he'd been at the ends of the earth.

"It was too dangerous," Stavr explained, wiping away her tears with the pads of his fingers. "The men who pulled me from my grave didn't tell anyone for fear they'd be blamed if I died. And when I finally regained my senses—I didn't know whether"—his voice trailed off, not wishing to mention her husband's name, determined not to give voice to their deadly struggle. She might blame herself.

"You didn't know whether he was still looking for you."

Stavr nodded. "I asked about you in the last village I passed today and heard he was gone."

"He died of his wounds on his journey home."

Stavr's nostrils flared. "I'm glad."

She shivered slightly, as though touched by the demons in her past, but almost instantly rallied. She lifted her chin. "I would have found a way to rid myself of him."

"I know." Stavr didn't say—only if the tsar let you and the courts and Shuisky himself. "The spirits have been kind to us," he said instead.

"You mustn't tempt them and go off to war again."

"I won't." His voice was unyielding in its finality.

"So I have you all to myself, my lord," she lightly noted, hoping to erase the grim look that had come into his eyes.

It took him a moment to compose his sensibilities, and a moment more for a lazy smile to appear. "Consider me completely at your disposal, darling," he drawled, "in any way at all . . ."

"I didn't intend to imply"—her face flushed red—"in any event, you're not sufficiently recovered from your wounds . . . to—"

"I'm sure I could muster the strength," he interposed, his voice velvety and low.

"Do you mean, that is"—she trembled—"are you sure? No!" She took a small breath of restraint, trying to suppress the shimmering heat curling in the pit of her stomach, reminding herself they had a lifetime ahead of them. "We can't," she asserted, pushing at his chest.

With an indulgent smile, he let her step back; he, too, understood time was no longer at a premium. "I'm not an invalid, darling." Moving toward the bed, he began unbuttoning the muzhik neckline of his shirt. "And I don't want to argue on my first night home, but I hope you'll change your mind."

He stood near the bed, intent on his undressing, tall and beautiful, broad-shouldered, more lean than she would have wished, but so irresistibly tempting, she found herself almost willing to jettison good judgment without a qualm.

He looked up, the buttons undone. "I'm going to be ahead of you." His smile was pure seduction. "Although the thought of undressing you was great incentive on my ride home. I'd always start with your stockings." He grinned. "My fantasy would last longer that way. So, I'm more than willing to help you take off your clothes. Just give me a minute..." He kicked off the embroidered slippers she'd given him and reached for the fastening on his breeches.

"This isn't fair. How am I supposed to resist"—she waved her hand toward him in a little twirling motion—"when you're—"

"Getting ready for sex?"

"Well—yes ... it's not fair when I'm trying very hard to be unselfish and compassionate, and—"

"If you really want to be compassionate, sweetheart"—his fingers worked the ties at the waistband of his breeches— "you'll come just a little bit closer." His gaze was heated, his smile inviting, his erection clearly visible, lifting the soft wool of his breeches away from his body in the most enticing way.

Selfish motive overwhelmed Tatiana's hard-pressed scruple in a tidal wave of desire and try as she would, the throbbing deep inside her only heightened. "You won't regret this later?"

His gaze held hers for a potent moment and when he spoke his voice was husky with need. "You're exonerated from all blame, darling."

"Completely exonerated?"

He laughed. "I don't recall you being so restrained."

"The word grave sometimes has that effect on me," she replied with a small smile.

"The grave is long past." He winked. "Come closer."

"How close." A piquant longing trembled beneath her words.

"Preferably right here," he said, softly, a faint sweep of his hand indicating the outline of his arousal beneath his garments.

"Because you want me," she whispered, a shiver racing up her spine.

He drew in a breath of restraint. "Oh, yes . . ."

"You're sure I won't hurt you if—" his scowl stopped her and when he said very softly, "Come," she went.

The silk of her dress brushed against the soft wool of his breeches, the heat of their bodies warming the fabrics and then his hands closed on her waist and hers on his and they met— his lean taut body against her voluptuous softness, his erection hard against her belly.

His head dipped and he kissed her gently—in welcome and promise, in hope, and the sweetness of the moment overset even the urgency of their desire. Love took on texture and form, scent and taste, enveloped them in its rareness and beauty, disposed them to believe again in the goodness of the world.

And for long blissful moments, it was enough to simply hold each other and feel the glory.

But for a man who had never been saintlike, Tatiana's soft, redolent purr was triggering decidedly carnal impulses and when she smiled up at him and murmured, "Welcome home," in a particularly inviting tone, his mouth curved into a smile.

"You sound as though you missed me."

Her eyes were half-lidded, their violet depths heated. "I missed you in a thousand different ways."

"Like this?" he whispered, sliding his hands down her back, the silk of her gown luxurious, the warmth of her body his talisman and lure, his delight. As his hands slipped lower, coming to rest on the curve of her soft bottom, she melted against him with a sigh, the delicate utterance a heated, liquid pianissimo that brought his erection surging higher.

"Just like that," she whispered, swaying against him.

"And this?" he murmured, pulling her closer so they both felt the lush pulsing contact.

"Oh, God . . . oh, God . . ."

He knew that delicious breathy sound from their summer at his dacha; he remembered it with delight. Drawing her to the bed, he fell back onto the soft mattress, pulling her with him—stifling a gasp as she landed on his badly damaged sword arm.

She jerked away in alarm. "I'm sorry . . . I'm sorry!"

"It's nothing," he lied, pulling her back. "A twinge, that's all," he gently added, ignoring the caustic pain streaking down his arm, hoping his wounds wouldn't begin bleeding again. "Although, if I pass out, you have my permission to punch me back into consciousness."

"Stavr!" Shoving herself up on her hands, she gave him a sharp look of reproof. "We should wait. Really, we"—

His grip was astonishingly strong as he eased her back atop him and arched his hips so she felt his arousal. "No more waiting," he murmured, intense and impatient, beginning to slide his breeches downward, not having survived what he had to be stopped now by solicitude. "I'm done talking," he added, gruffly. As his erection sprang free, he was gratified to hear her low, feverish moan. "You're not going to hurt me," he whispered, pulling her skirt and petticoats upward, lifting the folds of silk and muslin away from her body. "This is about being alive."

She suddenly understood what had seemed to her rash and foolhardy. "So I shouldn't argue with you."

"I wouldn't recommend it." He delicately caressed the curve of her hips, his long slender fingers splayed wide. "You'd lose."

"Or win," she replied in a sultry whisper, moving her hips faintly beneath his light grip.

He laughed softly. "We'd both win."

"Beginning now?" she asked, her voice lightly teasing, stirring faintly against his rampant erection.

"Now would be good," he murmured in vast understatement.

Rising on her knees, she reached for him. "I see nothing was hurt here . . ." She traced the length of his engorged penis with her fingertips.

"Everything's fully operational," he replied, drolly.

"We'll have to see," she said, flirtatious and playful. She watched his penis swell and rise as her hand moved downward, the gleaming crown throbbing with his heartbeat, darkening to a deep crimson. His eyes shut, his back arched against the soul-stirring ecstasy and she smiled at her handiwork. "You're wonderfully healthy," she murmured, tightening her grip, his arousal visibly lengthening with the added pressure. "And so beautifully eager," she purred.

His lashes lifted marginally, his green gaze smoldering. "I'm glad you approve, because I may not let you out of bed for a month." He slid his finger over the slight swell of her mons, then lower, delicately tracing her slick, wet cleft. "I hope you can keep up." Nudging her upward slightly, he slipped his finger into her honeyed sweetness and she melted around him, succulent and warm, drenched with longing. "Because I want this to last and last . . ." he breathed, easing in another finger.

Preoccupied with the intense throbbing ache between her legs, she gazed at him blankly, trying to absorb the full impact of his words. "Last?" Preorgasmic hysteria was mounting, making it impossible to consider the word, last, reasonable in any way. "Please . . . don't say that," she panted, moving against his fingers, wet, frenzied.

"Maybe next time," he murmured, withdrawing his fingers, quickly rolling over her, so anesthetized by lust, he came to rest between her legs without feeling any pain.

"You don't mind, do you?" she gasped, easing her thighs

wider, arching her hips upward, frantically rubbing her slick labia against his erection.

Not inclined to reply with pleasure spiking through his brain, he forced her hips down, swiftly guided himself to her welcoming heat and entered her, plunging headlong into her honeyed sweetness.

Clutching at his shoulders, she urged him deeper, engulfed him in her silken flesh, pulsed around him with the splendid, sublime, hot-blooded passion he'd dreamed of in the harrowing months of his recovery.

"Are you feeling alive?" she breathed, touched by the unutterably vital sweetness of life.

A low rumble in his throat was the extent of his reply, riveting sensation washing over him in waves. Flexing his thighs, he drove deeper, his grip hard on her hips, the rhythm of his lower body exquisitely fluid, indulgent, skilled, his senses automatically attuned to the rhythm of her response. She was racing to orgasm, as always, although they both had reason for unbridled passions after so long . . . and he hastened to meet her. Seconds later, their climaxes broke on a perfect, fever pitch, tumultuous instant, the wildness momentarily blotting out the world, the breath-held essence of life rapturously reaffirmed in all its vaulting glory.

Happiness and bliss melting through their bones.

Afterward, Tatiana found her breath first. "I'm sorry. You wanted it to last," she noted ruefully.

His chest heaving, he shrugged and bent to kiss the tip of her nose. "It doesn't—matter," he panted.

"Because we have all night."

He grinned. "At least."

"Or a thousand nights," she noted with unalloyed delight.

He drew in a deep breath. "Or ten thousand thousand."

Pulling his head down, she kissed him joyously. "Isn't it just grand?"

He nodded, suddenly struck by the thought of many of his men not so fortunate.

His expression had turned grave. "Did I hurt you?"

"In thirty seconds?" he said, shaking away his melancholy. "I don't think so." Chance and destiny was every soldier's fortune; he knew it, they all knew it.

"I'll try to be better."

"You're excellent in every way, sweetheart. You couldn't be better."

"Really?" Her experience was limited, she had no way of knowing.

"Really."

"How gracious you are."

"I'm glad you think so."

"Are you tired?"

He looked at her expectant gaze and gave the required answer. "Not in the least."

"Oh, good—that is, I mean . . . you did mention—er—next time," she said, blushing in the most adorable way.

"Tell me what you want."

Her blush deepened. "I don't know; don't ask me."

"You'll have to learn to tell me what you want. You'll like it more."

"I like it very well indeed already."

He laughed. "You always do. I'll go first, then. Why don't you take off that gown."

"Is that all?" She offered him a coy, teasing glance.

He shook his head. "Take off everything."

"You must too, then. You haven't taken off your shirt. I won't be frightened," she added, with a discerning gaze.

Rolling off her, he didn't immediately reply. He sat up and leaned against the headboard. "It's not as bad as it looks," he said, the restraint in his voice plain.

"I understand."

"The wounds are just slow to heal with the manner of my convalescence."

"Darling, I'm not a child."

He grimaced faintly. "This could wait, couldn't it?"

"I'm capable of looking at a wound," she noted, gently, half-turning on her side to better see him.

"Don't say I didn't warn you," he murmured, shifting forward slightly, gripping the back of his shirt at the neckline.

"For heaven's sake, Stavr. Do you think I'm some faint-hearted female?"

He hesitated still.

"Stavr!"

He jerked his shirt over his head.

And her gasp was less conspicuous than the horror in her eyes.

"I told you," he said in a flat voice, beginning to slide his shirt back on.

"No, don't." She reached up and stayed his hand. "It's fine. You're alive. That's all that matters," she added, softly, tracing the outline of a scar on his arm. The awful puckered flesh was an angry red, the sword cut so deep it had left an indentation in the flesh. Coming to her knees, she smiled at him. "You'll be healed in no time now that you're home." She tried not to stare at the multitude of wounds criss-crossing his upper body, the dagger and sword cuts distinctive, the most life-threatening one, the sword thrust just under his heart. It still hadn't scabbed over and she suspected the point of exit in his back was equally gruesome. "Now I'm going to put some salve on your wounds and don't tell me no," she added, jabbing a finger at him. "Olga's babushka is famous for her healing ointments. Don't you dare move. I'll be right back."

Even had he wished to, Stavr wasn't sure he could. In the aftermath of euphoric lust, his senses were refocusing on his pain and he was trying very hard not to faint.

"There now, that's very sensible of you," Tatiana murmured on her return, seeing that he'd slid down on the pillows. "You just rest, and I'll put this salve on you. See, it even smells good." She thrust the pottery container at him. "Your favorite, cherry blossoms."

His pain visibly diminished. Whether it was the memorable

scent or Tatiana's solicitous attention or just the fact that he was where he most wished to be, he felt every muscle in his body relax. The salve was indeed soothing, Tatiana's touch exquisitely gentle, her frequent kisses the best medicine of all. She covered all his wounds, brought him a clean shirt, helped him pull it over his head and then said, proudly, "You're feeling better already, aren't you?"

"Thank you, yes. In a number of ways." He glanced downward. "A nude nursemaid always has a predictable effect on me."

"Always?" Her voice was tart as she surveyed his rising erection.

"Let me rephrase that."

"That might be wise," she noted, a telling edge to her gaze.

"Your nudity always has a predictable effect on me."

"Thank you, but you're in no condition to—"

In a flashing moment, he'd rolled over, picked her off her feet, lifted her up and deposited her on his thighs. "Consider, darling, if you do all the work, I won't even have to move."

She glanced at his blatant erection.

"It might even be therapeutic. I'm sure it would be."

"What if your wounds start bleeding?"

He smiled up at her. "They won't."

"How can you be so sure?"

"If you move very, very slowly, they won't. You like when I go in and out slowly, don't you?"

Drawing in a breath, she gazed at his beautiful stiff, thick penis, the word slowly, a particularly tantalizing word. "You can't move at all," she commanded.

"Yes, ma'am."

"I mean it, Stavr."

"Whatever you say, darling."

"I hope I won't regret this."

He could guarantee she wouldn't, but he knew better than to voice his thoughts.

"Just this once now and then I want you to sleep."

"Yes, dear."

But when she was impaled on his rampant penis, he held her captive, his hands tight on her waist and after her third orgasm, she proved less difficult to deal with. In fact, she proved incredibly docile after that.

They made love all through the night—his way and her way and their way.

It was the very best of curatives.

It was the very, very best of homecomings.

It was the glorious beginning of their new life together.

HER LORD AND MASTER

Thea Devine

Chapter One

London, 1810

The Earl of Wick was bored.

He was a man of five and thirty who had inherited his title young and had spent the ensuing years sampling everything his world had to offer. He was said to be jaded, dissolute, and unstoppable. Money bought him the freedom to be a libertine, and it did nothing to temper his appetites or imbue him with any sense of responsibility.

"There must be one thing," Ellingham mused one evening when they had all retreated to Heeton's back parlor and were fair on the way to drinking themselves into a stupor while Wick watched and listened to them with the irritated look of the unutterably weary.

He *was* tired, he thought, tired of the endless round of flirtations, seductions, beddings, women and wine, propriety and promiscuity, and gossips ever nipping at his heels.

There had to be something more. And would that it didn't involve his dowager mother's ceaseless demand that he marry and get an heir.

But what other challenge was left to him?

"There are always the virgins," he drawled as he tilted his glass to the low light of the candle to admire the deep ruby color of the expensive claret.

Even that which gave surcease to life's travails looked better than it tasted, he thought mordantly. And that, perhaps, was the leitmotif of his life: things were never as good as they looked, and he was always doomed to disappointment. His friends thought him jaded, but in point of fact, he was just tired; sometimes he wanted nothing more than to just lie down and sleep because his dreams were much more interesting than anything his life had to offer.

But this circle of his most intimate friends, the crème de la crème of society, was always on the lookout for anything new and novel to amuse him. It was in fact their entertainment, to provide for Wick what he couldn't seem to find for himself at this point in his life.

Something that didn't bore him.

Like virgins.

Except men married virgins.

As Ellingham immediately pointed out. "Incorruptible, my dear Wick. Bred to purity, white as white. You touch a virgin and you die."

"Certain road to hell and marriage," Max Bowen muttered. "You don't want to travel that road, Wick."

"Now wait, now wait . . ." Ellingham interposed. "Let's just think about this. After all, Madam Mother is avid to find the hot piece who will by choice agree to wear blinders, in order to get Wick an heir."

"I've had enough of that," Wick said dryly.

"But here's the point," Ellingham said excitedly, "you haven't. You've had every available toss and tart who's struck your fancy, but that's quite another proposition from having a *proper* piece, someone you can take home to Madam Mother. Yes, I'm talking about *cloistered* virgins, my dear Wick. The mice on the marriage mart. The ones whose mothers would kill to have them marry an earl. It makes one wonder just how far a virgin would let loose if there were a real possibility marriage was in the offing. Marriage to *you*, Wick. The Unmentionable, the Unobtainable. The ever-corrupt, endlessly debauched, but always acceptable—if not indeed sought after—Earl of Wick . . . who in his expressed desire never to marry, has now come to the conclusion that he must find someone he can tolerate so he can mate and get an heir. What would a girl, an untouched, unstained virgin, trade for that?

"Gentlemen, think of the possibilities: she will obtain money, position, a title. A bottomless well of luxury and pleasures to be plumbed once she provides the heir . . . and all at the cost of one small insignificant body part that women have willingly surrendered or the price of a night's pleasure since time immemorial.

"Could a well-bred English rose do any less? *If* her prize were to be the Golden Bull? Could *any* woman resist? Oh, they'd be beating down the doors, every last wanton one of them, from Lancashire to London. God, what fun. Can you see it? All those delicious, untouched, untried virgins, spreading themselves for your delectation? Wick! The idea of it is positively obscene. You *have* to do it. Oh, you must. All that luscious new flesh . . . it makes my mouth water just to think of it."

"My dear Ellingham," Wick interposed gently. "Don't *you* get carried away when it is *I* who must perform."

Ellingham dismissed that statement with a wave of his hand. "The legendary Golden Bull? Never a problem. Did we not ourselves witness your masterful pump and spew of not less than five hot-tailed toddies two weeks ago? Didn't even stop for breath. Amazing performance. Amazing. But this—what I'm proposing—this is different. It's—an experiment. We seduce these sanctimonious unsoiled maidens of propriety who hide behind their purity, innocence, and spotless reputations, and offer them everything in the world they could want. Including Wick—because, after all, there must be a prize for such a massive and triumphant corruption.

"But that's hardly of any moment, my dear Wick, because your Madam Mother will love this fallen angel who will have by that time gotten you an heir, and Madam Mother will keep her suitably occupied raising the brat while you fuck and cat around as you always have."

Wick yawned. "What's in it for me?"

"Why, the challenge, dear boy. You underestimate how many vestal vessels are really whores under their skirts. We'll put out the word, we'll swear them to secrecy—they won't want to admit they've failed to captivate the mighty Wick in the first go-round anyway. We'll find three untouched, un-stained, untrained beauties for you. Three desperate-to-wed-an-earl goddesses who would do anything for you, if only you would . . . well, you'll teach them all the *if onlys,* Wick. You'll define what they need to do to excite your interest. Whatever your imagination dreams up, my dear boy. And we all have cause to know how inventive you are.

"And in the meantime, we'll have the fun of watching the perversion of innocence. Fine sport all around and bets will be taken, gentlemen, once the contenders are chosen."

"A momentary diversion at best," Wick murmured lan-guidly, but his penis was already rigid with excitement at the thought of it, and ready to plow the nearest toll-hole. He reached for the waitress who was refilling their goblets, and pulled her onto his lap. The waitresses were very accommo-dating here: they wore no underclothes and they took every poke and thrust they could get for the lavish gratuity that came with their willingness to spread their legs.

It was but one more movement to settle this willing trull onto his penis, and another to thrust and blow to relieve the pressure in his nether parts. A perfunctory performance at best, over too soon, and too easily come by at that.

But what did he expect? He tucked a handful of notes into the woman's bosom and pushed her away.

Life was a momentary diversion at best, he thought, pick-ing up his goblet and tipping it to Ellingham. But he needed that diversion, and the idea of corrupting a stainless virgin had great appeal after all the practiced courtesans he'd seduced.

And, there was something to be gained, which was never

the case in the normal course of events. And this was the thing that made him prick up all over: at the end of Ellingham's great *experiment,* there would be an heir, and his Madam Mother would cease her haranguing and finally leave him alone.

Jenise Trowbridge stormed into her family's London town house so choked with fury she could barely speak. "The *beast,* the *bastard.* The *gall.* The . . . *outrage* of it all." She slipped off her cloak and heaved it onto the sofa for want of having something heavier—a vase would have done, the bastard's dead body would have been better—to express her rage.

And she stopped cold.

Julia was there, curled up as usual in a corner of the sofa, staring out the big bow window that overlooked the street.

The garment had settled like a cloud on her sister's lap, and the distressed look on Julia's delicate face stemmed Jenise's tirade instantly.

Damn and damn. She had thought herself to be alone, and here was Julia, the abandoned object of the beast's attentions, poised like a siren to hear her clarion call.

The beast would marry after all.

How could she tell Julia?

"Things are that bad?" Julia asked in her fairy-thin voice. "What could be *that* bad after all the bad there has been?"

Jenise came into the room slowly. It seemed to her she had never appreciated this room so much as at this moment. It was a room made for confidences, a small room at the front of the house just off the entrance hallway that was cozy, warm, intimate.

The family called it the blue room because of its blue painted walls and blue satin upholstered furniture. It was a very restful room, not a room that one barged in on uttering unladylike curses and throwing things.

It was Julia's room, her refuge, her *home,* the place of all the rooms in the house where she felt safest and most content. The room where when the door was closed, the family knew not to intrude because Julia's grief at having been jilted by the Earl of Wick had overcome her once again.

Stupid beast, Jenise thought as she pulled up a chair close to the sofa and regarded her beautiful sister. How could he *not* have married her beautiful, tenderhearted, gentle, loving sister?

Her *younger* sister, who had not yet learned there were liars and libertines in the world and promises made could just as easily be promises never meant to be kept.

How could he have so callously destroyed this beautiful flower without a thought or care of her feelings, her delicacy, her *life?*

And yet, he had, and in all probability he probably didn't even remember who she was, if the accounts of all his conquests were even half true. So many women. London was strewn with broken hearts tromped all over by the dissolute Earl of Wick, but after he'd gone through that first year of ravaging the wealthy, more worldly maidens in their first season on the marriage mart, he'd gone on to bigger, more experienced game.

Not for him leg shackles and domesticity.

Did one thank heaven he'd come to that conclusion in time?

But not in time to spare Julia.

She had never recovered from the blow.

And now the daunting news that the Earl of Wick *would* marry, and he wanted not the gamey, wanton women whom he'd bedded and banged to a fare-thee-well for the past four years.

Oh no. Even the mighty earl of debauchery wanted a virgin, pure and lily white. Damn the man. Damn, damn, damn the bastard, when Julia was everything a man of breeding and taste could want. He had had Julia melting and yearning for him not four years ago. He could have married her, set up his nursery, become a man of esteem and honor and substance.

Ha! Not for Wick—not then, in any event. The only thing of substance he was ever interested in was how fast a woman would spread her legs for him.

Or at least that was what the gossips said.

And now this.

The earl would marry. And to carry on the line, only the most beautiful, the most accomplished, the most pristine of virgins would do.

She wondered why, as she took Julia's hand reassuringly in her own.

She wondered if there was a mother in London who didn't think her daughter fit the bill. She wondered if their mother might believe that this was a second chance for Julia.

Oh no. No. Did that happen, I would sacrifice my body, my virginity before that beast would ever see her, ever touch her again.

"Jenise? What can be that bad that you must vent your annoyance by throwing things?" Julia's light voice was like butterfly wings, fluttery and evanescent. The beast had destroyed her, just murdered her spirit and her confidence, and the bright young thing she had been.

She ought not need to tell this awful news to Julia. And yet, Julia would hear, one way or another, whether it was a friend, or her mother, who, Jenise sometimes thought, secretly believed that Julia herself had done something to make the earl cry off the commitment.

Had it been a real, formal engagement? Julia had thought so even though it had not been a public thing.

Well, not yet, she'd said. He must tell his family, his mother, his friends. It is no small thing for the Earl of Wick to come to point.

No small thing, indeed. A very big thing. A very wicked thing for him to promise marriage to get what he wanted. Then.

He had no need to do so now, for he'd plowed and furrowed every available and willing woman in all of England, it seemed, and he had no need of promising anything if he didn't wish to do so.

So therefore something must have changed, Jenise thought suddenly as she stroked Julia's hand and tried to think of some way to impart the news that wouldn't send Julia into a deeper mope.

Something was different. For some reason, marriage was on the table for real now, and the earl meant to carry through. He would not have gone public with it, were it not so.

Oh dear God. Imagine what that would mean. Every mother, every fair maiden with lineage to the Stone Age would be casting lures for the earl.

Her horror must have shown on her face because Julia tugged her hand and demanded once again, "What can have you in such a temper that you cannot even speak of it?"

"Something you could not possibly want to hear," Jenise temporized.

"Please, Sister—what could I not want to hear after having heard the worst, most debilitating thing a woman could ever hear?"

Yes—and that was the other thing—everything in Julia's world was related to *that event*—the event of the earl's rejection of her. Which made telling her this news that much more appalling.

But it had to be done—or someone else would tell her. Someone vicious and unkind, or someone who wanted to hurt and eviscerate her. Someone like their mother, even.

But she couldn't quite utter the words, knowing that after a while, she wouldn't have to. Julia would divine the topic very soon just by the set of her jaw and the determination in her face. Julia would know part of it without her having to say it.

And indeed, several minutes later, Julia said, "... Oh ..."

"Yes."

"The gossips are at it again?"

Delicately phrased, Jenise thought. "The beast has gone to

a new level in his desire to debauch and destroy every woman in the whole of England," she said carefully.

"How can that be? I thought he had already done that."

Oh, there was a new sharp awareness? Could it be that Julia's heart was mending, that she finally perceived the truth of the matter?

Too much to hope for, especially after she heard this news, for certain. And hear it she would.

Or read it . . . Would there not be a tidbit in the gossip columns in the coming week?

Oh, worse and worse.

Julia must hear the news from her, there was no other choice.

"But he has not ever—*ever*—declared publicly that he will marry," Jenise said.

"*What!*" Julia turned white, looked faint, looked at Jenise as if she were responsible, as if she were the devil.

"Don't—stop that! Don't you dare faint!"

"Oh, how could you . . . how could you . . . ?" Julia moaned, wrenching her hand from Jenise's and falling back on the sofa pillows. "To hear this from you . . ."

"And who else?" Jenise asked brutally. "Who else would impart this news without malice, without the vicious desire to hurt you? You would have heard in no time at all because I heard within hours of his having told acquaintances that this is his new and most urgent desire. How could you *not* have heard within this day, and perhaps from someone who cares not for your feelings and sensibilities? How dare you even *think* I would tell you because I wished to hurt you?"

Julia swallowed convulsively, trying to get control. "I can hardly assimilate the news, or what it means to anyone so unlucky as to capture *his* interest. She will be debilitated within a month and take to her bed forever."

"Surely she must get an heir before—" Jenise said astringently, and stopped abruptly. *That is what has changed. Even a hedonist must grow old and lose his vigor. And he is the last of his line. What pressure must there be for him to get a legitimate son after all the bastards he's littered around the countryside.*

Yes . . . that makes sense . . . that explains why—marriage and a virgin. The unconscionable beast—

". . . that," she finished distractedly.

"Poor girl," Julia muttered, "if she does, and then comes to this point with him . . ." She waved her hand at herself and cried, "Oh, dear heaven, how can I bear this news after what he did to me? I should never have come . . ."

"But it was time, my darling," Jenise said. "It was time to come out of the grave and into the light where some wonderful man will appreciate and love you."

"And yet, here I sit, yearning for the one man I can never have. And now with this news, I might just as well be—"

"Don't say it, don't think it, don't open your mouth . . ." Jenise interrupted violently, "Oh God, if only I could flush the thought from your brain, if I could destroy it somehow, some way—if I could find for you that one perfect one who would adore you and make you forget the beast . . ."

"He can never be forgotten . . ." Julia moaned. "Never. Not the things he said, the things he promised, the things he did I will never tell—and I will never forget . . ."

Jenise went cold. *Things he did . . . ? Julia, too? He had corrupted Julia on top of everything else?*

She would kill the man. She would conquer him, flay him, destroy him, cut off his head, his private parts, hang him from the tower. Dear God, if only, only, only there were some way to wreak vengeance on a man who was so completely above all moral law . . .

There had to be a way—she couldn't bear to look at Julia and believe there was no way. Julia suffered. Julia took nothing lightly, so trusting was her nature. And the beast had taken it, disrespected it, used it, abused it, and tossed it away.

Someone had to teach the beast a lesson. Someone had to pierce his heart, destroy his confidence, and toss *him* away.

Could she . . . ?
How—?
Could Julia stand it?
What was *she thinking?*

"We'll go home," she said despairingly. There was no other answer for Julia's distress. "We'll just pick up, pack up, and leave before this gets so out of hand it can't be dealt with. Just you and I—mother and father can stay in town, and we'll go spend the season quietly at Wanford, and you need never know anything about wh . . . what is going on."

"Would that it were that easy to forget . . ."

"Well, you must. Four years, Julia. Four years the beast has had this power over you . . ."

"Has it been? Four years? It feels like four weeks."

"Never say so. Dear Julia, you *must* wipe every vestige of the beast from your soul."

"Could you?" Julia asked mournfully.

"I would like to hope so," Jenise said cautiously, "but I have never been so much in love that it has mattered. And I have found most men easy to excise from my consciousness."

"He could seduce even *you,* his appeal is that powerful, that strong."

Jenise thought not but it seemed as if Julia's words were an omen, a challenge almost, and she leaped on them without thinking, without caution.

"Then perhaps I should seek to be among those he considers for this new stage in his life."

"My dear, my dear, my dear . . ."

Jenise froze.

Her mother's voice from the doorway as she bustled into the room.

"Was I not just thinking the same thing? How attuned we are. My two daughters. You both have everything to recommend you, with sensibilities as different as day and night. So if the gentler daughter would not do, perhaps the more aggressive daughter would suffice."

Julia burrowed down farther against the pillows as her mother sank into the other end of the couch.

"I have been trying to tell your sister this age that a man like Wick . . ."

"A beast like Wick," Jenise interpolated maliciously.

Her mother raised her eyebrows. "You cannot be thinking like that if you are even half serious—but you aren't, are you?"

"I don't know." And she didn't—except that it was such a perfect vehicle for avenging her sister, she almost felt beside herself with the need to do it. But that was not for her mother to know. Nor Julia, for that matter, until she could ascertain how upset her sister would be if she pursued such a course.

"In any event, I have tried and tried to tell Julia that a man like Wick needs a headstrong woman to go toe to toe with him at every patch. A nature such as Julia's is far too easy for a man to ride roughshod over. He will trample her every time. And then what? She withers and . . ." Her mother glanced at Julia and decided not to finish that thought. "Well, for myself, I'm grateful for Wick's uncommon consideration *not* to put Julia through that, and for crying off before things went too far. But I cannot convince Julia of the delicacy of his feelings, and that her union with him would have been misery personified, and a complete and utter disaster."

"The beast—delicacy? Mother—too droll to say his name and those words in the same sentence. He is an animal, ever sniffing around until he catches the scent of some willing prey. And what does he do then? He *pounces*, he takes his pound of flesh and then throws the doe away. Delicacy of feelings? He's an abomination, a beast . . ."

"Oh no, you are wrong," Julia piped up. "There is no want of feeling within him. Except of course, at the end . . ." her voice petered off. "But he wasn't brutal, even then . . . he just . . . went away—"

"Oh good God," Jenise said disgustedly. "I wash my hands of this. Let Julia pine away forever for the beast, and let him go and disgrace and defile some other gobbleheaded girl who does not know better."

She rose to leave and her mother put out a hand to detain her.

"But he will marry," her mother said softly with maternal practicality. "*Some* gobbleheaded girl will be his wife and share his fortune—why can it not be *you?*"

Jenise was horrified. Her mother was *truly* thinking that way, in those terms?

Never mind she had just had that same thought. Her desire to lay into him was something very far apart from that hard-headed matronly approbation that saw the opportunity in the negative, the gold in the dross, and saw it in spite of Julia's experience, and his reputation . . .

She turned away—her mother couldn't know, her mother could not have heard the worst of the scurrilous gossip, could not know the depths of licentiousness and hedonism to which the beast had descended even before his abortive ghost engagement to Julia.

Nor could her mother begin to comprehend his depravity, which was only whispered about at balls and parties, and generally by eligible virgins, appalled mamas, and disapproving dowagers who were both in awe of and utterly terrorized by his legendary prowess.

Her mother couldn't possibly know any of it if she could even suggest Jenise might be as eligible to marry Wick as anyone. She was as good as giving her carte blanche to play Wick's game.

But then, she thought trenchantly, none of it mitigated this one fact, so dear to a mother's heart: nothing about a libertine earl mattered, as long as the man was marriage-minded, had fifty thousand a year and could pay penance in pin money.

And it oughtn't matter to her either, because a man would ever be a man, and a woman always had to pay.

She looked at Julia, who had shriveled back against the cushions and closed her eyes to hide the tears trickling out from under her lashes.

Not this time. Not this time.
If only Julia would give her tacit consent as well . . .
. . . then, oh then—she could think long and hard about pursuing her plan to avenge Julia's honor.
And this time, in sweet vengeance, Wick would be made to pay.

Chapter Two

And then, it was one thing to consider it emotionally, and quite another to parse out the practicalities. Simpering virgins were just not in Wick's line, and none of Jenise's friends, who were turning the news top over bottom, could see him with some slender pale Venus who hadn't any conversation, style, or wit.

Or was he just trolling for a breeding sow?

There was something more there, Jenise decided, as she settled herself at the table for yet another round of dinner and cards. Wick was the sole topic of conversation at every gathering; how could he not be when his *volte-face* was so intriguing.

And yet, he hadn't come forth himself. All of this gossip and speculation had been fueled by something in passing he'd told a friend who'd told another and another until the news spread like wildfire.

No one dared ask Wick, who moved about the normal societal doings with his usual air of cool disdain, and every once in a while taking his quizzing glass and looking over a bevy of naïve young things as if they were cattle.

"God, this is the most fun we've had in years," Ellingham declared late one night at Heeton's when they'd all come from the Gladneys' annual masquerade ball. "Everyone circling around Wick, everyone speculating and gossiping. No one daring to ask, to question, to censure . . . My dear man, were you in business, you'd be launched to great success and pots of pounds just on the way your name is on everyone's lips."

"And not a pair to kiss within a league of here," Wick said repressively. "I am not in harmony with this idea that I must keep myself pure until my vestals are chosen."

"We are narrowing it down." This from Max Bowen. "There are too many sweet, young eligibles this season. So we made a list of qualities we thought were Wickian . . ."

"Do tell," Wick drawled. "*Wickian?* Qualities? In a green girl? There's only one quality I care about—will she spread her legs without coaxing, prodding, or pretty pleas. But do go on—this might have some amusement value."

"Well, there it is," Max went on. "You've viewed them all now, and even we can see that no one vestal stands out above the other. They are all very much alike—too coy, too restrained, too pale, too dark, they giggle too much, they have little conversation, not that *that* necessarily is a point on our list . . . but it comes to this: no one of them can be recommended above the other. And we have not yet found three who would do for the parameters of our experiment. So . . ."

"Yes, so . . ." Ellingham took up the thread. "We come to round two. And with it, the list." He pulled out a piece of paper and brandished it in Wick's direction. "To hone in, to refine it down to the three most luscious virgins in the whole of London who might—just might—have the capacity to appreciate this grand scheme of corruption and reward. But to do that, they need to have these qualities—to wit: they must be beautiful beyond beautiful; they must be approachable; and better still if they would be flirts—you can easily coerce a kiss from a flirt; they must be, in a word, touchable without all the usual maidenly fussing and blushing; and if you can proceed from there in the cloakroom, you have the perfect girl who is biddable, trainable, and ready for the Wick stick."

"And who is going to test all the green girls?" Wick asked lazily.

"Why, we *all* are," Ellingham said with a trace of indignation. "You didn't think we would leave you to go through this terrible ordeal alone, did you? We'll feel and fondle your virgins for you, and we'll come up with just the right girls for the grand experiment. Remember, under the skin, they're all whores. One just has to give them permission to be. Give us time—and we'll have them primed. And then, my dear Wick, they're yours . . . while we get to watch the fun. I swear, I'm frothed already that you'll have the pleasure of humping them first."

"All these promises, and yet the well is dry," Wick said caustically. "Abstinence does not become me. It's draining."

"Just store it up, dear boy. And then let it loose in a virgin hole in the name of queen, country, and your putative heir. There is something to be said for restraint."

"*I* can't say a thing for it," Wick interpolated irritably. "I'm bored. *Stiff.* So this virgin cattle prod had better turn up a likely cream jug—and soon."

The rumors flew thick and fast. Wick was looking. Wick was not. His friends were looking. His mother was exerting pressure. His fortune was not all that healthy. He was looking for an heiress. He was looking for the purest of the pure. He wasn't looking at all. The whole thing was a hum and Wick was off in the usual dens of depravity doing all the obscene things he usually did.

Wick, Wick, Wick—he wanted a virgin. No, he wanted a woman with some experience. A proven breeder. No, he wanted a maidenhead. She didn't have to be rich. She had to be mannered, of good breeding *stock,* she had to sign some agreement to look the other way once she'd got him a son.

The amount of money he was willing to pay grew astronomical. Thousands of pounds for one virgin to spread one time to get an heir. His mother was desperate. He was desperate. He was growing old and had to set his affairs in order.

And where was Wick? In his town house in St. James, amused, but by no means laughing as the noose tightened around his neck. The moment was coming soon when he would be presented with three nubile virgins willing to sacrifice themselves on the altar of his, reproducing a son like himself.

One might choke at the thought, except that the grain of truth within was somewhat galling. He might well get a brat that would turn out very like him, even with the civilizing influences of Madam Mother and the gilded lily who would ultimately consent to marry him.

He ought send them all to purdah when the deed was done. Out of sight, out of mind. Gone and forgotten within a fortnight. His mother still held sway in the dowager house at Holcombe. The least he could give her was a brat and wife to dominate as well.

And indeed, he had to admit there was some pleasure in restraint. In knowing he could just summon a maid within his household and bang her on the floor, but choosing not to. In electing to tame his nature, save his cream, and savor the moment when he would pour it into the pure, undefiled hole of a virgin sacrifice.

The thought almost made him weak with anticipation. The only thing worth doing in life, fucking. And even that had its limitations . . . the partner, the time, the energy, the drain.

Yes, this restraint business had something to recommend it. He couldn't stop thinking about the demands of his penis. His imagination ran riot at the thought initiating a virginal innocent into the pleasures of her flesh.

Yes, a pair of innocent eyes adoring him would be a novelty after all the experienced, vain and self-centered trulls he'd had. And none of them worth the time spent on them.

And her inexperienced hands all over his body—groping, seeking, grasping, holding . . . it made him squirm to think of how it would feel to be handled by an untrained *houri* who wanted just him, his body, his juice, his child.

His money.

Her reward.

It dulled the prospect after all.

"Negative thinking," Ellingham chided him.

"And how far along are we?" Wick asked, his voice deceptively gentle.

"We're having a delightful time digging for virgin treasure," Ellingham assured him blithely. "It won't be long now, my dear Wick, until we present you with the cream of the crop in which to spend your fill."

There wasn't anywhere in London that Wick was not being talked about. From the mercantile stores to the lending libraries, Wick's wife-to-be was the ongoing topic of conversation.

Jenise could barely hold her irritation in check. "How has the beast managed it?" she wondered aloud to her mother as they made their rounds one morning. "His desires are now so in the consciousness of everyone that no one can avoid hearing about them. As if we had not heard enough before. I would give what fortune I have to be the one to teach him the lesson he so richly deserves."

"You?" her mother murmured. "Oh, my dear, you do not want to be thinking in those terms, if you wish to excite his interest; you are no match for the likes of him on that level."

"I would be more of a match than Julia. You said so yourself. He fair devoured her for breakfast. And now he's serious about matrimony; every mother in London is plotting and planning this very hour how to catch the eye of his sycophants to gain his favor. And I should be among them."

"So I said," her mother said. "I do not disagree."

"Except for Julia," Jenise said. Except for Julia and the *things he did* that Julia would never tell. "And her knowledge that the marriage, did he come to point, would have to be real."

"Fifty thousand a year can smooth away many things," her mother said. "A woman adjusts. Julia's feelings can be of no consequence if it comes to pass."

"But *I* cannot bear to see his rejection of her go unavenged. Yet how will she feel if I am chosen to be among those presenting themselves as candidates to be his bride?"

"She understands why," her mother said. "She as good as said so the other afternoon over tea."

"And still it would mitigate nothing," Jenise said wretchedly. "But I can't stand by and watch this circus, knowing he will choose some mealymouthed creature with no wit and much guile who will slough him off as soon as she gets him an heir. He must be punished somehow for this travesty. Someone has to do it, Mother. It is the only reason I would even consider it. It is killing me to stand by and watch it, and watch Julia suffer every day like this."

"It might as well be you, as anyone else," her mother repeated. "And you are fooling yourself if you think you will dish out vengeance in a heap. You can have no conception of what he might require of a potential wife."

No, she hadn't thought that far ahead. At least in concrete terms. All she knew was that she would do anything to humiliate the beast. Go to any lengths to pay him back in his own coin for what he had done to Julia—what he was about to do to yet another innocent and unsuspecting girl.

"So you'd best keep those feelings hidden when you step up onto the public stage of consideration. There could be much benefit to it," her mother added.

Jenise couldn't think of one thing. But the fact remained that Julia must be informed. "I will be Julia's avenging angel," she said at last.

"In his marriage bed?"

"I will smite him long before things get to that point."

"My dear girl, I'm truly in favor of any girl casting her lures to attract a man of status and wealth such as Wick. But this romantic notion of vengeance ill suits you and will color your appeal to him. Leave off all such notions, and proceed as if the one thing in the world you wish is to marry him. Then, all will go well."

Jenise snorted. "Well, under whatever guise I wish to proceed, I cannot do so without Julia's knowledge. Painful as it will be, it is time to talk to Julia."

* * *

And yet, it was the most delicate question. How did she approach Julia with the notion that in the name of revenge, she wished to attract Wick's notice?

It was one thing to theorize about it, quite another to make the plan concrete.

Not so easy, after all. And perhaps an unrealistic product of her overheated imagination. No one was a match for Wick. He toppled women like dominoes, never looking back. And who was to say what was the truth of his motives now? Did he truly want a wife, a child, an aura of respectability at last? Or was it purely an exercise in obscenity—corrupt a virgin, get a child.

For that alone, he ought to be punished, but she didn't think there was a girl or woman in the whole of London—or England for that matter—who thought in those terms, or even thought it was possible to bring down the mighty Wick.

Except her.

And what chance had she? Even with her mother's confidence that she qualified on all the counts that mattered.

But the idea had rooted so strongly, she could do nothing less. It was an abomination to listen to the gossip, to the thread of lust and longing that wove through every account by every friend, and every friend's mother who had any kind of hope that her daughter might be The One.

When even her own mother believed that *her* daughter could be The One.

"And so on it goes," she closed her account to Julia of this day's *on-dit,* after she and her mother had returned from shopping and appropriating some books from the library with which they hoped to tempt Julia out of her gloomy mood. Julia, who was where she always was, in the blue room, feeling blue, and waiting to hear the news of the day.

Jenise went on, phrasing her next thought with care. "And one just feels there ought to be something *someone* could do to stop it—to stop him somehow, in the name of every innocent girl he's ever defiled."

"Oh, how I wish—" Julia said wanly, running her fingers

over the leather-bound volumes of romances arrayed on her lap. She looked up as their mother entered with the tea tray. "Yes, I picture it all the time, I dream of it—an Amazon to cut him off at the knees, to render him impotent, begging, mewling for mercy . . ."

"Exactly," Jenise murmured. "An Amazon, bold, brazen, fearless . . ."

"And who would this be?" their mother asked. "And why would she be so stupid as to enrage a man with fifty thousand a year?"

"Julia agrees *something* must be done," Jenise said defiantly.

"Yes?" their mother murmured, pouring tea. She handed a cup to Julia. "Did you like the selections we found for you?"

"I particularly like stories about revenge," Julia said, her voice seeming stronger because of either the tea or the idea of Wick prostrate before some superhuman fury of a woman who had finally bested him.

"I'll keep that in mind next time," their mother said. "Jenise?"

Jenise took the cup and sipped thoughtfully. She hadn't thought that Julia had such strong feelings about decimating Wick. "What if we could make the story real somehow?" she asked lightly, cautiously.

"Jenise . . ." Her mother's tone said, *not here, not now. Don't tell her. Don't hurt her . . .*

Julia's gaze darted from one to the other and settled long and hard and speculatively on Jenise. "You? Would you—?"

"I want to do something. I *need* to do something. But how can I not take your feelings and your experience into account? However, this is the one chance anyone has to bring him to his knees. And there is no one riding this bridal carousel who would wish to do so—except me. And yet—how can I, when we all know what it must entail?"

Julia seemed to crumble. . . . *the things he did . . .*

"I cannot bear to think . . ."

"I will say no more," Jenise said instantly. Brave talk, all of it. Julia's Amazon, her thirst for revenge.

"But Mother's thinking that it could be you—"

"It would be horrific, if I were to present myself and if he would even choose me. It couldn't be borne. How would you bear it?"

"So much money," Julia whispered. "It could have been mine . . ."

"Shhh—no more talk . . . I will never mention it again."

"Wait . . ." Julia put out a limp hand. "Wait—do it . . ."

"No. Your brain is addled. You're not thinking straight."

"No, I am. Truly, I am. Do it. I want you to do it. Mother is right. Let him atone by marrying the right daughter, the strong and brave one. The best daughter. The best of all eligibles. Show them all, Jenise. Show the gossips. Show him . . ."

Her hand tightened forcefully around Jenise's wrist. "Show *me*. And above all . . . make Wick pay. . . ."

Jenise fretted. "I've got such a late start. They are two weeks into the process already. His acolytes have taken no notice of me. I've no clothes to speak of. This can't be done."

"Anything can be done," her mother said placidly, as she elbowed Jenise toward the most fashionable dressmaker on Bond Street. "It wants some ingenuity, certainly, but with three heads working and the right invitation, you certainly can put yourself in Mr. Ellingham's way. And that will be the start of it."

"Perhaps it's already the end of it."

"Let's not think like that. In any event, the gossips would have had a field day if that were true. Come . . . there's much work to be done."

It was a whirlwind afternoon of winding, draping, pinning, and pulling gauzy and sophisticated materials into a half dozen figure-shaping gowns.

"You can be sure Wick is up to the nines on feminine fashion," her mother said with her usual practicality. "It does not hurt to cut a dash in one's evening wear." She flashed a look at Jenise. "To attract attention, of course. The *right* kind of attention, I mean."

Jenise knew just what her mother meant. Her mother was eminently practical, and now that they had decided to go ahead with presenting Jenise, she was like an army commander, plotting every move, countermove, and possibility.

Her mother was taking this seriously; Jenise was to be a serious candidate for consideration by Wick's friends, who, by some accounts, were culling the ranks to narrow down the choices.

"After all, not everyone who styles herself an heiress or a gentlewoman of good breeding has the background or the attributes to make Wick a good wife," her mother pointed out. "A wealthy ninnyhammer would bore him to tears within a sennight. A beauty too full of herself would demand he pay more attention to her than he does himself. Not a good idea. A true young innocent—like Julia—would, and did, drive him to distraction. I truly do not hold him at fault for *that* disastrous connection. He thought there was more there than there was. Don't look at me like that, Jenise. Julia is a water sprite, as ethereal as the moon. And what he needs is just the combination of breeding, beauty, wit, practicality, and intellect as you possess, my dear girl. And if you approach this exercise on those terms, and leave off this odious idea of revenge, you will surely win his regard and, more importantly, his proposal."

"His pounds sterling, you mean," Jenise said contrarily. She was not going to go starry-eyed over the idea of Wick. It would be naïve to do so. His casting for a bride did not make him any less objectionable, when his obscene behavior was so well known. There was nothing to say he wouldn't test a bride-to-be rigorously on that level.

Oh dear God. She hadn't really ever considered that. What if he did? What would it entail? Was she even willing to go that far? Even for revenge?

Did a man's money gloss over every humiliation?

Her father's money certainly bought the most elegant and beautiful of ball gowns, she thought the next night as she surveyed herself in a dress of clinging jonquil-yellow silk. The neckline was square and low, and the construction of the bodice plumped her breasts to an obvious swell above the dainty ruched edging.

There were slippers to match, and a frill of ribbon to wind through her hair. She looked innocent and bold both, exactly the tack her mother had determined her to take.

It was a strange sensation to be outfitted in such a gown; it was just on the edge of improper. In a certain light, her body was completely outlined. If she leaned forward, she was in danger of exposing a bare breast. The hem was just a little shorter than was respectable, so that she flashed a beribboned ankle every time she moved. And then, her hair was so tightly upswept that the nape of her bared neck could have been deemed too tempting for a man to resist.

This was what it took to attract a man like Wick. And those were just the superficial things: the pleasing feminine shape, the artfully displayed breast, the ankle crisscrossed and bound with ribbons, the nakedness of what was allowed to be revealed: the arm, the nape of the neck, the ear.

There was a subtlety here that was not taught in finishing school. Rather it was the school of experience, things some women knew and most did not. And those with the awareness and the knowledge were locked into a sisterhood of silence, letting innocence fall where it would.

That knowledge conferred power. It was the first lesson that Jenise perceived the next night as she stepped into the ballroom of the Cavendish House on Regent Street.

The sisterhood was there, staring at her, wondering who now had come to throw her expectations into the ring.

They didn't want competition from any other one. This stamping ground was theirs; they had claimed it, they owned it, they congregated on it nightly, hoping and waiting for Ellingham to decide.

And that was the second lesson Jenise learned this night: that unknowns and usurpers like herself had better be prepared to be devoured alive.

Chapter Three

"And who is that tasty morsel?" Ellingham murmured, lifting his quizzing glass as he gently elbowed his way into Cavendish House two hours later. "Do look, Max, my dear boy—such a crowd, such a succulence of sirens, all waiting on our Wick. It's too delicious for words. Would that he were here to see it. But all that fawning would bore him to tears, whereas it lifts our spit and spine to hitherto unparalleled heights."

They were deep in the crush now, enough to know there was music playing, there were knots of lovely women trying hard not to look as if their every dream of happiness hung on their being noticed by Ellingham, and there were the jaded ones, who tried hard to pretend they didn't care.

And then there was the morsel, a column of sunlight in the soft glow of the candles. The bare neck. The curving breasts. The clinging dress. The simplicity. The gleam.

Oh the gleam—that was the key. The intelligence was there, Ellingham could see it in her eyes. And the body, the style, the dash. Not too forward. Not too innocent. Ladylike, and yet—just a little brazen, and completely aware of the way her breasts spilled over that tantalizing frill around her bodice; and the temptation of the naked line of the back of her neck, all unadorned for every man to admire—no, covet—from afar.

She knew what she was about, the morsel. No jewelry to

distract a man's concentration on her form. No artifice—even here, where everything artificial was the norm.

What manner of Venus was this? One of the innocents, or one of the coquettes?

He would have to test her, to be sure, but he found much enjoyment in watching her move through the crowd, greeting friends and acquaintances, and in ascertaining that she was someone who was known to this *crème de la cite* assemblage, above all.

Then why had he never seen her before?

Or was she that clever that she had waited until he sampled all the insipidity in London, before she put herself forward?

Oh, what a sly, cunning morsel she was. She piqued his interest, especially because she didn't seem to be making any attempt to cross his path or make herself known to him. And yet surely she knew who he was and why he was there.

Did it irk him, just a little?

"She carries herself like a duchess," Max Bowen observed.

"Oh, she's a fatuous piece of fruit like the rest of them," Ellingham snapped, just a little peeved with her now. "And will prove to be just as humdrum and tiresome as they are."

"It is indeed hard to find a toothsome virgin for the corruption. There hasn't been a likely candidate yet."

"I never thought it would be so tedious, vetting the virgins," Ellingham said petulantly. "I thought they all would fall into our laps."

"Would that have been the case, I would have burst my britches three weeks ago. And there's not much time left to initiate this experiment. Wick is getting impatient. We will go forward with two of them, if necessary, and if you can find one more who meets the criteria—as your morsel would seem to—then we shall have our three. All that remains is to test her and I'm already up for that."

Ellingham eyed his friend balefully. "Then stand down, my dear Max. I am now officially intrigued." He sought her golden figure deep in the crush, and eyed her speculatively.

"There might be some sport there, after all. I'll take the morsel on. She's got a look in her eye and reticence in her manner that, despite the way she's dressed, could be exactly the template we're seeking for Wick."

Jenise felt Ellingham's gaze on her incessantly throughout the evening. It was like the slam of a fist, that first assessing glance; it made her feel too out of her depth, too uncertain of her course, too gauche, and yet, at the same time, his interest cemented her resolve.

And that being so, it also necessitated that she quickly arm herself with some information as to how to proceed.

The artless ones, she discovered, the ones well protected by the mamas who had gauged and dismissed their chances, *they* were eager to tell what they'd *heard,* as she quickly found out. And they were not at all unwilling to share, almost as if dispensing that information gave them entrée into some forbidden world.

"Oh, you are so right in your assessment," they said. "Ellingham's the one—he's gone gleaning, we call it, when he starts to cull the women. He'll come up and talk to you, rain lavish compliments upon you, touch your arm perhaps, and then, suggest a stroll around the room that will inevitably lead into a more private space where he may try to take further liberties."

"And that is the whole of it? Compliments and liberties in the retiring room?"

"Is that not enough? If he is able to steal a kiss from a well-bred virgin, is it not a triumph? Is she not then worthy of Wick's notice?"

"That is the test?" She couldn't believe it. It was a game, a perversion. "This is how Wick will choose his life's companion?"

"Oh no. It is said these little auditions are but the first gauntlet to be run to even be considered in matrimonial contention. It is said he will not even consider a shrinking vine, as fruitful or wealthy or well-favored as she might be. That he wants only the most beautiful, the most refined, the most elegant, educated, well-spoken, and pure virgin for his wife."

"And has anyone yet passed the test?"

"It is said there are only two so far, of different styles, temperaments, and desires. And that they seek a third to present to Wick, and there it will end, at least insofar as the public portion of his search is concerned. All else, they say, will rest on Wick's desire and inclination, and any other standards and measures will be applied by him in private, at his whim, and nothing further will be revealed, they say, until the banns are called."

"Oh." It was a stunningly masculine plan, with Wick wholly in control once the brides-designates were chosen. Jenise felt her insides curdle. How did one combat such a satyric plan? What mother, comprehending those circumstances, would give her daughter's innocence to the Golden Bull by way of Ellingham's golden tongue?

Apparently many. They were all watching him with hawkish eyes, waiting for the moment to attract his notice.

And if she were to do so, which she would not have the slightest trouble in accomplishing given Ellingham's covert interest, she had better have some stone-hard design in mind for Wick's payback, and the determination to follow it through, brick by brick.

Could she? Now she had been noticed, now that she was on the precipice of being tested, she saw that it would require much more of her than the fury of exacting vengeance on the rutting bull.

For the first, it would necessitate responding to Ellingham without giving in to him, inviting his interest and rebuffing his touch, promising everything, and giving nothing.

She could not be the same as the others, and she could not be that much different. She had to stand out, and be reserved. She had to be both willing and coy.

A tightrope walk at the very least.

And if that was all it took to be numbered on Wick's list of worthies, what would happen once any of them was subject to

his *private* standard? What would a man like Wick require—
in private—of a woman he might choose to wed?

Everything . . .

Meaning . . . ?

Everything.

And there were dozens of women perfectly prepared to give
him that.

Whatever *that* might mean.

Was she one of them?

But *that* would be rewarded; he had publicly committed
himself to marrying some *one.* Whatever the means and mode
of him choosing a bride, he would her wed, and he would do
so on a public stage.

Fifty thousand a year smooths over many a man's sins . . .

It wasn't the money. It was a cause—Julia's cause—and that
of dozens of other innocents whom he had seduced into his depraved world.

*And was it—just a little—flirting with that forbidden
world?*

She took a deep breath and . . .

"There you are, my pretty." She whirled to find Ellingham
practically breathing down her neck. "I've been trying to effect an introduction for this hour. And here I have my Lady
Cavendish herself finally, come to my rescue."

Lady Cavendish was standing behind him, lavish in satin
and lace, and a headdress that almost brushed the chandelier.
He pushed her forward, and she took Jenise's hand, and made
the introduction. "Mr. Ellingham, Miss Trowbridge. Miss
Trowbridge, of course, is the daughter of Sir Osbert of the
shipping company. There you go, my dear."

"And so here we are," Ellingham murmured as Lady
Cavendish retreated. *Banalities first, to see if the morsel even
had any wit or style.* "Such a crush."

Jenise froze. The moment was at hand and all Mr.
Ellingham had in the way of conversation was the merest commonplace comment?

What was the game? And there most certainly *was* a game. What, by that question, was Ellingham seeking to discover? That she was as insipid as the rest of the marriage-minded mice?

That would gain her nothing, she saw at the instant. She must set herself apart, she must be herself, or at least a version of the outspoken self she was in private.

Private again. Everything meaningful—and illicit—was done in private.

She girded herself. "Oh, it is a crush indeed. It begs the question why you are even here, Mr. Ellingham."

Bold baggage. The gleam was there. A certain spirit. And those creamy, dreamy breasts . . . he would lick that faint whiff of vinegar in her.

"You are not so ill informed you do not know the circum stances of my societal to-ing and fro-ing, Miss Trowbridge."

"Not in the least. You are in want of good company. I completely comprehend, Mr. Ellingham. It is hard to secure in any circumstances. So of course you must troll among the best people in town to find it."

Clever morsel. "I do believe I have," Ellingham said appreciatively. *Wick would appreciate an immaculate who could bandy words.*

"You do me too much credit, Mr. Ellingham, for I can see that you've been fair taken in by my feminine attributes. If you could but look past that, you would strongly desire more scintillating conversation which my bosom, I am sad to say, cannot provide."

"*I'm* not so sure of that," Ellingham retorted. "But I hardly can ask for that privilege on first meeting. We are still yet strangers, so come. Take a turn with me around the room and we shall gossip about everyone we see."

Or he would, she thought, as she placed her hand on his arm. *So far, no gaffes. But now what? Dear heaven, now what?* "And so we dance a quadrille across the ballroom, Mr. Ellingham," she said tranquilly, "and do-si-do with whom we will."

"I only wish to waltz *you* in," Ellingham said as they paced slowly around the perimeter of the dancers.

"How droll. I am but a wealthy sea merchant's daughter. What have I done to excite your interest?"

"No, no, no, Miss Trowbridge. Don't go missish on me. You know exactly the circumstances of my interest."

"So I do, Mr. Ellingham. Who can help but know in this tattletale climate."

He smiled faintly. "Yes. Who can help . . . ? So you *will* let me have a private word with you?"

Private—again. Her heart started pounding. The moment was at hand. Her playful plain speaking intrigued him. At least enough so that he was blunt with her.

And now what? *What? Could she go the course?*

"To say what, Mr. Ellingham? That I am so desirable, you can't help yourself, you must steal a kiss? Sample the wares and then report back to he-who-cannot-take-the-time-in-his-arrogance to vet the one he might choose to marry? I think not, Mr. Ellingham."

There—she had stepped well over that fine line she tread, rejecting his advance, and wanting, needing, dreading to be among those in consideration.

And she didn't fool him either, with her indignation.

"I think you protest too much, Miss Trowbridge. Come— here we are at the cloakroom. A word with you only, you shall see my hands at all times."

She allowed him to lead her into the brightly lit room.

"And so here we are, Mr. Ellingham, toe to toe. What is it you find necessary to say away from the crowd and crush of the ballroom?"

"I need to say, Miss Trowbridge, that you are beautiful."

"Pointless for you to say, Mr. Ellingham. I know that."

Oh, he liked that. A goddess should be imperious and sure of her allure. And yet—a virtuous vestal she was, with just a tremor in her hand as she faced him down.

"Are you interested?" he asked bluntly.

"In?"

"Don't be coy. It does not become you, nor does it square with the spit and candor of your true person. I won't joust with you, Miss Trowbridge. I've never once asked a one in consideration so frankly, so soon. But I've seen your mettle. You've passed the test. So—shall I? Add you to my list?"

Oh Lord . . . too soon, too successful. How had this happened? And yet—

"And what exactly was the test?" she asked, amazed that her voice was not strangled with her dismay.

"Whatever I wish it to be at any given moment," he answered, his voice hard. "Yes or no, Miss Trowbridge. I have not much time to complete the list. You came here tonight for a reason. You've accomplished your goal. You have only to accept your fate."

A stone-hard coldness washed over her. He had put it so well. She was in just the place she could waffle no longer.

Her plan. Her fate. Her folly.

She had willingly put herself over the line, and now she had no choice.

She lifted her chin. "How perceptive you are, Mr. Ellingham. Of course, the answer is yes."

And now, she must wait. Wick would send for her, for all the chosen ones, very soon. And this was the beauty of the plan: that none of the three would be known outside of his circle of friends, and that whatever means Wick chose to evaluate them was his design alone, and then the certainty that the two who ultimately were not chosen would not be willing to confess it and risk public ridicule.

So the public game was over. Speculation ran rampant as to who had made the list. Ellingham had been seen talking in private to a dozen likely candidates. Every one of them admitted it, no one said whether she was among the chosen.

It was as if they had all banded together and made the determination that no one would come forth at the expense of the other.

A different kind of sisterhood of silence.

The fun was over. The wait had begun.

"The man is demonic," Jenise said one rainy afternoon as she and Julia played piquet in the blue room. "What is it meant to do but incite one's anger . . ."

"Or anticipation," Julia said softly.

"Anticipation of what? Standing toe to toe with the bull and being gored and gutted in the process? It is a monster, pure and simple, and it deserves to die."

Their mother, however, was ecstatic at the turn of events. "And so I told you," she said complacently. "What man of refinement and sense could not be taken by your beauty and your intelligence?"

"What? Ellingham? What is he but a puppet, mouthing all that Wick puts into his head."

"You will intrigue Wick every bit as much as you did Mr. Ellingham," her mother said. "I know."

Oh, but what her mother did *not* know—or *chose* not to know, Jenise thought. And what Wick knew was beyond comprehension altogether.

The summons came two weeks later, as prim and proper as an invitation to a ball. The vellum on which it was penned was thick, creamy, clotted with compliments and assurances that Miss Jenise Trowbridge, invited to a country weekend at Holcombe in the company of several other friends and acquaintances, would be properly chaperoned by his Madam Mother, a stickler for manners and propriety, who would be in strict attendance at all times.

"And so it begins," Jenise whispered. "And where it will end, no one can know. . . ."

Holcombe Manor was the stuff of gothic fiction—all stone walls, thick wooden beams and buttresses, and slitty little windows into which daylight could not possibly infiltrate.

All of a piece for Wick, Jenise thought as her carriage barreled up the long winding drive to the manor. She was by herself, with trunks full of dresses and embellishments and adornments she was certain she would not need, and which her mother insisted a well-bred, well-ordered houseguest must have.

There was a certain naïveté in the way her mother had approached her country-house weekend. A certain blocking of the realities of what Wick was about. A certain trust that all would be as he had promised in his invitation.

But nothing was certain with Wick. Everything with him had solely to do with his depraved whims. Getting a wife did not eliminate his vaunted immorality from the equation. It merely sank it to another level.

She comprehended that, and that her innocence was no drawback to him in his mission to get a wife. But it would not constrain him, either. She must be prepared for anything, *everything*, be prepared to surrender every part of herself in the name of vengeance.

Whatever it might mean. Whatever it entailed.

The carriage drew up before the thick, worn, wooden doors of Holcombe Manor just as the sun was setting. It had been a tiresome trip, given that she was alone with her musings and forebodings, and in one respect, she was relieved to finally have arrived and to pitch herself into the reality of the situation.

Ellingham met her at the door. "So here you are, Miss Trowbridge, full of spit and fire, I hope. I know the journey is wearying, and you shall have an hour to refresh yourself before dinner. Your rooms are situated on the gallery, and here is Mrs. Wilton to show you there."

Mrs. Wilton was as long and thin and sour as a pickle, and she wordlessly led Jenise up the stone steps to the gallery as a footman followed with her trunks, and to the second door to the right of the steps.

It was a commodious room with a four-poster bed of indeterminate age immaculately swathed in virgin white bed dressings, and heaped with pillows. There was a fireplace, with a fire already lit, and a comfortable upholstered chair beside it; opposite, there was a small mahogany table and chair next to the bed, a chest of drawers against one wall, and a massive armoire on the other. A fitted carpet covered the floor overlaid with two other smaller carpets by the bed and fireplace.

And there was one other door, Jenise discovered, which led to a dressing room fitted out with a mirrored table on which there was a glass tray with an assortment of empty jars, a matching chair, a built-in wardrobe, and a washstand.

"I'll send a maid and a footman with some hot water," Mrs. Wilton said with not a nuance of expression on her face.

But at least there were other presences in the house besides the guests, Jenise thought with some relief as she began to unpack. And Ellingham, for whatever buffer he might supply.

And Max Bowen, she discovered as she came down to dinner, an hour later; and the two other favored ones who were slightly known to her, and who looked at her with distinct animosity as she sat herself at the table.

"Just a nice cozy *diner à cinq*," Ellingham murmured, rubbing his hands together. "I will make you known to each other by first names only. We're all friends here, after all, and discreet as death. Nothing will ever go beyond these walls."

He looked around meaningfully and saw they understood precisely, and that no one of them would ever confess to being considered or rejected by Wick. They would keep the silence.

"Exactly." He nodded as if they were children, Jenise thought resentfully, who had assimilated an important lesson.

"Now do let me introduce you . . ." He waved at the blonde with the sweet, ingenuous face who immediately looked relieved as he pronounced her name, "Innocenta. And this—" a willowy brunette dressed in the height of fashion— "Virtuosa."

Virtuosa smiled a secret little smile as Ellingham pointed to Jenise. And here . . . is Chaste."

"I like that name *better* than mine." Innocenta pouted.

There was always one, Ellingham thought, *who didn't immediately get onto the game. Always one who was the most selfish and wanted everything everyone else had for herself.*

Well, he had thought, *perhaps this one might do for*

Wick—*a creature as grasping and self-indulgent as Wick him-self.*

He ignored her. "Ladies . . ." he said benignly and reached for the bellpull, "let's eat."

And she had thought there would be more to it than that, this first meeting. Jenise was not a little surprised that the first order of business was food, but then, she found, she was al-most ravenous, as the footmen began to serve.

Or was Ellingham fattening them up for the kill?

She almost lost her appetite on that thought. Still, she did justice to an ample but plain bill of fare that included a first course of soup, fish, savouries, and rice casserole, removed with breast of lamb and sweetbreads, wine sauce, accompany-ing vegetables, and finished off with cheeses, apple pudding, and plum pie.

There was too much wine flowing, and too little sense at work; Virtuosa and Innocenta helped themselves liberally, a fact not lost on Ellingham.

"Now two of my pretties are nice and warm, and ready to begin," he said. "Wick awaits, did you not guess? One by one, you will come with me to the library for the first meeting with he who would marry one of you."

He eyed Virtuosa and Innocenta speculatively. Who was the most foxed on two small glasses of wine? The pouty Innocenta. Let her drink some more while Wick had his fun. He motioned to Virtuosa, who rose gracefully from the table with her goblet and followed him into the shadows.

"And now what?" Innocenta demanded. "He leaves us alone. He leaves us together to piddle and pout? I think not. Don't you think not, Chaste, or don't you think altogether?'

"I . . ."

"You're a fool, Chaste. You cannot compete with me. And Virtuosa—pablum-mouth—will charm our Wick for certain with her nonexistent conversation." She jumped up from the table and began pacing—and drinking. "*What* is happening in that room? I would give—no . . ." she amended craftily, "the point is not to give; the point, my dear Chaste-mouth, is to get. You must leave and I must get. You see the simplicity of it. And—well, yes . . ." She waved her goblet at Jenise. "You may take your turn, but it's useless, I will tell you. I mean to have him, whatever he might require me to do."

Whatever the price. Whatever he might require—in private. . . . What if he was watching this tawdry display? What was he demanding of Virtuosa even as they waited, and Innocenta lurched around the room proclaiming her superiority? What must either of them do to pique his interest and make him come to point?

And how far were they willing to go to accomplish that?

How far was *she* willing to go to exact revenge?

It was an imponderable question, heightened now by Innocenta's insistence Wick would choose *her,* and by Jenise's own deliberate and calm silence. It only served to enrage Innocenta more as she emptied the decanter and continued her rant.

And finally, she sank back into her chair, and Jenise put out her hand, and said gently, "Did it never occur to you that someone—Wick—might be able to see us and hear everything we say?"

Innocenta paled and choked.

And Ellingham appeared just outside the shadows.

"Chaste, my dear, come. It is your turn to meet Wick."

She had of course seen him from afar now and again. But up close, the lines of dissipation and weariness were that much more pronounced on his angular, ascetic, and extremely handsome face.

He was tall, well but plainly dressed, and so bored, it seemed, as he hunkered down in a worn leather chair, that he didn't even condescend to look at her as she entered the room.

She had been dreading this? A spoiled, jaded, and patronizing nobleman without grace or manners or even commonplace politeness?

This was a one with whom she could deal. And Innocenta could have him. A lifetime of legacy could not pay her to consider wedding him. The first cut was done, and it remained only to see the path by which she could exact some penance for his seduction of Julia.

"You did well to hold your peace with that virago." His voice startled her; it was rich as syrup and honeyed as a hive. Danger lived in that voice, and a thousand surrendered hearts.

So she *had* divined the truth. Everything in this manor was bent to his perversions, and nothing was secure or secret from him. Truly, it didn't do to underestimate him at all.

She held her tongue, and Wick slowly eased himself up from the chair to get a better look at her.

Up close, he was not a little intimidating. There was something in his height, in his face, in his opaque black eyes. He walked around her, viewing her form from every angle, and stepped away from her so that he could see her face and her figure taken as a whole.

"Chaste, is it?" He moved directly in front of her. "Are you? Chaste?" He cupped her chin and lifted her head one way and the other. His touch was hot, his fingers long and strong and commanding against her skin. So he would be in his life—strong and commanding. And too easily distracted.

"I am not a melon to be poked and prodded to test my ripeness, my lord. Mr. Ellingham has done a thorough job of that. And that should be your answer."

He let go of her abruptly. "Ah, so it has a voice—and some spleen, too. But that is the point, my dear Chaste. To poke and prod your virgin fruit, else why are you here?"

Oh, now was not the moment to cave under that voice and those eyes. Now was the time to stand up to his nonsense, his sense of entitlement. Now, now, now—

"Why *am* I here, my lord? You have had your fill of women to last an eternity. You surely cannot have summoned me merely to observe my face or my demeanor. Mr. Ellingham vetted those already. Tell me what you require of me, and we shall go on from there."

"Oh, my lady Chaste is quite the romantic," Wick drawled. "Can't wait to drop her drawers and let me fondle the merchandise. If my lady is even wearing drawers. Which I would think she is not." He circled around her again, appraising her from every angle. "No, this chaste mistress has quite the curvaceous figure under that narrow skirt; quite the trim ankle; and a delicious, swanlike neck. Quite clever the way you have neatly outfitted your body to excite a man's interest. I think I am taken with such forethought. So considerate of my pleasure, when I've gone without it for so long. Yes, I think . . ."

He cupped her chin and lifted her face. "I think Ellingham was exactly right . . ." Slid his hand down to stroke her throat. "A man's pleasure . . ." Slid his hand still farther to rest on the swell of her breasts. ". . . a man's pleasure is incalculable when he's foresworn it for weeks in order to possess such white-hot purity . . ."

He stared into her eyes. "Such white-hot fury . . . such . . ." His fingers rooted in her bodice and found one taut nipple, that stiffened as he caressed it. ". . . a hot, luscious nipple. . . ."

Her body shuddered with shock at the first feeling of a man's fingers invading a private place. She utterly froze, her mind shifting apart from her body, almost as if it couldn't contain the reality of what he was doing, and even though she had known it would come to something like this at the outset.

But how could anyone be prepared for something like *this?* Not an inexperienced woman alive could be prepared for this: his will and his whim worked on her body however he wanted, wherever he wanted, whatever he wished to do with her.

Things I can never tell . . .

She felt as if she were standing outside herself, watching, assessing, forcibly keeping restraining her first strong impulse to flee.

Here, at this moment, the question must be answered—just what was she willing to do, how much was she willing to bare—of her body, of her nature, and her soul—to exact revenge?

It was far easier to contemplate than to experience the reality; she wasn't experienced enough to know how to repress her shame and repugnance as he expertly fondled her breast and watched her, a fox savoring the fear of the doe.

But worst of all, that which was meant to disgrace and degrade her instead generated intense feelings of swamping pleasure within her, and that was the most unexpected, the most horrifying thing—that sumptuous sensation emanating from his flicking his fingers back and forth all over her virgin nipple.

She was transfixed by it, seduced by it, helpless in the face of it; her body went weak, and some other sensation, utterly foreign, spiraled downward from the pressure of his fingers like liquid silver.

And then he didn't move; just held her there like that, his fingers surrounding her nipple, as if he knew, as if he was completely aware of the stunning shaft of pleasure still piercing her deep in her core.

She felt naked, wholly and completely naked. She felt invaded, and she felt the power of her body and what it could do, what it was meant to do. A woman's secrets, the things men knew by which they had seduced every willing woman since Eve. Empires had fallen for this, women enslaved themselves for this.

And this was but the first taste of what was to come.

This was the moment where there was no turning back, the place where she had to commit her mind and body to whatever excesses he might demand of her, where she had to shake off the paralyzing and decimating fear of the unknown and surrender to the inevitability of what was to come.

This was the turning point. He was watching her closely, seeing every nuance of feeling that played across her face, knowing what his caress of her nipple made her feel. She could hardly think straight—she hadn't expected this, not at all— could never have conceived of this slow, lush seduction by this one hard point of pleasure she never knew existed.

"Ah, Chaste, you are a revelation," Wick murmured. "There is nothing like the hard, hot thrust of a virgin nipple. . . .

I need to see that which gives me so much pleasure. . . ." He waited a moment, a palpable beat in the thick silence of the room, to see if she would protest.

She held herself preternaturally still; this was the moment of no return, and she made no protest as he pushed aside the frill of her bodice and pulled the thin gauze down over her breast.

Heat suffused her body, tingeing her neck, her breast. Her exposed nipple tightened still more as she stared down at it as if it were something alien.

But it was—it was a thing apart from her, with a sensational greed all its own that was mindlessly seductive—a thing if virgins knew, they would throw themselves on a man's mercy and do anything for one naked caress.

Things he did I'll never tell . . .

Oh dear heaven—this? Of course, this—and so much more . . .

She closed her eyes. This. Part and parcel of all the things she did not know, and would soon find out. And what next, what?

"You must let me nip and lick," he murmured as he gazed at her nipple, and then, as she said nothing, just stared at him with flashing eyes, he bent his head to her breast and slowly took the nipple into his mouth and compressed his firm lips around the hard tip.

The liquid silver turned molten between her legs, hot and thick and melting like tallow as he expertly sucked and squeezed her nipple . . . the way he must have expertly sucked and squeezed and licked and tugged . . . pulling the pleasure from deep inside her, inside who?—until it was something tangible, explosive, and sweet.

And then, as he sucked hard on her nipple one last time, her body caved; he caught her with one arm, never relinquishing his possession of her nipple as he pulled every last ounce of pleasure from her with his mouth and tongue, and she hung onto him as if he were her savior.

But this was no savior; as he slowly eased his mouth from her breast, all she saw was a certain triumph in his eyes, and she instantly turned cold and pushed him away. This was commonplace for him, women melting for him like that. Women fell all over him, displayed themselves for him, begged him to do exactly what he had just done to her, responded in the same way, holding him and fawning all over him for his skill with his lips and tongue.

This was not for her, to be one of *them*. She must not lose sight of that in the maelstrom of new sensations that threatened to overcome her reason. He would know just how to make any of them capitulate; he would win them over with his hands and his mouth, with his body, with *their* desire to do anything he wanted in the name of getting him a son, and getting themselves a life of luxury predicated on fifty thousand a year.

They—no, she alone—must never forget this was a man bent on finding a virgin sow, and responsive nipples were presumably low on the list of attributes he required of the mother of his heir.

"Don't cover up that succulent nipple," Wick said, coming at her as she began to set her gown to rights. "You will sit—at the edge of the desk, I think—and allow me to admire it."

Damn the man; this part of the test was not yet over? She felt the edge of the desk hit her thighs and she braced herself against it.

"Yes, this is good, your back arches just so, your nipple entices me yet again. It is no small thing for me to desire a woman's breast so quickly after I have had it, Chaste. And yet, I'm avid to suck the other one, to see if that nipple is as hard and—come—let your untutored hands bare that luscious breast to me."

She took a deep, shuddering breath. This was it—she wanted to flee; she wanted to stay. She wanted to feel his mouth on her breast again, to feel those mind-sapping sensations of pleasure and submission that even at this moment warred with her flaming desire to bring him down.

Who knew? What sheltered virgin could ever know? This was the commitment, the moment, the *now*—

The things I did I'll never tell . . .

She slowly lifted her hands and pulled the bodice away from her breast.

Chapter Four

He was not done with them yet Jenise and Virtuosa sat primly at the dining room table, not even acknowledging the other was there, while Ellingham escorted Innocenta to Wick.

It was the most hateful thing, for Wick to take each of them on in private while the other two waited, knowing, imagining all that he might do in the name of his will and his whim.

How had he tested Virtuosa? What would he do with Innocenta? Jenise furiously shook off the thought. Don't play his game; that was what he wanted, for them to be curious, competitive, combative. They were the final three after all. He must choose one. So keeping them together in the aftermath of his first test of their tolerance of his advances was meant to make them all the more eager to please him and best the others.

Dear heaven, it was a wicked and wily devil they were dealing with.

How did one deal with the devil when he had all the sensual power to render them wax in his hands?

She couldn't stand the suspense, or Ellingham's amused glance as he rejoined them at the table.

"Dessert, my ladies? Wick is particularly fond of strawberries and clotted cream."

Jenise slanted a covert glance at Virtuosa; Virtuosa of the stone-hard determined look in her burning eyes.

They all meant to win, to become his bride. And he could only choose one of them.

What was he doing to Innocenta? Innocenta who was certain she would be the one . . . was he tasting her nipples now? Sucking them and tugging them as hard as he had hers, demanding of Innocenta everything he had taken from her?

Self-absorbed Innocenta—would she please him with her virginal worldliness or would her temper come to the fore?

No, of all of them, Innocenta had the most invested in pulling a proposal from Wick. She would not do anything that would cause him to reject her.

What *was* he doing with Innocenta?

Stop it! she told herself. She ought not care. Her emotions were not at risk in this. But dear heaven, she had not expected to feel this thrill of rivalry with these women. She hadn't expected to be so utterly seduced into giving Wick her breasts. She had expected to resist and repel him, she had expected to make him work for the privilege of even touching her.

How naïve was that? And even worse, she had never expected the shimmering, shattering sensations he aroused just by sucking at her. That was more shocking than anything. It had taken nothing at all for her body to betray her, and Wick was such a master, she had never seen it coming.

And the sheer hell of it was, she secretly yearned for more. Why did no one ever tell them?

Now that she knew, she was in a deeper place with this plan of revenge than ever she had contemplated. And more susceptible to him than any of them. Pleasure and anger went too well hand in hand and at any given moment, one easily overrode the other.

And she wanted to win. How could she win, divided as she was like that? She must win. For a dozen good reasons, and half of them to do with his too-easy conquest of her breasts. She vowed she would win, no matter what he required of her, no matter what she had to do.

And so, she was intensely heartened to see that Innocenta

returned to the table much sooner than had either she or Virtuosa, with Wick following at a leisurely pace behind.

"So," he said, seating himself at the opposite end of the table from Ellingham, "I trust you've called for dessert."

"I had assumed you'd had that," Ellingham said, casting him a knowing glance, "but it seems you've only dined on the first course."

"A luscious first course nonetheless," Wick murmured. "The appetizer can be amazingly filling to a starving man. But now—dessert . . . my favorite, I trust."

"We are served even as you speak," Ellingham said, nodding as Mrs. Wilton entered bearing a large silver tray on which there were five cut-glass plates, and two serving bowls full of fruit and cream. These were set out and she retired from the room while Ellingham served.

This was a play, Jenise thought, and he and Ellingham had done some variation of this scene throughout Wick's libidinous career. Ellingham was too well versed at it, and Wick had that smug, satisfied look of a cat waiting to leap and lap.

What would his next whim be? One could easily imagine—one or all of them naked and laid out on the table, perhaps, all covered in cream . . .

No—dear Lord, such an unladylike, such a salacious thought; it had to be the atmosphere, thick with anticipation and nuances, and each of them with her own approach to him, her own sense of what had just transpired between them.

What had that man done to her? And if he could do it to the most skeptical of virgins, someone like herself who abhorred and despised him, how had someone like Julia stood any chance against him?

He must be paid in his own coin. She could not let the fact she was in this isolated place with no witnesses to her own weakness sway her desire to bring him down.

That was the point. That was the promise.

. . . He was speaking, and she hadn't heard a word.

"Come, my beauties, I need to taste cream on your tongue. A creamy kiss for me. Who will come to me first?"

Now there was reticence. Now neither Virtuosa or Innocenta rushed to the front of the line. And Jenise was so im-
mersed in her own thoughts, she barely comprehended what
he was saying.

"Chaste, then, I will taste Chaste's kisses first," Wick decreed. "Come to me here, Chaste, and give me your tongue."

She rose up slowly, aware of the vicious looks she was getting from Virtuosa and Innocenta, as she made her way to
Wick's side.

He lifted his bowl full of fruit and cream and spooned off a
dollop of cream. "Lick that, right on the tip of your tongue,
don't swallow . . ." as she made a move to retract her tongue.
"Now bend your head to me—just so . . ." He slanted his head
and met her tongue with his own, foraging and sucking cream
from the tip, and then hotly enveloping her mouth with his.

She almost swooned at the shocking heat, and total subjugation of her tongue to his; she braced her hands against his
chest, and he caught her just at her knees. As he deepened into
the kiss, she felt his hands sliding down her legs and working
the hem of her dress up, until he could stroke her naked flesh.

She shuddered at his touch, but he wouldn't relinquish her
mouth.

Nor did she want him to; she liked it too much, and she felt
a pure revulsion at the fact that she liked it *that* much.

And then she felt the shock of his hot hand sliding up her
legs to her bottom, felt him cup the soft flesh, and feel the firm
set of her buttocks. Felt him stroking them lightly, coaxingly,
all over so that she didn't want to move, didn't even feel that
this was any kind of violation, felt as if she had been waiting
her whole life for some man to discover this precious erotic
point of her body.

How did he know—how could he know how much her body
loved this light, lush touch; how everything inside her seemed
to liquefy as he continued his beguiling fondling of her bottom?

How could she give herself to him so easily?

Because she must, to do what she must do . . .

What was it she must do?

She pressed in tighter against his mouth, canting her body slightly outward to invite his caresses, even though she knew there was no gentleness in Wick, and this erotic persuasion was meant solely as a way to prepare her for—for—

She gasped—she tried to wriggle away from him, but there was no escaping the incursion of his most expert fingers in her buttocks crease, and then, hard and demanding, up between her legs, so insistent and compelling all she could do was helplessly spread her thighs to ease his way.

She was so tight, his fingers were so demanding, probing and pressing against her tight virgin cunt, stroking, seeking . . . and suddenly, pushing with emphatic possession, into her hot, honeyed core.

Her body jolted in dismay—and something else—

Revulsion? Fear? Acceptance? Need? Want? *What she must do*— The sensations warred within her. Push him away, pull him in tighter. This was such a jolting invasion, she felt faint; this was so familiar, it seemed as if she had been waiting her whole life to feel him there.

He pulled slowly away from her lips. "Do not tempt me so, Chaste. I am but a man, and how can a man resist what awaits him . . ." he pushed his fingers more tightly into her "*. . . there.*"

She couldn't help herself; she was leaning tightly against him now; they all could see his fingers embedded in her cunt from the obverse position. They could see her expression, part terror, part astonishment at experiencing something so intense, and unexpectedly pleasurable, and so new.

Not so new . . . she had been waiting for this, she had been born for this one moment of hard male possession. . . .

He took another dollop of cream and licked it from the spoon. "Your turn to taste me, Chaste. Come . . ." He rimmed his lips with his cream-coated tongue, while he pulsed his fingers inside her, and bent her to his will.

She leaned down and licked and lapped the cream from his tongue, and he played with her, dueling with her, sucking her, and fucking her with his fingers . . . and all she could do was thrust against those long, insatiable fingers, pushing them deeper and tighter, until she was swallowed by his voracious mouth, and the swoon of sensation spiraling between her legs.

He felt the gush of her come, and he eased himself away from her mouth, while he held her tightly to him with his fingers still possessing pushed tight and deep within her. "My dear Ellingham, you were so right; there is nothing to compare with such hot, willing virgin flesh."

He maneuvered his fingers from her body then, and immediately she felt empty, cold, filled with longing to be fingered again. "Chaste, you are a revelation. Your virgin kisses, your tight virgin cunt, your willing body . . . For me to have such a choice virgin—indescribable—and yet we have not sampled all my beauties have to offer. Come, Virtuosa, your name says it all. I can't wait to feel you lick the cream from my tongue."

And Virtuosa came and ate him voraciously, and let him feel and fondle her womanflesh until she, too, surrendered to his expert handling.

Make them compete, Jenise thought furiously. *Make them outdo each other in what they would accept, what they would allow.* It was positively Machiavellian—and yet, and yet—the seed of jealousy was planted now and was growing exponentially as she tried not to watch Innocenta brazenly lift her dress, and climb onto his lap and just devour his tongue while she directed his hands to her buttocks and cleft.

It was impossible. She was fascinated. And she could see so clearly that he liked exactly what Innocenta was doing. What man would not like a woman throwing her naked self onto him and showing him what she wanted?

This was the way. Or was it? Was it? Innocenta pumping herself up and down against his groin. Was that what he wanted? Innocenta, noisy in her appreciation of his kisses, his questing fingers, his hot, clothed body in contrast to her nakedness, her eager, avid mouth all over his. Was this a lesson for the chaste, the virtuous?

Had they come this far to lose already to a woman who was too well-versed in the ways of a man's sex?

And Ellingham, savoring his berries and cream, lounging his chair, leering at everything, leaning forward now and again to get a better glimpse of Innocenta's heaving breasts and naked thighs.

"God, what a show . . ." he breathed as Wick finally pulled away from Innocenta's wild mouth. "It begs the question what our darling Innocenta really does behind closed doors. She knows too much. Not so innocent, our Innocenta. Take her, Wick. If she knows enough to get naked for you, you just spread those creamy thighs and poke that hot hole and give her what she's begging for."

Wick grasped Innocenta's arms and eased her away. "Not . . . yet. A lovely thought, mind you, noting in your blowhole, but—not yet." He got her off of his lap and back to her chair. "It would spoil everything to tuck and fuck the first night. I'm only living up to your lesson, my dear Ellingham," he said to his friend as Ellingham was about to protest. "You drummed it into me often enough: hold your butter, hold your cream, and ere I see the benefit of doing so, you want me to spend it inconsequentially? No, this I will not do. No, I when I blow— it will be volcanic. You will want to bear witness, my dear Ellingham. It will be—a sight to behold, a wonder of the world. It will be the reward for my patience and prudence in this erotic process of choosing a mate.

"And now we've begun, now that I see the benefit of hoarding and abstinence—I need to see more of my beauties. I need them naked, Ellingham. Naked, and all mine to probe and prod and do with as I will. Tomorrow." There was a promise in his voice that none of them could possibly miss. "Tell Mrs. Wilton. She knows what to do."

She knows what to do . . .

Was there ever a debaucher like this? His object of desire could not even have the cold comfort of knowing his own house was sacrosanct. But no, even here, he had the willing complicity of the sour-faced housekeeper in his depravity.

That alone should tear the blinders from her eyes.

Had she not learned the harshest of lessons here today? That seduction was seductive in its own right, and so enticing and entrancing that no one, no woman, no matter how determined, how innocent, how righteous, was immune to its pleasures?

Not even *her* . . .

Especially her.

And then there was Innocenta, strutting and preening, taunting her and Virtuosa as Ellingham escorted them to their bedrooms. "He likes me the best. He can only choose me. I can't wait for tomorrow when I can offer myself completely naked to him. He will not want another . . ."

"Oh, be quiet," Virtuosa snapped. "It is not as if you were Aphrodite herself. Your breasts are small and mangy, and your nipples soft and spongy. What man wants to suck a calf's breasts? A man likes big bosomy women, like myself. With wide hips that can carry the child he will surely get on me the day that he takes me as his wife."

"And yet, he spent so much time suckling me. So much time fondling my body as I sat on his lap. Did he take you on his lap? Did you feel that monster between his legs? No, I didn't think so."

"Oh, did he only scat you on his lap?" Virtuosa asked provokingly. "Well. He *showed* himself to *me*. Let me slide my hand all over his hard shaft. Innocenta, I tell you—he was so hot for me, he was ike iron; wanted to show me what I had to look forward to. Apologized that there wasn't time for me to . . . have something to eat. . . ."

"Liar," Innocenta interrupted heatedly. "You're lying. He didn't show himself . . . he didn't invite you to eat . . . *he did not* . . . !"

"And what about sweet, silent, chocolate-wouldn't-melt-in-her-mouth Chaste?" Virtuosa interrupted her. "What about Miss Shimmy Shammy Virgin who pretends she's never been touched by a man? What a lie. Did you see the way she enticed him? Did you see how her cunt swallowed his fingers? Someone else has plowed that furrow before today. She knew just what to do when he penetrated her. And that kiss. Oh, our Chaste has been kissed before, I can guarantee you that. And not in the cloakroom either. This one is deep, thinking to outwit us with her maidenly airs and her coy, virginal ways. Thinking if she is not brash and bold, if she is submissive and pliable, she will captivate him where we cannot."

"I think not, Virtuosa. I think now we understand her plan, we can circumvent her. I would rather one of us win his hand than her. I would rather it be me. It will be me. I am set on it."

"And I am determined it will be me," Virtuosa snapped. "It will be a fight to the death then, Innocenta. Because you will surely die when I win."

"And I will step over your dead body on my way to the altar," Innocenta retorted furiously, pushing Virtuosa. Virtuosa stumbled, and then lurched forward and pushed back. Innocenta went down, Virtuosa dove on top of her, and began pulling her hair and tearing her clothes.

Innocenta fought back, cursing and screaming, and the two of them rolled around the landing like two animals in heat for a good three minutes, while Ellingham watched in utter enjoyment.

"There's nothing like a little cunt fight," he murmured to Jenise. "Those lovely legs, those dirty mouths . . . it makes for fine sport. But I must step in—I must—for Wick's sake. . . . *I'd* rather watch them tear off their clothes, but we have Wick to consider—"

He stepped into the fray. "Here, ladies—stop—*now.*" He grasped Innocenta's arm and pulled her to a standing position. "Wick would not appreciate a naked body marred by scratches and blood. You must be at your best tomorrow, rested, refreshed, and eager for his caresses. How can that come to pass if you are venting your anger, and your eyes are bloodshot from crying, or worse? You—Innocenta, now—to your room."

Innocenta threw Virtuosa a venomous glance and stalked off.

"Virtuosa—calmly now, like the lady you are . . . Remember, a man likes to play with danger, but he sets up his nursery with a virtuous *lady.*"

Virtuosa nodded, Ellingham relinquished his grasp, and she straightened her shoulders, pulled up her torn dress, and went her way to her room.

"And dear, deep Chaste—what can you be thinking?"

"That *my* dress is still intact," Jenise retorted. "And my dignity—such as it remains the same even after this night."

"Pack your dignity away, Chaste. There is no place for it here. Only your willingness to give Wick what he wants and let him do anything he desires to your naked body. Nothing will be intact after tomorrow, except for the decision as to whether you will still wish to be his bride. If you survive this trial with your *wits* intact. And if, in the end, you are even the one he would choose."

So there it was. He would choose one. And the eager, worldly Innocenta was the most likely of the three.

How could she compete with Innocenta? Innocenta's breasts were perfectly fine—small round globes with hard pointed nipples that were eminently suckable. And her body knew the secrets of a man's touch, her avid mouth the nuances of a man's kiss.

And Virtuosa—with a body as round and shapely as a brood mare—was Wick envisioning his putative heir at her ample breast? Perhaps that was all he really cared about, and the rest of this elaborate plot to choose a wife was just a game to debauch a trio of virgins.

If indeed Innocenta were a virgin. Or Virtuosa, for that matter.

What did she, aptly named Chaste, have to offer him?

Her innocence? Her wit? Her *virginity?*

What would a man like Wick treasure the most?

Not privacy. Not if he were pursuing his pleasures here.

Not family. Not honor. Not—anything?

She had nothing to compete with. And now she had an inkling of the pleasures of her body, she was more vulnerable even than Julia. And the thought of Julia, and how he must have played with her, did not provide her with any consolation. Or any ideas. Especially after how easily she had welcomed his encroaching caresses.

The fault for that was within her. The submerged and fatal flaw.

She was one of *those* women, a soiled dove in the making, destined to become a mistress of lustful wealthy men after Wick got through with her—or she with him.

She liked it too much, what he had done to her. And that was wholly irrespective of her desire to defeat him. She liked it. She wanted more.

Dear heaven, more—the *more* of which she could not conceive except in a hazy kind of way, but the *more* of which Innocenta and Virtuosa no doubt had vast experience.

Innocenta would win any contest in which sensuality was the test; she was certain of that now. Innocenta knew all the secrets of men. And Innocenta was determined.

No, she amended that thought, they all were determined, but in entirely different ways. Interesting. Because Innocenta and Virtuosa would use their obvious sensual knowledge to try to captivate him. Whereas she knew so little about that, it was almost a joke that Ellingham had even chosen her to be among the chosen; and while she might be willing, she was not experienced enough to initiate anything.

Yet.

That was important, she thought, but she didn't quite perceive how.

But witness how Innocenta had brazenly climbed on his lap, and how even though Ellingham encouraged Wick to fuck her, he had declined to do so, even with her legs spread so enticingly. He had said no. And he had come back so soon after she went into the library for the first meeting with him.

What didn't he do or say to Innocenta?

Perhaps Innocenta was *too* eager. *Too* sure of herself. *Too* experienced for the mother of the heir-to-be.

And Virtuosa—no—he'd relished her kisses, and he had penetrated her with ease . . .

No reluctance there. No shock or dismay at the first feel of a man's fingers invading her most private place.

Hmmm . . . they were both so intense, so eager, almost frantic in their desire to outdo each other. There was no passion there, only a certain aggressiveness and security in their femininity, their beauty, and in whatever experience and knowledge they possessed.

And they—and she—were the best of all the eligibles on the marriage mart? Or was it that they were game, not insipid, and had some backbone?

What *had* Ellingham been thinking? Whatever it was, however it had started, it was now something for real: Wick was committed to it, and as determined as they to get the most out of it. The most out of them. And in the end, his wife and an heir . . .

So what had she to—

You have to stop looking at them.

The thought flashed through her mind like a comet.

Stop comparing yourself to them.

Remove yourself.

Enjoy yourself.

Don't let him see how much you want it . . . any of it—

And you do want it . . . that's the thing you're resisting.

You yearn for it, now that you know how good it feels—and now that you've been so expertly felt and fondled, and penetrated, you want more, you can't wait for more—and that is the most daunting thing: you can't wait to be naked so he'll do more—

So remove yourself. Don't let him see that hot yearning. Be elusive, be willing, be malleable and coy—but just a little removed—and enjoy it, everything he will do to your naked body—let yourself sink into the pleasure . . . take everything you can from him . . .

Why not? He is the most experienced man in the art of pleasure in the whole of England . . .
Soon enough you'll be gone—
And no one will ever know.
But the best part will be, you never have to tell . . .

Chapter Five

In the morning, she awakened to find herself lying naked on her bed, with her clothes gone, and nothing in her room to wear except a pair of black heeled booties and a long strip of black lace, which were laid out at the foot of the bed.

Ellingham barged in a few minutes later. "Oh, excellent. Everything is as it should be. Good morning, Chaste, I trust you slept well. Don't say a word. The day has begun, and you see before you the elements of what Wick requires. You are to fashion an accessory from the length of lace that will set off the part of your body you think is your best feature. You will wear the boots, of course; Wick loves, loves the contrast of the naked body and the fully enveloping booties. And you need to be ready in—oh, twenty minutes. Mrs. Wilton will come for you. I must say, by the way, you are just lovely naked. If Wick doesn't choose you, I want to fuck you. I love a woman with a bushy mound." He exited on that observation, leaving her a little nonplussed.

He would probably tell all of them he wanted to fuck them, she thought mordantly, picking up the piece of lace and considering what to do with it. He probably told all the women he wanted to fuck that he loved a bushy mound.

Even if they didn't have one.

But she did, and it was interesting to her, in this new tack she had decided to take, that such a thing provoked a man. Perhaps she should emphasize it, just to play with him. And to see if Wick was of the same mind.

Some ten minutes later, after she had washed and devised her focal point, there was another knock at the door—a maid, bearing a cup of morning chocolate, averting her eyes from Jenise's blatantly naked body. And some minutes after that, Mrs. Wilton came in.

"Stand up, my lady," she commanded sharply. "Let me see what you've done."

Jenise climbed out of the bed. "Will he approve?" she asked insolently, turning so that Mrs. Wilton could see the circlet she had fashioned which she'd tied around one thigh, and from which the delicate ends of a bow caressed her leg and her bush.

"That's for him to say, my lady. It is only for me to give you this veil which you will wear over your hair and face—thusly. . . ."

"And why is that?" Jenise demanded as she allowed Mrs. Wilton to pull the black lace veil over her head and obscure her face.

"So my lord can concentrate solely on your naked body, my lady."

"And how will we be presented to him, Mrs. Wilton?"

"All together this morning, and then one by one as he chooses."

"I see." Yes, she saw. More turmoil between Innocenta and Virtuosa, especially when they would see each other naked. So she must find some way that he would choose her first. And then, she must keep him so occupied, he would not have time for the others.

She was dreaming; what did she know about seduction and how to fascinate a man like Wick who had seen everything, done everything, and had seduced everything that moved?

"Come."

She slipped her feet into the booties and followed Mrs.

Wilton out into the hall, down the steps, into a salon with a half-dozen sofas scattered around.

"Wait for my ladies and my lord here."

There were mirrors all around, and for the first time, she saw herself as Wick would see her. Saw that her features were obscured by the lace veil, which made her body that much more prominent. Saw the drift of lace on her thigh that emphasized what was between her long legs. Saw her flat belly, her round full breasts, her nipples, rosy and pebble hard with excitement.

Everything Wick would see, everything Wick would want. And more. Whatever *more* might be . . .

What struck her forcibly was that she was not appalled by this. Not unnerved or nauseated. She wanted never to dress again. She was stunned to the point of breathlessness by her reaction: she loved being naked. She loved the waiting and the anticipation. Nothing about being naked disgusted her, only the circumstances, only why.

But it was her own choice; she must never forget that, even if she had discovered something about herself that totally confounded her.

"Ah. Chaste."

Damn, Innocenta . . .

"Look at our Chaste. Not so chaste, is she?"

Jenise watched her in the mirror, mincing toward her in the heeled booties and lace veil. Slender was the word for Innocenta, but rounded in the hips and fuller in the breast than Virtuosa's words might have anyone believe. Her bush was blonde, as was she, and not nearly as full as Jenise's. She had chosen to wear the lace band around her neck, and she exuded a sensual confidence that was almost intimidating.

"Well, you strip down very well, Chaste. I would not have thought. Of course, your breasts sag just a little, and your pubic hair—you must have that trimmed—men don't like to taste a mouthful of hair when they come to get you there. Turn around—turn around . . . you'll do, I suppose, if he must make a meal of contenders before he chooses me. . . . And now, our Virtuosa . . . look at how her nipples turn down toward the floor, and how wide her hips are. Well, there are men who admire such things. Oh? Is there a little pouch to her belly? A thickness in the thighs? She did well to place her lace on her arms, which draws attention to her bosom; her bush would not do—there is such a thing as too little hair— Oh, I cannot look any longer . . ." And Innocenta turned away to seat herself on one of the sofas.

And there she sat, rubbing her breasts, adjusting her lace veil, stroking her thighs while Jenise and Virtuosa looked everywhere else.

Surely, Jenise thought, this was not the point, that they should play with themselves while he watched from some other room. But she ought not discount anything perverted when it came to Wick. Everything was possible, even that.

I am no match for them. I cannot compete—

Or is he testing our imaginations?

Virtuosa seemed to think so too—for suddenly she chose a couch and began preening and posing.

And now Jenise must, whether she wanted to or not. What to do when it was only your naked body you must entertain? And *his* eyes, hiding in the shadows.

Waiting for them to do what?

Ellingham admired your pubic hair; it is not a far cry to think Wick might do the same . . .

She lifted her right leg onto a couch and began massaging her thigh, stroking closer and closer to her mound, running her fingers delicately through her bush, cupping herself there, and knowing he watched, slipping her fingers into her cunt to feel the seductive wet heat that he already foraged with his long penetrating fingers.

It was too easy to imagine a shadow-lover watching, melting, aroused beyond forebearance as three naked virgins posed and postured in an effort to seduce him.

It would take nothing at all to seduce Wick.

There was something in that thought . . . She stilled her hand and shot a covert look at Innocenta who was on her hands and knees, stretching like a cat.

So desperate . . . so sure when nothing was certain about what Wick really wanted . . .

Yes, yes—

She couldn't be like them. Even if it cost her a proposal, she could not be like them.

Exactly. Not like them.

Her heart started pounding. She would change the rules of the game. One of his chosen virgins would not be the fawning exhibitionist he expected her to be. Would not be so free to expose all of herself to him. Would have some backbone, some mettle. Would make *him* come to her.

Would make him work for it, damn it, work for *her*—whatever that might mean.

He could expel her from the mansion in a minute, Jenise thought, with some dismay as she considered the ramifications. You didn't play with a man like Wick, who fully expected everything he desired to be laid at his feet at his command.

But how else to differentiate between them, when they were masked, when they were so much the same in all ways, and only their naked bodies were on display?

No more display. She sat primly at the edge of the couch, her arms crossed over her breasts. She felt breathless at this bold move, her heart felt like it would pound right out of her chest. She was taking an enormous risk now. To flaunt the rules of Wick's game. To demand that he come for her.

She knew he was watching, but what did he see that was any different from any other woman he had fucked in his long career? A naked body would hold no novelty for him. He must, in all his years of debauchery, have seen every size, shape, coloration there ever was. So it could not only be her body that must attract him.

Dear Lord, this was crazy. Anyone would say it was beyond all reason to flout his authority, his wishes. But so she would do, because there was no other way: she must be the one who was different, the one who piqued his interest, she must be the one who took the trick.

She took a deep breath to steady herself. There was no turning back the moment she spoke. "And where is Wick?" She was amazed her voice wasn't shaking. "Why do we wait and pretend to be puppets, when I fully expected he would have come among us and chosen one of us to play with?"

Her words echoed in the high-ceilinged room, and Innocenta and Virtuosa paused in their posing, shocked.

"Excellent," Innocenta whispered. "Keep going, Chaste. Learn that a man like Wick abhors a brassy mouth."

"If Wick does not wish to avail himself of my naked body, Mr. Ellingham has offered his services. He tells me he likes a bushy mound." Jenise looked down at herself. "And indeed, I do believe I qualify."

"*Enough!*" No mistaking Wick's bellow from close by. "Ellingham, you bastard . . . I'll make you suck your own cream if you've been propositioning my virgins—"

He came striding out from the near end of the room. "Where is the bitch who dares to command me?"

As if it weren't easy to tell, with Innocenta arching her back and spreading her legs wide, and Virtuosa cupping her breasts as if she were offering them to him now he had come in person.

Jenise sat, as tense and tight as if she were at a tea party, her hands folded on her lap, and waited.

"Ah, our Chaste," Wick sneered. "Who hides her bush even as she claims men lust after it. Ever a revelation, our Chaste. Never did I think my fingers could penetrate a virgin so deeply. Such heat, such elasticity to take my fingers like that. But is there gratitude today? No. Our Chaste instead makes demands. Our Chaste, having forgotten she came willingly to vie for my affections, now thinks she is in command. It is ever so with virgins—they give a man a taste of their bodies, and then they all think they can exert control."

He was but inches from her, and he tilted her veiled face up to his. "There is no control, honey-cunt. There is only my will and my desire."

Now—*now*—the greatest risk of all—

"And yet you are here."

The words hung in the air with a pulse all their own. But Wick was not a man who caved to provocation.

"Indeed, to show you what one ungrateful mouthy virgin will be missing." He started stripping, one item at a time, while Innocenta and Virtuosa panted, until he had divested himself of every piece of clothing, right before their eyes, and stood before Jenise naked, except for one thing: a leather scrotum pouch from which his penis angled like a jutting rock.

He grasped the shaft and moved himself closer to her, his penis almost directly level with her lips. If he had thought to shock her yet again, he had not.

This was the essence of a man. This proud, hard object of desire, endlessly throbbing with the insatiable need to possess the most intimate and deepest part of a woman . . .

Yes, yes—that made such sense. Where his fingers had penetrated, this thick, long, hard shaft would follow, would fill her in a way no other part of him could.

She felt no fear of it. She wanted to touch it, caress it. Her mouth watered with a swamping desire to enfold it.

She felt her body seize up, as if it, independent of her mind and her will, were readying itself for that inevitable reaming.

She swallowed her fear. She was too far gone with him already; the risk had not paid off, and it only remained for him to banish her. She had nothing to lose. Nothing at all.

"And indeed, what Wick will be missing," she dared to murmur, still unable to keep her eyes off of his massive manhood.

She heard him growl and she looked up at him. His eyes glittered in his dark, impassive face.

Elusive—

"Take me . . ." Innocenta whispered loudly behind her.

Remove yourself . . .

"No, me..." Virtuosa panted. "The very sight of you makes me weak with longing..."

Wick heard them, Jenise was certain he heard every urgent word, things he must have heard a thousand times and more from a thousand different women of every shape and bent. And not a word that would dissuade him from his course.

Yet his eyes never left her face, all the while Innocenta and Virtuosa moaned and begged him to come and mount them.

"Ellingham! Take those two away..."

Ellingham entered swiftly, as Innocenta and Virtuosa started shrieking and crying. "You'll have your turn," he murmured consolingly. "He means to try you all out equally before any decision is made; do hush and not let him see you in such a temper. Come, I will comfort you both, as you desire..."

That *sotto voce* promise sent Jenise's imagination reeling.

"He may fuck them to oblivion," Wick said unfeelingly. "And I will drown myself in his juices after. It is all of a piece between friends. But you—Chaste... you offer some amusement in your naïve, naked way. I mind how deeply my fingers penetrated your cunt, your innocent pleasure in my finger fucking, and the taste of your rash tongue, and only for that do you escape my wrath at your brazen mouthing-off.

"Now"—he positioned himself before her, so that his penis pushed at her lips—"take my penis head into your mouth, and honey-suck your tongue all over it."

She licked her lips. *Things I'll never tell. Never have to tell...*

Dear Lord, he was so big, so thick and long— How did one do this?

She lifted the veil just above her lips so that all he would see was her mouth closed over his penis head; and with no qualm or hesitation, she pulled it between her teeth, and started lapping it with fairy-light licks.

He didn't think he could get any harder, but the sight of her virgin's mouth working him so urgently was so arousing, he almost came. "Harder, Chaste..." He pushed himself against her mouth, grinding himself in deeper, demanding she eat as much of him as she could hold.

Not that deep—she would choke; a little panicked, she pressed her lips tightly around his shaft to contain him, and then began sucking at him for all she was worth.

That was the way—his hips undulated to the motions of her tongue, to the unconscious little sounds at the back of her throat, to the innocence of the way she pulled and tugged and sucked at his penis.

This, this, this . . .

A novelty, this—he had been sucked up by the most experienced of whores and the most elevated of virgins who had learned early on to use oral congress to get what they wanted.

But never in recent memory had he been sucked off by a naked virgin such as this, this—he had nothing with which to characterize her. She was here to be chosen, and yet she acted as if being chosen was the last thing she wanted.

Her mouth was unskilled, but it was as thrilling to be swallowed by her as any courtesan.

He felt himself bubbling up as she began pulling at him hard, hard, hard. He wanted to ram himself into her mouth, but it was such an inexperienced mouth. . . .

Hell and horns, when did he ever have compunction for any woman? Damn her eyes—oh, but that lush, hot tongue—those moans . . .

He thrust his hips, perfectly aware he was connected to her solely by his penis head and her grasping lips. There was something very erotic about that, as if she had the control of him and not the other way around.

But soon, too soon, he would blow—

All his resolutions to hoard his cream until that one explosive moment when he would . . . would . . .

No! The game must be played until he could not contain one exquisite drop of come—and then, and only then . . .

He wrenched himself out of her mouth, leaving a smear of his ejaculate for her to taste on her tongue.

"No, not yet, succulent Chaste. I have much more of your

naked body to plow before you get any reward from my penis."

She licked her lips and he followed the movement avidly. Such an innocent gesture. Such an eager tongue. Who was she? Why didn't he know her? What was it about her?

"That was but a small taste of the cream that will saturate and soak your honey cunt. When you earn it. When I decide you deserve it."

She drew herself up. "I deserve it now. I wanted to eat all of it, Wick; why would you, of all people, stop me from swallowing every last drop of your come?"

He felt a flash of—what, anger? For that audacious mouth that only wanted to eat his cream? Of course, she didn't understand he was conserving himself. That he was aching to spew and determined not to until he had come to his decision about his putative wife.

She didn't need to comprehend any of that, this one.

But right now, the only thing he wanted to decide was where, in that luscious naked body, he was going to plant his fingers. She still needed to please him, and if she were standing, he would have greater purchase to penetrate her.

He pulled her to her feet. Yes. In profile, she had the perfect breasts, the hardest little nipples, the bushiest mound, the longest legs. He slipped his hands between those legs, one from the front, one from behind.

Immediately, her body went weak at his touch—his three fingers slipping into her pubic hair, probing for her slit; and the long slide of his palm against her buttocks, feeling for her crease.

Her body arched involuntarily as he found what he sought, his fingers ramming upward into her hot soaked cunt. "Oh, our innocent Chaste doesn't need a man to make her wet and hot, does she?" He twisted his fingers and her body spasmed. "No. Our Chaste knows all about the pleasure between her legs." He pushed harder and deeper into her. "I haven't yet plumbed the depths of my succulent Chaste...." He began stroking her from behind, deep in her crease, moving downward to that nether part that had never been touched—and now he stroked it and pushed at it, and she convulsed again.

He made a guttural sound. His penis throbbed and jammed against her hip. He held her eyes which were glazed with pleasure as she writhed and shimmied against the feel of his fingers.

He couldn't get enough of that—her undulating body, her heat, her honey, her pleasure, her innocence, her elusiveness. She loved everything he was doing to her, he saw it in her eyes, and yet, and yet—

He was rubbing himself against her, his need building, rushing like a torrent, ready to erupt. She erupted, so suddenly he wasn't prepared for her pulling so violently against him, as if she were desperate to get away from the pleasure—the spiraling, golden, molten, sweeping undertow of pleasure that threatened every sense, every sensibility, her very being.

She went limp, with his fingers still possessing her. She was so hot, so thick with honey deep in her core. He could take her now, so smooth would be his way within.

But not yet. Not yet. He bent to suckle one taut nipple and her body came awake as it stretched toward his mouth. "Ah, not-so-innocent Chaste loves a man sucking on her nipples. . . ." He pulled away from her breast, leaving surrounding the nipple a bubble of hot saliva that dissipated immediately in the cold air so the tip hardened even more.

He made a sound, as she tried to entice him to continue sucking. He licked the tip instead, and she was suffused with heat as he forced her legs farther apart and his fingers pressed deeper.

"The most naked part of a woman . . . I will embed my penis *there* . . ." he moved his fingers, ". . . that deep inside you, Miss Insolence. When I'm ready."

"I'm ready," she whispered.

"You're ready for one thing only . . . and that is whatever I decide . . ."

"*Oh!* . . ." she breathed. "Decide something then . . ." *Oh*

Lord, mouthing off again, when she was so suffused with the pleasure of his fingers fucking her, she could hardly speak.

He took her other nipple in his mouth. Now he meant business. His mouth worked on the tip in concert with his fingers playing deep inside her. His body rocked against her as she rode his fingers, front and back, and thrust her breast more tightly against his pulling, sucking lips.

Who would have dreamed she would ever willingly put herself in his arms, at the mercy of his mouth, his tongue, his fingers? Who could have conceived of such pleasure? In what lifetime would a gently reared woman ever discover the depths of her body?

Only with him, only this—only . . . her body seized, and she rode his fingers down as the pleasure billowed up and broke inside her, curling and swirling down her body to pool right between her legs where he fondled her.

"No more, no more . . ." She could barely breathe, hardly speak. "Oh, go away . . . go away—" Everything he touched now was tender, ravaged. And he didn't need to care. He didn't.

But there was something about her—the pleasure at least seemed so pure—there was just something about her—he eased his way out from between her legs, and he lifted her in his arms.

Even then the honey scent of her sex was on his fingers, in the air, and he had to have more of her. There had to be something more.

He kicked open the salon door and took her straight to his bed.

Chapter Six

Chaste . . .

God, who thought up those names for those women? Innocenta—too smooth and slick by half; Virtuosa—not likely. He could not nearly imagine either of them as the mother of his child. Nor even in the same room with his own mother.

But this one—this one, damn her eyes, didn't seem to be after his money, his title, or his skill. There was something else. What?

She was such an intriguing combination of artlessness and guile. Or was she a consummate actress, a fallen angel whom Ellingham had introduced into the mix as a joke, a ringer, to trip him up?

Wouldn't that fuel the gossip fodder for months? And Ellingham wasn't beyond doing it either, damn his soul.

Who was Chaste? She lay on the bed watching him pace around the room, everything but her eyes obscured by the obliterating veil.

Who was she, this voluptuous daughter of some crème de la crème London family, who was so willing to offer herself up to him for so little emotional gain? This was no avaricious piece like Innocenta or Virtuosa.

There was a look in her eyes that bothered him and challenged him, as if she were seeing him from a distance, even while she fully intended to comply with everything he might demand of her.

What was she seeing? Damn, he wanted to know what she was thinking, and her every thought was concealed behind that glimmer in her eyes and that blasted veil.

Did it matter? She was beautiful, willing, pliant, and his erection was still stone hard with need. That was all that mattered. The depth of her cunt and how many times and how many ways he could fuck her until he tired of her.

Luscious Chaste, naked but for her booties and veil; it kept her at a distance, just the way he liked it: it gave her a certain anonymity, made her just a vessel to get a child.

That was all this was about. Getting a child with a body he could stand to occupy for more than thirty seconds.

Ellingham could fuck the other two to oblivion for all he cared; he'd drench himself in their juices after the supreme pleasure of plowing the hot, endless honey pot that was Chaste.

What did it matter if, beneath all that innocence and guile, she *was* really an actress and a whore? All women were, beneath the skin.

And Chaste had such lovely skin. Soft, smooth, pliable. And those nipples—he wanted them next. Just the nipples, to tug and twist and play with as he would.

She wriggled impatiently on the bed. Just the way he liked to see his women: edgy and needy. "Are you tired so soon, my lord?" There was that voice, soft, insinuating, brash. "Three were too much, and for one alone you can barely summon the energy—and you haven't even spent your seed. I do wonder at all the reports of your legendary prowess, my lord."

Wick smiled wolfishly. "Rest assured, most virginal and chaste—you shall not be either when you leave this room. Come. Now." He pointed to the edge of the bed where he stood, his penis poking majestically out of the erotic leather pouch. "Turn your back to me so that you are facing the head of the bed." And so that his penis head could slide along the soft cushion of her buttocks. Just like that, yes.

"Put your arms up and around my neck. Yes, like that," he said as she leaned back against his chest, and he slipped his arms around her and cupped her breasts.

She shuddered at his touch.

Good. He fingered each hard nipple simultaneously, and every muscle in her body contracted violently.

"Ah, that's the way, Chaste. Such sensitive nipples. Just how I like them. Now . . ."

Now, what? she wondered wildly. For all her bravado, *now* was scarier than she wanted to admit, especially with her naked body just haywire with all the pleasure he was inflicting. And now she'd come to the point of being alone with him . . . he could do anything to her—anything—and she couldn't say she hadn't walked into this unknowingly. This was the endgame with Wick, always, and she had only her own wits to protect her.

But if he continued fondling her nipples like that, she would become a puddle of pure hedonistic surrender in a matter of moments and nothing else would matter.

His large hands covered her breasts. A moment's respite from his incessant attention. A creaking sound, she didn't expect, and then the elaborate headboard tilting and turning to reveal a mirror in which she and Wick were reflected erotically entwined.

Oh dear heaven, was that her? Naked, enveloped by his hands, her bare bottom rubbing against his massive erection as he rubbed his palms against her nipples . . .

"Oh, yes, you will watch your downfall, Chaste."

And so, the moment of truth. Everything else was but a prelude to this moment, Jenise thought frantically as he began his seduction of her nipples. And there was no way out.

And in truth, she wasn't sure she wanted a way out: she loved it too much, what he was doing to her body. She had long past decided to let him do whatever he wanted at whatever cost to her, even the ultimate unknown.

It was the only way. And it would be worth it to captivate

him, to be his chosen wife, and then, when he made the commitment, to just turn around and walk away.

If indeed she *could* walk away after such a complete capitulation. Would not a woman sacrifice everything in her life to experience such pleasure? Women did, all the time. And she had thought she would be different.

No difference. No backbone or spine. Touch her nipples, pull at them, tug at them, roll them in his fingers, and she was his, every nerve ending, every inch of her naked skin . . . squeeze one and then the other as he pushed his iron bar of an erection between her legs, giving her a hard ledge to grind her cunt down on, and she would give him her nipples forever.

What manner of woman was she?

She could see herself riding his hot length as it poked out from the thick bush between her legs; she could see his every last nipping and stroking of her nipples that turned her body into a pool of molten submission.

She couldn't keep from watching her writhing hips and bottom shimmying against his body as his fingers pulled and played with her nipples.

"Ah, Chaste . . . you *are* an experience. . . ." he rasped in her ear. "Who could have conceived of such extraordinary virgin nipples? I never want to stop fondling them. . . ."

"Then don't," she whispered—*who* whispered? Who was this wanton who was a slave to her naked body? Who? Oh, it didn't matter; nothing mattered but this skeining pleasure streaming throughout her body from those pleasure points he knew how to manipulate so well.

"Whatever my naked Chaste desires. . . ." And he tugged at each nipple one more time, and sent a bone-cracking spasm of molten gold streaming through her body.

Omygod, omygod, omygod . . . She bent over double at the sheer force of it. She felt like she would dissolve if he touched her. She felt him hard and tight between her legs, his hands at her hips, the eddying pool of pleasure, the lingering sensations in her nipples.

Felt his hands cupping her bottom, stroking her there. Felt him maneuvering himself onto the bed behind her.

"What a revelation is a naked Chaste," he murmured. "I keep wondering at it. Who could have known? And the pleasure is yet to begin. . . ."

Yet? *Yet???*

She felt him push her over onto her belly so that she faced the mirror with him covering her. She lifted herself to see, and there he was, the bull, his naked prey, and his rampaging erection looking for a hole in which to root.

"And now the hard part, my creamy Chaste. If you indeed are as chaste as you have been represented to be . . ." He slipped his arm under her belly and lifted her so that her body—her cunt—canted toward him in the obverse position. "This is the point I need to know . . ."

She felt his penis head probing between her legs. *Oh dear Lord* . . . Lifted her head again so that she could see him, rising like a monolith behind her body, holding it irrevocably against him with his absolute strength for the length of his penis.

She felt it rend the most naked part of her, felt him insert it just inside her labia, felt his fingers follow, testing her wet, heard his male growl of pure guttural arousal, felt him grasp her buttocks, and—

Push—and pain—her protest; his shudder of excitement as he pulled back and then . . .

Thrust—her cry, his primitive drive to possess what he had breached, her frantic instinct to crawl away, just escape the thing that wanted to take over her body . . . what was this? . . . what—God, he was so big, so thick, her body couldn't stretch to accommodate this, this, this—

She had to get away, get away . . . lifted her head again to see him mounted on her, her buttocks slanted upward, her veiled head, his male triumph at the conquest of her body . . .

He would not let her get away. He covered her body as she tried to escape him; he owned her body with that hard thickness of his penis still embedded in her.

"Ah, Chaste . . ." he murmured, his voice just a little un-even with something she could not define. "Your cunt is mine. I can barely hold myself in. I want to drench you in my cream. Flood your hole with it. Drown you in it. And then spew it all over your naked body. I want you to bathe in it, I have that much cream to spend." He ground his hips against her but-tocks, pushing himself deeper. "How do you like the feel of your master reaming your virgin pump?"

How did she *like* . . . ? She never expected anything like this, this blast of pain, this awful discomfort as he stretched her sheath to fit his lethal-thick cock deeper and deeper within her.

But how she liked it wasn't the point. She liked being naked. She liked him fucking her nipples. And, to play this game, she had to like his rooting in her like some preening cockerel, because there was something about his breaking her virginal barrier that seemed to arouse him beyond all reason.

He would not seek out Innocenta or Virtuosa anytime soon if she accommodated all those desires he had named. He would spend himself in her. Drown himself in her at her com-mand. She would keep him occupied for hours, for days, just juicing that tremor of excitement she had felt in him as he punched through her maidenhead.

It would be nothing, after all she had already done, to give him her naked cunt to do with as he would. She would make him feel, make him believe, he *was* her lord and master.

And then, at the moment of jubilation, she would just walk away.

He rode her, slowly, thickly, tightly, pushing his engorged penis to the hilt and then even farther. Taking his time. Slow, slow, slow—she didn't think there was another inch to plumb, but he kept finding it.

She was on her knees now, her head buried in the pillows, and he watched in the mirror as he took her, slowly, thickly, tightly. Holding himself back, rigid with a voluptuous need to prolong every thrust, every moment he was embedded in her hot hole.

She was different. For the first time ever, there was someone different, there was someone who lived up to what she promised to be, and he wanted to savor the moment, to indulge himself in it, to absolutely luxuriate in her nakedness, the thick honey between her legs, the depth of her hole that his barge of a penis kept expanding and deepening with every stroke.

It was but the first time; the next would be so much easier for her, if the response of her incredible nipples was any gauge.

God, a respectable virgin, innocent yet bold, and wily enough to give in to the passions of her body, while guarding her maidenhead to the last moment. Ah, a puss beyond price, his naked Chaste.

And she *was* his; no one else would ever have her. Only him. Somehow he would arrange it. Set her up as his mistress. *Make her his wife . . .*

No, no, too soon to decide that—

But maybe not, the possessive way he was feeling about being the first to fuck her. He was absolutely insensate with the desire to ream her wholly and fully over and over, and to mark her body as his own.

He rode her slowly, tightly, thickly. He didn't want to give up his pudding, not yet. He wanted her to become accustomed to the feel of his ramrod between her legs, because he was going to root his rock head deep—deeper than deep—inside her . . . He kept rocking his hips against her, pushing, plumbing, feeling for the end of her and finding nothing but the tight, hot accommodating walls of her saturated cunt stretching to accept him.

He grasped her hips, and thrust into her suddenly, ravenously, almost as if the slower pace were stifling him somehow.

She gasped at the unexpected and pleasurable sensation of the movement. Oh. So. This was not just for his heat and heft. It wasn't just pain and the unbearable weight, his possession. There was something in it for her . . .

Oh. The idea stunned her, but then why should it, she wondered hazily, when her body reacted so keenly to his fingers playing with her nipples?

There was much *more,* she thought, easing her head up and staring at his reflection, which showed him utterly engrossed in his handling of her buttocks and the slow, tight movement of his hips as he ground the long, hard length of his penis into her.

This might be the moment, she thought. Say the right thing, do whatever he wanted, and he would never remember that Innocenta and Virtuosa would kill for his fuck. Keep him so busy, he wouldn't even remember who they were.

"You, my chaste hot cunt, are pink beyond naked pink," he rasped, almost as if he couldn't help it, his hips shimmying with urgent need.

This was the moment. Something beyond his slow, hot fuck was happening to him. His body strained against hers as he fought to contain himself.

She wanted his cream. Suddenly and inevitably, she understood that if she could provoke his cream, she would win. She would have him. And he wanted to choose her.

And so she looked him dead in the eye through the mirror, and not even the veil could obscure the hot, knowing glitter of her gaze.

"But you," she whispered, "are my lord and master."

It took only those words, and he couldn't contain himself a moment longer: he erupted volcanically, his hips gyrating wildly as he melted inside her and poured out his cream.

She lay flat on her back not five minutes later, his ejaculate oozing from between her legs and his penis rammed right back deep in her cunt.

"You didn't get it all, naked Chaste, hard as you tried. And I haven't yet found the end of you."

"Feel free to poke around," she murmured, staring at the connection of their two bodies—hers, poised just at the edge of the mattress, her legs wrapped around his waist, and him standing just there, embedded tightly within her.

"Oh, I will poke you every conceivable way, naked Chaste, now that you've forced me to melt my tallow. I don't take that lightly when I was determined I would not."

Wet, sticky, arousing to view the physical joining of their bodies, reflected again in the see-all mirror. This time, there was no discomfort; this time, he just levered her body upward slightly to take the lengthy jut of his penis into her drenched cunt, and his slick, thick cream eased the way.

Her pubic hair was clotted with it. And he meant to make more, to drench her naked body in it, and fill her to her core.

"I'm not sorry," she whispered.

"And why is that, creamy Chaste?"

What to say, she wondered wildly, when she knew nothing of such things. Nothing of the words that would incite him to keep her in his bed for as long as it took Innocenta and Virtuosa to give up.

"Because I want more."

"More what?" he asked silkily as he grasped her thighs and thrust for the first time in this position.

"More—of—ohhhhhh—*that* . . ."

He made a small sound of satisfaction and pulled back into another hard thrust, and another, as he watched her veiled head move back and forth and her hips bear down on the hard, hot length of his penis.

This time, he would make her beg for mercy, and he would keep his cream. And then, he would feast on her nipples while cradling his penis between her legs. And he would make her come again, and then—

He caught himself as he felt his melt ooze from his penis head. Just in time. He had to stop thinking about what he would do to her naked body, how deep he could drive into her naked cunt, and just pound into her and prime her and make her explode.

He lay rooted between her legs, soaked in his cream. Not exactly what he had planned, that galvanic orgasm that produced this sea of musk he was drowning in right now. It was

Chaste's fault—it was her luscious body, and the way his penis filled her cunt to the very hilt, the way she moved, and enticed him with her heat and her wet and the grip of her thighs.

She slept now, having teetered on the edge of her first orgasm, and all he wanted to do was ride her again. His penis was still stiff, still eager, and the more he thought about Chaste and how deeply his penis nestled in her tight, hot cunt, the more he wanted to fuck her again.

She was made for fucking. Those nipples alone . . . His hips writhed against hers, seeking a response. Who would have thought such a well-bred virgin would have nipples that would respond to finger fucking like that?

Damn—every time he thought about her nipples, his penis head oozed, and he couldn't think about her nipples or her cunt without wanting to jam himself into her. So, what was a greedy penis to do while the object of its desire slept?

Goddamn wake her up was what.

She must have sensed his impatience to fuck her again; she moved, she stretched, and then she felt him rammed deep inside her and the restrained way he was pushing against her slit, and she opened her eyes.

"My lord and master," she murmured sleepily, undulating her hips to the movement of his. "Give me more cream."

He gave her more, first taking her like a storm, and then taking her nipples into his mouth and fucking them one at a time, while he cradled his penis tight in her soaking, naked core.

And after she convulsed in his mouth, he pumped her cunt again, after which they both slept, interlocked and intertwined.

This is the way of it, Jenise thought as she lay entangled in his arms. This nakedness, this penetration and possession, this heat and wet, and obsessiveness. Her master. Who still, because of the interminable veil, only saw her body.

Which, perhaps, was just as well. He still wore the pouch, she still wore the booties. His whole focus was on her nipples and her cunt, on sucking and spewing, and all the pleasure that entailed.

For him. And for her? Unimaginable. Even the loss of her maidenhead, just unimaginable . . . she was a traitor to every well-bred woman on the marriage mart.

And worse, she liked it all too well. And she was easy. Easier than ever she could have imagined. And fair on the way to eliciting that almighty proposal from him.

All she had to do was pretend to be as insatiable for him as he was for her. Not hard to do, when he was a master at teaching an innocent the pleasures of her untutored naked body.

God, what had she gotten herself into? And if she failed, however would she go back to the way she had been?

She must not fail, then. She must remain elusive to him while giving him every part of her body he demanded, and by acknowledging his mastery.

There was something about a man's cream—or this man's cream. It was a symbol of a multitude of things, and so she must want it beyond reason so that he would keep wanting her.

Simple.

And maybe it was . . .

He was stirring on top of her; she moved her hips, and pretended to come slowly awake in tandem with him.

"My lord?" she said sleepily. "My master? I have been too long without your cream."

She watched him fuck her in the mirror.

What an exquisite dance it was between two naked bodies. She was panting for it, riding him hard, making him work her body exhaustively until she was once again on the brink of that thundercrack of pleasure. What would it take? She bent her knees and levered herself up to meet his greedy thrusts. That, there—oh, just so high, there, ride it—*there* . . .

It bolted out between her legs and broke over his hardness, rhythmically pounding like a wave on the rock of his penis. There, there, there—oh, undescribable, irresistible . . . more,

more, more . . . and washing into the spume of his white honey as he unleashed into her core.

And over. Limp. Tired. Rest.

No. More. It was the only way to keep him from being bored.

"Who is the master of my naked body?" she demanded. "More cream."

"I'm soaked out," Wick muttered.

"This cannot be. My lord and master has an infinite amount of cream to give me." She didn't even think she could take more, but she felt a desperation to keep him engaged on this sexual level. "Or so he said to me. I believe he boasted he would cover my body with his cream, there was that much of it; that he would drown me in it. That he would . . ."

He pushed her down the bed. "That he would . . . what, my voracious Chaste? You have yet to eat me, if you're so avid to have my cream."

"Then I will be the master of you," she retorted.

"Take me, then." He brushed his bone hard penis against her mouth. "Take all of my cream. . . ." He swung himself out of bed, and she levered herself up onto her elbows. "There will be more to fuck you—if that's what worries you."

There was a gleam in her eyes behind the veil as she got to her knees. "Whatever my lord and master desires," she responded with a coy lilt, reaching for the jut of his penis. "That is what I desire too." And she lifted the veil once again and closed her mouth around his bulbous penis head and began sucking it hot and hard.

He braced his hands on her shoulders, and gave himself to her—but it didn't take long at all, not watching her voracious mouth: he blasted into her mouth and she swallowed it all.

They lay in the bed, each facing the mirror, and she was watching him idly play with her nipples. His penis, rock hard and ready to go, was pillowed between her thighs, and she could just see the head poking out from her thick bush, enticing her to handle it.

She almost couldn't think, with his fingers nipping at her sensitive tips. But she couldn't get enough of it either.

She had no sense of time now. They had been fucking all day as far as she could tell, maybe all night. And she still hadn't diminished his cream.

And that was the essence of all things Wick. His prowess and his stamina.

And for some reason, he was enthralled with her. For the moment. So she couldn't let up on her demands. It was that simple. The more she wanted it, the more avid he was to give it to her.

"Every time you tug at my nipples, I want more cream." She made her voice low, breathy, intimate. "Give me more cream."

"God, you are greedy," he growled in her ear.

"But you're so hard, I just know you have more cream to lavish on me."

"I never knew how much cream I could spew until I fucked you."

"You're not finished fucking me by any means, my lord. I haven't had nearly enough."

"How much does a rapacious virgin need?"

"Every drop, my master."

"My voracious Chaste doesn't want too much, does she?"

"I just want my lord and master to keep his promise to drench my body in his cream."

"I've flooded your body with my cream."

"Not in the last ten minutes, he who is master of my body. Unless of course you . . ."

"I—what, insatiable Chaste?"

"Don't have enough, my lord."

"I've proved dozens of times I have more than enough cream for you, and I have more than enough for you now. Spread your legs."

He positioned himself just at the juncture of her thighs. Pushed his penis head into her slit. Just the bulbous head of his long, hard length as she watched in the mirror. Just kept the

head enfolded in her labia. Let her watch the way he manipulated himself just inside her slit, not even holding his shaft, just
by the long, hard length of his penis and the undulation of his
hips.

Impossible—she needed the whole of him embedded deep
inside her cunt. She fought to take him into her and he wouldn't
let her. Kept himself inside her just at the head by wriggling his
hips to ward off her thrusts, a secret smile on his face.

"I want more," she panted. God, this wasn't fair, this
wasn't. . . .

He rode her slit, pushing and pulling his penis head back
and forth, letting her feel the hard ridge just at the ingress between her legs. Watching her body writhe with insensate need
for his possession. But he gave her only the bulbous head to
ride, until she was moaning and begging for him to penetrate
her wholly and fully with his thick length.

"Oh no, my naked Chaste. This is about you wanting
cream. And so, my beauty, you shall have cream." And as he
said it, his body seized up, and he pulled his penis head from
her and grasped and pumped his shaft so that cream spurted
all over her breasts, her nipples, her belly, her bush . . .

Oh yes, she thought as she levered herself up so that she
could cup one breast. That was all good and well, my lord. For
you.

And she looked at her nipples, all wet and sticky with his
ejaculate, and she slanted that glittery gaze at him before she
lifted her breast to her lips and deliberately licked the thick
essence of him from one nipple, and she murmured "Yes, I see
you have more than enough cream. But you comprehend, my
lord, I have now had you, but you didn't have me."

Chapter Seven

He froze. An erotic trick right out of the bag of the most experienced and expensive lease-piece. Damn, damn, damn, and damn—nothing was ever what it seemed—*ever* . . .

He moved off the bed furiously, eyeing her as she lay there covered with his residue. No. She *was*—had been—a virgin. He'd swear on his life; there was no mistaking that once-in-her-life cleaving of that barrier in Chaste's unsophisticated body. And she had been appropriately frightened and overwhelmed by his possession of it, and then properly submissive to his whim and will.

And yet, she knew a whore's artful enticements. How? Why? The inconsistencies infuriated him.

Why?

Because on some level, he wanted to choose her while he was still fascinated by those contradictions?

What did it matter in the long run? Whomever he chose of the three would bore him to tears within days. It was just a matter of getting an heir, and with Chaste he was already well on the way, and his penis, if not his intellect, was humping for more.

Who was she? The daughter of a whore? His imagination ran riot with that scenario for a good minute. What did a whore of a mother teach an innocent daughter, the *theory* of pleasing a man? Chaste must have taken *that* lesson to her bosom, judging by the intensity of her responses.

No. Not the daughter of a trull. Ellingham had vetted them all; they were all the purest of the pure, however much they might have fiddled and twanged in the cloakroom. He had to take that on faith. It was the corruption of that purity that was his first purpose. And subsequent to that, choosing a wife and getting an heir.

Who was she then, this Chaste, with that elusive gleam in her eye and a fair hot desire for his fondling her body, now she discovered just how much she wanted it? Lying there, rubbing his ejaculate into her silky skin, looking at him with that look. What was she thinking? That he had wasted all his seed?

Damn her eyes. It made him hot again, thinking of all that seed; it made him eager to mount her again and fill her with every ounce of his essence.

Who was she, Chaste, who was there, but not wholly there; alive to him, but seeming far away, even as she moaned and clutched him and demanded more and still more of what only he could give her . . . ?

His penis elongated incrementally with every hot thought of her.

The hell with where she had learned those harlot's blandishments. She was here, she was his for however long she aroused him like this, and his sole function was to fuck her as much and as often as he wanted.

Bam! Bam! Bam!

The knocking was like thunder at the door.

"Let us *in* . . ." Innocenta, the voice unmistakable, in a rage. "You cannot fuck her all day and not try *me* on . . . damn it. Wick, open up—it's our turn now . . . do you *hear* me . . . ?"

And Ellingham's voice, trying to soothe her. "Come now, come, Innocenta, this isn't the way. Leave off this noise and insanity. Wick will come for you."

"He will *not*. He's coming for her, and it's not fair. It's not.

We haven't had a fair chance. He's been fucking her for hours while we sit and twiddle our thumbs instead of him diddling us. Well, I'm tired of waiting, do you hear me? I came here to be fucked and I mean to be fucked."

The door blasted open and Innocenta in a naked fury stormed into the room to see Wick in all his glory reflected in the headboard mirror.

The sight just stopped her in her tracks. *"Oh . . . !"* Her eyes widened. "Ohhh . . . It's been hours . . . lifetimes . . . Virtuosa—tell me, isn't he even harder and thicker and longer than when we saw him this morning?"

"Of course he is," Jenise broke in, just a little tired of all the coy wordplay. "Why do you think? Because he's been fucking *me.*" She swung her legs over the bed. She had to make her move now, to get this rival out of the way, before Innocenta jumped on him. "And we're not near to being finished . . ."

She edged her way behind him and wrapped her arms around his hips. "In fact, we were just . . ." she reached for his penis and began stroking it from behind, "in the middle of something—"

"Well, you're now in the middle of giving Wick up to me," Innocenta snapped.

"Am I?" Jenise could feel the tremors going through his body as she worked her hands all over his shaft. "I don't think so. I think my lord is enjoying what I'm doing very, very much." She grasped him with one hand and came around so that she faced him.

And then she knelt, and with delicate hands she began stroking and fondling the length and breadth of his penis as Innocenta shrieked in the background. "Stop it! Stop her! Ellingham—you promised he would fuck all of us—and look—just look . . . !"

Ellingham was positively goggling at Jenise's handling of Wick's penis—the slow, languorous strokes, the brief tight squeezes, the way she grasped the base of his shaft and held it like it was the root of all her desire. The way she rubbed and twisted his bulbous penis head, playing with the very tip, and licking just where pearly drops of ejaculate oozed.

The long, erotic strokes up and down his thick length, almost as if she were kneading him like bread. And all the while, she looked up to him and at him as if he were the master of her world.

And while they were all staring at her delicious and dexterous manipulation of his penis, she slipped the fingers of one hand between his legs and up into the leather pouch cradling his scrotum, and slowly worked it off.

Now she could caress and squeeze those tight, luscious balls. Now she could stroke that delicious fold of skin behind them.

Now, she could bring him to his knees . . .

"*Stop it!*" Innocenta lunged. "Bitch! Whore! *Tweat!* Who knows to do such things? Only an experienced lay-a-back is who. Wick—wake up—don't you see? She is not an innocent, nor a virgin—look at her—*Stop her!*"

Too late to stop anything then. Wick ejaculated softly, slowly, powerfully, at the first touch of Jenise's fingers between his legs, and as his cream flowed over, she rubbed his penis against her body, against her breasts, her nipples, and her mouth, and smeared herself with his essence.

And Innocenta collapsed into Ellingham's unwilling arms, sobbing.

"Get her out of here," Wick ordered. "Get her back to her family. Virtuosa too. I've made my choice."

The two in the doorway froze, a tableau of disbelief and anger all directed at Jenise's naked back as she still knelt at Wick's feet.

"Good choice," Ellingham murmured. What he wouldn't give to find such a one as this, so malleable, so obviously in love with the scent and taste of a man's body and his spunk. God, Wick had all the luck, all the time; the only setback was the commitment. The man would be leg shackled in no time, which had its compensations as long as he remained fascinated with Chaste.

She had surely entertained him royally today. He couldn't count the hours they'd been closeted in Wick's bedroom, and Wick still looked like he hadn't had nearly enough of Chaste's nakedness.

Innocenta and Virtuosa just couldn't compare.

"Come, ladies. The contest is over."

"Is it?" Innocenta demanded wrathfully.

"Wick always compensates those he *cares* about for their disappointments. You wouldn't want to put yourself in the category of those who might become bothersome to him, Innocenta. It wouldn't pay to do so."

"How much would it pay *not* to become Wick's wife? Fifty thousand, my dear Ellingham? Times how many years a wife might live—or a man for that matter . . . ?"

"Oh, you were ever a greedy baggage, my dear Innocenta. Trust me, you will not want this talked about, Wick's rejection, and that is very easily done, you know, no matter how much you might deny it. I'll see to it personally, my dear. On the other hand, Wick is always generous in the letdown."

"Tell me how generous."

He named a sum. Innocenta looked as if she were about to protest, then she looked at Wick and thought the better of it.

"She will live a life in hell, that one. She has no idea what kind of man this is, or how to deal with him."

"That is her problem then," Ellingham said as he closed the door behind them. "Yours is to be as gracious in defeat as possible."

And then they were alone, Jenise still on her knees as if she were worshiping him, adoring his penis.

He rather liked the picture that made. Already, he was elongated to a thrumming hardness, excited by the notion there would never have to be another interruption.

Who was she, this Chaste? She was still veiled, as he

wanted, even though she had removed the last vestige of what he wished to conceal from her. No longer. Every part of his body was hers, now that he had declared her his choice.

But he still wanted the mystery of her intact. He wanted her just as she was, submissive at his feet, but with a hot, creaming desire for his penis. And that was all he wanted from Chaste.

She looked up at him. Still, he couldn't tell anything about what she was thinking. Her hands told him what she was thinking as she grasped him again with the surety of one who knows what she wants.

She wanted his penis. And that was all he wanted her to want.

A match made in heaven, he thought a little derisively, as he toppled her, spread her legs, and mounted her on the floor.

Done. Oh Lord, done. He had chosen her. She could barely breathe thinking about it. She could barely hold still for want of doing something that might make him change his mind.

It was early hours yet, even though he had fucked her ferociously on the floor, against the wall, and subsequently on the bed. And now they lay entwined once again, his arm around her, his one hand cradling one breast, the other slipping subtly down her belly between her legs, and working to part her labia.

Her body heated up instantly. The feel of his questing fingers was the most arousing thing. No. His thumbing her taut nipple was. No—both—*oh* . . . as he fingered the tight, hot nub of her desire deep between her legs.

Inside her now, his long expert fingers, sliding, feeling, making her wet; his thumb back and forth on her nipple, tweaking it, pressing it, feeling its contour . . . sweet moans of encouragement—his penis rock hard against the pillow of her buttocks . . . streaming pleasure—anything he wanted, anything—

She came—hot, succulent, thick against his shaft, she came . . . and as she melted into the throes of her pleasure, he pushed into her from behind, humping her between her legs with his penis and his fingers, and his thumb incessantly at her nipple.

It took nothing but a couple of thrusts to catapult him into a long, slow, effusion of unspeakable sensation that he discharged deep into her throbbing core.

"The hot, naked, sex-hungry Chaste is endlessly fascinating to me," he murmured in her ear. "What does *she* think?"

"That my lord's penis is endlessly fascinating to me," she whispered back.

"Good, because it wants to plow you again."

"Just what I was thinking . . . "

And in he came, endlessly hard, with that legendary stamina and the bottomless well of his cream spurting into her yet again.

He wanted to watch her in the mirror. He cradled her against his hips, his penis plowed deep and tight in her cunt from behind, and he watched himself as he played with her nipples.

She watched the unimaginable tableau of her body so erotically connected to him, writhing and undulating against him, her one leg angled over his and the tiny thin heel of her bootie digging into his.

She could just see a bare, hard, muscular inch of his penis embedded in her under the spread of her leg and it made her catch her breath. And those insistent fingers tugging at her nipples, tweaking, pulling . . . she felt so erotically charged, she might explode. And she didn't want him to stop. She wanted to float on the sensation of his possession and his expert fingers manipulating the rock hard tips of her nipples.

Just that, just there—

I love this too much . . .

Dear heaven . . . I would subjugate myself to his will forever for this pleasure—

I can't . . . I shouldn't—

I want to . . .

Women have done this for centuries—given themselves up to this naked carnality.... I could do it—it's all mine, already. He chose me. He's given it to me....

I can't, I can't, I can't...

What is the victory in submitting to him? What will he have learned?

What have you learned?

She made a deep guttural sound of approval. Whatever he was doing, she didn't want him to stop. Even watching him could not explain the mystery of how his fondling her nipples produced this cataclysmic jolt of pleasure. How his delicate circling of her aureolae made her want to melt.

"Promise you will always be naked for me," he whispered in her ear.

"Promise you'll always play with my nipples like this..." she breathed. It was a spell, she thought. Her response to him was contrary to everything she'd vowed to accomplish by undertaking this subjugation in the first place.

Never could she have imagined she would be so enthralled by him, by his touch, his sex, his ability to give her pleasure. Never had she dreamed she would be talking to him like this, begging him to take her naked nipples whenever he wanted, craving, pleading for the incessant penetration of his rock of a penis.

It was so deeply rooted in her now, she didn't want to move, and she couldn't help moving as his fingers teased and tantalized her nipples.

And then suddenly he rolled onto his back, taking her with him so that she lay sprawled on his body, with his penis still hard, thick, and connecting them deep in her core.

He worked her breasts, cupping them, palming them, rubbing his hands over her nipples and then immediately seeking the hard tips once more to just hold them.

Softly, delicately, he held each of her nipples in between two fingers so that she could just feel the pressure. Just feel the voluptuous sensation of him possessing them like that.

Watching him in the mirror as he positioned his fingers just so around her nipples. Seeing them move as one as he undulated himself deeper inside her, her legs draped widely over his thighs, and he still holding those hard tips, breathless, soft, gentle, meaningfully *there* . . .

And then he squeezed, and it was like hot gold roaring through her veins, slow, thick, bright wave after overlapping wave of sensation, cascading down to her very core and drowning in the backwash of his explosive climax.

She was awash again in his cream. She felt him shift her onto her side again so that they were facing the mirror. Felt him rock hard inside her, not nearly depleted by that galvanic orgasm. Felt his insatiable possession of her undiminished.

She closed her eyes. How could she give this up? She didn't have to give this up. Of course she had to give this up. The point of the exercise was to induce him to choose her.

And then reject him as he had rejected a hundred others before her.

How could she reject this unspeakable carnality between them? Men died for it; women destroyed their lives for it, and here she had it, given to her on his will and whim just because she had been that little bit different, that much more responsive.

And he would make it legal; he would call her his wife.

She hadn't counted at all on this dilemma. She had supposed she would hate everything about succumbing to him. She had thought she would be pretending, that everything he would want to do to her would be utter anathema to her.

She hadn't even supposed she would get as far as his bedroom, in truth, given the two other candidates' greater experience with men.

And yet here she was, and she must revile the thing she most desired in the name of all the women he had ever compromised. That was her vow and her promise, and his seductive eroticism was totally beside the point.

She felt a shudder of regret. She almost couldn't bear looking at them in the mirror, and yet, what memories would she have after but those reflected back to her in these lone, carnal moments.

And there she was, connected to him, cosseted by him, drenched with his come, cradled in his hands.

Or was she there? She still wore the veil. He still referred to her as Chaste. There was no kissing or petting, or a moment when she was not naked to him or he to her.

In the raw light of the room, she was just a body, a cunt, and one that was particularly susceptible to him.

He knew her not other than as a vessel, a repository of his seed.

This was the end, then, for every woman he had ever known. This was what she must remember, not the shattering pleasure, or the ache to be possessed by his stallion of a penis.

No, the thing about Wick was his careless, heartless obliteration of a woman's identity in subjugation to his carnal needs. And if her desire was in concert with his, why then, he would praise her to the sky and pay her more than an hour's worth of attention.

So long as she kept him occupied.

Yes, that was the thing. That was Wick. And did she stay and truly become his wife, it would be one thing after another just like that when he became tired of her.

She had to go.

She absolutely *had* to go, because women did not leave Wick—he abandoned them. Carelessly. Heartlessly. With thousands of pounds of jewels to console them. But still, he abandoned them.

So it could not hurt that she would reject him. It would do wonders for her pride if nothing else, and then Innocenta could have another shot at him, once it was revealed, in an underground way, that her union with him was not to be.

Oh—the torrent of regret threatened to drown her.

But a man like Wick would never come to heel, never behave, never believe that there was honor in family and marriage and staying a faithful course.

And she must, by her leaving him, honor every woman of whom he had taken advantage who had believed he might be changed.

Chapter Eight

"Where is she?"

Wick bolted to the door, his roar echoing down the hallway. The empty hallway. Somewhere a clock struck five in the dead silence. The empty silence.

"Wilton!" He did not stand on ceremony with her, or try to dress before she entered the room. Nor did he even try to hide his convulsive anger. "Where is the woman?"

"Sir?" He didn't intimidate her. She'd had years of coping with his whims and wants and tantrums. "And how would I know?"

"How wouldn't you?" he growled. "You know everything that goes on in this house. Where is she?"

"I don't know."

"Find out," he bit out succinctly, and reached for his trousers, shirt, and boots. He didn't even stop to wash or bathe, he was in such a fury; he wanted the scent of that bitch all over him, and her betrayal to seep into his very pores.

Now for Ellingham, that son of a bitch.

"My dear Wick," Ellingham said conciliatingly as he was unconscionably routed out of bed. "This is no way to treat a guest, especially your best friend and prime procurer." He shook his head as he began to comprehend Wick's agitation. "What do you mean, where is she? Where is who?"

"The pristine piece you vetted as pure and pink with pussy

to please. She's gone, do you hear me? Left my bed, my house, and my heft—*mine*—and who knows where she's gone, or what lies she's spreading besides her legs. Damn it to hell and Haliburton . . . get out of bed, Ellingham! It's your head, literally and figuratively. I'll lop it off if you don't tell me who she is and where she's gone."

"Now, now, Wick, don't jump your fences. You don't yet know she's not in the house—in the kitchen, perhaps, or the library . . ."

Wick threw him a baleful glance, but Ellingham wasn't even looking; he was too busy pulling on his clothes and fussing. "At five in the morning, you dolt? I think not. Who is she, Ellingham?"

"Dear God, you chose the chit to be your wife—you mean to say you never asked her name?" Ellingham was appalled. This was behavior over and beyond, even for Wick. To fuck the girl day and night, and never even want to know who she was? Even as he was conceivably planting his seed?

Too distasteful. He didn't want to think of it. The girl was in the house, she had to be. "Did you never even remove that damned veil?"

"Why would I want to?" Wick answered insolently. "She was beautiful, pliable, and her cunt was hot and eager to please. What else did I need to know?"

"Her goddamned name, you jack shit. You're going to marry her, for God's sake. This is too much, even for you, Wick."

"I want her back . . ." Wick bit out, and then amended, "in my bed."

"You want a hot blowhole," Ellingham muttered. "And for that, either of the two flat-backs you sent home would do."

"*I—want—her.*"

"Ah . . ." Ellingham breathed. "Her."

"Who is she?"

"She is Chaste, she is Diana, and she's gone to the sun."

"Ellingham . . ." His tone brooked no argument, his hands

flexed as if he wanted to crunch Ellingham against the nearest wall. "Who—*is*—she?"

"Violence will get you nowhere," Ellingham chided. "Remember, there are great sums of money at stake here, and the honor of queen and country."

"Who is she?"

"Someone, perhaps, too good for you."

"I—will—kill you. . . ."

"It will kill me to tell you—I rather enjoy seeing you sweat for a change."

"I will rather enjoy sweating the life out of you, my dear friend. That woman *will* be back in my bed within the day, and will be my wife within the month. Whether she wills it or not. That was the agreement, and I do not want to think this has been an elaborate practical joke on your part because the consequences would be beyond your comprehension."

Now there was a threat that made him just a little afraid. Wick's consequence in society was above the angels no matter what his behavior. It was the money, the title, the lineage, the *connections*. It was any number of intangible things, among them the glitter that rubbed off on anyone associated with him.

It was the most potent of threats, as far as Ellingham was concerned. He'd had too much fun being Wick's acolyte and factotum, and he wouldn't defend Chaste as far as it would take for Wick to rescind his friendship.

There *were* limits, after all.

But to see Wick in such an uproar was highly entertaining, and something that would be forever for his delectation alone. And something with which he could blackmail him anytime he needed the upper hand.

"Hold easy, my dear Wick. It is too early to storm the barricades in any event. You truly don't yet know she's gone. Let us look first, take some breakfast, calm down, and then, if necessary, we'll confront the lioness in her den."

*   *   *

220 / *Thea Devine*

"Did he kiss you?"

Now it was Jenise's turn to wallow in the blue room. And blue didn't adequately describe what she was feeling the morning after she came reeling home, half dressed and half sunk in remorse.

God, what it had taken to get out of the environs of Wick's domain, and even then, all her luck had depended on a moonstruck stable boy who thought the whole runaway adventure was romantic and never gave a thought to Wick's wrath should he discover the boy's complicity.

She had slept, had some breakfast, slept some more, and now, in the early evening hour of the day she left Wick, she felt as if a month had passed.

And then there was Julia, ever solicitous, knowing Wick, and wanting to know all the gory details.

Well, she could spare her that, at least. "No, he didn't. Kiss me." Liar—he had, but could you call licking a dollop of cream off his tongue a kiss—*really* . . . ?

And then his fingers, probing, feeling . . . don't think about it—don't let yourself remember . . .

"Did he touch you?" There was a tremor in Julia's voice as she asked that question.

Damn. But she should have expected that question too, Jenise thought futilely. The trick was—no details. Less was more, especially in Julia's case.

"I liked it not," she answered, her voice carefully neutral. Not a hint of how much she had craved his touch after . . . with? . . . *dessert.* "It was not worth the hoops he put us through to discover that fifty thousand a year would be no compensation for a bartered marriage."

"He touched you." Julia's voice was wispy now, like a candle that had been snuffed.

"What did you expect?" Jenise demanded, suddenly out of patience. "He is seeking a wife. Someone he will surely make demands of. Someone he will touch and kiss and . . ."

. . . will not care who she is as long as she spreads her legs for him willingly, endlessly . . .

. . . I am that woman—
And I can never tell . . .

But he hadn't removed the veil either. And he hadn't wanted anything more than complete and total access to her most intimate naked parts. Even now, the day after her return, her body reeked with the scent of him because she would not wash it off. She wanted it to soak into her skin, her very vitals.

She never wanted to forget, but what it was she didn't want to forget, she did not want to define.

"Oh," Julia said faintly. "Oh."

"You did say . . ." Jenise began simultaneously.

"Yes, I did. I'm sorry. I just—I want . . ."

". . . to know," Jenise finished for her. "Of course you do, having come so close yourself to being annihilated by him. He is lethal, he is dangerous, he is seductive, and spoiled and evil beyond repair. And I am just as happy to have escaped the vile fate of possibly having been chosen as the one he would take to wife."

"Who was, then?" Julia demanded, brightening. Here was news, here was gossip, and she might even be the first to know.

Oh Lord. The traps . . . There was no answer for this question; it was a quagmire, pure and simple, and she must skim the surface in order to reach the other side.

"He kept us sequestered. We didn't know each other's names. He interacted with us individually. It was the wisest course because whoever was not chosen must be able to return to society with her reputation intact. It was the one commendable thing about the whole process . . ." Jenise trailed off.

Such lies. Even now, her body pulsated with need. This time last night, in the mirror, she had been naked in his bed, slave to his magic hands, and that was all, in the aftermath, she was going to remember.

That was the curse: her body craved his hands and the possessive ram of his penis, and no reality about him would ever touch that.

And well he knew it.

How could she have done this to herself? Bold, adventurous Jenise, daring to take on the beast only to be utterly seduced by him.

How stupid. How inutterably naïve of her.

"Jenise . . . ?"

And now—she was ruined for any other man, *ever* . . .

"Yes, Julia?" Was that her voice? In her mind, she heard only him; her nipples tightened in anticipation, her body creamed.

"Would you like some tea?"

Thump . . . reality beckoned; and the mirror only reflected what was the truth: that she was the most foolhardy woman in the whole of England for having abandoned his bed, rejected his sex, and tossed this once in a lifetime chance away.

"My dear Wick, we shall call her Chaste until such time as we ascertain she wishes to be addressed as something else."

"I have offered her the ultimate name," Wick growled, "and she will take it if I have to tie her up and stand her at the altar. I will meet those expectations and I will not be a laughingstock. I *will* fulfill my duty. And she is likely knocked up already with how much cream I spent in her. . . . Damn her eyes—who is this woman, *who,* who would defy me and revile my name?"

It was early evening, and they had been traveling for a good two hours, and had only just arrived at Wick's London town house.

And he hadn't let up for the entire trip, Ellingham reflected with a covert smile. He didn't know whether Wick's fury was pure selfish possessiveness of a thing he believed to be his, or whether something about this woman bit deeper in his soul.

Whatever it was, Wick was not bored, and there was something to be said for that.

"We will go round to her father's house *now.*" Wick said as they debarked from the carriage and followed the footmen and a half-dozen trunks into the house.

"We will *not,*" Ellingham said emphatically. "We will spend the night, and you will contemplate whether you truly want to leg shackle yourself to this woman. After all, what can happen in the course of a night? She won't have run off to Gretna with someone else."

"Won't she?" Wick growled. "She ran out on me . . ."

"And in the morning," Ellingham continued unflappably, "we will send a note, and then, if she is amenable, we will see her."

"*If . . . ?*" Wick roared. "And it is not *we* who will *see* her. . . ."

"Of course. Meantime, tonight you can sit and ruminate on all her bad qualities to prepare yourself for jilting her. Or, you can enumerate all the things you quite liked about her to prepare handing yourself over to the parson's purse. Either way . . ."

"If you will not tell me who she is," Wick said with a dangerous edge to his voice, "you will assign someone to watch her house to make certain she does not sneak off with the footman."

Ellingham looked a little taken aback at that demand. "As you wish, of course, my dear Wick. We'll get Max on it. He hasn't quite lived up to his part in this whole to-do. Let me send a note posthaste so that there isn't one moment when my lady is not under observation."

"My lady?" Wick grabbed that observation in a minute as Ellingham scribbled a note, summoned Wick's butler, and sent the thing off.

"She is a lady, Wick. Nothing less would do."

"So I was led to believe. But ladies don't run away in the middle of the night."

Oh, this desertion was killing him, was it? Ellingham wondered which was the worst of it—the betrayal or the rejection. Maybe both. There hadn't been a woman in recent memory who had had the guts, the nerve, the daring to repudiate Wick. They fell all over him; hell, even this innocent piece was wax in his hands.

And yet—and yet—there was backbone there as well. She hadn't followed the path of the other two. She dared to speak her mind and will. And when things were not to her liking, she had taken action.

Perhaps this was one with the strength and cunning to tame a libertine.

Wick on a leash, by God—

Wick was pacing the room. The fire was lit, the butler had brought the port, which sat untouched on a side table. And Ellingham sat by the fireplace, watching him with glee in his eyes.

"You are enjoying this, aren't you? God, if I find out you had a hand in this, I will draw and quarter your nether parts, my erstwhile friend. It *was* your idea, after all is said and done."

"Brilliant, too, if I do say so," Ellingham murmured. "I do believe I will have some port. This is great sport, watching your agitation."

"*My—what . . . ?*" Wick stopped in his tracks. "No. I am not agitated, I am in a rage that the bitch took everything and left me with nothing, not even the possibility of a wife, which is the greatest prize in the whole of England. *Who* is she, to scorn such an honor? *Who?* And to leave me hanging like this in public . . . I swear to God, Ellingham, if you don't tell me . . ."

"So that is the whole of it—Wick's public embarrassment that the cunt he has chosen to wed would not have him? You could remedy that in a heartbeat, my dear man. Send around to Innocenta. There will be no discomfort, she will understand perfectly, and no one need ever know. She, certainly, would never tell. And Virtuosa is smart enough to know that social ostracism is but a word away, should she choose to gossip."

"*I—do—not—want—Innocenta. I—want—Chaste.*"

The words echoed in the room. Resonated somewhere outside of every rule by which Wick had lived. Insinuated themselves somewhere deep in his craw, because suddenly the thought of anyone else in his bed was repulsive.

. . . I want Chaste . . .

He had never thought to ever speak those words about any

woman. The moment he said them, he felt total shock, surprise, and he instantly wanted to take them back. Because hovering in the air—they were real. They had meaning.

They had a witness.

. . . I want Chaste . . .

He rolled the words around in his mind for a few moments.

What was it about Chaste? But he had been asking that question from the first, setting her apart from the three who had come to him supposedly on equal ground.

Would he be so adamant if Innocenta had been the one to leave him?

What was it about Chaste?

Beautiful, witty, elegant . . . yes. Aware of what her being chosen to compete for his attentions meant on the most basic level. Willing, yet reserved. Bold. Restrained. Attuned to her body in spite of her innocence. Truly a virgin, yet eager and receptive to everything he wanted to do to her once he claimed her maidenhead. But still something elusive about her. Something she was withholding, was standing back and watching from afar even as she opened her most intimate secret places over to his questing sex.

Yes, that was Chaste. Chaste, whom every time he so much as thought her name, he got hard and hot, and thunderous inside with wanting her. That was Chaste too—with the boundlessly fascinating body that he could not stop fondling. Chaste of the rock hard nipples, and the hot, tight cunt whose depths were endless and enthralling.

Where even now, he might already have planted his seed . . .

Or ought he wait until that was proved a reality? Make her come to him, as well she should after what she had done.

Yes, that was the way of it. He would make her crawl, make her come until she screamed for mercy . . .

But what if instead, she utterly repudiated him and someone else married her, took on his child, and got to plow that supple, compliant body and suck those hot, luscious nipples—

No! It didn't bear thinking about. He wouldn't think about it.

It was inconceivable. He had chosen her and chosen she would be. It didn't matter what she wanted.

Ellingham perfectly understood. And that was the end of it.

And tomorrow, he would make her see . . .

And so, the last thing Jenise expected was the creamy vellum with Wick's seal and a request, signed by Ellingham, ever discreet, that she consider meeting with Wick.

Nor was this something to be kept from the family. Not with Wick's carriage and footman and the whole artistocratic formality of the presentation of the note.

Julia was fair jumping over her shoulder trying to read what Ellingham had written.

"No, it is *not* from Wick," Jenise snapped as her mother inquired yet again. "Wick must have a go-between even for this. He cannot lower himself to publicly choose a mate. He cannot, apparently, speak for himself."

Jenise's mother raised an eyebrow but forebore to comment. She was as curious as ten cats about what had gone on in the past days at Holcombe, but all things Wick were never subject for anything but speculation or gossip. Anyone involved never would tell, and neither, she suspected, would Jenise, although she had a fair idea what Wick would have required of any female he invited to his home.

That certainty aside, it was curious still that a note had been sent in the aftermath, and she held high hopes that perhaps something had transpired which would be to the good of Jenise's future.

Of course, Jenise being curled up in the blue room, looking utterly vexed and angry by turns, was not a hopeful sign.

"If I see him—*if*—I must have that time with him alone," she finally said to her mother. "Do not even try to inflict yourself as a chaperon. You cared nothing about that when I went to Holcombe."

"But Wick went to great pains to assure us his mother would play that role."

"Yes, from the dower house twenty miles away. Or whatever. He will charm you all to a fare-thee-well, Mother. But now I have some sense of the wrongs he has done to Julia and every other woman within his orbit, and I will never cave in. There is nothing the ogre can say after these blighted days in his company that will sway me."

Ellingham came anyway. Wick didn't think he could have kept him away. And it was only when they were but a block or two from Chaste's home that Ellingham even told him her name.

"Trowbridge? *Trow*bridge? I believe I know that name . . ."

"Indeed you do," Ellingham agreed, "but I'll let you remember just what it was."

"Games. I hate games. Chaste is playing a game. Trowbridge, Trowbridge—wait—a slender wispy blonde . . . Oh, Lord all bleeding mighty—one of those cool, catch me, coddle me virgins who go cold cock, thinking to force a proposal from me. That icy little chit? I did her the biggest favor dropping her like a hot stone. Hell and bloody damnation. Chaste is her sister?"

"There it is. And perhaps the cause of Chaste's defection?"

Wick contemplated that for a moment. The scenario was clear: Chaste was out for sweet vengeance. And she had served it with a hot, savory sauce and a plateful of promises *she* never meant to keep. "Shit."

"Well, we'll just turn the carriage around and . . . send round to Innocenta, who will be ecstatic to receive you."

"We will not." Oh, the steel was in his voice, along with determination, purpose, and not a hint of ennui. Chaste would not get away this time, Ellingham thought gleefully. He couldn't wait to see.

But what he didn't expect was Julia. Not this Julia, who was nothing like the wounded pigeon that Wick had discarded by the wayside.

Who was this Julia, standing confident and tall, a faint wash of color suffusing her cheeks, her bright blue eyes glit-

tery and defiant as she showed Wick to the blue room and ushered Ellingham into the drawing room?

He could not stop staring at her.

"My Lord," she murmured, her voice low, rich, musical.
Had he never noticed that about Julia in all the weeks of
Wick's pursuit. Or her well-rounded body, her beautiful pos-
ture, her lovely manners, her innate poise.

She was so elegant, proud, and beautiful. Something about
her had changed: she had learned something from those travails. She had grown, and she was worthy, and he didn't expect this. What was *this?* It had nothing to do with him, in any
event. He didn't want this. And he knew that was a lie.

His gaze glanced against hers, to repudiate what he was
feeling, but Ellingham knew in that moment the game was
over, the rules had changed, and that he, without ever having
played a hand, had lost.

Julia. Everything he had ever sought was embodied in that
name and in that person, even considering he had never
known he was looking. But of course, he'd been looking—
there had just never been a woman who excited his interest.

And yet Julia had always been there, in the backwash of all
of Wick's conquests. Blast the man for not appreciating what
he'd had. And thank God, he hadn't, because Julia was the
one.

Julia. Everything had changed. He had to earn her respect
now or suffer to lose her forever.

Julia. He never wanted to leave her. He sat down beside her
on the sofa, feeling in his heart of hearts as if he had finally
found home.

And so she was letting him languish, Wick thought furiously, pacing the room with no control, and no Jenise on
whom to vent his fury. He was beginning to think he had spent
too much of his time and too much of his tallow on the bitch
already.

That was the thing with women. They absolutely thought

that men were brought to their knees by what was between their legs.

Ha. Not he. Countless women had tried. And failed. And the only reason he was here was because of Ellingham's campaign to get him a wife and heir. If that had not been out in the air for the past months, if the whole of society were not expecting some denouement, if he had not used his mother's good name in the quest for a virgin to corrupt and impregnate, Chaste would not have a chance in hell at his name.

At least he had some conscience, he thought. He wasn't totally off the line himself. And Chaste had some refreshing qualities. He might be able to stand to live with her as long as it took to birth an heir. They'd come to a settlement. She'd lead her own life, and he would continue as always.

What woman could resist such a proposition? Not any of the hundreds he had casually fucked. So who was Chaste to go running off like that?

Immediately his fury engorged him.

And at that moment, the door slowly opened and Chaste slipped into the room.

Or he thought it was Chaste, but since she was enveloped head to foot in a long cloak with a hood that covered her head and face, he couldn't be quite sure. It might be that fragile sparrow of a sister—except he didn't think she was quite that tall.

And then she parted the edges of the cloak to reveal that she was naked beneath, and she waited.

". . . Chaste?"

But there was no question. He knew that bush, those nipples.

"A body, my lord. What does it matter if it is Chaste or Innocenta or one of your ladies in waiting . . . ?"

"It is Chaste I have chosen to be my bride."

"No, it is a body you have chosen, my lord. A place to root and a nipple to suck and nothing more. Therefore, any body will do. Go and choose one from the roster of willing bodies you have already possessed, and leave this body in peace."

She was too calm, too still. This was not going anywhere near how Wick had imagined it. Was it not true that in the lending library romances a woman capitulated the moment her beloved came after her? What was wrong with Chaste? Did she not understand how utterly out of character this was for him?

Damn Ellingham's hide. To have put him in this position because of this frivolous competition. To bring him to this, the torture of having to look at Chaste's breasts and belly and the bushy entrée to heaven and not touch . . . not possess—Any other woman would be on her back by now trying to entice him, and here was Chaste rejecting him all over again.

A man could only take so much.

And a woman. Jenise was near faint with fear at her aggressive stance. This was not the way to deal with Wick—Innocenta had had the right of it. But she could do nothing less. As easy as it had been for him to master her, she was determined that on every other ground they must be equals. To capitulate now, she would lose all pride and never regain any footing with him.

In this room, in any event.

Truly, just for these moments he would give her before he became unutterably bored with the game of getting a wife, she must stand toe to toe with him and not give him any ground. Then Ellingham would steer him toward Innocenta, who had no emotional investment in him as a man, and too much experience with other men, and would comfortably rub along on his money as his wife.

"I've chosen you—Jenise—and the choice is irrevocable."

Oh! The tone was implacable, and to hear him say her name—dear heaven, it did give credence to the fact he was serious if nothing else.

"I believe I have said no."

"No. You said come and get me if you really want me. You have won, Chaste. I am here, and running out of patience looking at your nakedness and knowing that in this house I cannot touch you, I cannot savor you. And you well may be carrying my child."

"Truly, that is all you want," she said frostily. "The heir. The rest can go hang."

"You too, Chaste? You demand that I change my nature?"

"What is man's nature, or a woman's for that matter? No, I would ask you shoulder some responsibility. It isn't enough to carry the title and then strew your bastards all over the island while your *chosen* wife looks on. That is one condition I would never accept. On the other hand . . ." she looked down at her body, "who could have known that I, as genteelly raised as I was, would embrace sexual congress so completely, with all my body and soul. It might well be that *I* would be strewing the countryside with bastards while *you* are relegated to the closet . . . now there's a thought. All those lovers with whom I might never have a chance but for the fact I was Wick's wife. Just on that condition alone, I might reconsider . . ."

Her words made his blood run cold. That was never her. He didn't know how he knew that, but he did. She could never do that, not to him, not to any man to whom she had pledged herself. He knew it like he knew his own name. He was counting on it, in fact.

Wick crossed the room like lightning and grabbed her shoulders.

"You are NOT Innocenta . . . I know it—I know you . . ."

The words, the words—echoing, resonating . . . even as he spoke to her hooded face . . . even as he comprehended what he was saying—and that it *was* true—and again, it took him utterly by surprise.

. . . *I know you* . . .

He did. He *did*.

"You know me not," Jenise said, her words dropping like stones.

They stood for a long moment; he made no move to uncover her face. This was the moment.

"I know you," he said, his voice hoarse. "I chose you."

"Until you weary of me."

"I will not tell you what is not true."

"I'm seeing what is true: you talk to my body, it's as if I am not here."

He lifted his hand and pushed back her hood, looked into her eyes, touched her soft cheek, her lips. Beautiful. Intelligent. Sensual.

His.

"I see you, Jenise. I know who you are. I know you."

"Brave words to get you what you want."

"I want you." And that was so true at this moment, the thought startled him. She was so perfect, in all ways, everything about her the epitome of his dream of the woman he had always envisioned as his wife.

He felt a hot urgency not to lose her, and a deep gnawing fear at even the thought. And it had nothing to do with his status or his money. "You want me. We may have already started a child. This is a beginning, then. And the rest, perhaps, we both have to learn. And this is what I can promise you: I will try to learn."

Jenise caught her breath. He was serious. He meant it, he would do it for her, for however long it held his attention, because nothing yet had come close to the appeal of having a wife and a child, two things that would be irrevocably and wholly his.

She looked into his eyes, and there, for the first time, she saw the vulnerability and just a hint of the child, the indulged, precocious, and perhaps unwanted child, who really, truly craved love and had yet to find it; and she saw, too, the man who had everything, of whom people only wanted the pieces that would give them countenance.

Did he not then, in all his amorous adventures, yearn for someone and something to love beyond the superficial and the ephemeral?

She saw him in that instant as lonely and lost, and she knew she must continually challenge him to keep vows and keep faithful, life-affirming things that would change him for the better forever.

There was no more time than that to parse it out, or contemplate how it worked into his character. Suffice it that she felt the first tremor of feeling for him that went far beyond the physical, even as she was swamped with desire for his touch, for his sex.

This was the moment. If she had thought she must live without his caresses and his sex, she would not. If she had mourned the loss of their sensual connection, it was now resurrected. And more than that, he had already done things so outside his usual behavior, he had proved his determination to keep his end of the bargain.

Not the least was, he had come. He had sought her out. He had chosen her and he meant to stand by that choice and all that it meant. He would try to learn to be better.

And he was a lover beyond compare. It seemed to her in that moment, with all she had perceived about him, that it was the best bargain in the whole of England.

"Jenise?" He took her hands firmly, drew her to the sofa and pulled her onto his lap. Onto the iron bar of his erection and the evidence that he still wanted her beyond all reason and was still utterly enthralled by her sex.

It was enough. That, and his pledge, and the promise of tomorrow. Some women didn't even have that much.

She couldn't bear to be apart from him for another minute. Her lord and master. He was all that and more, now. She'd been waiting so long for him. She settled her cunt tight against his penis, offered him her nipples, and the bargain was met.

Erotic Déjà Vu

Katherine O'Neal

Chapter One

S.S. Oceania
Off Gibraltar
August 4, 1888

"There she is!"

The small group of tourists perked up as the woman passed, as if they'd just been turned on by the flick of a switch.

"She isn't at all what I expected."

"Nor I. From reading her books I thought she'd be more . . . well . . . bawdy, I suppose."

They took in her appearance critically: the stylish traveling suit that reined in her feminine curves to suit the fashion of the day; the upswept wealth of hair—rich brown shot through with copper glints, like the gleam of firelight on mahogany; the confidence of her carriage, the subtle sway of her walk. The women, in their country tweeds, noting her understated glamour with envious eyes. The men squirming uncomfortably because for all her warmth, sophistication, and grace, they felt an innate and unconscious sensuality smoldering beneath the surface. She was, in fact, the most seductive woman they'd encountered in their stodgy, uneventful lives.

Naturally they knew all about her. Who, in the far-flung reaches of the British Empire, *hadn't* heard all there was to know about Lady Celia Wybourne? Married at twenty to a much older earl, a respected member of the House of Lords. Widowed within the month when the poor man had dropped dead of apoplexy, leaving her well-fixed and a countess to boot. Martyred by a mourning nation until, scarcely a year later, she'd shocked them all with the publication of her first book. Certainly not the sort of thing they'd expected. Set in scorching desert sands, it was a spirited adventure in which a dark and daring—and roguishly unscrupulous—hero swept the heroine to ecstasy in a most *suggestive* manner, its sly innuendo and undertones of sexual mastery leaving her readers breathless. One young woman, devouring it in the Underground on her way home from the G. H. Harris Bookshop, was said to have fainted dead away when she'd read the part where the lusty cad had forced his attentions on the heroine— and the shameful wench had actually loved it and begged for more!

Oh, how London tongues had wagged. Earl Wybourne had ruffled feathers when he'd championed women's rights, but surely his wife had gone too far! In the wake of the sensation the book caused, rumors began to spread that she'd been too much even for the forward-minded earl; that he'd died in bed ("And I don't mean *sleeping*," they'd add with meaningfully arched brows) trying to keep up with his amorous young wife.

In the fifteen years since his death there had been many additional books, each more scandalous than the last. Some called them smut, of course. But they read them all the same. Yet, for all that she traveled the world—alone for the most part—seeking new stories to tell, there wasn't a breath of scandal linked with her name. If she took lovers—as surely she must, for how else could she write with such . . . *abandon?*— she was undeniably discreet.

"Do you see the way men *fawn* over her?" one of her observers whispered now. "I should be embarrassed to *death* to make such a fool of *my*self."

"She was most charming to me last evening when I bumped into her on deck. Quite the lady, really. Surprisingly so."

They watched as she placed delicate, gloved hands on the ship's rail and looked out at the view beyond.

"How then," wondered one of the women aloud, "does such a *lady* write such *naughty* books?"

Celia heard their whispers as she passed. It was nothing new. She'd long ago become an object of curiosity and speculation. Talking about her in those hissed whispers that carried farther than if they'd spoken aloud. As if she couldn't hear what they were saying. As if she were a phantom floating in their midst, not a flesh and blood woman with feelings and desires every bit as real as their own. She'd encountered their type in all the corners of the world—drab English tourists who journeyed to exotic places seeking diversion, yet who spent the majority of their holiday complaining that things weren't "like home." Until she—authoress, adventuress—swept in and made them forget their discomforts in the titillation of her presence.

She tried to ignore it all and concentrate on the view she'd come to see, gazing out across the Straits of Gibraltar with the fresh wind in her face. Not what she'd anticipated when she'd imagined Gibraltar. A more gentle peak than she'd envisioned rising from the mist of the deep blue sea far off in the distance. Hardly the dramatic rock of legend. But strangely familiar. As if she'd looked upon it before, perhaps in a dream. It wasn't the first time this had happened. Sometimes . . .

"Where *do* you think she gets her . . . inspiration?"

The voice drifted to her, interrupting her thoughts. She realized only too well what they wanted to know. It was *the* question, the one that inevitably sprang to mind whenever someone met her. What inspired a lady of culture and refinement to write prose that, without really saying it, so thrillingly evoked the most shocking, carnal images in the whole history of English literature? The one question she never answered, deflecting their impertinence—their rudeness—with a mysterious smile. Consequently, it was what fascinated them most.

The women secretly envying her freedom, the men dreaming of possessing her for themselves.

How stunned they'd all be should they learn the truth. For, while everyone assumed she lived the life of her tempestuous heroines, the kind of mystical love and sexual adventures she wrote about had eluded her. Oh, she'd had some affairs since the death of poor Robert. But she'd found that men were ultimately intimidated by her, made tentative and clumsy by the conviction that they couldn't possibly live up to her standards. The joke was they hadn't breathed a word of their encounters with her because their masculine pride shuddered at the thought of anyone guessing the magnitude of their inadequacy. They'd sensed her disappointment and had simply slunk away. In the absence of boastful confession, they'd left the world to wonder: *did she, or didn't she?*

So she'd given up. Because, as people were fond of pointing out to her, men such as she wrote about didn't exist. So she'd concentrated her attentions on the hero of her books: the man she wrote about again and again in different guises with altered names; the faceless force who thrilled her even more than he did her readers. Bringing him to life with her pen so effortlessly that it sometimes seemed as if she were *remembering* rather than inventing him. Assuming the role of heroine in her imagination.

And yet it wasn't enough. Once she was finished with a book, the temporary contentment she'd found while writing vanished. She was once again seized by the wanderlust that had nagged her all her life, compelling her to go out and search the world for . . . what? Something grand, audacious, larger than life. Something that was hers alone. Something . . . unique. She didn't know what she was seeking. But without it, she felt restless, miserable, lost. Even the stories were beginning to elude her now, as if she'd exhausted all the fantasy she could conceive. So that this time she'd traveled across Northern Europe, down through the Near East, and around the Mediterranean in one seemingly endless journey, waiting for inspiration to strike. For another fantasy, another story to tell.

Except that sometimes her stories didn't feel like fantasy at all. And sometimes she knew, against all logic, that what she was really seeking was the hero of her books. Something kept whispering that he *did* exist. That all she had to do was find him.

But she'd searched for so long. She was thirty-five years old. Tired of seeking. Tired of asking herself the same unanswerable questions. *Was* he real? Or was she destined to live out her life in some demented daydream, endlessly re-creating a man who resided only in her mind? Living vicariously through her heroines, perpetuating her image as a glamorous fraud?

How much longer could this go on?

She felt a presence at her side. Turning, she saw a steward who'd paused as he was passing by with tray in hand. "Yer on the wrong side, mum," he informed her gently. "Gibraltar's on the other side. That's Morocco yer lookin' at."

Celia glanced back at the misted view. *How peculiar.* That she'd been drawn to this outlook when what she'd come to see was on the opposite side of the ship. Perhaps she was more muddled than she'd thought.

She rounded the bow and suddenly there it was. The mighty Rock of Gibraltar. Jutting from the water off the southern coast of Spain to tower high above like a grand, jagged sentry. Dominating the horizon, as if rising from out of nowhere like some enchanted realm of legend. Powerful. Erotic. Undeniably phallic. As singularly exciting and unique as the Taj Mahal or the pyramids of Giza. What must ancient mariners have thought when they suddenly came upon this magnificent site at the edge of the known world?

It stirred in her such emotion that she shivered with longing. Utterly mesmerized. Her heart pounding as if she'd just seen the face of her true love. Everything forgotten but this.

She didn't even know how long she stood transfixed, staring at the shape and solid form of it, feeling its raw, magnetic power. *Perhaps what I've been searching for is here . . .*

"I say," a male voice boomed behind her. "You *are* Lady Wybourne, are you not?"

She wheeled around, feeling jarred, as if she'd just been ripped from the clutches of some deep, enduring trance. Struggling to adjust to the abrupt shift in mood, she realized two of the tourists—a man and woman—had followed her.

"We'd heard you were on board," the man continued, oblivious to her consternation. Barely taller than the woman beside him, he had a round, good-natured face that was sweating profusely, thinning hair, and a paunch belly flirting with the rotund. "Caused quite a stir, I don't mind telling you. Never met a famous authoress before. I'm Homer Clifton. This is my wife . . ."

His voice droned on. It required all of her training to smile politely and shake the eagerly offered hands. *Was it possible that they actually stood there gawking at her without even bothering to glance at the majesty before them? It was beyond belief!*

Mrs. Clifton piped up then—too thin for beauty, but just attractive enough to feel she should garner more attention than she did. "I've read all your books. Except, of course, the one set in India. Beastly place, India. But I've read the rest."

"She has," Clifton concurred, bobbing his head. "Keeps 'em in a locked drawer where the servants won't find them. Brings 'em home in brown wrappers, wot?" He nudged Celia with his elbow. "'Course I don't read that sort of thing myself. But it keeps the missus happy."

"You're too kind," she murmured, covering her distaste with a gracious smile. Using the façade of a lady to disarm them and still their wagging tongues. Never letting them know that she'd understood the implied insult, even if *they* hadn't. The mask of aloofness distancing her from their ability to wound, keeping them from guessing the answer to the question they wanted most to ask.

That at heart she wasn't a lady at all, but a secret slut, desperate to be fucked.

"Are you here to write another book?"

"Perhaps." She glanced at the ghastly man who didn't read that sort of thing, himself. "Perhaps I shall write a book about *you.*"

"Me?" The man colored, giddily flattered, glancing at his wife to make certain she'd heard. "Good heavens, I should scarcely think . . ."

He didn't think. *That was the trouble. Otherwise he'd be standing quietly at the rail, breathing in the spirit of this amazing place, instead of pestering her.*

The ship lurched. "Gracious. We must be docking soon," Clifton said. "Charming to have met you. Simply charming. Hope we meet again." As they toddled off, she heard him hiss, "Lovely is wot she is. Did you see how she looked at me? With those smoldering eyes."

"*You?*" scoffed his wife. "As if the likes of her would look at *you!*"

"You heard her. She says she might write a book about me!"

He'd read that one, no doubt.

Celia turned back to the view of Gibraltar, soaring above her now. Instantly, she felt soothed, the encounter falling away like rain from its surface. There was something about it that continued to thrill her. As if this almighty rock understood her and was encouraging her, once again, to dream. As if it were calling out her name.

It seemed there would be no respite from her celebrity. The manager when she checked into the hotel: "It's an honour to have you here, my lady. We've been expecting you." Lowering his voice to add: "I just loved *The Pirate and the Princess*. It's my favorite. And that pirate . . . such a *brute!* It jolly well scorched my hands! But we'll just keep that between the two of us, shall we?" Winking conspiratorially before regaining his formal demeanor and ringing for the bellman. Everyone staring at her in the lobby because word of her visit had preceded her. A woman in the lift breaking the awkward silence by attempting to compliment her: "I read one of your books once. I can't remember which one." Her room filled with flowers, the telegram from her publisher tucked into a basket of exotic Spanish fruit: "When may we expect the manuscript? Your deadline, after all . . ." She crumpled it without reading the rest.

But the suite was nice, spacious and quiet with a separate sitting area leading to a balcony beyond, decorated in muted shades of creams and gold. A safe and pleasant haven from prying eyes. Where she could let down her hair and be herself.

She removed her jacket and tossed it to the bed. Unbuttoned the high, restrictive collar of her blouse. Tossed off her coquettish bonnet and pulled the pins from her hair. Fluffing it so it fell about her shoulders as she opened the terrace doors and stepped onto the balcony to a glorious view of the harbor. Azure sky, sapphire sea. A steep drop from where the hotel was perched atop a rocky ledge amidst palms and pines, the sheer face of the cliff rising behind her. Gibraltar. One of the legendary pillars of Hercules . . . guarding the entrance to the Mediterranean . . . crossroads of Europe and North Africa. An enclave prototypically British, yet gleaming in the brilliant Iberian sun. She absolutely loved it.

She stretched her arms above her head, feeling the stiffness of travel ease. Put her elbows to the balustrade and leaned over to peer down onto the terraced garden below.

And saw him standing there.

She recognized him with a shock. She'd seen him months ago among the ruins of old Babylon—a man with striking salt-and-pepper hair, gazing at her intimately. He'd seemed vaguely familiar. She'd wondered if he was an acquaintance from her travels, but had put it out of her mind when he disappeared into the crowd. Until she spotted him weeks later at the Forum in Rome. And yet again a fortnight ago on La Rambla in Barcelona. Each time it was clear that he'd been watching her in that oddly personal way until she turned and looked at him.

But since he always left immediately, never bothering her, she'd dismissed it as coincidence.

This time it was no coincidence. This time he was standing below her balcony, looking up at her as if he'd been waiting for her to appear. Taking in her disheveled hair and loosened clothing with a slow burning gaze and the hint of an amused smile. As if he knew everything she was thinking. As if he saw through the guise she showed the world. As if saying with his eyes *I know who you really are. And you're mine.*

Her initial impression, as she perused him with a writer's eye, was of a man of contrasts. Tall, but not imposingly so. Handsome, but unconventional. He didn't look like any of the men she'd known, yet once again he seemed familiar. Although she sensed he was a few years older than she, he bore an ageless quality, as if he defied the march of time. He wore his silvered hair longer than was strictly fashionable, exhibiting an individual disposition that appealed at once to the rebel in her. Utterly masculine, but elegantly so—his dashing sophistication infinitely more appealing than blustering machismo. While his demeanor was casual, one hand in the pocket of his trousers, it struck her as deceptive. She detected a faintly theatrical flair to his stance, as if leashing his true power like a sideshow mesmerist, in the form of mirrors and smoke. A man who, if he chose, could hold an audience in the palm of his hand.

But it was his eyes that riveted her. Piercing eyes, so dark they appeared black from where she stood. Proprietary . . . amatory. Boring into her with the unflinching stare of a man who'd come to claim what was his. As if he had the right. An unfathomable power emanating from their depths. Hypnotic . . . mysterious . . . dangerous?

Sorcerer's eyes.

Willing her to do his bidding. To obey his every command.

And as he held her gaze captive, she felt herself begin to succumb. Lulled as if he dangled a swaying pendulum from his hand. Deliciously drowsy, losing all sense of place and time, yet incongruously more aware than she'd ever been. Of her breath deepening until it began to come in helpless little pants. Of her lips parting . . . moist . . . trembling . . . Of her pulse pounding in her head, her blood rushing through her veins, heating like wine simmering on a flame. Of her juices flowing to some timeless rhythm until she felt them spill over in the fulsome wet heat between her thighs. Conscious of a hunger that swept everything away—all thought and judgment, all caution and shame.

She closed her eyes. Her breasts were throbbing, the nipples hard little points pulsing beneath the crispness of her blouse. She was seized by an impulse to cup them in her hands. To let him see her playing with them as he watched with those devil's eyes.

Where was this coming from?

It shocked her so much—*she who thought she was unshockable*—that she jerked back abruptly, breaking the pull of his unholy force with every ounce of strength at her command. Lurching away, out of his sight. To retreat into her room and lean back against the wall, breathing hard. Her body alive. Her cunt so juicy that she rucked up her skirts and thrust her hand inside. Feeling the proof of stark desire. Her steaming cleft leaping at the contact of soft fingers. So hot, so ravenously starved that, as her other hand came up to squeeze her bound breast, she exploded in a shattering climax, throwing back her head and gasping aloud.

It took some time for her to come back to the room in which she stood. Her limbs felt weak. Shivering violently, although it wasn't cold. She dropped her skirts, her hand still damp with the juices of her lust. Taking in deep breaths to try and calm her battered spirit.

What had just happened?

Slowly, she gained control over her quivering limbs. Bit by bit, her breath returned to normal. And yet the hammering of her heart refused to slow. Because all the while she knew she had to go back to that balcony and look again. Force herself to gaze upon him—this stranger who'd done this to her. Somehow convince herself that . . . what? That it hadn't been real? That a man she didn't even know hadn't really exerted this power over her? That he hadn't willed her to orgasm like a shameless whore? Because that was the only explanation.

She took a step. And then another. Holding her breath. Her body rigid with dread. Fearful of what she might find, yet irresistibly lured. What would she see in his eyes? Would he guess what had happened?

One more measured step. Until at last she reached the rail and looked down at the terrace below.

To find him gone. As if he'd never been.

Chapter Two

She was soundly shaken. Had she imagined what had happened? Had this man—*this stranger*—really done that to her? Or had she done it to herself? Had the depths of her loneliness and longing played tricks with her mind? Her body? Was she going insane?

There'd been something so . . . mysterious about it all. Like nothing she'd ever experienced. Certainly she'd never felt this level of arousal, so fast, so . . . *consuming*. Driving away the world so that only he existed. It was as if he'd exerted some hellish persuasion over her. *Had she been bewitched?* She recalled something hard and ruthless in his gaze. As if he'd willed her with an evil eye to yield herself to him.

She unpacked slowly, allowing the mundane activity to anchor her. Trying, all the while, to make sense of it all. In her research, she'd come across stories of legendary lotharios throughout history. Some of them seemingly ordinary men, but with such innate animal magnetism that they could throw it over a woman like a net and bend her to their will. She'd written books about such men. Masterful lovers who, with a blazing look, could turn her heroines into lustful slaves. The critics had scoffed. Unrealistic—pure fantasy—stuff and nonsense. Not like real life at all. Even she was beginning to wonder if she'd gone too far.

But *this!* This made every scene she'd ever written pale. Because it was real. And it had happened to her!

Not only had it happened. It had been . . . *thrilling!*

Who *was* this man? What was this power he had over her? And why was he following her? For she was certain now that he was. He wanted something. But what could it possibly be?

She went downstairs to ask about him. The manager, the bellman, the barkeeper—none of the staff could remember ever having seen him. So he wasn't staying in the hotel. She ventured out into the charming British town at the base of the rock and glanced in the shops and cafes. Over the next two days she made a round of the tourist spots along the flats: the convent, the city center, the old parson's lodge. Nothing. No sign of him. As if he'd vanished without a trace.

Or never existed.

Had he really been there? Had she really seen him in those other stops along her journey?

By the end of the second day she began to relax. If he *was* real, and not a figment of her writer's imagination, the Crown Colony of Gibraltar was too small for him to hide for long— just two and a half square miles, most of it towering rock, craggy and inaccessible. If she hadn't found him yet, chances were he was gone. After all, she'd never spotted him twice in one place.

She let it go. Because Gibraltar continued to call to her like a siren's song. Everywhere she went, she found her gaze drawn to the upper rock—gently sloping and richly verdant on the western face, dropping in a sheer limestone cliff to the east. Below she felt restive, impatient, barely noticing the town around her. She didn't want to be there. She wanted to climb to the top of that beckoning cliff, to look out across the Straits toward Morocco. The call was so strong that, with some inexplicable instinct, she felt she'd know the way.

She rented a horse from the hotel livery. Riding sidesaddle, she set out alone into the blazing Mediterranean sunshine, picking her way upward, always upward, past the old fortified walls, the military barracks, winding her way along narrow paths as she left the community behind. Higher and higher, pausing now and again to savor the stunning views and dizzying heights. Rugged splendor everywhere she looked.

It was like a dream. As if she'd tread these paths before. She remembered then that she'd dreamt of a magnificent rock as a child. Was it Gibraltar? Yet how could she have dreamt of it, when she'd never been here before?

And if she'd seen this rock of ages in her dreams . . . had she dreamt of *him* as well? Was that why he'd seemed agonizingly familiar?

Had she been dreaming the other day when she'd seen him standing in the garden below her balcony?

She paused at the old Moorish castle, now abandoned, and felt that she'd seen it before. Smiled at the brash, tailless Gibraltar monkeys who roamed the countryside as if they owned it. Made her way to the entrance of the tunnels that crisscrossed within the womb of the rock. Dismounted and went inside like a sleepwalker. Moving through the dimly lighted tunnels with the ease of one who'd explored them before.

Then she rounded a turn and came abruptly upon a group of tourists, listening to a guide.

"The hillside above you is honeycombed with tunnels, built by His Majesty's engineers during the Great Siege of 1779— the greatest defense system ever conceived. Directly below you, at the base of the rock, you'll see a cemetery. It's where most of the British citizens of Gibraltar have been buried for the past two hundred years. We'll be stopping there after we see St. Michael's cave."

Celia spotted the Cliftons then with the group from the ship. She ducked into one of the recessed outlooks, hiding herself, waiting for them to pass, not wanting her dreamy mood spoiled by conversation. When the group had trudged past, and she was once again alone, she went to the grilled window and looked down. Far below, she saw the cemetery the guide had pointed out. And felt a peculiar flutter inside.

She'd often perused graveyards looking for interesting inscriptions or names to spark ideas for books. But this one seemed to have a particular lure. As if it were no accident that she'd arrived here in time for the guide to point it out. As if there were something waiting for her there. It wasn't unusual. Often, along her travels, she'd found that she was called to the very things that would ignite her imagination. She'd learned to trust that intuition.

If she hurried she could reach it in plenty of time to rummage through it before Clifton and his gaggle of star-struck tourists arrived.

It was empty. Ghostly despite the hotly beating sun. Tying the horse, she wandered through the hodgepodge of graves, idly reading headstones in an attempt to discern what had enticed her here, finding nothing of particular interest.

She was beginning to feel that she'd been mistaken when she turned a corner and saw him. *Him!* Standing at the far end of the park, stock-still, staring down at a grave. His hair gleaming like silver in the sun. Sorrow permeating the air around him.

She was so stunned to see him there, all alone in the spectral stillness, that she stayed rooted where she was. He didn't move. Just stood engrossed by the tombstone before him as if mourning some deep loss. She watched him, breath held, her heart pounding.

He hadn't been a dream after all.

Finally she found the strength—the courage—to move. Walking toward him slowly, through the maze of vaults and crypts. Losing sight of him occasionally as she rounded some portentous monument to the forgotten dead. Passing through a group of bushes to come out the other side.

To find him gone again.

She stopped in her tracks. Where was he? It unsettled her,

this ability he had to seemingly disappear. She knew now that he was real. And she knew she had to find him.

Spurred on by an urgency she didn't understand, she began to walk quickly, up one path and down another, searching with mounting panic, past statuary and tombstones, seeking out places where he might hide. Increasing her pace, faster . . . faster . . . desperate lest he get away. Finding nothing . . . *nothing* all around her but empty lawn and looming shrines. Rounding a statue at a run, nearly colliding with him.

She reared to a halt, standing before him, breathing hard, her lungs on fire, her corset cutting into her ribs. Conspicuously aware of her lack of dignity at having chased him down like some unseemly hooligan. He regarded her intently but with no trace of surprise at finding her here. His eyes burning into her.

"Who are you?" she breathed, her voice sounding strained and whispery to her ears.

He gave a small, worldly smile. "You know who I am," he said simply. His voice, in a cultured English accent, as hypnotic as his eyes.

"How could I know you?" she cried. "I haven't the faintest idea who you are."

"Yes, you have," he told her in that same irritatingly steady tone. "You've known me in many forms. In many different lifetimes."

It was the last thing she'd expected him to say. She'd envisioned . . . what? Evasion certainly. But never this outlandish statement, presented as matter-of-factly as if he were imparting the time of day. "I . . . beg your pardon?" she stammered.

He was studying her face intently, as if looking for something. "I believe you and I are soul mates. That we've come together in different places, in numerous lifetimes. That we've been lovers in a number of different guises through the ages, most of which have ended tragically. I believe that you've intuitively caught glimpses of this past. That in fact, the books you've written have been shadows of the lives we've shared."

She took a step back. "You must be daft!"

"Am I?" He peered at her with his sorcerer's eyes and she felt a shiver tingle up her spine. "Don't I seem familiar to you? Even though we've never met?"

She was so befuddled, she couldn't bring herself to speak.

"Haven't you often felt as if your books were writing themselves in some inexplicable way? That they were more like half-remembered experiences than made-up fantasies? Or as if you'd lived them in a dream?"

The color drained from her face. *How could he possibly know this?*

He took a step closer and cupped her chin with his hand. "Haven't you," he ground out ruthlessly, "suspected in your heart-of-hearts that the hero of your books really exists?"

She gasped. The pressure of his hand scorched her, sending treacherous spirals of longing shooting through her loins. In her mind's eye she saw him pulling her to him and crushing her lips in a blinding kiss.

She wrenched away. Her breath coming in scalding gasps. Battling for sanity. Not certain who was more unbalanced: he or she.

"I want you to stop following me."

He shrugged as if her wishes were of no importance. "I can't do that. I've followed you with a purpose."

"I don't care what you think your purpose is. I demand that you stop."

"Your place is not to make demands, but to obey."

She gulped. "Obey . . . ? *You?*"

"Me, Celia. As you always have."

She felt once again as if she were drowning. Felt the shocking urge to surrender to the dominance in his tone. Madness, surely. "I've had admirers approach me in outrageous ways before, but none more preposterous than this."

He crooked a smile. "I *am* an admirer. But not in the way you think."

"And my . . . soul mate."

"Yes."

"My tragic lover . . ."

"Yes again."

"You're either lying or you're mad. You've read my books, obviously. For some deranged reason of your own you've concocted this travesty, thinking it might appeal to the dramatist in me. I'm afraid you've miscalculated."

He swept her with a biting glance. "I doubt it," he said and walked away.

She stood for a moment, reeling. Then turned and caught up to him with quick steps. Catching his arm to wheel him around to face her. Snatching back her hand as a shock passed between them, seeming to bind them together for one explosive instant. "I don't believe you," she declared, her chin rising a notch in regal defiance.

"Do you want me to convince you?"

"I want . . ." What *did* she want? She was so damnably confused. "I want you to leave me alone."

"Ah, but it was you who followed me here."

"I did no such thing!"

He perused her for a moment more. "Go to St. Michael's cave," he suggested. "See what happens."

With that, he left her, walking off with casual ease. This time she let him go, along the path toward the entrance where the group of tourists from the tunnels were just arriving.

Nothing seemed real. Stranger still, as she looked after him, she saw Homer Clifton leave the group and approach him. To speak to him excitedly, much the way he'd spoken to her on the ship. To scoot back to his wife and urge her forth to speak to the man, only to find that he was walking away. To stare after him just as she was doing now.

In a sort of daze, she made her way through the sun-drenched afternoon, this time seeking out her tiresome admirers.

"Why, Lady Wybourne," Clifton greeted, using a stained handkerchief to mop his brow. "This is, indeed, a privilege. The missus and I were just—"

She cut him off, too disconcerted to concern herself with manners. "Mr. Clifton, who was that man?"

Clifton scowled at her. "Him? I should think you'd know him, sure. Thought all celebrities knew each other, wot?"

"Who is he?" she repeated.

"Why he's Royce Tyler. The famous psychic. He's all the rage in London. Demmed clever, he is. Tells folks things no one else could possibly know. Spooky, like. I went to him myself. Told me beware of horses. The very next day, I was felled by a runaway team along the Strand. Broke my leg in two places. Oh, he's a wonder, he is. Though wot he's doing here I couldn't say."

Royce Tyler. She had, of course, heard of him. The "Medium of Mayfair." Society's clairvoyant darling. He was, in his own way, as notorious as she. Some said he was brilliant. Others claimed he was a colossal fraud.

A mesmerist! That would explain the power of his presence. And how she felt like she was in a trance every time she came near him.

Clifton chattered on, but she'd stopped listening. The things Royce Tyler had told her couldn't possibly be true. And yet . . . how had he known the secrets of her soul?

Of course you can't go. The voice of her mother, the conditioning of society, cautioning her. Yet, when had she ever listened to those warnings? Even as the tug-of-war in her mind raged on, she knew she had to go. As rash as it might seem.

She spent the afternoon preparing. Asked directions of the manager. Borrowed a lantern from the stable. Ate a light early supper in her room. Bathed in a steaming scented tub, feeling her body quicken as the silky water caressed all her tender female spots. Not certain what she would find, but compelled all the same.

Leaving on her rented horse before twilight, so she could find her way, the lantern tied to the saddle. Riding once again up into the lofty heights of the mountain, feeling the heat of the day recede with the cooling sea breeze. Apprehensive as she approached the entrance to the cave just as the sun was setting gloriously over the Spanish coast.

As she dismounted and tied her mare to an olive tree, native monkeys advanced, peering down at her from precipitous ledges, adding to the eerie feel of being up here all alone in the gathering dusk. The curious primates clustered around as she lit the lantern, scrambling to be the first to pick up the matchstick as it dropped from her quaking hand, thinking it a bit of food.

She left them, drawing near the entrance of the cave. A wooden barricade held a sign that proclaimed it closed for the day. Not much of a barrier, apparently trusting that the sign would keep people out. Ignoring it, she ducked beneath and went inside.

It was as dark as a tomb. She held the lantern high and gasped aloud. Mighty stalactites dripped from the ceiling in a staggering display, reflecting the light from the lantern in sparkling prisms. On and on through the vast cave, like grand icicles in some winter wonderland. The shapes varied, ancient. Nature's cathedral.

She ventured inside, her heels resounding on the stone floor in the serene silence. And as she did, she was overcome with a sense of deep, abiding love.

She placed the lantern on the ground and touched the limestone wall. Feeling her palm fuse into its embrace. Feeling that the splendid cave recognized her. Welcomed her. That it loved her as much as she loved it.

That it had been waiting for her.

St. Michael's cave? she thought. *Oh, no. My cave.*

She laid her cheek against the wall, feeling the cool moist succor. And then, as she'd somehow known would happen, she felt a hand on her back. Strong. Warm. Possessive. Claiming her as she had claimed this mystical grotto. She hadn't heard him come up behind, but the touch of his hand felt like . . .

Destiny come to call.

A thrill shot through her. She felt herself melt into him. Time stood still. As if it had never existed. She didn't know in that moment who she was, or when this was. Only that he was touching her again. *Again?* That all she wanted was to dissolve into him completely. She felt herself resurrected after having been dead inside for far too long. Needing nothing. *Wanting* nothing but the touch of his hand. Sublime. Leaving her breathless. Completing her.

And as she leaned back into him, it seemed as if bits and pieces of forgotten dreams flicked through her like flashes of lightning. Raw. Electric. Shattering her. The touch of him—so warm, so vibrant, so wonderfully illicit—flowing through her like the river of life. Amplifying the sense of heightened reality, all her senses screamingly alive. Nothing existing in all the world but this enchanted cave.

And him.

She felt him move closer, his hand still at her back, his mouth coming to rest against her ear. "Your name was Charlotte Lansdowne," he told her. His voice enthralling in the redolent hushed air. His breath seductively hot. "You were a beautiful, rebellious, intelligent young woman. You were born here, on Gibraltar, over a hundred years ago. Your father was an English colonel in the Royal Gibraltar Regiment. Your mother was Spanish. He was cold and unfeeling, she hot-blooded and quick-tempered. They fought continually, often about you. You were lonely, confused by the conflicts at home. To escape, you went out by yourself, exploring Gibraltar. You knew and loved every inch of it as no one ever has or will. This rock was more than your home, it was a living part of you. You were its child as you'd never really been the child of your parents. You didn't know that rocks and crystals have special energy, and that this, being the most spectacular rock in all of creation, would possess a mystique and vital force greater than any other. You just felt it as no one ever had before. Its power vibrated within you. It called to you and you answered that call by devoting yourself to it like a loving custodian. You explored its hidden tunnels and knew them all by heart. You discovered this cave."

"My cave," she whispered, dancing to his spell.

"Yes. This you loved more than anything else. It was your secret. Your treasure. The beating heart of the Rock. Where you came to be alone."

She could see it all in her mind's eye. "But I wasn't always alone. I brought someone else here."

"Yes. This is where the two of you would meet."

She took a shaky breath. "Who?"

"A Moroccan man. Handsome, exciting, forbidden. Ruthless. The two of you had a passionate affair."

"Meeting here secretly. I'd never brought anyone here before. But I brought him."

"Yes. You brought him."

She was breathing deeply now, caught in the web he was weaving. "What was your name?"

His hand contracted against her back, noting the change of pronoun. What was *your* name, not his. Then it moved and he was close behind her, both hands coming round to capture her breasts in his palms. A jolt of lust rocked her.

"Rashid Abdel Aziz," he said.

"*Rah-sheed,*" she repeated, sounding it out. Then quoted, "'A proud and noble name, from a proud and noble family.'" Hearing him say it to her, standing before her in all his arrogant glory, hands on his hips. Proud. Boastful. As if wanting her to know it wasn't just some Moroccan upstart she was addressing, but a prince in his own right.

Not certain if she were really seeing the vision, or if it was just her imagination contributing to his tale. Not even caring anymore.

His hands tightened on her breasts as his lips nuzzled her neck, causing her to quiver.

"You trusted him. Loved him. Fiercely. As you loved Gibraltar. With all the passion in you. But he wasn't a good man. He used you."

"How?"

He moved into her and she felt his erection, hard as flint, against the crack of her ass. "Used your body for his own selfish pleasure."

She dropped her head back and moaned. She was wet and wild. Thrilled to the bone by the picture he painted of this rugged, pitiless Arab who'd swept into her solitary life, bringing with him heart-pounding excitement and outlawed love.

"Used my body . . ." she repeated, prompting him, wanting more . . .

"Introducing you to sex like you'd never dreamt existed. Training you, teaching you, priming your body. Making it crave his touch. Until you were so addicted to what only he could give you that you'd do anything . . . for him . . ."

"Anything?" she croaked.

His hands moved from the soft, quivering mounds of her breasts. She felt their absence keenly. She wanted to grab hold of them and put them back, to feel the delicious force and pressure against her nipples. But he put them to her shoulders and turned her slowly instead. She was so besotted by his words that she swayed as she moved. Peering up at him as if through a haze. Seeing him, but also seeing Rashid—savage, untamable Rashid, desert warrior, dashing chieftain of scorching sands. *Her* Rashid.

"Anything," he told her in a voice like ground glass. "Until you were so deeply under his influence that you became his slave. Begging him for the honour of pleasing him. Following him willingly into a world of passionate abandonment and forbidden sex. And he—mastering you. Making you do things you'd never even imagined. All for him. For his pleasure."

"What things?" she panted.

"Things you're not ready to hear."

She mewled deep within her throat. "I am. I'm ready. Tell me." Feeling that she'd been waiting for this all her life.

He took her face in both hands and studied her with an accessing glare. "Not yet."

"Yes. Now. Show me."

She felt so drunk with lust that she could barely see his face swimming before her eyes. He tightened his hold, tipping her jaw and shaking her once until he filled her sights in sharp focus. Holding her gaze hostage with the black magic of his eyes. Then his mouth curved in a sardonic smile. "Beg me."

Pride pierced the fuzziness of her mind. She'd never begged for anything in her life. She wasn't about to start now. It was well and good for her heroines to plead and whine. But never she.

In the lantern's light he saw the willful glint in glazed green eyes. He gave a slow blink then dropped his hands from her face. "Very well."

Just like that. His sudden retreat was more surprising than his attack. What would her hero do, were she writing the scene? Impose his will until the heroine caved in. But never once had he just stepped back. This man had gone to considerable trouble to arouse her with his words, enflaming her senses as her own written words had ignited her readers. Yet here he was, perfectly willing to drop the game—if game it was—because she'd offered this tiny bit of resistance.

She felt bereft, her disappointment flooding through her to mingle with her desire. Would he walk away once more, leaving her like . . . *this?*

"What do you want?" she asked as he turned his back.

He paused, then faced her once again. Quietly. Calmly. As if he weren't standing before her with a ramrod poker in his pants.

"The question is, what do *you* want? What have you always wanted? Why do you write the kind of books you do, about those kind of men? Cruel. Possessive. Masterful. Why?"

"Why?" she repeated, trembling unbearably.

He stepped to her and once again took her face in his hands. "Because you want what you had before. What you've had again and again. What you've lost."

"What?"

"To be my slave."

Her knees buckled beneath her. He held her up with the grip of his hands.

"How was I your slave? Show me."

"Beg me."

Her lips parted but no words came. She was so flustered. She knew only one thing for certain: If he left her now, she'd die.

Don't leave. Don't walk away . . .

He lowered his head and brought his mouth to hers. Barely grazing it. Enough that she could feel the texture of his lips, nothing more. Moving back ever so slightly as she lunged forward, seeking his kiss. Not breaking the contact, but neither giving her what she sought.

"Beg me."

She whimpered again. Must she say it? Wasn't it enough that everything in her was crying out for him? When she was so fucking hot that she'd lay down now, this minute, on the cold stone floor of this grotto and spread her legs for him like a bitch in heat?

He had to know what he was doing to her.

"Don't make me," she pleaded.

He pulled away. She was so afraid he'd leave that she gave a strangled cry. And then, suddenly, he yanked her to him and claimed her mouth. Crushing her lips. Parting them with a thrusting tongue. Stealing her breath.

And she knew as he kissed her that she'd known this kiss before. The kiss she'd dreamt of, written about a hundred times and more. Longed for in sweat-soaked sheets through endless, lonesome nights. The kiss she'd given to her heroines, and never experienced herself. Hot. Consuming. Possessive. Branding her as his.

She was desolate with need. Wet and slick and starved beyond redemption. His mouth on hers like the fulfillment of everything she'd wanted and hoped for and sought to obtain. Aroused to the point of explosion. A hair trigger primed to go off at the slightest touch.

"Beg me," he commanded against her mouth, his breath one with hers.

His words in the cemetery came back to her.

Your place is not to demand, but to obey.

Obey . . . as you always have . . .

She lost the will to resist. He was too strong, his lure too primal to refuse. She sought his mouth again, but he moved away, denying her. And then she felt an odd stirring . . . as if someone residing inside her was rising to the surface . . . as if Charlotte was asserting her will, wanting this more than Celia wanted to deny it. It burst forth from her with a force as old as time, resounding with the full thrust and madness of her desire. Spilling from her lips on winded breath. "Show me, teach me." She who had intimidated other men. Her lips finding his—warm, firm, unbearable enticement. "I beg you. *Please!*"

She caught the brief flash of a smile before he kissed her again, rewarding her. His tongue in her mouth turning her to putty in his hands, to mold and shape as he willed. Beyond caring, beyond pride, beyond anything estimating rational thought. Lost . . . lost . . .

She was barely conscious of him taking her hand in his. Thrusting it against his erection. The rigid length and breadth and width of him against the soft material of his trousers. Confined like a serpent ready to strike.

"This," he rasped, jutting his piercing lance against her palm, "is what you're slave to. This dick. The pleasure of this dick. The worship of it. Do you understand?"

She nodded quickly. *Yes, yes . . .*

"Get on your knees."

Her gaze flashed to his. He wasn't jesting. The hard, trenchant gleam told her so. She sank slowly to her knees. Watched as he yanked off his jacket and let it drop to the floor. As his shirt followed in its wake. Baring a torso that made her mouth water. Lean, muscular, manly. Following the path of his hair with her eyes, from his chest as it veered ever downward, like an arrow pointing inexorably to that hidden treasure she'd briefly held in her hand. His . . . dick. The nasty word—a man's word, virile and succinct—making her juices flow.

Watching his fingers as they slowly—too slowly—unbuttoned his pants. Licking her lips in anticipation. Hurry . . . hurry . . . *hurry* . . .

Sighing as she saw him for the first time. Dynamically

veined, perfectly formed, huge and hard. More beautiful than she could have imagined. Tool of cruel seduction. Symbol of her submission.

She had the urge to reach beneath her skirt and stroke herself. "Yes," he said, startling her, reading her thoughts. "Play with yourself. Let me see."

How had he known? Then she remembered. He was psychic.

Was he?

Could he read her mind? Did he know—did he have any *idea*—what he was doing to her?

Did it matter now? She'd gone too far.

She tried to obey, but on her knees as she was, she couldn't disengage her skirt.

"Take off your clothes."

Watching her patiently with hot eyes as she did, stroking his erection. Nodding when she'd taken off her outer layers, but not her corset or stockings. Telling her silently it was enough for now.

She used her skirts as padding and once again knelt before him. Spreading her knees wide so she could reach between. Stunned by how wet she was, how glazed and sticky. How greedy . . .

"Lean back," he told her. "Show me your cunt."

She did so, anchoring herself on one hand, spreading her knees wider still. Arching up for him to watch as her fingers played in the downy folds. Finding her clit and moaning shamelessly. Closing her eyes. Giving herself over to each feverish sensation. Feeling disgracefully opened and exposed before him.

Loving it.

She felt a stirring of the air around her. And then he was before her, rubbing his dick against her mouth. Velvety soft, solid as steel. She could smell his sex.

"Take me in your mouth."

He didn't wait, but pushed himself between her lips. Her moist mouth closing in on him, relishing the feel of him swelling and straining against her tongue. Sucking the head, licking the tip, wanting more of him . . . more . . . all of him . . . everything he had to give . . . more, more, more . . .

"I'm going to teach you something you learned from Rashid."

She froze. Suddenly frightened. Rashid! Who'd heartlessly used her . . . used her woman's body to satisfy his own selfish needs . . . who'd made her his slave . . . who'd taught her things she wasn't ready to know . . .

What could this be? Could she handle it?

She felt her throat close. Convulsing on him in a seizure of fear. Her heart slamming in her breast. It had gone *too* far. *What am I doing?*

He sensed her panic and stilled. She felt his hands in her hair, gentling her. Stroking her firmly but with such tenderness that it surprised her. Holding himself motionless within her mouth. Not pushing. Making no demands. Just telling her with his soothing hands that everything was all right. That she was safe.

His gentleness touched her so deeply that she believed him. Somewhere along the way she felt herself relax. Felt her mouth thaw to him once again. Opening. Inviting. *Trusting him.* This man who for all she knew could be a—

"Just feel Rashid," he coaxed. "Open your mind. Let him come to you. Speak to you. Feel what he wants. If you let me, I can channel his energy into you, so you can relive it."

She slid back, letting his dick fall into his palm. "Is that what you did that first day? In my suite? Channel your . . . energy into me?"

It was Royce's turn to be surprised. He hadn't expected that level of perception. He watched her for a moment, weighing his choices. She looked so beautiful kneeling before him with a mixture of trepidation and a longing to trust him in the dazzling depths of her eyes. *Achingly beautiful.* He felt a rush of tenderness that caused him to stroke her lips with the tip of his finger. Before he realized what he was doing.

Stop it, he warned himself. She was more desirable than

he'd bargained for. *She was sensational.* He couldn't afford to become distracted. Couldn't forget why he was here. Despite the fact that all he wanted at the moment was to bury himself inside her. He'd come with a purpose. He *had* to succeed. Everything was riding on his ability to pull this off.

"Is that what you did?" she prompted. Looking, for all her sophisticated splendor, almost childlike in her desire to believe. Vulnerable as she admitted something she hadn't intended: that she'd already succumbed to him once before.

"Yes," he told her cryptically. "That's exactly what I did."

She lowered her lashes, concealing her thoughts from him for an instant, then looked up at him again. Her eyes like richest emeralds in the lantern's flickering light. A seductive warmth replacing the dread. "I loved it," she purred, her voice husky with renewed arousal. "Do it again."

Sweet Jesus. He hadn't counted on this.

He used the pads of his fingers to close her eyes. Cutting himself off from the irresistible temptation within their depths. As long as he didn't look into her eyes, he was safe. He could regain his supremacy.

He held his hand fastened on her like a blindfold. Protecting himself.

The enforced blindness electrified her. She opened her mouth, willing once again. Trusting him . . . why? Because Charlotte had trusted Rashid? Or because she loved the helplessness? The release from responsibility. From the need to decide, to think, to understand. All she had to do was feel.

And obey . . .

Then he was in her mouth once more. Harder than before. Just holding himself there, allowing her to reacquaint herself with the feel of him.

And as she did, an odd thing happened. The mood in the cave shifted. The lantern's light seemed to flare suddenly, then recede. It seemed to her that the cock in her mouth altered imperceptibly, changing in shape and feel. It seemed to her—incredibly—that she recognized the texture of it as something much beloved. Something dearly missed.

It was her last conscious thought. Suddenly he was moving in her mouth. Gently—so gently that she scarcely noticed it— he began to slide down her throat. She gagged a little once and drew away. But something took her over. She'd never done this before, yet all at once she was holding him deep within her throat. Easily. No strain, no effort. Loving the feel of him filling her absolutely. As if her throat had been fashioned for his shape. As if that was where he belonged.

It happened so seamlessly. There wasn't a moment when she didn't know how, then did. It was as if she'd been born knowing. Holding him lodged in her throat, then pulling back, slowly . . . slowly . . . feeling him swell and pulse in her mouth, sucking the head, the ramrod stiff shaft, back and forth, lost in the rhythm, then lunging forth and taking him deeply into her throat once again. Knowing by some unfathomable instinct that it was more exciting for him if she varied the strokes. Not taking him completely all the time, but every once in a while, making him wait, anticipate it. When would it come? Now? Or now? *Oh, now!*

"That's it. Take it deep. Take it . . ."

Even his voice seemed changed. She felt him burgeon, the whole great length and width of him, too large now for her mouth. Felt him pull free, his hand grabbing her hair and jerking back her head, her mouth opening, tongue out, famished now, ravenous, starved for his cum . . . crying out her joy, discharging beneath her own fingers in wave after wave of undeniable bone-melting passion as he shot a hot load into her mouth.

Delicious. The stuff of gods, source of all his mastery. Hers, because she'd driven him past the point of discipline. She reached for him, still hard, still pulsing with lust and life. To rub his creamy staff reverently along her face, her cheeks, her chin, worshiping him, luxuriating in his essence. Kissing its source. Feeling such a rush of love fill her that she felt on the verge of tears.

"I love this dick," she whispered, taking a long, slow swipe with her tongue. Feeling the empowerment of her submission.

Her true womanliness, as she'd never known it before. Her ability to cast a spell on *him* with her desire.

He stilled for just an instant. Feeling her ascendance now. Fighting for control. He should leave her, the first step of his task complete. But she looked so ravishing with his cum on her face. The urge to fuck her was stronger than his resolve. He hadn't counted on her being this willing . . . this enticing . . . this intoxicating . . .

With a curse, he made the decision. He'd do it. But his way, not hers. Not with tender words. Not with loverlike concern. His way.

He shoved her back into the folds of her clothes. Spread her legs and entered her with a ramming thrust. Heard her breath catch as he filled her to the hilt. *Christ! It was like coming home . . .*

Moving roughly, pounding her senseless. Feeling her open to him, loving it, her moans echoing off the cavern walls. He clamped a hand down over her mouth. Silencing her as if to silence the need he felt inside. So deep a need that it left him feeling stunned.

Stunned? It terrified him.

She wrenched her mouth from his hand and lifted her lips toward his. But he denied her the kiss she sought. Exerting his will. *My way . . . not yours . . .*

Slamming into her. Trying not to notice how right it felt. Fighting with himself not to give in. Leaning close with his mouth at her ear to dispel any romantic notions she might have.

"I told you Rashid made you his slave. But that's not all he did."

"What?" she cried. "What did he do?"

He thrust into her some more—*good God, had anything felt so right?*—and then he spoke, rasping in her ear. "I trained you to give carnal pleasure to men. All the forbidden things a girl like you—so fair, so unsullied—would never know. *For me.*"

Saying it to test her. To see what she could take. Intending to say "he." Never noticing that he'd said "I."

Never dreaming that she'd gasp in ecstasy. That she'd arch beneath him with unabashed exhilaration. That she'd explode with his hot hard dick fucking her cunt, begging now, unashamedly.

"Please . . . I beg you . . . kiss me . . . please . . ."

A last brief hesitation. Then, losing the battle, he drove forth and gave her what she wanted. Crushed her mouth with his and rammed himself home.

Chapter Three

The next morning Celia sat in the hotel dining room in a daze. Nibbling on scones she didn't taste. Sipping cold tea without noticing that it had chilled. Feeling her heart race as she thought of him.

She realized with a start that she was happy this morning. Deliriously so. Exultant yet . . . serene. She couldn't remember any other time in her life when she'd truly felt at peace. The sense of unease and discontent had vanished. Today she felt astonishingly as if all was right with the world. All because of him.

Royce.

She still couldn't sort it out in her mind. The intensity of it all. No introductions, no idle chitchat. Just "I'm your soul mate." No courtship or tender kisses leading up to the inevitable tussle in bed. Just "Get on your knees and beg." Like a scene from one of her books.

It was too incredible to believe. That the books she'd written had been reflections of lifetimes she'd shared with him. And yet . . . was that why, while writing them, she'd felt that sense of momentary peace? Because she'd connected with some aspect of her true self? Because she'd connected with him?

Last night, she'd felt that all he'd told her was true. She'd looked up at the cave's dazzling ceiling and felt that she'd seen it just so before. On her back, with her legs spread. Looking past him as he moved within her, absorbing its eternal beauty as they'd merged and become one. A strangely mystical union, the sort she'd written about repeatedly. One body, one mind, one soul. It had even seemed to her that she remembered Rashid. Remembered having loved him, trusted him. Being *thrilled* by him.

I trained you to give carnal pleasure to men . . .

She shivered, forgetting her breakfast altogether.

A moment later, she was startled from her reverie when someone took the seat next to hers. Mrs. Clifton scraped the chair closer with a sense of urgency and whispered, "I haven't much time. Homer's quibbling about the bill as usual, bloody cheap bugger that he is. I don't want him knowing what we're talking about, so I have to be quick."

"My dear Mrs. Clifton—"

"Call me Maggie, my lady. I told you I'm an admirer, otherwise I wouldn't bother. But because I am, I've come to warn you."

The woman seemed genuinely frazzled. She kept casting glances back at her husband who stood by the dining room entrance arguing with the maitre d'. Her thin face was flushed and puffy, her eyes bearing dark circles as if she hadn't slept the night before.

"Warn me? About what, pray tell?"

"About him. I saw you with him yesterday." When Celia gave a blank look, Mrs. Clifton hissed, *"Him.* Royce Tyler. Fraud that he is. His own father, the Earl of Cunningham, disowned him, you know. Psychic? He's the devil himself! He's a . . ." She struggled for a moment, then peered quizzically at Celia. "What did you call Remington in *The Duke's Revenge?* That creature that changes his colors?"

"A chameleon."

"That's it to a turn! He's a bloody chameleon. He charms women so they don't know which end is up. Makes each one believe he's just what she's been waiting for all her life. Why, he did it to Homer's own dear sister. She fell for his good looks and smooth tongue, and he conned her proper then tossed her aside like yesterday's rubbish. But did Homer see through him? Not on your life. And why? Because he's an idiot, is what Homer is. But I saw Mr. Royce Tyler for what he really is. He's duped half of Mayfair society, and others like my poor sister-in-law besides. And if you don't watch out, he'll con you, too." She darted a glance across the room to see her husband finishing up his transaction. "I have to scoot. But mark my words, my lady. He's a dangerous man. You stay away from him, if you know what's good for you."

She rushed off, leaving Celia feeling as if the woman had just tossed a glass of icy water in her face.

A fraud . . .

She'd heard such conjecture about him before, of course. There would always be those who believed in the supernatural and those who didn't. Celia had seen enough in her travels through the mysterious East to entertain the possibility that such inexplicable forces did exist. She certainly wasn't going to take the word of a ridiculous woman who hadn't read *The Raja's Prize* because she thought India a "beastly place." Still, Mrs. Clifton's warning had touched off Celia's own latent doubts about the man himself. Now she wondered: How much of what had happened last night was an authentic connection to a past life, and how much of it was his particular skill at casting a hypnotic spell?

But if he *was* conning her, what could be his motivation? Sex? Money? What did he want from her?

He's a dangerous man . . .

Mrs. Clifton's vehemence left no doubt that she believed every word she'd said. Yet . . . wasn't it the fact that Royce *was* dangerous that thrilled Celia so? Wasn't it the edge of intrigue that she'd found wanting in every other man? Wasn't that what made him so like the heroes of her books?

The question, then, wasn't so much if Royce was dangerous. But was he a danger to *her?*

If you don't watch out he'll con you, too . . .

Too . . .

She felt a flash of fury. If that's what he was up to, by God, she'd show him she wasn't just another hapless female waiting to be duped!

She paused in front of the door to room 325, collecting herself. It had taken her most of the afternoon to find him here, at the oldest hotel in Gibraltar. Small and far removed from the town, it wasn't on the usual list of tourist accommodations. They catered to a discriminating clientele, mostly wealthy Moroccans. A Berber jewel fashioned around a charming tiled inner courtyard. She'd only found it because the manager of the final hotel on her list had suggested it as a last resort.

She rapped on the door. It was a moment before she heard the lock turn. Then the door opened slowly, and he was standing before her. Casually dressed in white trousers and shirt with sleeves rolled to just below the elbows. His exposed wrists and forearms—sleekly muscled, strong and hairy— looking so sexy that she almost faltered and forgot the vehemence that had fueled her throughout the afternoon.

"Mrs. Clifton says you're a fraud."

She hadn't intended to begin so abruptly. But then, nothing about their encounters had ever been customary or genteel.

His bold mouth formed a derisive smirk, as if running through his mind some private joke. "I suppose she would."

"She said you're a chameleon who becomes for every woman what she wants most. But only for a time. Only long enough to swindle her."

He raised a brow. "And how do I do that?"

"She said, for instance, that you charmed her unsuspecting sister-in-law into falling in love with you, then dropped her flat when you'd had your fill of her. She didn't specify whether it was the woman's dowry or her virtue that you took as payment."

She caught a flash of irritation before he lowered his gaze. "Poor Maggie."

Not the denial she'd expected. She certainly hadn't thought he'd sound so sympathetic and sincere. It threw her off. But at the same time, it irritated her that he knew the woman's first name. Her decidedly female reaction surprised her so that she had to wonder: Was she angry because Maggie Clifton had accused him of being a charlatan? Or because she'd implied that Royce wielded his power over *all* women, and not just Celia? *Was she jealous? Was that why she'd come barging in here? Because he'd made her feel that he belonged to her alone? And because that silly cow had implied that other women felt it, too?*

He gestured for her to enter. She did, cautiously, stepping into a room fit for a caliph. The walls and floors elaborately tiled in varying shades of deep and restful blue, scattered with thick-piled rugs in hues of indigo, black, and gold. The sofa and chairs of the lower sitting room amassed with luxurious pillows in sapphire silks. The tables inlaid thuya wood or mirrored mosaics. A large bed raised high on a pedestal below a Moorish arch, draped all around in diaphanous royal blue. Similarly arched glass doors thrown open to the breathtaking vista of sea and sky and Morocco spreading out in the distance beyond a cerulean tiled balcony that seemed an extension of the view itself. The ceiling fan whirring soothingly above, stirring the warm air, enticingly fluttering the transparent bed curtains as if offering invitation.

As if stepping into a blue heaven. The last sort of environment in which she'd expected to find him. And yet he seemed strangely at home in these otherworldly surroundings.

She heard his voice behind her. "This is the room where Rashid used to stay, when he came to Gibraltar."

She spun around, glaring at him with blistering eyes. As furious now with her own foolishness as she was with him. "I've just told you I have reason to believe you're a fraud, and you tell me *that?*"

He shrugged. "It doesn't matter to me what people think. What matters is you. And me."

"She said you'd been disowned by your father."

A flicker of something unfathomable stirred in his obsidian eyes. "Disowned *and* disinherited. Does it matter? You, too, had a strained relation with a family member. Does that make you any less credible?"

"What do you know about that?"

"You had a domineering mother who sought to crush your rebellious spirit with harsh discipline and constant criticism. An ineffectual father you wished would protect you from her rages, but who didn't."

"How do you know this?"

He gave a self-deprecating smile. "I'm psychic, remember?"

"Perhaps. Or perhaps you've heard some gossip along the way."

"Are you in the habit of telling people your business?"

Celia flushed. She'd confided these things to no one but her husband years ago. Keeping her friendships light and casual. Revealing little of herself. Still, things got around . . .

He moved into the room and went to a mosaic sideboard to pour some amber liquid into two snifters. One he held out to her. "Drink it. It will help you relax." When she eyed him suspiciously, he drank from the other glass to show her it was safe. He continued speaking as she tentatively took a sip, feeling the brandy burn through her.

"My father didn't know how to handle a son who saw things people weren't supposed to see. He tried to beat it out of me. When that failed, he did the only thing a self-respecting earl *could* do. To save himself from humiliation, he disowned what he couldn't understand. That's my story. But we were talking about you."

"Were we?" She liked the warmth the brandy brought and took another sip.

"You married young to escape an untenable home life. But your husband was just the catalyst to set you on the path to your destiny. He gave you the means for the freedom you needed. His money allowed you to travel the world looking for stories to tell. Your status as his wife dispelled the necessity for a chaperone, and kept you free from gossip. When he'd fulfilled his purpose, he conveniently died. And you began to write. But not just any books. Books about passion. And pain."

"Stop it!" she cried, because he'd described it all with frightening precision. "What do you want from me? Why *me?*"

Royce considered her, taking a sip from his own brandy. She expected him to dodge her questions with fancy words. But instead, he spoke simply, directly. As if he had nothing to hide.

"I was in a bookstore some months ago in London when I picked up one of your books. I can't tell you why I chose it, except to say I was compelled to. I began to glance through it and I knew I had to read it. Once I had, I read the rest of them. I recognized in your writing flashes of my own past lives. Nothing concrete, just bits and pieces. Enough to know that I had to know more. I inquired after you and found that you'd left the country. So I set out to follow you. Caught up with you in Sumeria. Again in Rome. And Spain. And each time I saw you, I glimpsed impressions of the two of us together in these places, in the past. Again, these flashes were indistinct. Just enough to realize that you'd chosen these very sites for a reason. That you were looking for something, too."

"Too?"

"It wasn't until I came here—to Gibraltar—that things really started coming together. I think it was here that we shared the most recent life, and the most intense. Since arriving here, I've been flooded with memories from several of the lives we've shared. Feeling them keenly. And I'm beginning to see that there's a pattern to these lives."

"What sort of pattern?"

"I don't think we've ever had what you'd call an ordinary experience together. I don't see us married with hearth and children. They were always highly dramatic, passionate affairs. I've come to see that we've been going through a cycle which has held us as karmic prisoners."

She squirmed irritably. "What does that mean?"

"It means that we've been repeating the same tragic pattern again and again. Differently each time, but the end result has been the same."

She drained the brandy from her glass, and set it aside. "You still haven't explained what you want from me."

"I want peace."

Her gaze flew to his. Utterly stunned.

"Because I, like you, have been doomed to a life of searching and unrest. Tormented. Unfulfilled. Finding no peace of mind, no matter where I look. In agony, without knowing why. Always searching . . . for something . . . but what? Not even knowing where to look. You've felt it, too. Haven't you?"

She continued to stare at him, too staggered to speak. He crossed the room in three great strides and took her shoulders in his hands. *"Haven't you?"*

"Yes," she cried, as if the word had been wrenched from her.

"What we've been searching for is each other. But for some reason, every time we find each other again, something awful happens. I haven't been aware of this before. But this time things are different. This time I was reincarnated as a psychic. And you were reborn as a highly intuitive author with glimpses of the past. So we both have the means to see what's been going on. I don't know how to change things. But together, maybe we can find a way."

"To break this pattern?"

"And end the torment each of us has felt."

She could see that torment now in his eyes. The same torment she'd always felt inside, without knowing why.

"Don't you see?" he rasped, tightening his grip. "I need to be set free."

Set free . . . without realizing it, that was what she'd wanted all her life.

"It has to be now," he insisted, shaking her. Intense. Frightening. "We might not have this chance again."

His desperation touched her profoundly. He appeared to

her, standing alone with his inner turmoil, like a vision of the heroes from her books. A man secretly afraid. Needing help. Needing *her*.

And she knew in that moment that she loved him. Against all reason. Despite the fact that she'd known him just a few short days. But then, she'd known him longer than that, hadn't she? She'd known him through the ages, through countless lifetimes. And she'd always loved him. Even before she'd known he existed. The tortured hero she'd written about repeatedly, driven by his own demons, driving her to ecstasy in his bed.

"When I'm with you, I want to trust you," she confessed.

"Then do." He leaned into her, resting his forehead against hers. "Please, Celia. Before it's too late."

"Too late for what? What's going to happen?"

"That's what we have to find out. And if we can, perhaps prevent it from happening."

It felt so good to have him close. So right. "How may I be of help?" she asked.

He was still and quiet for a long moment. Then he sighed and lifted his head. "By opening yourself to me. By reliving together what happened in our last lifetime. And seeing if it doesn't reveal the answer."

Despite the thrill she felt at this prospect, she was still afraid. "How do I know you haven't told me all this to get me into bed?"

It broke his despair. He straightened to his full height, his strong jaw tilted at a proud angle. She could swear in that moment that the spirit of Rashid stood before her. He flicked her with a heated gaze that caused her toes to curl. "Because I don't *have* to tell you all this to get you into bed." Supremely confident. The Master once again.

"You said you'd use me."

"I intend to use you. For my pleasure. But there's something you're forgetting. You love it as much as I. You always have."

Behind him, the sun was setting, painting the sky in extravagant hues.

"So our way of connecting," she ventured, "has always been . . . carnal."

"Always."

"You've taught me . . . mastered me . . . many times before. But there has to have been more to it than that."

"Why?"

"Because . . . it's not what people do."

"Forget what others do. You've never wanted the sort of life others have. Forget everything your mother told you about what's right and wrong. Forget what nice girls do or don't. When you come to me, the rules change. This isn't about being nice or ladylike or like other people."

"What's it about?"

"Surrender."

"And the rules are . . . ?"

"Obedience."

She was trembling, alarmed and excited all at once. "I'm not a woman who's naturally given to obedience."

"Ah, but that's the point. You don't obey everyone. That would be ludicrous. You only obey me. And only in my bed."

Oh God.

She turned her back so he couldn't read the vulnerability in her eyes.

"A strong woman who is willingly submissive to a sexual master is the most delicious thing imaginable. When a woman makes the *choice* to be creative in bed, no matter that she's a lady elsewhere."

He ran a finger down the length of her spine, turning her to liquid.

"I know the secrets of your soul, Celia. I know you play the lady, but in your heart you're disposed to be my slave. It's what I've always known about you. It's what I've given you— the gift of being your true self with me. That's why you can't resist me. That's the true power I hold over you. That I know about you what others would judge as the worst—and I love it."

Oh God . . . oh God . . .

He took her shoulders in his hands. "It's what you want, too. It's why the only time you've ever forgotten your unrest is when you've been with me."

Oh . . . dear . . . God . . .

It was happening again. That feeling of being drawn into him. His words unleashing such a hunger in her soul that she was trembling with it. His voice a force all its own.

"Go to the bed."

She glanced at him. Saw his searing gaze. Obeyed. Stepping up on the dais with shaky limbs.

"Take your clothes off first. Slowly, while I watch."

She did so in a trance. Letting each piece of expensive Worth clothing—lavish silks, whisper-thin lace—drop to the carpet like charwoman's rags. Feeling lush and gloriously aroused as she felt his gaze scrutinize her naked curves. Ripe breasts, tapered waist, rounded womanly hips.

"Now get up on the edge of the bed and kneel, facing me."

She did as he directed, feeling her flesh jiggle deliciously as she moved. Kneeling at the foot of the bed with the transparent blue bed curtains fluttering all around her in the swirl of the ceiling fan. Concealing yet revealing her like a harem veil. Voluptuous. Seductive.

He walked toward her slowly, his eyes taking her in. Then went to the bedside table in the encroaching darkness to light a single candle. When he stepped before her once again, the candlelight bathed him in a spectral glow, his white garments and silvered hair causing him to seem spotlighted against the deep blues of the room beyond. The flame dancing across his face, obscuring his features in shifting shadows.

"Hold your tits in your hands."

She flinched at the word.

"'Breasts' is too clinical. Save that for your readers. When you're with me, you call them tits. Say it."

She cupped them in her hands. "These . . . tits . . . are . . ."

"For me."

Her loins began to tingle at the pitiless edge in his voice. "Because I . . . belong to you?"

Was this Celia speaking, or Charlotte?

"Exactly. Because you're mine. To do with what I will."

She played with her tits, rubbing them, pinching the nipples until they hardened beneath her fingers, raising one high and lapping at it with the tip of her tongue. Putting on a show for him. Smiling triumphantly as she saw the sudden bulge in his trousers.

Like a torrent, he thrust the bed curtains aside. Took hold of her hands and shoved them behind her back. Locked them in the prison of a powerful fist.

Her sense of control vanished. Replaced by a feeling of helplessness that was so highly charged, so intensely erotic that she melted completely beneath the overwhelming strength of him. Feeling unexpectedly like a fragile flower offering homage to the towering mountain before her.

When his other hand found her between her thighs she was already drenched.

"You came here before," he said, his voice an enthralling pulse, like the beating of her heart. "Just as you came to me today, Charlotte came to Rashid. Because she needed more of what she'd experienced in the cave. Do you remember? How much you loved it? How much you needed it? How you would break down that door to have it?"

Her head dropped back. Her mouth slack, opening to allow her to gulp precious air.

"There was champagne on the table. You drank. I took it from your hand. You stripped for me just as you did now. I began to stroke you. Like this. Telling you how much I desired you. How just the sight of your naked body set my blood on fire. Telling you that when you were ready, I was going to have my way with you. Sucking your tits. Making you crazy." He leaned and took her nipple in his mouth. She gasped with the delectable play of sensations. His strong hand confining her wrists. His mouth soft and moist on her nipple. Relentlessly fingering her juicy cunt, driving her mad.

"And then I did take you. I turned you over." He rotated her, positioning her facedown at the edge of the bed, planting her feet on the carpet, slapping her thighs to spread them wide. Open to his eyes. All the while pinning her arms behind her back with the pressure of his fist. She felt him unfastening his trousers with fierce tugs, felt the velvet and steel of his erection rubbing her dripping core. "I took you from behind, like a bitch in heat." He slammed himself into her and she moaned uncontrollably. As he drove into her, sending her breath hurtling from her at every heartrending thrust, he reached around her so the fingers of his free hand once again found her clit. Working it with exquisite mastery, bringing his mouth to her ear. His voiced hushed, intimate, pure power. Sounding for all the world like an Arab sheik storming the desert on a mighty steed, brandishing his sword. The force of his presence exhilarating. "I asked you, 'Would you do anything for me?' And what did you answer?"

"Yes," she panted. Caught up now in the fantasy so that every word he uttered seemed real. So aroused now that she felt it all, the past merging with the present, her consciousness spanning the two worlds in a seamless flow. One moment Celia, the next Charlotte, then feeling both of them at once. His manhood huge and plunging within her. His fingers sticky with her cream.

"Anything," he emphasized. "If I ask you to leave your home and run away with me, you would. Your family, your people, your home, they mean nothing compared to the delight only I can give you."

Celia was panting, licking her lips.

"Suddenly there was a knock on the door. You froze. It might be your father's men. Gibraltar is a small place. Maybe you were seen coming to this hotel frequented by Moroccans. Maybe they'll break down the door. You want to run and hide. But no. I hold your hands captive as I'm doing now. I force you to enjoy the delicious, forbidden danger of it all.

Thrilling you like nothing has ever thrilled you before. Still humping you from behind. Still using my fingers to arouse you beyond caring. Knowing they may be outside waiting, listening. You attempt to resist, to keep completely quiet as they stand outside that door, trying to determine if the daughter of Colonel Lansdowne could possibly be in this outlaw's room. You know you should get away. Climb out the window, anything. But you can't tear yourself away. The thought that they might break down the door any moment—the very danger of it all—enthralls you. So instead of fleeing, you drop to your knees and take me in your mouth. Do it! Yes . . . like that. All the way in. Finding that the pleasure you receive is even more exquisite than it was in the cave. Finding . . . that you're *addicted* to it. That you *must* have it."

She was breathless now, completely carried away. Seeing it all, feeling it, as if it were happening this minute, in this very room. Loving it. The sense of being helpless to his domination. The surfeit of decision. Just doing, feeling, sucking, held down like a captive relishing the brazen shameless feel of doing something so forbidden under the very noses of those who sought to wrest this illicit delicacy from her. Her clit throbbing, aching, spiraling with heat, desperate for release. Coiling with need.

With a sudden, animal-like lunge, he yanked her to her feet and tossed her onto the bed. He shed his clothes and hurled them aside, then fell atop her, shoving her legs apart and entering her with a thundering thrust. As he glided in and out of her, his voice droned on, establishing a rhythm that was at once lulling and electrifying. Carrying her higher with every whispered word. "You love this so much, you'll do anything I say. Grovel at my feet for the privilege of feeling that you're my possession. You belong one hundred percent to my will. I'll teach you what it's like to be totally owned. Designed only for one thing: whatever is important to my cock and my lust. Your function is only to spread your legs and service my will. I'll use your body in every conceivable way. And you'll love it."

She surrendered completely, exploding beneath him. Held down, gasping for breath, feeling him in her, all around her, a part of her. Her senses spinning dizzily. Crazed with hunger and delight. Shattered by the intensity of her fulfillment in knowing she belonged completely to him.

He held her caressingly then. Stroking her hair back from her face. Grazing her lips with his. Kissing her endlessly until once again she was swimming in succulent desire.

"I love this," she gasped. "I've never loved anything more." And then, beyond reserve, past fear or inhibition, she begged, "Train me. Show me all the things you taught me once before."

He did. In the hours that passed, he tutored her in the forbidden arts, introducing her to things few people even talked about. Avenues of prurient delight. Shocking delicacies. Teaching her secrets that only the most practiced courtesans had known since the beginning of time. Showing her that it was a woman's eagerness and adoration that transformed an act of passion into art, that made her irresistible to even the most skilled and worldly of men. Marveling at her capacity. Her willingness. Her joy. At her gift for turning flights of fancy into the reality of the moment.

She was insatiable. Impatient for more, alluringly eager for all he had to give. Adding her music to his words so that together they created a symphony of body and spirit. Reveling in even the most prohibited pleasuring of his body with her tongue, doing everything he demanded, adding riveting touches of her own. So quick to love it that it was easy to believe she'd learned it all before and was but remembering it now. Lush, sumptuous, voluptuous temptation in her eagerness to give, in her propensity to receive. Looking so sophisticated, so wickedly divine in the now damp and rumpled sheets, her hair loose and wild, her body ripe and inviting. Yet devouring him with touching devotion and an ingenuous sense of fun. A woman truly designed for love.

Asking him always, with accelerating enthusiasm, "What's next?" As if she couldn't get enough. Of the whimsy he wove.

284 / Katherine O'Neal

Of him. Despairing when he left her side, as if he might magically disappear.

"And when I've had my fill of teasing you," he murmured against her lips, "I'll make you spread your legs for me. And fuck you . . ." He took his erection in hand and plunged inside. She was so slick that, big as he was, she took him easily, her body rising to meet him, welcoming him back where he belonged. "Until you can't remember your name. Until all you want is me."

"All I'll *ever* want is you," she sighed.

He kissed her again, deeply, passionately, searching her mouth. Distracted once more from the spell he was weaving as the scent of her filled him. Taking the time now to touch her like a lover, to marvel over the silky feel of her, to leisurely taste her mouth with his. Unsettled by the utter and profound contentment he found while buried deep inside her. How his erection felt as if it had been made just for this.

He shook himself and tried to get it back. The thread of what he'd been saying. Troubled by how much he needed her beyond his intentions. Drawing back in alarm. He hadn't planned to get involved like this. Emotionally. There was too much at stake. This had to work, or he could lose everything. He must fortify himself. Regain his control.

But she reached up and pulled him back to her. Back to the warm haven of her arms. Back to the lips he'd tried so hard to resist. He didn't want to be tender with her. He wanted to see his handprint on her ass. Not enough to hurt her—just to see her branded with his palm. But he couldn't resist the impulse for affection. He, who'd always prided himself on his discipline. Because the lure of her was far too strong. Because he'd set out to put a spell on her, but it was she, in the end, who'd enchanted him.

Because he wasn't in control. If he hadn't understood that when he'd started, he knew it now. He was no longer the director of this drama. Destiny was controlling *him*.

She threaded her fingers through his hair and held him

close, feeling his heart beat in harmony with hers. "That was wonderful," she murmured. *"Beyond* wonderful."

"What did you see?" he asked, surprising her. She *had* seen something. How had he known?

"Something . . . unsettling."

"Tell me."

"I think I know why Rashid wanted to get Charlotte so addicted to sex that she'd do anything for him. As you said, Charlotte knew Gibraltar as no one ever had. The hidden crevices where ships could land. Caves where they could hide and store ammunition. Secret ways in and out of the British fortifications. All the things an invading armada would need to know in order to take it over. And that's exactly what Rashid was sent here to find out. He was the envoy—the spy. Sent from Morocco to seduce her into divulging the secrets only she knew. He wanted her to betray her family, her nation. Gibraltar. Don't you see how devastating that would be to her?"

He thought about it quietly for a time, trailing the curve of her shoulder with his finger. "Yes. That makes sense. That must be what happened. But I can't see what happens next. Does she do it? Betray Gibraltar?"

"Surely not. Loving it as she does, how could she?"

"Then he has to find a way to convince her."

"I think he took her somewhere. I saw something else. Charlotte and Rashid together, but not here. In a different place."

"Where?"

She closed her eyes and concentrated. "A city built on a hill, behind walls. White buildings beneath a fierce sun. Winding streets, like a maze. Men in caftans, women wearing veils. Camels, open markets. And one building in particular. Narrow, wooden stairs. Colorful beads in the doorway. A small, stuccoed room. I was lying on a bed, but . . . I couldn't really see. It's as if the room was dark, or . . . something was covering my eyes. I know Rashid is there, sitting beside me, but the rest of it is murky."

Royce had stilled as she'd spoken. Now he disengaged himself from her and sat up on the edge of the bed, his back to her. She rolled onto her side, propping herself up on an elbow, her firelit hair cascading all around her.

"Do you know where it is?" she asked.

He nodded. "Tangier."

She sat up, excited. "Yes. That must be it. The answer we're looking for. It's in Tangier."

He said nothing.

She touched his back. "It isn't far from here, is it?"

"Seventeen miles across the Straits of Gibraltar."

"Then we must go. If we're there, perhaps we can pick up the rest of the story. We can leave tomorrow. It can't take more than an hour by ship."

Again, he was silent. As if wrestling with something in his own mind.

She wrapped her arms about him and laid her cheek persuasively on his shoulder. His muscles were rigid and tensely flexed. "That must be it. The answer's there, I feel it. We have to go. Please, Royce. I want to help you. To help . . . us."

He turned then. It was impossible to read the look in his eyes. What was disguised in their opaque depths? Trepidation . . . or some bleak triumph?

"Very well," he agreed at last. "We'll leave tomorrow."

She felt a flutter of excitement. To Tangier.

To their destiny.

Chapter Four

Tangier.

Resting like a crown atop a high, dusty hill. Whitewashed buildings and antiquated walls glistening in a wash of golden sun, like a colossal mirage shimmering before a background of brilliant blue. City of contrasts: ancient Berber traditions set against the new concepts of artists, writers, and visitors who flocked to the city from around the globe, lured by the hedonistic pleasures of North Africa, imparting an international flavor to the spice of Moroccan life. Flamboyant sensuality and passionate spirituality flowing hand in hand like two rivers joining one vast sea. Mystifying. Mesmerizing.

Celia took it all in eagerly. The men with their bronzed skin and mustaches, wearing striped caftans and pointed leather slippers. *(What did Rashid look like?)* The conundrum of the women with their heads covered, their beauty hidden by veils. *(What would they, in their modesty, have thought of Charlotte who'd so shamelessly lusted after one of their bold, impassioned sons?)* The reed-roofed souks, alive with vibrant, clashing colors, displaying their wares: brightly woven textiles, handcrafted baskets, olive jars, multihued painted boxes and chests, ceramics, pottery, embroidered silks, vegetables, flowers, fruits. The camel market invoking romantic images of sand dunes strewn with luxurious tents where sun-scorched chieftains waited out the heat of the day. A land beyond time.

Bejeweled mosques with soaring minarets, the mournful song of the muezzins calling the faithful to prayer. The lavish hotel where they sat on a shaded tiled terrace listening to the splash of the sea and breathing in the perfume of orange blossoms and jasmine as they sipped mint tea from glasses etched with embossed gold. All of it exotic, glamorous, stimulating.

"I wonder what that building is," she mused as her eyes scanned the horizon from what seemed their own private oasis. "The one that dominates that hill. It looks very nearly like a fort."

Royce gazed at her thoughtfully. Was she picking up more than he'd intended? "It's the sultan's palace."

Something in his tone made her look at him. "You've been here before." Then grinned and teased, "In *this* life, I mean."

He acknowledged her sally with a grim smile. "Yes."

So he was a traveler, just as she was. There was so much she didn't know about him. But every time she'd tried to question him about his life on the ship from Gibraltar, he'd deflected her inquiries, insisting they'd be more successful if she knew as little as possible about him, returning her focus to the task at hand. Intriguing her even more with his penchant for mystery. But she realized now that, while he'd been fairly quiet on the trip over, he'd become noticeably moody ever since they'd set foot in this tantalizing city. Wary. As if something were still weighing on his mind.

"You're troubled," she said now. "May I help?"

"You may help by keeping your mind clear for what's ahead. Let go of any expectations you might have. Don't think, don't analyze. Just feel the spirit of Tangier."

In some ways they were so alike. He, too, understood that every place had a spirit all its own. Unlike the frivolous Cliftons, he wasn't one to fritter away the magic of the moment or the impact of his surroundings with trivialities.

"What do *you* feel?" she asked.

He closed his eyes. "Charlotte used to accompany her father every few months when he came here on military business. When she was here, she would meet Rashid at a caravansary—one of the old inns where caravans used to rest for the night. A place where neither of them would be recognized. The place you saw in your vision."

"*Was* it a vision? Or a writer's fantasy?"

His eyes opened slowly. "You still doubt me."

"I doubt myself. I'm not clairvoyant."

"Oh, but you are. You pick up impressions without realizing what they are at the time. That's why your writing is so vivid. Because what you're writing about is real." He took a sip of tea then added, "In fact, you're the most amazing receiver of psychic energy I've ever come across."

She was so pleased by his praise and faith in her that she came as close to blushing as she ever had. "Then you think I really saw this place?"

"I know you did."

"*How* do you know?"

"Because I saw it, too. *With* you."

"Is that possible? For both of us to see the same vision at the same time?"

He shrugged. "It's never happened to me before. I don't pretend to know everything about how this works. I don't know *why* I see what I do, I just know that I do. I can't control it. And usually I can see more clearly for others than I do for myself. What I do know is yesterday in my room you described everything I was seeing. So I would say that for us, yes. It's possible to share the same vision."

She liked the sound of that. Wondered if he meant it in the larger sense—sharing the same vision of life, the same hopes and dreams—or if he was referring to this instance alone. What did he feel for her? He acknowledged that they were soul mates, yet he gave no indication of romantic feelings, or even that the knowledge gave him any pleasure. She had no doubt that he wanted her—after all, erections didn't lie. But what of love? Had he ever really loved her, in any of the lifetimes he claimed they'd shared? Or had he, as he'd said, merely used her?

A horrible thought hit her then. Was *that* the tragedy? The repeated pattern? That she'd always loved him and had always discovered in the end that he'd never cared for her?

Was that the freedom he wanted? Freedom from *her*?

She felt a flash of fear. He looked so handsome sitting across the table from her. His salt-and-pepper hair a scrumptious chiaroscuro. The haunted look in his strangely dark eyes, as if seeing possibilities for pain that she couldn't even fathom. The long, artistic fingers that toyed with his glass. Fingers that had brought her such ecstatic pleasure. Suddenly she wanted desperately not to lose him.

At any cost.

"How will we find the place we're looking for?" she asked, not certain now that she even wanted to find it. Couldn't they just forget the whole thing? Abandon the search for something that, for all they knew, might lead not to freedom but to more tragedy? Discover each other as they were now, not as they'd been? Couldn't she just give him enough love that it would make up for the past?

It was a moment before he responded. Was he, too, feeling the dread? Finally he said, "I think I know where it is."

With those words he sealed their fate. If he'd been unsure, perhaps she could have convinced him to call it off. But as it was, she would have to go through with it. As frightening as it might be.

She took a full breath. *Do it now, before you lose your nerve.* "Then let's go." She stood up, the decision made.

But he shook his head. "Not now. Go to your room and rest. You'll need it. We'll leave at dusk."

"Where are we going?"

"To the Kasbah."

They ventured into the heart of the oldest part of the city, the sky darkening as they went. Here, behind the aged walls, was yet another world. Dank, tight corridors zigzagging deeper and deeper into a mind-boggling jumble of cramped lanes that left Celia feeling lost in no time. The buildings small and low and jammed closely together. No painted ceilings or colorful tiles here, just shadows and gloom. Men hunkered down in alleyways over charcoal stoves as the chill of evening set in. Watching furtively as they walked by—the striking European man with the stunning but obviously nervous woman at his side. Chickens scattering in their path. Dusty. Seedy. Foreboding.

The Kasbah at night.

Royce led her with unfailing instinct to an unspectacular building, coated with white lye like all the rest. A servant opened the door and beckoned them inside. Celia was left in the murky entrance while Royce made his arrangements in a back room. She caught quick impressions as she waited—the throaty sounds of women's laughter, the faint whiff of jasmine and musk.

"This is a brothel," she whispered when Royce returned

He nodded. "A hundred years ago it was a bit more respectable. But no less clandestine."

He led her to a narrow wooden stairway, the steps of which were scattered with multicolored rose petals. As they ascended, the crush of their shoes releasing the scent of the roses, Celia felt her heart beating fast. She'd never been in a bordello before. She felt awkward, conspicuous. Yet surprisingly aroused.

The way we've connected has been carnal . . .

Always . . .

The upper floor contained a long hallway with a succession of closed doors. Occasionally she caught a muffled moan or cry, brief hints of what went on behind. Royce opened one at the far end, saying, "I felt the instant we came in that it was room eight. Fortunately for us, it's not occupied at the moment."

Celia stepped inside and stopped short. A small vestibule led to an inner door with a colorful beaded curtain. Just as she'd seen in her imagination the day before.

The glass beads tinkled as they moved through them, the

sound of it stirring her inside. Evoking erotic images. Faint reverberations of what she must have experienced here in that other life.

The room beyond was as she'd envisioned it, but not as plush. Stuccoed walls. A high window. A plain wooden cot with embroidered coverings, a cushioned chair at its edge. Not much else.

Royce said, "They had to meet in privacy. If word of their relationship leaked out, Charlotte's father would have whisked her back to England on the first ship."

Celia swallowed, her mouth dry. Feeling ominous. As if she were about to discover something she'd rather not know. "What happened here? What did they do?"

"Come. Let's see if we can't discover that together."

He kissed her lightly. Then, feeling that she was skittish, he eased her into his arms, deepening the kiss, gentling her, patiently allowing her to feel the warmth of his body thaw her qualms. Intensifying the pressure of his embrace. Until gradually she lost all conscious thought and became pliable in his arms. Until his kiss—his magnificent, blinding kiss—was all that existed.

She was breathing deeply by the time he took his mouth from hers. Wanting him now more than she wanted anything else, more than she'd dreaded what was to come. Loving him more fiercely than fear.

"Rashid," he told her softly, "is unleashing a passion in Charlotte that she's never known before. Once she tastes of it, and experiences what she's been searching for all along, she'll belong to him body and soul. Step by step, he's drawing her deeper into a world where her darkest desires are realized. Helping her explore prohibited pleasures, helping her fulfill that part of herself that has been starved. Giving her what she wants most. What she really craves. What she'd never ask for on her own. The most forbidden longings of her soul."

He kissed her again. Warm mouth, masterfully drawing her out of herself, spinning her senses dizzily, delightfully. As he did, she was half-conscious of her clothes falling from her.

Feeling his hands everywhere, arousing her with touches that somehow knew where she most wanted to be touched. Just as he was exciting her with the erotic power of his words.

"No matter what he asked of her, no matter how she might protest initially, he knew she'd love it in the end. Love it as no other woman could, or ever had. As *you* love it."

She moaned aloud. She was already as addicted to him as Charlotte had ever been to Rashid.

Repeated patterns . . .

A karmic prisoner . . .

Prisoner to his lust.

"Would you do anything for me?" he asked.

"Anything," she breathed into his mouth.

He took a black scarf from his pocket and positioned it over her eyes, tying it securely at the back of her head. *Something was covering my eyes* . . . Then he came up behind her, taking her breasts—her *tits*—in his hands. Pitched into darkness, she felt her senses leap to life. Felt her nipples tighten beneath the demand of his palms. Caught the clean, male scent of him. Heard his breath at her ear. Tasted her arousal as she felt his erection rubbing alluringly against her buttocks.

"Just let yourself go," he coaxed her. "Feel this energy. Feel Charlotte and Rashid. There's no pressure. Just see where this takes us."

No pressure. She felt the tension drop from her, to be replaced by a force so potent that it shot through her, electrifying. The blindfold making her feel defenseless, yet freeing her at the same time. Liberated from the burden of sight, she could meld into the flow of energy that seemed to alter her surroundings. She breathed it in, making it a part of her, anchoring it in her soul.

And as the energy shifted, the touch of his hands felt different. Tightening his grip. Pulling her back into him now with fierce desire. Possessive. Claiming her as his property. Nuzzling her neck with hot lips, feasting on her flesh, caressing her with hands that probed and explored as if he did, indeed, own the body he fondled, as if he needed no permission to touch it where he wanted, in whatever manner he chose. Heightening her growing lust in the awareness that she was his to do with as he wished. *Whatever* he wished. Sending her blood roaring through her veins. Her flesh damp. All of her rife with need.

"Why have you put me in the dark?" she asked, feeling Charlotte alive within her.

"So you can feel your senses for the first time. So you can feel what I'm about to do to you without any of the distractions or limitations of the temporal earth. So you can feel the infinity of bliss." Royce's voice, but Rashid's words.

"Bliss," she repeated dreamily, the promise of it sweet on her tongue.

"Any initial fear you might have felt has now vanished. Gone is your tendency to judge primarily by sight. Gone is any sense of passing time. You exist in this one moment. This isn't about seeing, it's about *feeling*. Feeling a profound trust in me . . . a longing to do *anything* that will give me satisfaction . . . a sense of anticipation that is so exciting, so *thrilling*, that you feel yourself on the edge of a soaring precipice of pleasure."

He grasped her arm and led her forward. Disoriented, she had no idea where he was taking her until her knees came up against the cot. He eased her down on it so she was lying on her back, then sat beside her, tracing her exposed flesh with his fingertips, exciting her with a skill and power that refused to be denied. Patient. As if he had all the time in the world. As if he had the leisure to wait until she was truly ready. Touching her unrelentingly, until she was so hot, so wet, so ferocious with animal craving that she was reaching for him, whimpering.

He pressed her back, denying her. But still he stroked her, her heaving tits, her inner thigh, her throat, her lips. She sucked his fingers into her mouth, hungry for cock. His hand playing with her juices, toying with her clit, slipping inside to finger her, causing her to arch up ravenously against the luscious friction of his hand. Highly conscious that he watched her as she lay naked, blindfolded, helplessly inflamed before him. Transported to that other time and body. So entrenched in the energy of the past that it was happening all over again.

And when he'd had his fill of this, he climbed onto the cot. Spreading her legs, pushing them back to expose her to his feral gaze. She felt his lascivious inspection, even though she couldn't see him. Felt a salacious surge at the knowledge that he was greedily filling his sight with her in this most vulnerable position, spread open, panting with desire, wet with need.

"What I'm about to do, Charlotte has never done before. You've never dreamt anything could be so . . . intimate. The feel of a warm, wet tongue lapping at the citadel of your most hidden self. Turning yourself over to it, its willing slave. To pleasure so relentless that you can never get enough."

And then she felt his tongue on her. Warm. Wet. Soft. As light as a feather. Causing her to gasp in a shock of euphoria. Slowly following the contour of her cunt. Delicately lapping at her folds, causing her to arch herself up into his mouth. His fingers, moist with her juices, parting the tender nether lips, opening her to his exploration. Slipping inside her, filling her, arousing her as his tongue continued its journey. Leisurely exploring, searching, looking for just the right spot . . . finding it . . . there . . . there . . . oh yes *there* . . . oh my God . . . Slurping at her with rapid, hungry flicks, sucking the tight aching bud of her clit between his lips. So lovingly executed that he carried her to paradise. All of him—his body, his hands, his heart—concentrating on pleasuring her. And as her own hunger built, increasing the pressure of his tongue . . . faster, harder . . . eternity . . . never wanting it to end . . . oh God, don't stop, *don't ever stop* . . . taking her higher . . . higher . . . making her feel more voluptuous than she ever had . . . a goddess . . . hurtling her to a place she'd never been before . . . not Charlotte, not Celia . . . not any of the others whose faces began to flash through her mind . . . other places, other times . . . she could almost remember their names . . .

Sensing her digression, the voice called her back. "No. Don't think of them. Think only of Charlotte."

And then the mouth, tasting her again with rising intensity, the tongue digging into her cunt, fucking her . . . ferocious now, like a wild animal too long denied. Taking her higher . . .

Higher. Taking her somewhere beyond her reach, but nearly there. Where only the gods existed. Taking her to immortality. Almost there . . . almost there . . .

The drama, the mystery, the magnitude of it all . . . too much . . . too much. She surrendered with a cry to the explosive demand of her body, climaxing in an eruption of pulsing pleasure that spiraled upon itself in a succession of galvanizing orgasms, each more volatile, magnifying the one before, melting into the next. The ecstasy pure delirium. Feeling herself the spirit of Eros itself, mindless, timeless, basking in unending rapture and infinite bliss. Wicked sensual delight that clutched and curled her body in a single, ceaseless swell. Giving herself to him completely.

Royce rode the waves with her. Feeling Rashid glorying in his own skill. In the unequivocal success of his seduction. Reveling in the knowledge that at last she was the putty in his hands that he'd wanted her to be. And yet . . . even as he sought to master her, beginning to lose himself in the pleasure. Realizing that he'd never experienced a sensation so totally fulfilling. Loving it . . . loving *her* . . . her sweetness, her delicacy, her openness, her . . . *perfection*. Wanting to linger, to drown in it, to forget the imperative of his mission and bury himself in her welcoming flesh for all eternity . . . softening . . . weakening . . . relinquishing . . .

He wrenched himself away. Sitting up with a bolt, his breath coming hard and fast. Seeking to calm himself . . . seeking control . . .

"What is it?" she asked. When he didn't answer, she pushed the blindfold back off her head. It took a moment for her eyes to adjust to the onslaught of light so that he appeared to her at first through a blurred mist. But as her vision cleared, she detected the rigid, startled stance, the face of stone.

She sat up. "What happened?"

He passed a hand across his face. "I know how it ends."

"How?"

The bleak look he gave her made her suddenly afraid.

"Royce . . . what happened?" she pressed. Feeling the shattering shift of energy.

He searched her eyes for a moment, assessing her ability to take what was to come. "Charlotte found out that Rashid was plotting against Gibraltar. She turned him in." He paused a moment, then added, "He hanged."

A cry of horror caught in her throat. He'd been killed . . . because of her.

When she could speak she asked, choking on the words, "And there were other times . . . in other lives . . . when you died because of me?"

A brief hesitation. Then, "Yes."

Because of her . . .

A tragic pattern.

How many times had it happened?

God help her, she believed him. There was no doubt in her mind that *he* was what she'd been searching for all this time. The soul mate she'd longed for. *But not like this!* Not knowing they'd come to a bad end time and again. Not with the realization that, if this pattern continued, they were bound for tragedy once more.

She looked up and saw her own sense of horror and grief reflected like a mirror in his eyes.

And then, as she watched him, it seemed to her that she felt something stir inside. As if Charlotte, deeply buried beneath layers of consciousness, was revealing herself to Celia at last, as the characters in her books often did. She spoke in her own voice, but felt strangely that it was Charlotte who provided the words.

"I think Charlotte turned Rashid in not just because of her love of Gibraltar, but because her female vanity was so outraged. She'd trusted him—sexually—in a way she never would have anyone else. She gave him all her faith and all the force of her love and passion. To find that he'd been using her all that time for a sinister reason of his own—that he'd so heartlessly abused her trust in following him into the vulnerable world of—"

"Sexual bondage," he supplied numbly.

She felt his distance and touched his arm. "It sent her over the edge. I suspect she turned him in as quickly as she could, without giving herself a chance to think. But I also feel that Rashid loved Charlotte. More than he knew. That he was every bit as addicted to her as she was to him. That he needed her. But his pride wouldn't let him admit it."

Where was this coming from? Was it true? Or did she just need to believe it?

"I think, in the end, that she was more important to him than his mission. But it was too late. Had he told her how much he loved and needed her, things might have been different."

He averted his eyes. Left her suddenly to go to the window to stare out over the narrow Kasbah street. The same street Rashid had gazed down upon so many times. His knuckles white as he gripped the sill.

"Pride has always been my downfall," he said softly, his voice raw and weary. "It's something I'm . . . working on."

In that moment, she loved him desperately. And wanted more than anything to help him. To make it up to him.

She rose and went to him, putting her hands gently on his back. Feeling the stiffness of his muscles beneath her palms.

"You saw something else."

"No."

"Then . . . you started to. But something you saw, or were about to see, scared you and you pulled out of it. I can feel you holding yourself back."

He said nothing.

"It's all right," she soothed. "This frightens me, too. But we have to follow this to its conclusion, if we're going to find the answer we're seeking."

"What do you suggest?"

"We've been successful in bringing Charlotte to the surface. Now I want to call forth Rashid. Perhaps he can give us the answer. You're going to have to trust *me* this time. Give up control."

Over his shoulder, he gave her a narrowed look.

"What," she persisted, "if you were to lower your guard completely and just allow this to take you where it will? What's the worst that could happen?"

"I don't know," he admitted, still guarded.

"Then let's find out, shall we?"

She began to massage his shoulders in an attempt to ease his tension. But he shrugged her off and turned to face her. "Rashid is not the hero of this story. He's . . . dangerous. More dangerous than I knew."

She was touched by his concern, the first he'd shown in all of this. She raised a hand and used the pads of her fingers to caress his mouth. "I know you don't want to hurt me, and perhaps that's what's holding you back. As Royce, you're repelled by what you're seeing. But you have to remember it was Rashid's very danger that excited Charlotte most. And, too . . ." She brought both hands up and stroked his cherished face. "I feel even more strongly that Rashid loved Charlotte. That he was torn between his horrible duty and his love for her. I think he knew that Charlotte would love a forceful man in her bed. But I honestly don't believe he would hurt her."

She raised up on her tiptoes and touched his mouth with hers. He was still stiff, resistant. But she played with him, sweetly enticing, her lips imparting persuasive little kisses until at last he began to soften and kiss her in return. Until he began to warm to the touch of her palms on his chest. To the swipe of her wet tongue up the side of his neck. To her breath in his ear.

"Force me to my knees."

He put his hands on her shoulders, but there was no force or will behind his touch.

"No . . . hard! Grab my hair. Yank it."

He put his hands in her hair, but there was no fury to his grip. It felt more like a protective caress.

"Stronger. Rougher. You've got to make this daughter of

Gibraltar love the tight rein of the prince of the desert." His hand gripped her hair more forcefully now, giving it a slight yank. "Yes, that's what Charlotte needs. That's what I need. You've got to make me so addicted to this kind of lovemaking that I'll do anything for the man who can provide it."

Still he resisted. "No, I don't think this will . . ."

"Slap me," she coached.

He jerked away. "I can't."

It was true. He couldn't. What had changed in him? Why was it suddenly so difficult to go through with his plan? He looked at her through pained eyes. All he wanted in that moment was to cherish her, protect her. And yet, he had to overcome this. Shake himself free. Otherwise, how could he find the strength to follow through to the end?

She looked into his eyes and saw the play of conflicting emotions. "Royce, you asked me to trust you. And I do. More than my life. But unless you trust me just as much, we've reached an impasse. In order to break through, we must allow Rashid to tell us what we need to know. Otherwise, it's all for nothing. Please help me. Help me to . . ." Her voice caught on the words. She took a breath and tried again. "Help me to take away your pain." Slowly, carefully, she eased her arms about his neck and kissed his jaw. His cheek. The lobe of his ear. Then she began to whisper to him hypnotically, as he'd done with her. "Come to me, Rashid. I need you. Charlotte needs you."

She dropped to her knees before him then took his limp hand and used it to slap herself in the face. As she did, something flashed in his eyes. She saw the transformation in the straightening of his stance, the proud tilt of his jaw. His hands convulsed on her head and he tipped it roughly to look up at him. "So you need me, do you?" he demanded.

"You know I do," she said, speaking now to Rashid. "I've been too long without you. My body aches for you. Please, Rashid, don't torment me. Don't make me wait any longer. You *know* how desperately I need you."

He peered down at her, considering. "And you, my wild

flower of the Great Rock . . . sometimes I think I need you as well."

She rubbed her cheek against his thigh, relishing the confession. But once again, he tightened his grip, forcing her to look up at him.

"But no . . . I must drown out this treasonous weakness with the force of my power over you. To bind you not with the love I feel dancing at the corners of my heart, but with the more anonymous persuasion of animal passion. And yet . . . when you look at me so . . ."

He jerked her head, clearly fighting his more tender impulses. "Take your Master in your mouth . . . serve me . . . give yourself up to it completely . . . worship it . . . nothing else exists but its steely will . . . yes, that's it . . ."

Roughly grabbing her hair now, guiding her head in rhythm to his thrusts as he moved in and out of her mouth. "Tell me you love it."

She moaned, once again feeling herself merge with Charlotte. Feeling Charlotte's surrender. *I do love it . . . God help me, I do . . .*

"You will now prove yourself to me," he ground out with a ferocity that was intent on subduing any kinder emotion that might be stirring within him. "In a way you have not before."

Yes, the voice within her cried. *Something new. Show me, teach me . . . I want to do it all. Find the one thing I haven't done that will thrill me . . . fulfill me . . . release me . . .*

Release us.

Feeling his ardor build as the sheer irresistibility of it overcame her, as she reached for him fervently now, moaning her enjoyment, crazed with passion, desperate to be fucked. Spreading her legs like a rapacious slut, wanting more . . . more . . . any of it, all of it.

Swimming in desire, she reached up to put her arms about his neck, to draw him even closer. For a lingering moment, he didn't move. Then he turned from her, but at the same time moved close, coaxing her to do an unimaginable thing. Something no decent woman would ever do. Only a whore . . .

Tangling her hair in his fist and pulling her even closer. Demanding that she not only do it, but love it. Making her moan for more.

More . . .

Then he threw her onto her back and plunged inside, piercing her so that she cried out. Oblivious to the whores down the hall and the men they serviced not half as well. Clamping a hand down over her mouth to silence her, he rammed himself into her like a rutting stallion delirious with the scent of fertile cunt, leaning into her so her legs were thrust back over her shoulders, showcasing all her unprotected charms, swollen and clutching at his heaving dick, hurtled back, soaring, peaking, gasping against the pressure of his hand at her mouth. The gag intensifying her yearning until her entire body was vibrating with sensation. Swooning, escalating, bounding, pulsating, so full of him she felt that she would erupt. So close to exploding that she was losing control.

He fucked her harder, spreading her to the hilt, holding her down with the force of his hand over her mouth. As he did, Rashid rasped, "I won't give in to you. I won't fall in love with you. My mission . . . my people . . . must come first . . ."

She could feel Charlotte relishing the words. The denial too vehement, revealing the raw feelings underneath. She danced to their rhythm even as a wistful longing made her clutch him close. She'd give anything . . . everything . . . if only this were Royce vainly protesting against such an obvious love.

For even as he uttered the words, his body told a different tale. Even as his words tried to deny it, he pounded into her with greater and greater need, wanting more and more of her, going deeper and deeper into the core of her being until at last even his words changed. Until he lost the drift of protestation and began to growl, "You're mine . . . do you hear me? Mine. *Mine.* MINE!"

Branding her body with his own. Claiming her. Loving her. Until at last he bared his teeth and let out a primal roar. Cuming as she did, lifting her, enhancing her. Falling on her with all his weight. Breathing hard, his skin hot and damp against hers. Royce now, beyond the influence of Rashid. Kissing her warmly, appreciatively. Gently stroking her hair as if to make up for the vehemence of his previous incarnation.

She savored the feel of him for as long as she could. Shaken by the immensity of the feelings that had passed between them. Not wanting to speak. Not wanting to let him go. Wanting to cry because she loved him so dearly. The force of her love deeper than anything she'd ever felt in her life. Wishing fervently that this intimate silence between them could last forever, and that she could die right here, in his arms.

But finally, the compulsion to know surmounted her serenity. "Did you see it?" she asked, still holding him clasped to her breast.

"Yes."

"Something else happened between them, didn't it? Something that caused her to turn him in. She wouldn't betray Gibraltar, would she?"

He shook his head. "It was too important to her. And because he couldn't convince her, he was being pressed to take the next step. Luring her into the sultan's palace where her British nationality wouldn't protect her and the information could be tortured out of her."

This, after the emotion she'd felt from Rashid, jarred her. Had she been wrong about Rashid's love for Charlotte? Had she manufactured it for her own vanity's sake? Dreading the answer, she asked, "Did he?"

"I don't know. I can't see beyond this room."

"Then we shall have to go to the palace ourselves and find out."

He stilled. Stared at her with a strangely wary look. "Admission is forbidden to all foreigners."

"We shall find a way. There's always a way. I've written scenes like this a hundred times."

He moved from her, passing a weary hand across his face.

She sat up eagerly and tucked her legs beneath her. "Royce, we can do it. We *must* do it. I'm certain the answer lies in the sultan's palace. We have to know. I won't take no for an answer."

Still he seemed reluctant. Tormented. As if, once again, struggling with his own mind. Her heart ached with love for him. She put her arms about his neck. "But enough for now. Don't think about it yet. Courage will come with the light of day."

Kissing him. Soothing him. Enticing him back into her arms. Knowing she could never get enough of him in a million lifetimes.

Chapter Five

A persistent knocking roused Celia from sleep. Resisting, she buried her head beneath the pillow and sank into the soft comfort of the bed. But the banging resumed, beating an exasperating cadence. Jarring her from her drowsy dreams.

It occurred to her then that it must be Royce. But why this insistence? Struggling into a satin robe, she stumbled to the door, still foggy with sleep. And opened it to find, of all things, Mrs. Clifton standing before her, her raised knuckles red from rapping.

Maggie Clifton! In Tangier?

"I see you didn't heed my warning," the woman said. She moved past Celia, into the hotel room without invitation.

"Mrs. Clifton, whatever are you doing here? What time is it?"

"I heard you came here. With *him*. I knew he had to be up to something, but I couldn't figure out what it might be. I was so concerned, I wired Inspector Worthington of Scotland Yard last night. And did I find out plenty! So I talked Homer into taking the first boat this morning. And here I am."

This was taking on the trappings of a nightmare. Was she forever to be hounded by this woman and her ravings? "My dear Mrs. Clifton, I don't mean to be rude, but—"

"I know, I know. You think I'm a pest now, but you'll

thank me when you hear what I have to say. I've just discovered that your precious Mr. Tyler owes a whopping debt. And guess who to? I'll tell you. None other than the infamous Sultan of Tangier. And he can't pay it back. Not even a fraction of it. He squandered it. But the Inspector figures he's found a way to repay the sultan without so much as a ha'penny leaving his pocket."

"I can't imagine what this has to do with me."

"But that's just it, Lady Wybourne. It has *everything* to do with you. It just so happens this sultan has read every book you ever wrote."

"You must be joking."

"Inspector Worthington doesn't joke. He says the sultan's *obsessed* with you. When he was in London, he bought up every likeness of you he could find. He even tried to see you, but you were out of the country at the time. Not only that, *they say* he's acted out scenes from your books with his harem. Oh, he's a lecherous one, is *he*."

Celia rubbed her head, which was beginning to pound. "I need a cup of tea."

"The Inspector's fit to be tied. He didn't know you were anywhere near Tangier when I wired him. He says the sultan has—" She faltered for a moment, then fished in her pocket and retrieved the cable and quoted, "'The sultan has privately stated that he wants Lady Wybourne for his harem.' The Inspector's convinced your amorous Mr. Tyler plans to turn you over to the sultan to clear his debt. It's all here. Read it yourself."

Celia took the cable and read it hastily, then sank down onto her bed.

"If he does," the woman continued, "there's nothing anyone can do to rescue you. Tangier is an open city. Within the Kasbah, he's his own law. You fall in his clutches and there's not a bloody thing Her Majesty's government can do to get you out."

Celia was suddenly wide awake, her mind racing. Was it possible? It was so absurd. And yet . . .

Had Royce manipulated her into coming to Tangier? Had she cleverly taken his bait, thinking it her own idea?

I need to be set free.

His words took on an ominous new meaning. Was it the sultan he'd wanted to be set free from all along? Had he concocted an elaborate hoax to lead her to this? Was he clever enough—diabolical enough—to have read her books and deduced the perfect way of manipulating her? Knowing that she craved drama and excitement, guessing that she privately yearned for the sexual adventure that until now had belonged only to her heroines? Realizing that no mundane story would capture her imagination? Hypnotizing her, making her think it was *her* idea to go to the sultan's palace?

Had all of it been a buildup to this?

She wanted to deny it. And yet, it made a twisted sense. The fact that Royce had never so much as mentioned Tangier's ruler or his debt to him. The odd look he'd given her when she'd asked about the building on the hill and he'd told her it was the sultan's palace. Telling her Rashid had planned to take her there, then feigning hesitation. The perfect ruse that would make her want to go. For him.

I intend to use you.

He'd warned her with his own lips.

No wonder there had been no talk of caring . . . of love . . .

She sat on the edge of her bed, the cable clutched in her hand, trembling with rage. Maggie Clifton forgotten. Until the woman's voice brought her back to the room. "We have to get you out of here at once, my lady. Before the sultan finds out and stops you. There's a boat leaving in half an hour. You can make it if you hurry."

"Yes," she muttered. "I must hurry." Away from Tangier. Away from the sultan. Away from Royce . . .

"I'll help you pack, if I may."

Celia looked at the woman then—the woman she'd so clearly misjudged—and felt ashamed. "Mrs. Clifton, why have you done all this?"

Maggie looked down at her hands. "Bosh, my lady, you

308 / *Katherine O'Neal*

needn't bother to thank me. It's precious little to repay all the escape your books have given me. Come now, I can see you're upset, as well you should be. Let's get you out of harm's way."

Back in Gibraltar with two days to kill until her ship sailed for London. Two days with nothing to do but remember and fume. To look upon the once-loved vistas and chastise herself for being such a fool. What had she been thinking? Had she lost her mind completely? Falling for such a tale because she'd been lonely and had wanted so to believe.

Oh, he'd been clever. He'd left enough room for doubt, and yet had overcome those doubts one by one. What shocked her now was that it had been so easy for him to dupe her.

But then, Maggie Clifton had said he was a chameleon. That he became for every woman what she wanted most.

What had he thought when he'd come for her that last morning, only to find her gone? And why hadn't he come after her? She'd expected him to appear at any moment, demanding an explanation. She'd steeled herself for the confrontation. But apparently, he'd realized it was hopeless. In any case, he hadn't returned to Gibraltar. Just as well. She never wanted to see him again. She just wanted to forget him and go on.

Except that she couldn't forget. She found herself retracing their steps. Going to the cave where she'd first made love with him and had fallen under his spell. Going to look at the hotel where he'd so convincingly confessed his torment, and had made her want so much to make it up to him. And finally, to the cemetery where she'd first spoken to him. Meticulously retracing her steps until at last she found what she was seeking: the grave where he'd stood. Staring down at it with renewed shock as the name on the tombstone registered. Charlotte Lansdowne. He'd even had the presence of mind to choose a real name. In case she checked.

The sight of it broke her heart. She left with tears in her eyes. Although exactly what—or who—she was crying for, she wasn't certain.

Finally it was time to go. She called for the bellman, then went down to the lobby to check out. Only to bump into Homer Clifton as she was leaving the lift.

"Why, Lady Wybourne, good to see you again. We're only just returning from Tangier. Dreadful place, don't know what possessed Maggie to want to go. You must have found it so, too. Certainly left in a hurry, wot. Maggie hinted that your sudden departure had to do with Royce Tyler, though what it might be she didn't know. Not that I'm prying, mind."

Tiredly, wanting nothing but to be gone, Celia muttered, "I didn't want the same thing to happen to me that happened to your sister."

She was about to excuse herself when Homer gave her a quizzical glare. "But my lady," he protested, "I don't *have* a sister."

Celia stood in their sitting room as Homer paced before his wife, raging. "You shameless hussy! It wasn't my imaginary sister who was thrown over by Tyler. It was *you* all the time. You chased after him, made me a laughingstock behind my back. I should throw you out on your sorry ear. Cuckolding me—"

Maggie, weeping, cried, "I did no such thing!"

"Do you mean to tell me, woman, that you did *not* have carnal knowledge of this man?"

"No!" she shrieked, putting her face in her hands. "I swear it!"

Clifton perused his wife harshly. "I see. So you threw yourself at him, but he wouldn't have you, is that it?"

Maggie looked up at him bitterly. "All right," she hissed. "I admit it. I fell for him. I thought he loved me, too. But when I went to him, when I humbled myself and admitted my feelings, he said he was just being kind. *Kind!* As if that villain has a kind bone in his body. Leading me on, was what he did. He took advantage of me. He's a rascal and a rogue. So now you know!"

"Then everything you said was a lie," Celia accused. "The sister-in-law, all that business about the sultan reading my books . . ."

Maggie faced her. "No. That's the queen's own truth. I did you a service. That blackguard Tyler was using you just as he used me. He was going to turn you over to the sultan. What other reason could there be for him to risk his life and go to Tangier?"

Celia paled. "Risk his life?"

"The sultan," she spat out, "let it be known that if Royce Tyler ever set foot anywhere near his domain, he'd kill him sure as he'd swat a fly. You may be rich and beautiful, and you may have men fawning over you at every turn, but you're no different from me. You fell for that charlatan the same as I did, and he used you the same as he did me. Used your feelings for him so he could turn you over to that sultan to repay his debt."

As Celia struggled to digest all she'd just heard, Homer spoke in the tone of a man gathering together the shreds of his shattered pride. "Lady Wybourne, it seems I owe you an apology. It's clear to me that my wife has behaved like a jealous, spiteful woman. She was shown up for the ninny she is, and when she saw what was happening between you and Tyler, it obviously gnawed away at her."

"And what if it did?" Maggie demanded. "It doesn't change the truth."

"The *truth* is," Homer said to Celia, "I've known Royce Tyler for a goodly time. I know him to be an honorable man. It's true that he's in debt to the Sultan of Tangier. He won a small fortune from him playing cards last year in Monte Carlo. When the sultan found out his opponent was a psychic, he was furious and demanded his money back. The sultan, you see, takes especial pride in his ability at cards. It's his foremost point of vanity, you might say. He has always bragged how he's never been bested. He's also a spoiled and cruelly vindictive man. The fact that Tyler cleaned him out and humiliated him in front of the European cronies he was trying to impress stuck in his craw like nothing that's ever happened to him in his royal life. The only way he could justify the loss was to convince himself that Tyler had used his clairvoyant powers to cheat him. He's been nursing the insult ever since, to the point that it's become an obsession. He'll do anything to get revenge. And he has the means to wreak his vengeance without fear of interference."

"He could have given the money back," Maggie said.

"No, he could not. He won fair and square, and he needed the money. His father, the Earl of Cunningham, was on the verge of financial ruin. Royce used his winnings to anonymously help the father who'd disowned him. I only happen to know this because the banker who handled the transaction is a friend of mine, and told me so in confidence. Tyler never wanted his father to know it was he who'd bailed him out. Which should go a long way toward telling you the kind of man he is."

Celia suddenly remembered Royce's reaction when she'd told him Maggie Clifton had said he was a fraud. He could have told Celia the real story then. But he'd played the gentleman, saving the little fool the embarrassment.

"Furthermore," Homer continued, "I questioned Tyler about you when last I saw him. By the gleam in his eyes when I spoke of you, and the chivalrous and protective manner by which he refused to gossip, I could tell that he's very much in love with you. My wife, in a jealous fit, has done you a great injustice. But I can tell you the man I know would never do anything to cause you harm. The one bit of truth in my wife's addled story is that the sultan did threaten to have Tyler killed if he ever went near Tangier. I don't know what his reason was for going there with you, but whatever it was, you can jolly well be sure he risked his life in doing so."

Whatever his reason . . .

Suddenly Celia saw the events of the past week in a completely different light. The haunted look in Royce's eyes when she'd suggested they go to Tangier . . . his hesitation . . . his caution once they'd arrived, insisting they wait until dusk before venturing into the city . . .

He'd never intended to turn her over to the sultan. He'd gone to Tangier—at *her* instigation—knowing full well the danger to himself. He must have been afraid. And yet he'd put it all aside in a desperate attempt to keep the past from repeating itself. To try and spare them both the pain of losing each other tragically again. Knowing Tangier might bring the fulfillment of that destiny.

How could she have believed he'd planned such a vile conspiracy? How could she have trusted *Maggie Clifton* over Royce?

Suddenly she realized: *He was still there!*

She wheeled on Maggie as things fell horribly into place. "You told the sultan he was in Tangier, didn't you? The same morning you appeared at my door, pretending to befriend me . . ."

"No! I never—"

Celia grabbed the woman and shook her. "Tell me the truth, or I'll slap it out of you!"

Maggie was crying hysterically, but when Celia shook her again, she sobbed, "All right! I don't care who knows it. I sent a message to the palace. They came and dragged him from his bed. He's probably dead by now. And I'm glad, do you hear me? Glad!"

It was too ghastly to believe. That this awful, malicious woman could do such a thing!

And yet . . . it wasn't Maggie's fault. Not really. She was but an instrument of fate. Destiny had tricked Royce and Celia, as it had so many times before, into repeating the same disastrous pattern. Once again she hadn't believed in him. Once again, her actions had brought him to danger. Perhaps had even cost him his life.

All her fault. If only she'd listened to her heart and not her head. If only she'd trusted him more . . .

But it couldn't be true. Not when they'd come so far . . . when they'd been so close to finding a solution. She couldn't live with herself, knowing she'd caused him to suffer this way. She had to return to Tangier. She *must* believe that something could be done.

Please God, she prayed frantically, *don't let it be too late. I'll do anything to save him. Just let me be in time!*

Chapter Six

Abdulhamed the Resplendent, the thirty-fifth Sultan of Tangier, waddled down the opulent passageway of his palace on the hill overlooking the Kasbah. Never before had any of the hundreds of servants, retainers, and eunuchs that made up his retinue seen his three-hundred-pound girth move with such animated agility. He was a vision of corpulent extravagance: rings of precious gems stacked on fat fingers, the richest Damascus silk covering layer upon layer of portly flesh, diamond-studded slippers on stubby feet briskly carrying him to what could be the adventure of his life. Like so many of the idle rich who indulged themselves ceaselessly without discipline, the monarch was bored. But now . . . this!

Four days ago, his most loathed nemesis—Royce Tyler himself—had fallen miraculously into his hands. After months of plotting ways to lure him from the safety of England, the scoundrel had simply walked into the lion's den. Astonishing! Finally the humiliation the sultan had suffered at the hands of this mountebank would be avenged. It was just a question of deciding the most painful way to end the trickster's sorry life.

But then, this morning, something even more astonishing had happened. Lady Wybourne—the famous English novelist herself, the dazzling woman who'd occupied his midnight fantasies even longer and more powerfully than revenge against the devious psychic, this enchantress of erotic prose whose

writings had lighted a flame of passion within him like nothing
else in all of Allah's creation—had sent a note offering herself
in exchange for the villain's freedom.

He'd accepted in an instant. Taking her at her word—after
all, the women in her books *always* kept their promises—he'd
had the rogue beaten to show his contempt and hurled into the
street. His gamble regarding her character had paid off splendidly. Only moments later, his sentries reported that she'd surrendered herself to the guards at the front gate.

He'd spent the time while she was being prepared for him
in a fever of impatience. Scenes from her books, whole para-
graphs of which he'd committed to memory, returned to him
in a jumbled melee. Now, all those acts at which her books
had so exquisitely hinted would be brought to life in all their
sweaty glory, with their authoress playing the role of ravished
heroine! And this woman of elegance and imagination—so unlike these dull-witted beauties at his feet—would continue,
through the years ahead, to spark his exhausted appetites with
her unparalleled sexual creativity. The pearl of his harem.

As he approached the Chamber of a Thousand Delights,
two fierce guards armed with scimitars bowed and opened the
massive double doors. Beyond was a fantasia of saffron gyp-
sum, earth-toned embroidered silks, and piles of oversized cit-
rine and golden pillows. Slave girls, scantily dressed but veiled,
cooled the air with ostrich-feather fans. Muscular Nubian men
in white loincloths, their ebony skin oiled to a fine sheen,
stood in a line, awaiting their instructions. The sultan eyed
them appreciatively, thinking of the splendid contrast their
bodies would make with his fair-skinned captive.

He settled his bulk into the cushioned throne that was
slightly elevated over the lavish arena. As he did, five slave
girls rushed to his side, kneeling all around him, stroking him
in readiness for the spectacle to come. Trembling with lustful
anticipation, he clapped his hands and a small door at the side
opened to admit the Englishwoman, nude except for a thick
black leather collar about her throat, connected by silver
chains to the similar cuffs at her wrists. More lovely than he'd

316 / *Katherine O'Neal*

even imagined. Her mahogany hair tumbling about her shoulders in splendid abandon. Her creamy breasts riding high. Her hips and thighs womanly enticement to his accelerating ardor. Despite her slave chains, she walked in like the countess she was. Proud. Haughty. Her chin at an imposing angle, her eyes gleaming like Egyptian emeralds—cool green, but with an ineffable fire in their depths. Coveted womanhood daring him to conquer her if he could. Offering, as if sensing that his conquests were too easy, a challenge to appeal to the primal nature of his vanquishing forbears. As if she knew just how to appeal to a man seeking drama in an increasingly dull and soft world.

Celia heard the sharp intake of the sultan's breath, felt the eyes of all in the room caress the display of her shackled, naked form. She squared her shoulders, determined to be brave, reminding herself of why she was here.

When she'd returned and discovered that Royce was alive, it had seemed like such a miracle that the shock of it had cracked through her despair. She'd realized in a flash that Tangier had shown them the solution after all. That it was she who must break the pattern. She carried with her the guilt from countless lifetimes in which she had his blood on her hands. The only way to absolve herself was to reverse the situation: to put herself in danger to save Royce's life. To sacrifice herself. To set him free by her own actions: free from the sultan and yes, free from herself as well. The only way to break the tragic mold in which he kept dying because of her was to exchange her life for his.

And so she'd offered a deal. No longer caring what happened to her. Thinking only of him.

She'd waited until they'd released him before surrendering herself. Their eyes meeting as the guards whisked her past him. Seeing his bloodied face, the shocked look in his eyes as he realized what her presence meant. Her heart breaking as she grasped the sultan's perfidy in having him beaten. Telling herself it was all right now. His bruises would heal. And he'd be free.

And so she'd let them lead her away. Away from him . . . behind the fortress walls . . . into an Arabian Nights world. The harem, where she was bathed, massaged, and perfumed for her sacrifice to a demented admirer . . . the wait in the side room with the disinterested eunuchs . . .

And now it was to begin.

Two eunuchs led her before the sultan and pushed her to her knees to bow down before him.

"You cannot imagine how many hours I have spent waiting for this moment," he welcomed her in accomplished English. "But the results are worth the wait. Before this night is through, I will use you as no woman has ever been used. But first, I will entertain myself by watching my splendid Nubians ravage you"—he broke into a delighted grin—"*exactly* as you had Anna ravaged by the gypsies in *Duchess of Desire!*"

He rubbed his hands together in brisk anticipation.

But before they could begin, one of the guards entered the room, bowed before the sultan, and whispered something in his ear. His eyes widened and he laughed. "Truly? Why, the fool! How wonderful! By all means, bring him in. Let him join our little merriment."

Celia listened with only half an ear. Now that she'd made her choice, what difference did it make if one more joined the scene? She'd relinquished her own will the moment she'd set foot in the palace. So it was with vacant eyes that she glanced toward the door to see the new arrival. Until the guard returned a moment later . . . with Royce in tow!

Her world crashed in on her. *Everything in vain.*

She shot to her feet. "No! You promised you'd release him."

"I did release him." The sultan gave a philosophical shrug. "Is it my doing that he was so foolish as to return and attempt to rescue you?"

Rescue?

Stunned, she turned and looked at Royce. He'd come back voluntarily . . . for her . . .

But that wasn't the way it was supposed to work.

She stormed to him, shaking off the guards who sought to stop her. "You've ruined everything. Don't you see? The pattern was broken. You were free."

He shook his head. "Without you, I'm not free."

She felt tears flood her eyes. "But that's just it. Without me you *are* free. That's what we couldn't see. I'm nothing but trouble for you. I'm like some black widow spider who keeps leading you to your doom. And now it's happened again. I wouldn't blame you if you hated me. I hate *myself.* I hate what I've done to you over and over again. It has to stop. It's over for us now, but in the future . . . in any life we might have after this . . . I want you to stay away from me. I can't bear to go through this again. I won't."

She stepped back from him, seeking distance, seeking strength. But he came after her, taking hold of her hands. "I don't hate you, Celia. And I couldn't stay away from you if I tried."

She trembled, telling herself not to ask. What did it matter now? But in the end she had to know. "Why?"

He hesitated, as if still struggling within himself.

"Why, Royce? *Why?*"

For a moment more, his gaze pierced through her. But then his face softened and she felt his surrender. Felt the blockage inside him that had kept him emotionally distant from her dissolve. "Because I love you, Celia. Because I always have."

She swallowed the lump in her throat, staring at him wondrously through the mist of her tears. Unable to speak.

With the pad of his thumb, he wiped away her tears. "I fought it for as long as I could. But the moment I realized what you'd done—for me—I couldn't deny it any longer. I couldn't even think of anything else. I love you. I had to come back, if only to tell you."

He loved her! So much that he'd put her first, regardless of the consequences to himself.

Only then did she realize the truth that had eluded her: that in order to break the tragic rhythm of their fate, they'd both had to give themselves to each other. Totally. Completely. With no fear and no thought to their own well-being. Thinking only of the other.

And now that they had, surely the pattern must finally be broken. Surely in the next lifetime, they'd be free. Free of the residue of the past. Free to be together. Free to be happy.

But she didn't want to wait until the next lifetime. She wanted him now. She saw stretching before them the possibility of a life together. Time to get to know each other. To ask all the questions they'd avoided. Years to love and take care of one another. To travel, to explore the world—and each other—together. Laughter and adventure, passion and tenderness. Happiness, peace, fulfillment at last, reunited with their other halves.

If only it could be . . .

Her rebellious spirit stirred, born anew. There *must* be a way out. They couldn't have come this far, only to have it end like this. If only she could think of something . . . *something* . . .

"You are, indeed, a reckless man, Royce Tyler," the sultan was saying. "I was more than willing to accept the bargain that was struck, regardless of the fact that it cheated me of the pleasure of seeing you suffer for the distress you caused me. But with your return, it seems I am destined to, as you British say, have my cake and eat it as well. I will kill you—slowly, so I might savor every slice of the blade. But first you will watch the epic initiation of the woman you love into my harem."

He waved his hand and two guards grabbed Royce and held him pinned between them.

"Make certain he does not interfere," the sultan snapped out. Then, on reflection, cautioned, "Do not for an instant let down your guard—even mentally. He may be able to read your minds and thus gain unfair advantage. Again."

The guards forced Royce to the side as their monarch motioned to the Nubians. They came in a pack, surrounding Celia on all sides. Large black men bulging with muscles, standing sentry all around her like gigantic onyx statues. One by one they began to remove their loincloths, exposing large, tumescent cocks already hardening in anticipation of their feast.

"Be rough," the sultan commanded, stroking himself. "Show the haughty aristocrat how the gypsies do it."

Royce made a lunge toward them, but one of his sentries put a razor-sharp scimitar to his throat.

"Ah," the sultan chortled. "I see your protective instincts have been aroused. This will prove more entertaining than I imagined."

Royce faced him, breathing hard. "This is between you and me. Do what you want to me. Torture me, kill me. I don't care. But let her go."

"A pretty entreaty," the sultan said. "But why should I do that when I can have the both of you?" To the Nubians he added gleefully, "Put on a show. Fight each other for her. Like dogs fighting over a bitch."

Celia struggled to find a foothold that would help her. *Pretend,* she told herself fiercely. *You're Charlotte doing this for Rashid. Imagine him watching you.* But then she looked at Royce and saw both his anger and his frustration written on his face. And she knew that this time, she couldn't pretend. This was different from the games they'd played, the amusements he'd instigated. This was no longer for him—*for the two of them*—and because it wasn't, it was profane.

And yet, there had to be a way to survive this. *Pretend, as the sultan does, that it's a scene from one of your books . . .*

Wait a minute . . .

Her books . . .

Slowly, an idea began to form. A bored monarch who loved her stories to the point of obsession . . . to the point of *this.* Why not give him what he *really* wanted?

The Nubians were shoving one another in their impatience for her when she used the distraction to break from them. She ran to Royce and whispered feverishly, "I have an idea. Please, let me handle this. Don't do anything to jeopardize your safety. Promise me."

Some of the Nubians, thinking this part of the game, moved to follow her. "Swear it," she hissed.

Royce was watching her, unsure.

"Do you trust me?" she asked.

He gave a cheerless smile as if to say, *A fine time to ask.* But he answered aloud, "Implicitly."

"Then promise."

After a last brief hesitation, he nodded. With his pledge in hand, Celia turned to the sultan.

"This isn't worthy of you, Your Majesty. Why are you doing this to *me*? How much pleasure can this possibly give you?"

He flashed an expectant grin. "Oh, a great deal, I assure you."

"You're enjoying it now, but when it's over, it's over."

"I intend to make it last a very long time."

"But how long before you're bored again? You don't need me to act out my old scenes. Anyone can do that. What you need are *new* scenes."

He peered at her suspiciously. "What sort of trick is this?"

"No trick, Your Majesty, just reason. I can give you a much greater pleasure. I can give you what no other woman can."

"And what is that?"

"A story." She glanced at Royce tenderly and added, "In fact, the greatest erotic love story ever told. One that spans the ages. One that you will be the first to hear."

Within his moon face, the sultan's eyes were darting wildly. Confused, agitated. This wasn't what he'd planned, and yet . . . the prospect of such a story . . . from such a storyteller . . . for one who loved such stories above all else . . .

"The tale is within me now," she continued. "It's begging to be told. Tomorrow, it may be gone. You wanted me in the first place because of my way with words, not my body. If you merely use my body, it won't be long before you're as bored with me as you are with everything else. But this story will live within you forever. To be savored to the end of your days."

She'd pierced the heart of his character and peaked his curiosity. But still he was reluctant. She could see his contradicting thoughts flash across his face. In the silence as he pondered, she cast another look at Royce. Where a moment before he'd been the picture of gloom, he seemed animated now. He was looking at her with a light of hope shining in his eyes, with a growing pride and admiration for her resourcefulness and ingenuity. She could feel his energy pouring into her, and as it did, she felt the old familiar well of creativity rising in her, seizing her, making her its instrument. Stronger than it had ever been before.

She rushed to the sultan, falling down before him, putting her hands on his knees in eager supplication. "Your Majesty, this is the story of stories. You *must* hear it!"

For what seemed an eternity, the room was utterly still. Breaths unconsciously held, every eye fixed on the throne, awaiting the decision. The sultan weighing her through slitted eyes. Until finally he spat out, "Five minutes. I will give you five minutes."

Five minutes to hook him, or it was all over.

Celia let out her breath. She had to play this carefully. Use this opportunity to their advantage and, if possible, to save their lives. But could she do it? Come up with a story fascinating enough to captivate this evil man and change their fate? Trick destiny as it had so often tricked them?

She turned to Royce. He was watching her keenly. She felt the words he didn't speak. *Go on. I'll help you.*

He closed his eyes. And suddenly the images she needed began to unfold in Celia's mind.

She felt the shift within her. No longer was she a captive supplicant. She was the magnet upon which all attention was riveted. In her essence. All the years of creating fantasies culminating in this one moment, this one story. The story of her life . . . her *lives.*

Their lives.

She addressed the Nubians—those randy beasts so eager to defile her—with regal splendor, instructing, "Be so kind as to bring me a pillow, one of you." They jumped as a group to obey, each carting a large cushion to lay at her feet. Without rushing, she settled herself upon them, allowing the suspense to build.

And in her own time, she began to speak. Not certain where the story would take her. Following the images as they led her back in time, back to an ancient land . . .

Speaking in a voice that was mellow and seductive, skillfully pulling her audience into her narrative with a rhythm and flow that evoked a mood of primordial enchantment. Taking them back to ancient Babylon with words that caused their surroundings to vanish as the world she was creating unfolded all around them. Vast winged lion statues dominating city gates. Timeless flow of the Euphrates. Temple of Ishtar. A virile Persian warrior. A lovely Babylonian maiden.

"What does Sarna look like?" the sultan asked, leaning forward in his seat.

"Large raven eyes. Flowing ebony hair. Skin like porcelain. Full, lush breasts."

"Like Gwendolyn in *Ecstasy in Eden*," he supplied.

"Exactly like Gwendolyn."

The sultan slapped his fleshy cheeks in delight. "Gwendolyn is one of my favorites!" he cried. "But do you mean to say that a high-born woman would go to the temple to *prostitute* herself? Was this not sacrilege?"

"On the contrary. It was the custom in Babylon. Once in every woman's life, she must go to the Temple of Ishtar and serve her goddess. She did this by sitting in the temple court until she caught the eye of a stranger who would then buy her favors. She must wait until someone paid for her, no matter how long the wait. This was the sacred religious duty that every woman must fulfill. Even if it took years for her to be chosen."

"But with a beauty like Sarna, surely she was chosen at once."

"Very astute, Your Majesty. Ralik took one look at her and knew he had to have her. He made his offering to Ishtar and took her into the inner sanctum of the temple, where the liaisons took place. Custom demanded that within this private chamber, for this one time only, the lovely Sarna had to do anything Ralik commanded. To refuse any of his sexual requests would have been unspeakable blasphemy."

"A stranger," the sultan mused, growing more excited by the moment. "And in the temple, no less! Is it any wonder Babylon has lived throughout the ages as the very symbol of decadence?"

"Sarna wasn't inexperienced in matters of love. It wasn't the custom for Babylonian women to withhold their virtue. And yet she'd never had a lover like Ralik. While fighting with Darius's troops in India, he'd learned strange new lovemaking customs from the Hamana people of the Indus valley. He didn't take her quickly. He transformed the act of seduction into an art of dominance and submission. He bound her wrists with rawhide straps to emphasize her helplessness in his hands. He aroused her with a forceful touch, all the while letting her know that he wouldn't hurt her, that what they were doing was its own ritual, designed to take them to an undreamed-of plateau of pleasure. Teaching her captive body to love his touch. Arousing her to such a degree that she forgot everything in her desire for him. But even as she grew desperate for him, he bided his time. Making her beg, and making her love the begging for its own sake. It created a bond between them, a mutual exchange of power that fulfilled them both like no other carnal experience of their lives."

"But surely after such an experience, they would want more."

"That, of course, was where the trouble began. As a Persian, Ralik didn't grasp the strength of the taboo that forbade them from ever meeting again. But Sarna knew. Yet she was so taken by the exquisite pleasure of this new form of lovemaking—this bondage—that she went to him outside the temple and consummated their union again. Not once, but three times. Each time more intense. Each time flaunting the danger that they would be discovered."

"And they *were* discovered?"

"It was inevitable. Sarna was so addicted to this pleasure

that only Ralik could give her that she couldn't stop herself. She needed more and more, as if searching for a higher release that could only come with her total surrender to him. An informer alerted the temple priests. They were arrested and brought before the High Priest himself."

She paused for effect. As the silence filled the hall, the sultan pressed, "And what happened?"

"Ralik, though he loved Sarna, professed his ignorance of the taboo and, in his fear, blamed Sarna for leading him astray. But it didn't save him. He was put to death before her eyes."

"And Sarna?"

"The High Priest was unsure what to do with her. You see, no one had ever broken this strictest of taboos before, and death seemed an insufficient punishment to discourage this dangerous precedent. It was finally decided to let Ishtar herself settle the matter with her higher wisdom. Sarna was forced to lay prostrate before the statue of the goddess without food or water until judgment was rendered."

"You mean . . . until the goddess manifested herself?"

"Yes. Three days into Sarna's ordeal, Ishtar appeared to her and made an extraordinary pronouncement. She decreed that Sarna was free to go and live out the rest of her life. But from this day forward, she and Ralik were doomed to repeat the pattern of their blasphemy in all their subsequent lifetimes down through eternity. They would meet, share a fierce attraction, and feel the need to explore their sensuality in ever more intense situations, desperately seeking a release and fulfillment that would elude them. But they would keep trying until ultimately she would lead him into a dangerous situation that would result in his death. And even though they couldn't remember the past, they would feel its residue and recognize the bond between them, so each of their succeeding sexual relationships would build on what had gone before, and was more passionate than the last."

"This was to go on forever? Was there no escape from this curse?"

"Only one. The goddess let it be known that there was one

sexual act that was the most intimate, the most intense, the most satisfying experience possible between a man and a woman. Their quest was to find and share this act. If they did, if they succeeded in achieving this most precious of unions, their accumulated longing and frustration would finally find release and the curse would be broken."

"But what *is* this act? Were they given no clue?"

"Only that Ralik possessed the key to finding it, but he wasn't to know what the key was. That he must discover for himself."

"A riddle!" the sultan cried. "I love riddles! Go on. What happens next?"

Hours passed as Celia continued to captivate him. Along the way, she'd removed her chains without the sultan seeming to notice. As more time elapsed, he left his throne, settled himself on a massive couch, ordered a robe to be brought to her, then dismissed the Nubians and slave girls, so that only he, Celia, Royce, and the two guards remained. And still she spoke, taking him forward in time through three more episodes, a continuation of the same story, but each set in a different place and time. The same characters of Ralik and Sarna, but with new faces and names. Each encounter more breathless than the last, their bondage deepening, their sexual urgency for one another growing, its release becoming more elusive and frustrating each time. Carrying the sultan along so he couldn't help but empathize with their feelings, their hopes, their distress, their crushing need to achieve unity with one another. All the while making each segment more explicit than the one before.

And each time the sultan, aroused to an ever-increasing pitch, would ask, "Is *that* what they're looking for? Is that the act?"

And she would smile mysteriously and say, "Not yet." So that he had to hear more.

She'd been speaking for five hours straight when she felt the first onrush of fatigue. But the sultan was inexhaustible. He turned onto his side and plumped the pillows beneath his head. "Tell me more. Where do they next appear?"

Celia searched her mind, but nothing came. Alarmed, she rose and went to the enormous water jar and drank from the dipper slowly, stalling for time. She had to think. But she was so tired. And the words wouldn't come.

"Enough water!" the sultan barked. "Continue the tale."

Panic seized her. For the first time, she felt she couldn't do this. She was too drained. Her mind felt numb, her body ached from sitting in the same position for hours at a time. She'd been mad to think she could pull this off. And yet . . . she must. The alternative was unthinkable.

She turned and her gaze locked with Royce's. *Help me,* she implored him silently.

Chapter Seven

Royce rose and went to join her at the water jar, walking slowly to show the guards he offered no threat. He took the dipper from her, as if wanting a drink himself. But in the process, his hand touched hers. He held it for a moment. Fixing her with an empowering gaze. Focusing his energy, feeding her. She breathed it in. Felt his vigor transmitted through the touch of his hand. Felt herself infused with a new spirit and fresh images. Her emptiness filled by him.

"Where do they next appear?" the sultan demanded.

". . . Ancient Rome," she told him tentatively.

"What period?"

Royce was watching her intently. Something began to dance at the edge of her mind. "The reign of the Emperor Caligula."

"Ah! Magnificent! Rome at its most depraved! What was her name this time?"

Her connection to Royce was growing stronger by the moment, renewed by his touch, fueled by his faith. As if they were one mind, one soul, working together in one act of creation.

"Diana?" she asked.

He nodded gently, his eyes full of respect. She felt his love flow into her and returned to her seat. Relief and gratitude for Royce filling her heart.

Once again the threads of the saga began to weave themselves into a rich tapestry. Diana, patrician lady, taken by the corrupt and avaricious young emperor for his personal plaything. Guarding her jealously, watching her every move. Owning her in every sense of the word.

But Diana hated the sovereign and chafed under his restrictions. Especially when he would take her to the weekly palace orgies—mammoth affairs, fabulously staged, invariably lasting into the early hours of the morning. Diana would sit at Caligula's side, never allowed to take part. Being a naturally passionate woman, and growing increasingly restive under the loveless limits of her captivity, she would watch the carefree abandonment of the participants with yearning eyes. The pampered women in various stages of undress, hair piled high and cascading to their shoulders in streaming tendrils, dripping with emeralds and pearls, cavorting unreservedly with the hot-blooded soldiers and senators of Rome. Epic excesses. Wine flowing copiously. Ladies dancing in seductive invitation or gliding naked on gigantic silken swings dangling from the ceiling. Muscular men carrying them off in fits of laughter before the kissing, the petting, the rubbing of soft flesh against toughened sinew turned their giggles to impassioned sighs. Until they lined the hall of the grand playroom, hundreds of writhing bodies creating a carpet of undulating lust. Women surrounded by men with raging erections, taking them with fevered delight. Sucking dicks, being mounted from behind, thrown over men's laps and spanked before descending masculine hands began to caress, slipping underneath to toy with pouty nether lips, frigging them to new frenzies. Short-cropped, manly heads between tremulous female thighs, tongues lapping as the wealthy strumpets of the Empire stretched luxuriously and arched into their mouths with whimpered cries. Reaching for anyone who happened by, hungry for more, taking all comers eagerly, ravenously. Shrieking ecstatically as those studly appendages, rock-hard and ready, entered them, adding their male groans to the clamor as they thrust and slammed and fucked with all their might. Women kissing one another, sucking nearby breasts as they took the men in all positions. Stroking, fondling, fornicating like wild creatures, completely consumed. Rounded buttocks and shapely thighs wriggling and humping in ecstasy as fingers probed and cocks claimed the moist, furry caverns of their prurient aspirations.

Diana watched it all, her blood simmering, knowing Caligula had brought her here to tantalize her. Knowing the élan and revelry would stir her passions, would cause her to pine for such frolic as she saw around her—this spirited woman who hid her vivacity behind a mask of loneliness and pain. Punishing her for withholding the true force of her ardor from him, yet conversely submitting her to this week after week in the hopes that one day she'd crack and, driven mad with lust, would unleash her frustrated desires on him. Standing at the ready to reap the fruits of her capitulation.

But his sadistic plot backfired. One night, Diana noticed someone new at the orgy. A noble general, splendidly rugged and battle-scarred with an air of command that had led his legions to legendary victories in Gaul and Germania. Marcellus, champion of Rome.

He was scanning the spectacle with a mildly amused air when their eyes met. The attraction was instantaneous and electrifying. Leisurely, and with a detached assurance so at variance with his emperor's anxious fluttering, Marcellus joined the festivities. But always, no matter what woman he was with, his eyes would lock with Diana's and there was no question that, in his mind, it was *her* body his hands touched.

The next week, he returned to the party, but only because he knew she'd be there. As the months passed, she was forced to watch him with the ladies of the court. A magnificent lover whose legend grew and who was always much in demand. She could feel Caligula squirm as he caught her repeatedly caressing his most celebrated general with her eyes. But as time passed, the emperor concerned her less and less. She knew that somehow she must have the majestic Marcellus. That they must join their bodies in search of the sexual infinite . . . if only once . . .

One week, miraculously, Caligula was ill and couldn't attend. He ordered Diana locked in her room. But she bribed the guard and escaped to the grand hall. When Marcellus saw her without her imperial watchdog, he knew why she'd come. Stealthily, they slipped away. And when they were at last alone, they came together with a ferocity born of their enforced separation, throwing themselves into each other's arms, kissing madly, clutching, grasping, savoring the coveted flesh that had been denied them so long. Casting off their clothes and entwining their naked bodies, seeking the release they knew could only come with this.

And yet, once wasn't enough. They began to meet secretly whenever they could. Marcellus was such an exquisite lover that Diana blossomed quickly and fully, unchaining all her pent-up passions, lavishing on him all the love and devotion she'd thought never to have a chance to give to a man. Learning from him, exploring with him varied forms of pleasure that with Caligula had seemed an obscenity, but with her beloved Marcellus felt joyous and healing. Growing more and more enslaved to him. Both of them unconsciously driven to find something . . . but what? Taking greater chances. Diana certain that Caligula would find out in time and punish her, but beyond caring. Wanting only Marcellus, no matter the cost.

She begged him to take her away to some remote corner of Africa or Asia Minor where they could live together. Marcellus wanted to, but couldn't bring himself to give up his career, tarnish his family name, and live the life of an outlaw. Still, Diana harbored the hope that someday he would realize their love was more important than anything else.

Then, one night, she crept out of the palace for her moonlight assignation with Marcellus. As she went up the stairs of the little hostel where they met just off the Appian Way, the room was dark as usual and lightly scented with her lover's distinctive musk. She rushed into his arms, pressed her lips to his . . . but . . .

The lips were thin. The arms were bony and frail. His touch was clammy. It was . . . Caligula!

As she gasped, he threw her down on the bed. She fell against Marcellus's face. But his head had no body attached to it. She was forced to endure the horror of being ravaged by this monster in her lover's deathbed.

And so the pattern continued . . .

More hours passed. Royce had lost all track of time. He watched quietly as Celia spoke, using his vital force to nourish her, wrapped up in the unfolding saga, increasingly fascinated by the way her storytelling skill intuitively linked her to their joint past. And yet, he had no idea where she was going with this. Was she buying them time? Trying to lull her listeners so Royce could find some vulnerability in their defenses—perhaps try and overwhelm the guards and take the sultan hostage? He'd already run those possibilities through his mind and dismissed them as futile. What else could she be after? She couldn't keep talking forever. The sultan was clearly hooked on the unending chronicle, but at some point it would *have* to end. What then?

Yet eerily, Celia showed no more signs of fatigue or uncertainty. Now that things were flowing once again, she was gaining energy and power, in total command of the room as she took them to . . .

Spain in the 1500s. The Spanish Inquisition. This time she was Melda, flame-haired Barcelona seductress accused of witchcraft because she was known to bewitch every man who crossed her path. Brought forth to be interrogated by a panel of inquisitors. Stern men in black robes who questioned her ceaselessly, increasingly stymied and exasperated by her unconcerned contempt for the tribunal. Examining her with hostile yet covetous eyes as she sat in the chair before them, flaunting the seductive movements of her body, the crossing and uncrossing of her shapely legs, the thrust of her ripe bosom which threatened to spill over the scanty bodice of her gown.

Until finally, outraged, they resorted to the extreme means the inquisition employed when the witch in question was particularly stubborn—or beautiful. They piously assumed the guise of the devil to taunt his possessed maiden. They stripped her, fondled her, slapped her. Then, taking off their own clothes, their erections throbbing in the service of their god, they proceeded to force an admission from her. Shoving her to the stone floor, holding her down and spreading her wide between them, pumping their duly anointed manhoods into her mouth and rooting between her thighs, intent on driving out her evil lust and eliciting a confession of her abominable sins.

Only one of them, standing in the shadows, held himself back. Diego, proud, handsome, younger than the others by some years. His unrivaled piety making him chief inquisitor of Catalan, second only in command to the feared and all-powerful Torquemada himself. Regarding this unruly demonstration as one by one the interrogators succumbed to the witch's spell, transformed from judges to besotted suitors, amidst her taunting them with enticing obscenities and charges of hypocrisy. Until they'd spent themselves completely, leaving her unrepentant.

Incensed, Diego castigated them. "You have failed in your duty. I see that I must handle this. Leave us. I myself will break her and wrest from the siren the confession you buffoons neglected to attain."

When they'd gathered up their clothes and left, ashamed, Diego walked a circle around her, regarding her with hard, reproving eyes. "You won't find me such easy prey," he told her. "I'm impervious to your spells."

Naked, on her knees, her succulent flesh gleaming in the brazier's glow, she looked up at him and recognized in this man something elemental—an attraction, a vulnerability she knew she could exploit. Feeling curiously that heaven's larger purpose behind this vile inquisition was to bring them together. As if it were preordained. *"Are* you?" she asked.

Her confidence enraged him. But at the same time, he felt the stirrings of something hitherto unknown to his devout nature. Something that made him shudder in fear and hardened his determination to rout out the devil in this pathetic woman. Feeling strangely that this was a personal mission and that he'd been brought here to be tested in some way.

He called in some guards and ordered them to chain her to the heavy wooden chair, her legs stretched and draped over each arm so her sex was freely accessible to him, her arms lashed together behind the back of the chair so her breasts were thrust out in magnificent display. Then he took a short whip—much like a riding crop—in hand, dismissed the guards, and stood before her, slapping it ominously into his palm.

"Sorceress you may be," he informed her, "but you will soon learn that my power is greater than yours. I am master here. Sooner or later, you will submit to me and acknowledge your crimes. You might as well give in now."

"But if I *am* a witch," she defied him, "you have no power over me, do you?"

"We shall see."

"Are you going to beat it out of me?" she asked with a scornful glimpse.

"Worse than that."

She steeled herself to withstand whatever tactic he might employ. But he proved to be more skillful at this particular type of inducement than she'd anticipated. He began to trail the whip across her cheek, along her throat, around the generous mounds of her breasts. To circle her navel, then slowly, with deceptive delicacy, guiding it between her legs. Finding her cleft, testing it with the soft leather thong, teasing her with its touch. Observing her relentlessly as her breath deepened, her eyes closing, her mouth going slack. Working her clit, the soft caresses at variance with the stark room and the instrument of torture in his hands. Arousing her mercilessly, and so easily—she who'd always done the arousing—that it seemed to carry the force of some cosmic inevitability. His eyes singeing her. Exhibited so blatantly before him, bound and helpless now as she'd never been, twisting in her seat against her bonds, her body rising up and thrashing about rhythmically as he used the flick of the whip to incite her. Moaning now in sweet distress.

Realizing with a start that she was on the verge of climax. When she'd never come this close before, with any other man. The wonder of it filling her with exultation. But just as she felt the onset of delicious shivers, he took the whip away. Leaving her hanging with nowhere to go.

Her eyes flew open, crushed by the cruel abandonment, realizing his designs. "Fiend!" she spat out at him.

He said nothing, just gave a brief, sardonic smile. And when she'd cooled down the slightest bit, replaced the soft tip of the quirt. Playing with her pulsing clit once more. This time she tried to move away, but was thwarted by the bite of the chains. This time, he crouched down beside her and put his mouth to her nipple, taking it between his lips. Sucking on it, nibbling it delicately between his teeth, causing it to swell and throb as he slipped his fingers into her cunt. Fulsome and saturated, they moved within her remorselessly even as the whip continued its tyranny. All of her passion bubbling to the surface, unaccustomed to being in the clutches of some power greater than her own, wanting so to overflow and spill her release onto his hand. His fingers ruthlessly finding the spot that caused her to seize up and hump against him as her body screamed for mercy.

But once again, just as she felt the beginnings of blessed orgasm, he moved away, denying her satiation. She fell back into the confinement of her chair with an agonized cry.

He put his mouth to her ear. "Admit your crime," he growled. "Tell me you're a witch and I shall give you what you crave."

She collected herself and gave him a look of biting calm. "Whether or not I'm a witch, you will discover for yourself."

It unsettled him. He paused for a moment, then said, "Very well." And began again.

This time he stood before her and let his protective robes drop to the floor, displaying a body of masculine perfection. Taking himself in hand. Stroking himself deliberately as if building up a force of his own to counteract her spell. Making her watch, her tongue licking parched lips as she noted the brawn and beauty of him. And then . . . slowly, dramatically . . . he came closer and positioned himself between her extended thighs. Taking a moment to smear himself against her enflamed clit with the silky head, causing a sharp intake of her breath. Then he plunged inside, filling her more completely—more delightfully—than she'd ever been filled before. He drew back and fucked her slowly, so she could feel every minute motion as his steely rod invaded her inch by lovely inch. He touched her cleft again, supreme anguish, licking her flames. With the other hand, he put the cursed whip to her mouth and ordered, "Suck it, witch." She couldn't help but obey, parting her lips, tasting her own juices on its tip. Cast aloft once again as he drove into her with increasing fervor, until she was so desperate to climax that low, plaintive sobs punctuated panting breath. His flinty shaft like a battering ram that brought excruciating pleasure with every forceful shove.

"Confess, witch," he hissed. But she refused and again he stopped.

On and on it went, this licentious battle of wills, hour after hour. Each time, he found more persuasive and inventive ways of hurtling her to the point of bliss then snatching it away. Doing things to her that he'd done with no other woman, to prove to himself that she was possessed. Using her bound body like a toy, his power and his self-control driving her to the threshold of madness.

Yet even as he did, she astonished him. Because no matter what he inflicted on her, she loved it all. Growing riper and more responsive to his demands. Denying *him* release as she refused to give him the confession he sought. Dragging it out now, never wanting it to end, sensing that they were engaged in some epic ritual, searching for a release that wasn't just of the moment, but was larger and more fundamental. And gradually, without his realizing it, the balance of power began to shift. Until it was he who felt the domination of her spirit. Until he became possessed by *her*. Until finally he could contain himself no longer. Until he'd taken his fill and still couldn't get enough. Obsessed with her beyond reason, beyond the dictates of his training, beyond his dogged judgment. Disdaining—abandoning—all his stern authority in his need for her.

Until at last, he gave them both the shattering climax that could no longer be denied. Again and again. And then, finally spent, he set her free. Telling the others he'd proved beyond doubt that the charges were false. Protecting her. Hiding her away and coming to her repeatedly in the dead of night, his passion for her unquenchable. Searching . . . still searching . . . ever searching . . .

Frightened all the while that someone would discover what he'd done.

As their love for one another grew, Melda put forth a solution. "Marry me," she told him. "Torquemada can never harm us then."

But his pride was too stubborn even in the face of her charm. What would people think if he married a woman who'd been accused of sorcery? They'd say he'd let her go because she'd bewitched him, and that would benefit neither one of them.

And so he persisted with his secret affair. Until of course his jealous rivals learned of it and reported it to Torquemada, who found mercy in his heart for the sumptuous Melda, but promptly had his protégé Diego burned at the stake.

Then on to Gibraltar . . .
Charlotte and Rashid . . . the wild child of the Rock and

the dashing Moroccan spy ... their passion even more explosive this time, their awareness of their bondage greater than it had ever been ... their desperation for fulfillment even more aching ... the cave ... the blindfold ... seeking the one act that would free them ...

"Surely it comes now!" the sultan cried.

"No, Your Majesty. Not yet." Her voice husky now, her mouth dry, her throat strained. "Rashid fought his need for Charlotte and was determined to turn her over to the sultan. But she realized this and informed the British authorities. They arrested Rashid and hanged him."

The sultan fell back into his cushions in desperation. "*Again* no relief for the spirits of Ralik and Sarna? I can bear this no longer! When does the relief come?"

"In the next lifetime."

He pushed himself up. "Then tell me. What could it possibly be? No more stories, no more delays. Just describe this act that sets them free. I must know!"

His tormented eyes bore into her demandingly. As eager for relief as the tortured souls of the protagonists. So expertly manipulated by his Scheherezade that he empathized with them completely.

"I *demand* that you tell me!"

The time had come. The moment she'd been building toward for untold hours. Celia took a slow breath for courage. Everything—Royce's life and hers, and any chance they might have for freedom and happiness—depended on the next few moments. Everything else had been preparation for this.

Royce, feeling the subtle change in her, sat straighter in his chair. Still not certain where she was going. Alert for any opportunity to help.

Meeting the sultan's gaze steadily, she said, "I'll tell you, Your Majesty, when you set us free."

He shoved himself up into a seated position and glared his fury. "Strumpet! Do you dare to play with me? *Me?!* Abdulhamed the Resplendent?"

"What do I have to lose?"

"You will tell me now or I will . . . slay your lover before your eyes. I will slice him into a thousand pieces."

Affecting nonchalance, Celia shrugged. "Credit me with some sense, Your Majesty. You've made it clear that you were going to kill him in any event. So here is my offer. I'll write the conclusion for you to read and savor through the years. I promise it will be like nothing you've ever read before. But if you don't let us go, I won't tell you the end, no matter what you do. You may keep me captive for fifty years, and I shall never breathe a word."

"I will put you on the rack," he threatened, his voice rising. "I will torture it out of you! No woman can withstand torture."

Checkmate.

"I'd thought your memory better than that," she said with a cool smile. "Was the great Khan able to torture the information out of Lucinda in *The Mongol's Captive?*"

Tangier receded in the wake of the S.S. *Manchester*. Only minutes before, as she and Royce had stepped onto the London-bound ship, Celia had handed their former captor the envelope with the written conclusion to her story. Like an opium addict too long denied his pleasure, he'd ripped it open on the dock and was reading it even now. He scanned the pages hastily then clasped them to his heart and, meeting her gaze, kissed his fat fingers in tribute. Then he was borne away to savor the delectable ending in the privacy of his palace.

Standing at the rail beside her, Royce wrapped his arms about her and held her close. "You were absolutely magnificent," he told her, his lips in her hair.

She burrowed into his embrace, only now allowing herself to realize that it was over. All of it. Feeling the warmth and security of his arms about her, holding her, cherishing her. Looking forward to a future that held promise for the first time in her life. In many lives. And suddenly she laughed.

"What will we say when people ask us how we met? Do you think they'll ever believe this story of ours?"

"Probably not. Does it matter?"

She kissed his dear bruised face. "Not in the least."

He, too, smiled. It was as if all his tension and torment had been washed away. "You seem to have pleased the sultan with what you wrote."

She gave him a cheeky grin. "Naturally."

"So . . ."

"So . . . what?"

"The act . . . what was it? Did you make it up? I don't see it."

"That's because part of the curse was that Ralik would have the key but wouldn't know what it was. It was *you* who gave me the ending."

"How?"

"When you came back for me, when you admitted you loved me . . . when you made the ultimate commitment to me in a way you never had before . . . that was all you had to do. You had it in your power to break the curse at any time. But you had to put me, and our love, before your pride."

"And that's what you wrote?" he asked, still mystified.

"Part of it. I wrote that the most intense and daring sexuality can only flourish and find fulfillment when it's built on such a commitment . . . on unconditional trust. Otherwise, it's just . . . foreplay that never finds a truly satisfied release."

"So . . . there was no particular act?"

"Oh, yes," she cooed. "There was most *definitely* a specific act. An act so exquisite, so intimate, so unbearably erotic that it's only been experienced by a handful of men and women in the whole history of the world. But they could only experience it once they'd made the ultimate commitment to one another."

"Are you going to tell me what it is?"

"I don't know," she mused. "Weren't you the one who told me it's more delicious if you don't know everything? To always wonder . . ."

His dark eyes narrowed. "You vixen!"

"Yes," she laughed. "I think I shall keep you guessing. That way you'll never grow bored with me. There will always be a mystery to intrigue you."

"I can make you tell me, you know."

"Can you?"

"You know I can."

"I'd like to see you try."

He took her face in both his hands and looked for a long moment into her mocking eyes. Then, slowly, he lowered his head, bringing his lips to hers. Grazing them softly, then pulling away ever so slightly, making her reach for him. Until her merriment began to melt. Until she pressed her lips to his in increasing urgency. Until he finally crushed her to him, his mouth devouring hers, his hand surreptitiously sliding up her side so that his thumb grazed her breast. Out there on deck, where anyone who might happen by could see. Small but galvanizing public display of his possession of her.

"You *will* tell me," he told her, serious now.

"But I'm so tired of talking," she protested with a teasing purse of her lips.

"Then don't tell me. *Show* me."

She cocked her head and pretended to consider. "Give me the proper incentive, and I might."

It was what she'd wanted all along. To be persuaded.

Royce glanced around. Some of the passengers who'd stayed on deck to witness their departure were glancing their way through discreetly lowered lashes. One old couple, not as shy as the rest, beamed at them knowingly.

"Very well," he told her. "I will."

He swept her up into his arms just as Rodrigo had in *The Pirate and the Princess*. Ignoring her astonished gasp. Ignoring the startled looks that followed them. Carrying her across the deck and up the stairs toward their cabin. Opening it with her still in his arms and carting her inside. Placing her on her feet, then coming toward her with a magnificently wicked gleam in his eyes.

"I warn you," she said, already feeling breathless. "I'm terribly stubborn. You shan't convince me easily."

"That's all right," he assured her, taking hold of her shoulders and pulling her close. "We have nothing but time."